"We must escape while there is still time," the paladin whispered.

Cyrus resisted his pull to safety. He would watch this. He must.

"I gave my word," Magus continued once it was clear neither parent would offer up Cyrus's location. "A clear word, and a true promise. Accept this blood as a sacrifice to your memory. May it sear your conscience in the eternal lands beyond."

Cyrus knew fleeing was the wiser decision. He knew it was what his parents wanted. But it seemed so simple to Cyrus, so obvious what was right. He turned away from the door, pretending to go with the paladin. The moment Rayan's hand loosened, Cyrus shoved the man's chest, separating them. A heartbeat later he was out the door, legs and arms flailing as he ran. The distance between him and his parents felt like miles. His voice sounded small, insignificant, but he screamed it nonetheless.

"I'm here!" It didn't matter if it risked his life. He wouldn't leave his family behind. He wouldn't let them die for his sake. He crossed the green grass of the courtyard between him and the gathered soldiers. "I'm here, I'm here, I'm—"

Magus swung once for the both of them. His sword passed through blood and bone to halt upon the white brick. Only Cyrus's mother's injuries weren't instantly lethal, for the sword cut across her arm and waist instead of cleaving her in half. Her anguished scream pierced the courtyard. Her pain ripped through Cyrus's horror-locked mind. The Imperator, however, twirled his sword in his fingers and shook his head with disappointment.

"Why do I bother?" Magus asked as he cut the head from her shoulders. "It's always easier to rebuild from nothing."

Praise for
David Dalglish

"Dalglish sticks the landing with his final Keepers fantasy.... This is a worthy finale."   —*Publishers Weekly* on *Voidbreaker*

"Dark, gory, yet still inspiring.... Dalglish's approach to this third book in the series (after *Ravencaller*) keeps the returning characters fresh, relevant, and impactful in their necessary roles to both uplift and restrict the responsibilities of the Chainbreaker."

—*Library Journal* on *Voidbreaker*

"Fans will love the second installment of this dark fantasy about very human characters beset by inhuman dangers."

—*Kirkus* on *Ravencaller*

"With strong world building, imaginative monsters, and a capable system of magic, this series will please readers who enjoy dark epic fantasy with engaging characters."   —*Booklist* on *Ravencaller*

"A fast-paced, page-turning ride with a great, likeable main character in Devin Eveson. It's the definition of entertaining."

—John Gwynne, author of *Malice*, on *Soulkeeper*

"A dark and lush epic fantasy brimming with magical creatures and terrifying evil.... Dalglish's world building is subtle and fluid, and he weaves the history, magical workings, and governance of his world within the conversations and camaraderie of his characters. Readers of George R. R. Martin and Patrick Rothfuss will find much to enjoy here."   —*Booklist* on *Soulkeeper*

"A soaring tale that nails the high notes. *Skyborn* had me gazing heaven-ward, imagining what could be."   —Jay Posey, author of *Three*

"Dalglish raises the stakes and magnitude, demonstrating his knack for no-holds-barred, wildly imaginative storytelling and worldbuilding."
                    —*Publishers Weekly* on *Shadowborn*

"Fast, furious, and fabulous."
                    —Michael J. Sullivan, author of *Theft of Swords*,
                    on *A Dance of Cloaks*

By David Dalglish

VAGRANT GODS

The Bladed Faith

THE KEEPERS

Soulkeeper

Ravencaller

Voidbreaker

SERAPHIM

Skyborn

Fireborn

Shadowborn

SHADOWDANCE

A Dance of Cloaks

A Dance of Blades

A Dance of Mirrors

A Dance of Shadows

A Dance of Ghosts

A Dance of Chaos

Cloak and Spider (novella)

THE BLADED FAITH

VAGRANT GODS: BOOK ONE

DAVID DALGLISH

orbitbooks.net

Copyright © 2022 by David Dalglish
Excerpt from *Vagrant Gods: Book Two* copyright © 2022 by David Dalglish
Excerpt from *The Pariah* copyright © 2021 by Anthony Ryan

Cover design by Lauren Panepinto
Cover illustration by Chase Stone
Cover copyright © 2022 by Hachette Book Group, Inc.
Map by Sámhlaoch Swords
Author photograph by Myrtle Beach Photography

Orbit
Hachette Book Group
1290 Avenue of the Americas
New York, NY 10104
orbitbooks.net

First Edition: April 2022

Orbit is an imprint of Hachette Book Group.
The Orbit name and logo are trademarks of Little, Brown Book Group Limited.

The publisher is not responsible for websites (or their content) that are not owned by the publisher.

The Hachette Speakers Bureau provides a wide range of authors for speaking events. To find out more, go to www.hachettespeakersbureau.com or call (866) 376-6591.

Library of Congress Cataloging-in-Publication Data
Names: Dalglish, David, author.
Title: The bladed faith / David Dalglish.
Description: First edition. | New York, NY : Orbit, 2022. | Series: Vagrant gods; book 1
Identifiers: LCCN 2021031245 | ISBN 9780759557086 (trade paperback) |
    ISBN 9780759557093 (ebook) | ISBN 9780759557109
Classification: LCC PS3604.A376 B53 2022 | DDC [Fic]—dc23
LC record available at https://lccn.loc.gov/2021031245

ISBNs: 9780759557086 (trade paperback), 9780759557093 (ebook)

Printed in the United States of America

LSC-C

Printing 1, 2022

To my wife, Sam, who was calm when I needed it, confident when I wasn't, and helped salvage what would become of this new trilogy.

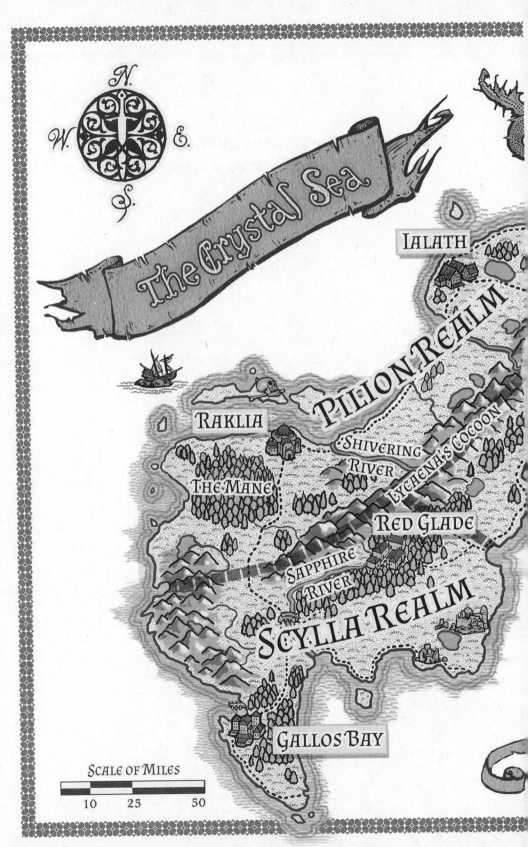

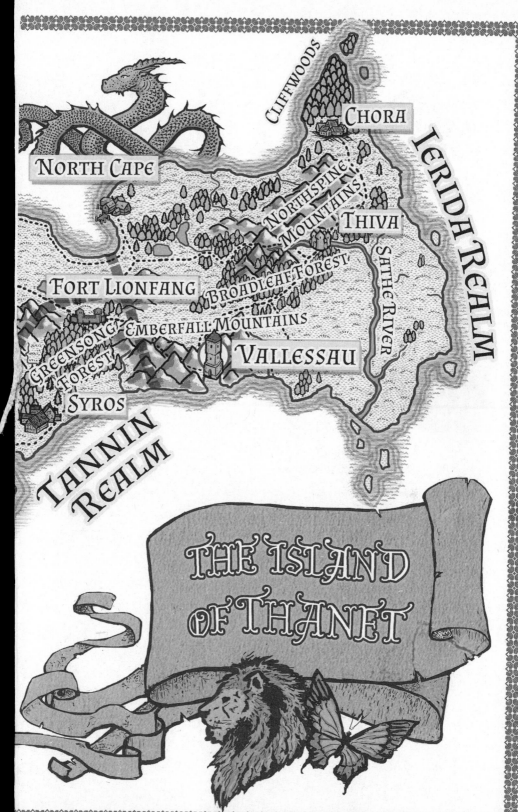

CLIFFWOODS

CHORA

NORTH CAPE

IERIDA REALM

NORTHSPINE MOUNTAINS

THIVA

SATHE RIVER

FORT LIONFANG

BROADLEAF FOREST

EMBERFALL MOUNTAINS

GREENSONG FOREST

VALLESSAU

SYROS

TANNIN REALM

THE ISLAND OF THANET

MAP BY SÁMHLAOCH SWORDS

CHAPTER 1

CYRUS

All his life, Cyrus Lythan had been told his parents' armada was the greatest in the world, unmatched by any fleet from the mainland continent of Gadir. It was the pride of his family, the jewel of the island kingdom of Thanet. Standing at the edge of the castle balcony, his hands white-knuckling the balustrade, Cyrus watched their ships burn and knew it for a lie.

"Their surprise will only gain them so much," said Rayan. The older man and dearest family friend stood beside Cyrus as the fires spread across the docks. "Hold faith. Our gods will protect us."

Smoke blotted out the harbor, but along the edges of the billowing black he saw the empire's ships firing flaming spears from ballistae mounted to their decks. Thanet's boats could not counter such power with their meager archers, not even if they had fought on equal numbers. Those numbers, however, were far from equal. Thanet's vaunted armada had counted fifty ships in total, though only thirty had been in the vicinity of Vallessau when two hundred imperial ships emerged from the morning fog, their hulls painted black and their gray sails marked with two red hands clenched in prayer.

"Shouldn't you be down there with the rest of the paladins?" Cyrus asked. "Or are you too old for battle?"

The man's white plate rattled as he crossed his arms. He was a paladin of Lycaena, a holy warrior who'd dedicated his life to one of Thanet's two gods. It was she and Endarius whom the island now relied upon to withstand the coming invasion. The castle was set upon the tallest hill in the city of Vallessau, protected by a wide outer wall that circled the base of its foundational hill. Thanet's soldiers massed along the outer wall, their padded leather armor seeming woefully inadequate. Paladins of the two gods gathered in the courtyard between the outer wall and the castle itself. Despite there being less than sixty, the sight of them gave Cyrus hope. The finely polished weapons of those men and women shone brightly, and the morning light reflected off their armor, be it the gilded chain of Endarius's paladins or the white plate of Lycaena's. As for the god and goddess, they both waited inside the castle.

"You are brave to call me old when you yourself are not yet a man," Rayan said. His skin was as dark as his hair was white, and when he smiled, it stretched his smartly trimmed beard. That smile was both heartfelt and fleeting. "His Highness ordered me to protect you."

Cyrus tried to remain optimistic. He tried to hold faith in the divine beings pledged to protect Thanet. A seemingly endless tide of soldiers disembarking from the ships and marching the main thoroughfare toward the outer castle walls broke that faith.

"Tell me, Rayan, if the walls fall and our gods die, how will you protect me?"

Rayan looked to the distant congregation of his fellow paladins of Lycaena at the outer gate, and his thoughts clearly echoed Cyrus's.

"Poorly," he said. "Stay here, and pray for us all. We will need every bit of help this cruel world can muster."

The paladin exited the balcony. The heavy thud of the shutting door quickened Cyrus's pulse, and he swallowed down his lingering fear. A cowardly part of him shouted to find somewhere in the castle to bury his head and hide. Stubborn pride kept his feet firmly in place. He was the fourteen-year-old Prince of Thanet, and he would bear witness to the fate of his kingdom.

The assault began with the arrival of the ladders, dozens of thick planks of wood with metal hooks bolted onto their tops so they could lock tightly onto the walls. The defenders rushed to shove them off, but the empire's crossbowmen punished them with volley after volley. Swords clashed, and though the empire's losses were heavy, nothing slowed the ascent of the invaders. What started as a few scattered soldiers fighting atop the walls became a mile-long battlefield. It did not take long before the gray tunics overwhelmed the blue tabards of Vallessau.

Next came the battering ram. How the enemy had built it in such short a time baffled Cyrus, but there was no denying its steady hammering on the opposite side of the outer gate. Even the intervals were maddeningly consistent. Every four seconds, the gate would rattle, the wood would crack, and the imperial army grew that much closer to flooding into the courtyard.

"It doesn't matter," Cyrus whispered to himself. "The gods protect us. The gods will save us."

The fight along the walls was growing thicker, with more ladders managing to stay upright with every passing moment. Cyrus could spare no glance in their direction, for with one last shuddering blast, the battering ram knocked open the outer gate. The invading army flooded through, and should have easily overrun the vastly outnumbered defenders, but at long last, the castle doors opened and Thanet's divine made their presence known.

The goddess Lycaena fluttered above an accompaniment of her priests. Her skin was black as midnight, her eyes brilliant rainbows of evershifting color. Long, flowing silk cascaded down from her arms and waist, its hue a brilliant orange that transitioned to yellow, green, and blue depending on the ruffle of the fabric. The dress billowed outward in all directions, and no matter how hard Cyrus looked, he couldn't tell where the fabric ended and the goddess's enormous wings began. She held a rod topped with an enormous ruby in her left hand; in the right, a golden harp whose strings shimmered all colors of the visible spectrum. Cyrus's heart ached at the sight of her. He'd witnessed Lycaena's physical form only a few times in his life, and each left him breathless and in awe.

"Be gone, locusts of a foreign land," Lycaena decreed. She did not shout, nor raise her voice, but all the city heard her words. "We will not break before a wave of hate and steel."

Fire lashed from the ruby atop her rod in a conical torrent that filled the broken gateway. The screams of the dying combined into a singular wail. The other god of Thanet, Endarius the Lion, charged into the ashen heap left in her attack's wake. His fur was gold, his claws obsidian, his mane a brilliant collection of feathers that ran the full gamut of the rainbow. Wings stretched from his back, the feathers there several feet long and shifting from a crimson red along the base to pale white at the tip. Those wings beat with his every stride, adding to his speed and power.

Endarius's paladins joined him in his charge. They did not wield swords and shields like their Lycaenan counterparts, nor did they share their long cloaks of interlocking colors resembling stained glass. Instead their gilded armor bore necklaces of fangs across their arms, and they wielded twin jagged swords to better support their ferocity. They bellowed as they ran, their version of a prayer, and they tore into the ranks of the invaders, the spray of blood and breaking of bones their worship.

In those first few minutes, Cyrus truly believed victory would be theirs. Thanet had never been conquered in all her history. Lycaena and Endarius protected their beloved people. The two divine beings rewarded their faithful subjects with safety and guidance. And as the imperial soldiers rushed through the gate with their swords and spears, the gods filled the courtyard with fire and blood. From such a height, Cyrus could only guess at the identities of the individual defenders, but he swore he saw Rayan fighting alongside his goddess, his sword lit with holy light as he kept his beloved deity safe with his rainbow shield.

You burned our fleets, Cyrus thought, and a vengeful thrill shot through him. *But we'll crush your armies. You'll never return, never, not after this defeat.*

The arrival of the twelve tempered his joy. The men appeared remarkably similar to Thanet's paladins, bearing thick golden platemail and wielding much larger weapons adorned with decorative hilts and handles. Unlike the rest of the imperial army, they did not wear gray tabards but instead colorful tunics and cloaks bearing differing animals. The twelve pushed through the blasted gate, flanked on either side by a contingent of soldiers. They showed no fear of the two divine beings leading the slaughter. They charged into the thick of things without hesitation, their shields held high and their weapons gleaming.

Cyrus knew little of the Everlorn Empire. Journey to the mainland took several months by boat, and its ruling emperor, arrogantly named the God-Incarnate, had issued an embargo upon Thanet lasting centuries. The empire worshiped and acknowledged no gods but their emperor, and claimed faith in him allowed humanity to transcend mortal limits. Seeing those twelve fight, Cyrus understood that belief for the first time in his life. Those twelve . . . they couldn't be human. Whatever they were, it was monstrous, it was impossible, and it was beyond even what Thanet's paladins could withstand.

God and invader clashed, and somehow these horrifying twelve endured the wrath of the immortal beings. Their armor held against fire and claw. Their weapons punched through armor as if it were glass. Soldiers and paladins from both sides attempted to intervene, but they were flies buzzing about fighting bulls. Each movement, each strike of an invader's sword or swipe of Endarius's paw, claimed the lives of foes with almost incidental ease. The battlefield ascended beyond the mortal, and these elite, these invading monsters, defied all reason as they stood their ground against Thanet's gods.

"No," Cyrus whispered. "It's not possible."

Endarius clenched his teeth about the long blade of one of the invaders, yet could not crunch through the metal. His foe ripped it free, and a crossbow brigade unleashed dozens of bolts to pelt the Lion as he danced away. The arrowheads couldn't find purchase, but they marked little black welts akin to bruises and frayed the edges of Endarius's increasingly ragged wings.

"This isn't right," Cyrus said. The battle had started so grand, yet now the defenders were scattered, the walls overrun, and the paladins struggling to maintain their attacks against wave after wave of soldiers coming through the broken gate. In the center of it all raged gods and the inhuman elite, and the world shook from their wrath. Thanet's troops attempted to seal off the wall entrance and isolate the battle against the gods. It briefly worked, at least until the men and women in red robes took to the front of enemy lines. Their lack of weapons and armor confused Cyrus at first, but then they lifted their hands in prayer. Golden weapons blistering with light burst into existence, hovering in the air and wielded by invisible hands. The weapons tore through the soldiers' ranks, the defense faltered, and Cyrus's last hope withered. What horrid power did these invaders command?

Time lost meaning. Blood flowed, bodies fell, the armies meeting and striking and dying with seemingly nihilistic determination. A spear-wielding member of those elite twelve leaped into the air, a single lunge of his legs carrying him dozens of feet heavenward. Lycaena was not prepared, and when the spear lodged deep into her side, her scream echoed for miles. It was right then, hearing that scream, that Cyrus knew his kingdom was lost.

"How dare you!" Endarius roared. Though one invader smashed a hammer into the Lion's side, and another knocked loose a fang from his jaw, the god cared only for the wound suffered by the Butterfly goddess. Two mighty beats of his wings carried him into the air, where his teeth closed about the elite still clinging to the embedded spear. All three crashed to the ground, but it was the invader who suffered most. Endarius crushed him in his jaws, punching through the man's armor, smashing bones, and spilling blood upon a silver tongue.

A casual flick of Endarius's neck tossed the body aside, but that was merely one of twelve. Eleven more remained, and they closed the space with calm, steady precision. No soldiers attempted to fill the gap, for what battles remained were scattered and chaotic. There was too much blood, too much death, and above it all, like a sick backdrop in the world's cruelest painting, rose the billowing smoke of Thanet's burning fleet.

"Flee from here!" Endarius bellowed as a bleeding Lycaena fluttered higher into the air.

"Only if you come with me," the goddess urged, but the Lion would not be moved. He prepared to pounce and bared his obsidian teeth.

"For the lives of the faithful," Endarius roared. His wings spread wide, unbridled power crackling like lightning across the feathers.

Cyrus dropped to his knees and clutched the side of the balustrade. He could feel it on his skin. He could smell it in the air. The overwhelming danger. The growing fury of a god who could never imagine defeat.

"Strike me with your blades," the Lion mocked the remaining eleven. "Come die as the vermin you are."

They were happy to oblige. The eleven clashed with the god in a coordinated effort, their swords, axes, and spears tearing into his golden flesh. The god could not avoid them, could not win, only buy time for Lycaena's escape. No matter how badly Cyrus pleaded under his breath for the Lion to flee, he would not. Endarius had been, above all, a stubborn god.

A blue-armored elite was the one to strike the killing blow. A spear pierced through Endarius's eye and sank to the hilt. His fur rumbled, his dying roar shook the land, and then the Lion's body split in half. A maelstrom of stars tore free of his body like floodwaters released from a dam. Whatever otherworldly essence comprised the existence of a god burned through the eleven like a swirling, rainbow fire before rolling outward in a great flare of blinding light. Cyrus crouched down and screamed. The death of something so beautiful, so noble and inseparably linked to Thanet's identity, shook him in a way he could not fathom.

At last the noise and light faded from the suddenly quiet battlefield. Two of the eleven elites died from the eruption of divine energy, their armor melted to their bodies as they lay upon the cobblestone path leading from the main gate to the castle entrance. Nothing remained of Endarius's body, for it had dissolved into light and crystal and floated away like scattered dust. Lycaena was long gone, having taken to the skies during the divine explosion. The paladins and priests of both gods likewise fled. A few entered the castle before it locked its gates, while the rest took to the distant portions of the outer wall not yet besieged by the invaders, seeking stairs and ladders that might allow them to escape out into Vallessau.

The soldiers of the Everlorn Empire filled the courtyard to face what was left of Thanet's defenses. Cyrus guessed maybe a dozen archers, and twice that in armed soldiers, remained inside the castle. Opposing thoughts rattled inside his head. What to do. Where to go. None of it seemed to matter. His mind couldn't process the shock. Last night he'd gone to bed having heard only rumors of imperial ships sailing the area. No one had known it was a full-scale invasion. No one had known Thanet's navy would fall in a single afternoon, and the capital along with it.

The nine remaining imperial elites gathered, joined by the men and women in red robes who Cyrus assumed to be some manner of priest.

One of the nine trudged to the front and stood before the locked gateway. He showed no fear of an archer's arrow, which wasn't surprising given the enormous gray slab of steel he carried as his shield. His face was hidden underneath a gigantic bull helmet with horns that stretched a full foot to either side of his head. He said something in his imperial tongue, and then one of the priests came forward holding a blue medallion. The gigantic man took it, slipped it over his neck, and then addressed the castle.

"I am Imperator Magus of Eldrid!" the man shouted, and though his lips moved wrong, there was no doubt that he somehow spoke the native Thanese language. "Paragon of Shields, servant of the Uplifted Church, and faithful child of the God-Incarnate. I command this conquest. My word is law, and so shall it be until this island bends its knee and accepts the wisdom of the Everlorn Empire. I say this not out of pride, but so you may understand that none challenge my word. Should I make a promise, I shall keep it, even unto the breaking of the world."

Magus drew a sword from his waist and lifted it high above him. He spoke again, the blue medallion flaring with light at his every word.

"I make you one offer, and it shall not be amended nor changed. Bring me the royal family who call this castle home. Cast them to the dirt at my feet, and I shall spare the lives of every single man, woman, and child within your walls. But if you will not..."

The Imperator lowered his blade.

"Then I shall execute every last one of you, so that only vermin remain to walk your halls."

And with that, silence followed, but that silence was like the held breath between seeing a flash of lightning and feeling its thunder rumble against your bones. Shouts soon erupted within the castle, scattered at first, then numerous. Screams. Steel striking steel.

Mother! Father! Cyrus's parents were both on a lower floor, watching the battle unfold from the castle windows. That their servants and soldiers would so easily turn upon them seemed unthinkable, but the sounds of battle were undeniable. Cyrus turned to the door to the balcony, still slightly ajar from when Rayan left.

"Oh no," he whispered, and then broke into a sprint. The door wasn't lockable, not from the outside, but if he could wedge it closed with something, even brace it with his weight...

The door opened right as he arrived, the wood ramming hard enough into him that he feared it might break his shoulder. Cyrus fell and rolled across the white stone, biting down a cry as his elbow and knees bruised. When he staggered to his feet, he found one of his guard captains, a woman named Nessa, blocking the doorway with her sword and shield drawn.

"I'm sorry, Cyrus," the woman said. "Maybe they'll spare you like they promised."

"You're a traitor."

"You saw it, prince. Endarius is dead. They're killing gods. What hope do we have? Now stand up. I will drag you if I must."

Nessa suddenly jerked forward, her jaw opening and closing in a noiseless death scream. When she collapsed, Rayan stood over her body. Blood soaked his white armor and stained his flowing cloak. His hand outstretched for Cyrus to take.

"Come," Rayan said. "We have little time."

They ran through the hall to the stairs. Cyrus pretended not to see the bodies strewn across the blue carpet. Some were soldiers. Some were servants. The king and queen still lived, yet the people of Thanet were already tearing one another apart. Was this how quickly their nation would fall?

Once at the bottom of the stairs, Rayan guided him through rooms and ducked along slender servant corridors hidden behind curtains. During their flight, treacherous Thanet soldiers ordered them to halt twice, and twice Rayan cut them down with an expert swing of his sword. Cyrus stepped over their bodies without truly seeing them. He felt like a stranger in his own skin. The entire world seemed unreal, a cruel dream no amount of biting his tongue allowed him to awake from.

Within minutes they were running down a lengthy corridor that connected a portion of the western wall to the castle proper. The corridor ran parallel to the courtyard, and at the first door they passed, Cyrus spotted the enormous gathering of soldiers surrounding Magus of Eldrid.

"I had feared the worst," Magus shouted as Cyrus continued. "Come before me, and kneel. I would hear your names."

Cyrus skidded to a halt at the next doorway. He pressed his chest against the cold stone and peered around the edge. It couldn't be. His parents, they were meant to escape like him. They had their own royal guard. Their own protectors. Yet there they stood before the Imperator, flanked on either side by blood-soaked traitors. His father was the first to bow his head and address their conqueror. With each proclamation, the empire's soldiers cheered and clattered their swords against their shields.

"Cleon Lythan," said his father. "King of Thanet."

"Berniss Lythan," said his mother. "Queen of Thanet."

Cyrus's stomach twisted into acidic knots. How could the world turn so dark and cruel within the span of a single day? Magus lifted his shield and slammed it back down hard enough to crack a full foot-deep groove into the stone and wedge his shield permanently upright. With only his sword swinging in his relaxed grip, he approached the pair.

"Cleon and Berniss," he said. "We are not ignorant of your kingdom and its history. Where is your son? The young man by the name of Cyrus?"

"I suspect he fled," Cleon said. The courtyard had grown deathly quiet. "Please, it was not by our order. We don't know where Cyrus has gone."

The Imperator removed his bull helmet. Cyrus had expected more of a monster, but Magus seemed remarkably human, with deeply tanned skin, silver eyes, and a magnificent smile. His long black hair cascaded down either side of his face as he spoke.

"I requested the entire royal line. Was I not clear? Did my word-lace mistranslate?"

"No," Berniss said. "Please, we looked, we did."

The man shook his head.

"Lies, and more lies," he said. "Do you stall for his safety? Feign at ignorance, as if your boy stands a chance of survival once this castle falls?"

Cyrus took a step, one single step out the doorway toward his parents, before Rayan grabbed him by his neck.

"We must escape while there is still time," the paladin whispered. Cyrus resisted his pull to safety. He would watch this. He must.

"I gave my word," Magus continued once it was clear neither would offer up Cyrus's location. "A clear word, and a true promise. Accept this blood as a sacrifice to your memory. May it sear across your conscience in the eternal lands beyond."

Cyrus knew fleeing with Rayan was the wiser decision. He knew it was what his parents wanted. But it seemed so simple to Cyrus, so obvious what the right course of action must be. He turned away from the door, pretending to go with the paladin. The moment Rayan's hand released from his neck, Cyrus shoved the man's chest, separating them. A heartbeat later he was out the door, legs and arms flailing as he willed his body to run faster. The distance between them felt like miles. His voice sounded quiet, insignificant, but he screamed it nonetheless.

"I'm here!" It didn't matter if he put his own life at risk. He wouldn't leave his family behind. He wouldn't let them die for his sake. He ran, crossing the green grass of the courtyard between him and the gathered soldiers. "I'm here, I'm here, I'm—"

Magus swung once for the both of them. His sword passed through blood and bone to halt upon the white brick. Only Cyrus's mother's injuries weren't instantly lethal, for the sword cut across her arm and waist instead of cleaving her in half. Her anguished scream pierced the courtyard. Her pain ripped daggers through Cyrus's horror-locked mind. Magus, however, twirled his sword in his fingers and shook his head with disappointment.

"Why do I bother?" he said as he cut the head from Berniss's shoulders. "It's always easier to rebuild from nothing."

Cyrus couldn't banish the sight. He couldn't stop seeing that killing stroke. His legs weakened, limbs becoming wobbling jelly that could not support him. His whole family, gone. Slain. Bleeding upon the courtyard stones with their blood pooling into the groove Magus had carved with his shield. Crossbow bolts hammered into the men and women who had turned traitor and brought the royal family out in custody. No reward for their betrayal. Only death.

Too late, he thought. Too late, too late, he ran too late, revealed himself too late. A scream ripped out of Cyrus's chest. No words, just a heartbroken protest against the brutality of the day and the terror sweeping through him as the ground seemed to shake at the approach of the Paragon of Shields. Too late, he had gained the attention of the monster from the boats. Too late to save his parents. Too late to mean anything but a cruel death. Cyrus prayed he would meet his father and mother on the rolling green fields of Endarius's paradise. Face wet with tears, he stared up at Magus and slowly climbed to his feet. He would die meeting the gaze of his executioner; this he swore. Not on his knees. Not begging for his life.

The golden-armored paragon grabbed Cyrus by the throat and lifted him into the air. Instinct had Cyrus clutching at the heavy gauntlet. How easily he carried him. As if he were nothing. Just a ghost. Magus, this man, this monster, towered above the other soldiers come to join him. Cyrus stared into the man's silver eyes and promised vengeance, even if it meant coming back as a spirit. Not even the grave would deny him his due.

"Cyrus?" Magus asked him. The necklace at his throat shimmered with pale blue light. "Prince Cyrus Lythan?"

Cyrus sucked in a shallow breath as the gauntlet loosened.

"I am," he said. "Now do it, bastard. I'm not scared."

One of the soldiers beside Magus asked a question in his foreign tongue. Magus thought for a moment and then shook his head. He tossed Cyrus to the stone, dropping him beside the bodies. Cyrus tried not to look. He tried to not let the blood and bone and spilled innards of his beloved parents sear into his memory for the rest of his life, however long or short it might be. He failed.

"Lock him in his room," Magus said. "We have much to do to prepare this wretched island, and too few years to do it. And one thing I've learned is that when it comes to keeping a populace in line, well..."

His giant boot settled atop Cyrus's chest, grinding him into the stone, smearing him upon the blood of his slain parents.

"It never hurts to have a hostage."

CHAPTER 2

MARI

Mari slid a word-lace around her neck in preparation for a meandering walk through the conquered city of Vallessau. The imperial tongue was still new to the island, and though she had learned much of Thanet's native language over the past few months she'd lived there, she found it much easier to rely on the word-lace's magic.

"Be careful out there," said Mari's older sister, Stasia. Sweat soaked Stasia's body, which was naked from the waist up except for a tightly wound strip of cloth tied across her chest. The two were in what had been dubbed the "training room" of their two-story house. The floor was heavily carpeted. Iron rods of various weights rested on hooks and shelves. A massive triple-wrapped sack of white sand from the nearby beach hung from the ceiling, and Stasia thundered her bare fists into it with a staccato rhythm.

"I'm always careful," Mari said. She removed a silken green band from her pocket and began tying her long brown hair into a tail. Mari was dressed opposite to her older sister, in a long, loose black dress over a thick chemise, a shawl for her head and neck, and long wool stockings. Whereas Stasia was more muscle than human, Mari would graciously consider herself plump.

"It doesn't mean I can't worry," Stasia said. She weaved back and forth to dodge imaginary punches. Mari knew she'd be at that sack of sand for at least an hour, beating it into submission. Her older sister always worked out when she knew battle approached. It was how she kept her nerves at bay. "I'm going to be at the front lines tomorrow, and I'd like you there with me."

"I'm trying," Mari insisted, as if she hadn't spent every day of the past months doing exactly that.

"Try harder."

"I'm communing with a god, Stasia. Either Endarius accepts my offer, or he doesn't."

Stasia flashed one of her cocky smiles that only an older sister could get away with.

"Don't give him a choice. You're Mari Ahlai. What's a dead lion compared to my little sister?"

"Stubborn, is what he is," Mari said. "But I'm attending a new ritual later today, so maybe he'll finally give me a listen."

Stasia wished her well and then returned to her training. Mari stepped out to the streets of Vallessau. If she was to hear the whispers of Thanet's fallen god, she needed to be immersed in its people, its back alleys, and its quiet dealings. She had a name and an image to focus upon, and let it direct her wandering steps.

"Endarius," she whispered as she closed her eyes while standing before a tavern not yet ready to open for the new day. The wooden sign sporting the tavern's name was scuffed beyond repair, but she saw the faintest hints of a red-and-white feather painted into a chipped corner. "You're lurking, I feel it, but where?"

Two years had passed since the Everlorn Empire conquered the island nation of Thanet. During those bloody years, the Uplifted Church and its priests and magistrates had scrubbed every reference to its gods from the land. To speak Lycaena's name was criminal. To bear an image of the feathered lion invited whippings, and you risked far worse if you carried any of the now-banned religious tracts. But no matter how hard the church tried, the people remembered. The imperials could not replace the old gods, not immediately. Given time, and the birth of new generations, the decay would sink in. The people of Thanet, like other conquered nations of the Everlorn Empire, would pledge their hearts to the God-Incarnate and disregard the old gods as blasphemous and irrelevant.

Mari traced her fingers along a red feather drawn with colored chalk across a stone wall. The image was hidden in a dark alley, far from potential patrols. A member of the church might find it, in time. Until then, it was a burning reminder of the slain god, and as the red rubbed onto her fingertips, she heard the faintest sound of a lion's roar.

"Not dead," Mari wondered aloud. "Not gone. Why won't you come to me then? Why avoid my call?"

Ever since arriving on Thanet, Mari had whispered for the Lion to hear her, to entreat with her. Yet he refused. He always refused.

"That's right, a great feast!" shouted a city crier. Mari's wandering path had taken her from district to district until she passed through the bustling heart of the city. The crier waved small, yellow-leaf pamphlets above his head and urged anyone interested to take them. "Feasting, songs, and games! Come early if you want the best spot to witness the ceremony!"

Mari pretended not to hear him. The idea turned her stomach. Nothing better exemplified the Everlorn Empire like feasting and gaming to celebrate a deity's execution. Criers throughout the city begged for attendance in the great field west of Vallessau, and imperial soldiers had strung up banners and streamers across every main road. Come tomorrow, the empire would celebrate the culmination of two years of work. Come tomorrow, with the entire city in attendance, the Uplifted Church's Anointed One would execute the goddess Lycaena.

That is, unless the resistance Mari's father commanded stopped them.

Mari's wandering took her through the darker and poorer parts of Vallessau. It wasn't intentional, but it was in the forgotten places that faith in Endarius dwelt. She didn't realize where she walked until the smell hit her, and she looked to the sky. Twenty-five poles had been hammered into the street at one of the cross-sections of two major roads in the southern portion of the city. Each pole was twice the height of a man, its sides perfectly smooth wood, its top marked by an upturned metal hook.

Corpses hung from all twenty-five hooks. Thick ropes were tied tightly about their necks and waists. Men and women hurried underneath their shadows, covering their noses and staring at the ground as if the foul stench were the only bothersome aspect. Mari forced herself to stare at the swinging bodies. Colored feathers fluttered from necklaces about their purple necks. Butterfly and harp tattoos marked their swollen hands and faces. This place was known as the Dead Flags, and it was the fate awaiting all who refused to abandon their faith in Endarius and Lycaena. Every morning, the Uplifted Church hung twenty-five new bodies. If rumors were true, the jails were full with enough traitors and religious protesters to keep the flags flying for another year.

"No other gods, no other faiths, only the one true God-Incarnate," Mari whispered, repeating the order given to every conquered nation's people. "Deny us worship, and we deny you life."

Finally Mari's stomach could take no more. She put her back to the Dead Flags and hurried away. Resistance groups were stationed all across Vallessau in preparation for tomorrow, and it was at one of them Mari would soon attend her first bloodletting ceremony. She passed underneath an archway, then paused to read graffiti written in a fading white paint meant to signal support for the resistance. It was in the imperial tongue, and while it was meant to read NO KILLERS, NO IMPERIALS, the writer, no doubt a native to Thanet, had botched the spelling so that it read NO KIILLERS, NO IMPRALS instead.

"I suppose it gets the message across," Mari said as she passed underneath it. Not far was a vacant two-story tenement. Though the residents had been cleared out weeks ago, a young man with dark hair hanging over his eyes kept guard at the door.

"What are you doing here, Mari?" he asked as she approached. "All of us are way too lowbrow shit for you to be hanging around."

"I've come for the bloodletting," she said. She didn't recognize the man, but it was no surprise that he knew her. There weren't too many outsiders on Thanet, let alone people like her and her family with the distinct red eyes of a Miquoan. These members didn't know her father was the mysterious "Coin," who funneled money into the resistance, but they knew she was a friend. More important, they knew her sister, and the vicious kills she had scored in the few short months they'd been on the island. It was a risk, coming here in the open during broad day-light, but having lived through so many rebellions, Mari was used to a bit of risk.

"You're cutting it close then," the man said, and he flung the rickety door open. "The paladin is upstairs. Should be starting soon."

They wouldn't start without her, though she didn't bother to explain that to the door guard. After three months of Endarius ignoring her prayers, this was her best idea at gaining the Lion's attention. The entire ceremony had been organized by her father. Mari entered the home, and the guard quickly shut the door behind her.

At least a dozen men were crammed into that bottom floor, and they glanced her way out of curiosity or mistrust. Pieces of armor lay scat-tered atop tables and couches. Freshly sharpened swords hung from two different racks on the wall. There weren't enough beds for them all, so instead, pillows and blankets were piled into haphazard nests. One such nest was occupied by two husbands, one curled up with his face buried into the chest of the other. Mari felt a pang of pity looking upon them. Had they been chased out of their home? Or were they here as a precau-tion, fearing the increased scrutiny their pairing would bring from the eyes of the Uplifted priests?

Mari made small talk with those who were awake, sensing their nervousness for tomorrow's execution, and doing her best to soothe it despite those waiting for her upstairs for the bloodletting. Here in the hidden dark, the symbols of Endarius and Lycaena were more bravely worn. She spotted several religious necklaces, the chains adorned with gold-and-silver butterfly wings. Several men sported Endarius's red-and-white feathers tucked into their hats or coats, and some lashed those feathers to their swords with strips of leather. There was fear in the air, certainly, an anxious dread at the coming battle, but there was faith, too. Mari smelled it like spilled vinegar. Since arriving on Thanet, she'd tried fasting. She'd tried prayer. She'd engaged in the little ritu-als the followers of Endarius practiced when no member of the church watched. Nothing had worked, so it was time to try something new.

The faith of your followers is strong, she thought. *So strong. Why will you not hear my whispers, Lion? I know you yet live.*

Stalling, she was stalling. Mari politely excused herself from conversation and climbed the stairs into the wide attic. Three men and two women gathered in attendance, sitting in a circle in the pale light. A single feather lay before each of them, and a sixth feather awaited her joining the circle. Of the five present, only one she recognized, a handsome man named Amhir. He was one of the leaders of the struggling resistance, and sometimes appeared at her father's house in need of orders. Of the others, one stood out by his garb. He wore gilded armor, a bearskin cloak, and a necklace of teeth, all of which would have him executed if seen wearing it in public. A paladin of Endarius, come to perform the bloodletting ceremony.

Though Mari's family had been there for only three months, it had been two years since the island's invasion, and she had missed much of the brief war. Near the end of the first year, the paladins and priests of Endarius had gathered in a deep forest known as the Mane, in southern Thanet, for a doomed final stand against the imperial army. The loss had devastated their numbers and, combined with their god's death during the invasion, had led to a near complete dissolution of their ranks. What few remained went into hiding, but with the planned execution tomorrow, several had returned to Vallessau for one last battle.

"What is she doing here?" an older woman asked. Her face was like leather, her dark hair tied back into a ponytail. "To invite a foreigner is an insult to our god."

"The Coin says she attends, so she attends," Amhir said.

The paladin drew a knife from his hip, and he watched Mari as he carefully sharpened it with flint from his pocket. His head was completely shaven, and tattooed across and above his forehead were rainbow feathers.

"There is danger in this ceremony to the unbelievers," he said softly.

"I fear no danger."

"But do you believe?"

Mari sat in the circle and smoothed out her skirt.

"I have walked your streets, heard your prayers, and felt the faith of your island settle upon me like a cloak," she said. "Yes, paladin, I believe. The Lion lingers, angry and eager to hunt."

"You believe he exists, but that is not belief *in* him. The difference may seem small, but it is a canyon. I pray you are not swallowed within."

"Not a believer, yet still to attend our most sacred rite," the first woman protested. "I do not understand why we must allow this."

"Because I come to offer myself to Endarius so he might live again." The circle fell silent.

"Impossible," the third man said, but there was a hint of hope within his whisper.

"But it won't be a true second life, will it?" the paladin asked. He had been informed of Mari's purpose, though how well he understood it, she did not yet know. "You aren't bringing Endarius back. You're letting him use your body like a puppet."

"More like 'share,'" Mari said. This was a conversation she was painfully familiar with, but she held the utmost confidence in her abilities. "There is a realm beyond life, and it is there your god now resides, without a physical body to grant him a presence in our world. I offer him that body. I will take his power, and his faith, into my heart and soul. Through me, he will live."

"Endarius lives in all our hearts," the first woman said. "Yet none of us would think to become the Lion."

"None of you are god-whisperers."

"Enough," Amhir said. "Begin the ceremony, paladin. The decision is made. Carry it through."

"You seek to create a pale shade of the mighty Lion's former glory," the paladin said. "But we dwell in the deepest, darkest of valleys. I shall extend to you a bit of faith, Mari Ahlai. May you repay it in kind. Now give to me your arm."

All others extended arms with the palms downward. The paladin retrieved one of the long feathers, then readied his knife.

"Pray for mercy," he whispered. "Pray for guidance. We come before the Lion."

The others in attendance took up a whispery chant. Each was unique, not a predetermined scripture but heartfelt confessions by each attendee. Words flowed over Mari, spoken in the Thanese tongue, and her word-lace struggled to translate them in her mind. Pleas for guidance, for mercy. Cries of pain and sorrow and fear for the future awaiting the island in imperial hands. The need for comfort overwhelmed everything. They were afraid, so afraid, and Mari yearned to give them some measure of peace. Their hope, their belief, would not die. Not even when they saw the Lion speared by a paragon, and witnessed his body break before the capital.

"Pray for strength," the paladin continued. "Pray for humility. We bow before the Lion."

The paladin cut a shallow line above the wrist and across the forearm of an attendee. Little murmurs and cries of pain accompanied it, but they only seemed to add to the chorus of prayers. Into that blood he dipped the feather, coating its white surface, before returning the feather to the center circle.

"By blood we prove our loyalty," he said with each cut. "By blood we offer our faith."

One by one, the paladin painted the feathers. The attic seemed to darken with every cut. The prayers, while still whispered, grew like an encroaching thunderstorm. A chill wind blew across her that no wall could ever stop. The presence of a god. The arrival of the divine.

At last, the paladin brought the knife to Mari.

"By blood we prove our loyalty," he said, and he paused to look her in the eye. "And it must be true."

Mari pulled back her shoulders and lifted her head.

"By blood I offer my faith," she said. "My blood, and I give it freely."

His knife sliced across her forearm. Red covered the white. Six feathers, each bathed in a splash of their blood, set into a circle. The paladin bowed his head, and he lifted his arms high.

"The circle is complete."

A fire burst between them. It burned, soft and small, and hovered an inch above the attic floor. The feathers shifted, each becoming a different color of the Lion's mane. The fire itself shimmered the spectrum of the rainbow. Mari sensed Endarius's presence clearer than she ever had before, so near, so close, as if he prowled just out of sight.

"Take our blood," the paladin said. "Take our prayers. Take our faith. Cradle us in your wings."

It wasn't part of the ceremony, but Mari leaned forward, fingers scooping up the feathers. With them in her grasp, so followed the rainbow flame. It hovered before her, casting its cold light across her face. She curled it to her breast as the others protested. The light swirled into her, and she gasped at the sudden influx of emotions. Love and loss, sorrow and rage. She smelled the grass of the highlands. The blood on the feathers flared crimson, and they burned hot between her fingers. All around her, the world darkened as if night had descended in an instant.

"Do you hear me, Endarius?" Mari whispered. "Because I'm ready to listen."

The darkness enfolded her completely, and a thunderous roar signified the fallen god's arrival. He towered before Mari, all the world fading away into a dark emptiness that stretched on forever and ever. She bowed her head, offering the divine being the respect he rightfully deserved.

"Ceaseless is your prodding," Endarius said. His voice was deep as stone and ageless as water. "I come, god-whisperer. What is it you seek?"

The others in attendance had vanished. There was only Mari, the Lion, and the six feathers she clutched to her chest. She looked into the beast's rainbow eyes. His wings spread wide, and they caught light that shone from nowhere. Red-and-pink waves shimmered across her, and her blood seemed to boil underneath the skin the light touched.

"I would take only what you would give," Mari said. "I offer you a physical form now that your old body is slain. I offer you a life to replace what you lost."

"And in return?" Endarius asked.

"Nothing you would not seek for yourself. The death of your enemies. The slaughter of the invaders, and the blood of imperial soldiers on our tongue."

The rainbow of colors that was Endarius's feathery mane swirled and shifted.

"I need not your human flesh. I need not the pity of a mortal. I am a *god*. I will not be mocked!"

His fury was beyond any Mari had experienced in her time as a god-whisperer. In other nations she'd visited, the slain gods were eager to regain a physical form lest they fade away into forgotten memories. Endarius, though? The Lion wasn't just refusing. He was insulted.

"I offer no mockery!" Mari shouted. Here in this otherworldly place she was a visitor, and her life was far from safe. "I only ask for the strength to defeat your enemies."

"My strength belongs to the paladins who serve me faithfully," Endarius said. He paced before her, a towering presence worthy of praise. "But you? You hold no faith. You grant no worship. I see your heart, girl, and it is bleeding."

Mari pulled her shoulders back, and she remembered the confidence that had brought the Lion to her in the first place.

"And what is it you would rather find in my heart?" she asked the god.

Endarius stepped closer, closer, until his flat nose pressed against her forehead. It burned her skin like fire. His warm breath washed over her, and she smelled the coppery scent of blood from those open jaws.

"RAGE."

Mari sucked in a sharp breath as if waking from a dream. The fellow worshipers of Endarius surrounded her, nervous and eager. They were watching for signs of a miracle, one she could not offer them. The fire was gone, as was the color of the feathers and the crimson glow of the blood. Faint daylight shone through the dirty window.

"Is that it?" Amhir asked.

Frustrated tears swelled in Mari's eyes. This was much worse than Endarius's previous refusal to meet with her. Finally, he had communed, listened to her offer of conjoining...and then found her wanting. The rejection stung a thousand times worse than the previous silence. Battle approached, the life of the goddess Lycaena on the line, and yet she would not be able to help. She did not have her sister's muscles. She lacked training with a blade or bow. She was a god-whisperer, one of few left from her conquered homeland of Miquo. If no god answered, she was useless in a fight. What was she to do if Thanet's slain god wanted nothing to do with her?

"Did it work?" the paladin pressed when she did not answer. "Did Endarius speak with you?"

"I'm sorry," she said, thrusting the feathers into the man's hands. It was the only answer she could give. "I'm sorry."

Mari fled down the stairs, her neck flushing from all the eyes watching her. The confidence she'd exuded at the start of the ceremony felt hollow and humiliating.

"I told you," a woman's voice followed her down the stairs. "You never should have let a foreigner partake."

Mari could not exit the house fast enough. She shoved out the door, ignoring the smattering of farewells she received from those within. Her eyes cast firmly to the ground, she wandered aimlessly through the street. She tried not to dwell on her failure, nor on how she would endure the following day. Lycaena's execution would come, and she could only watch. Not fight. Not protect her sister, or wage war against the empire. Just watch, useless and helpless. To make it worse, she felt Endarius hovering about her still. She could not shake the scent of tall grass, nor the feel of soft dirt beneath her feet despite the street's cobblestones. Why did he follow her? Why did the Lion god keep close, if she was so unworthy of his gifts?

Lost in her own mind, she paid no attention to the four imperial soldiers marching toward her. Mari sensed their presence too late, and she tried, and failed, to step out of the way in time. One of the four pushed her aside with her shield as if she were a stubborn horse.

"Move," the soldier shouted in broken Thanese. Mari lay where she'd fallen, careful to keep her expression calm and indifferent.

"My apologies," she said. The soldiers continued, paying her little attention. A crowd gathered ahead of them, and curious as to the reason, Mari followed after. A man was protesting the goddess's execution by sitting underneath an awning adjacent to the main road. One of Lycaena's priests, she realized. The elderly man sat with ashes sprinkled across his naked body, which he'd shaved from head to toe. His formerly colorful robes lay folded in his lap, and they, too, were covered with ashes. He said nothing, not a word of protest, as the soldiers shouted for him to leave.

"*Servitude*," the priest sang, seemingly oblivious to their presence. "*I am your servitude, your servitude, your servitude. Hear me, O goddess, your servant, your servant, your beloved servant.*"

The soldiers beat him to cease his song. They kicked his teeth to end the words. The priest continued in spite of the beatings. He sang despite the blood that flowed and the bruises that piled up.

"*Beauty*," he cried. "*I am your beauty, your beauty, your beauty . . .*"

The crowd was growing, filled with those disgusted by the violent treatment of a priest. Before the Everlorn Empire had invaded, these holy men had dedicated their lives to spreading their goddess's glory across the island. They were known for their love and joy, or so Mari had been told by her father when they first stepped off the boat after a three-month journey across the Crystal Sea.

"We said be quiet!" one of the soldiers shouted at the priest, though it was in the imperial tongue, and Mari doubted any present but her understood him.

"Forget it," said the lone female soldier in charge. "He knows what he's doing. End it."

Just like that, she swiped her sword across the priest's face, killing the song. The ensuing silence was heartbreaking in its emptiness, punctuated only by the priest's gagging. Some onlookers cried out. Others cursed. Mari cursed with them, but they were merely fifteen or so commoners facing armed imperial soldiers. The woman wiped her sword and sheathed it while showing open contempt for the onlookers.

The priest collapsed, the wound bloody but not fatal. Mari rushed to his side, doing her best to ignore the soldiers. *Stasia's going to be so mad at me*, she thought, but she had to get involved.

"It's all right," she whispered as she took the naked priest into her arms. "Let's get you somewhere quiet."

The man tried to respond, but only blood came out of his mouth. The sword had cut a gash across his cheek, and worse was the damage done to the tip of his tongue. Brutal to look at, but he'd live if mended in time, and perhaps even one day sing again.

"Get away from the heretic," the female soldier said. "Unless you want yourself branded one as well."

Mari pretended not to understand their imperial tongue. Feigned ignorance could be its own useful tool.

"Leave them," another of the soldiers said. "We shut the bastard up. That's all that matters."

Once they were both on their feet, Mari guided the priest toward the nearby alley. Stitching a tongue was awkward and often unnecessary, but with such a brutal wound, she'd need to ensure the man didn't choke to death in his sleep.

"We said leave," the third soldier said, this time in Thanese. Damn it, they'd already tortured the man. Why couldn't they leave her alone? He reached for her shoulder, but a quick shift of her feet avoided it. Still she pretended to be unaware. One of the two nearby buildings had a door ajar, and she guided the priest toward it. Perhaps when they were off the street, he would leave them be...

"Look at me, damn it!"

The soldier shoved her, and both she and the priest crumpled through the door into a little storage shed for the adjacent café. Blood splattered across the ground from the priest's split tongue. Some of it splashed across Mari's hands, and the smell of it awakened something deep within the pit of her stomach. Slowly she stood and faced the soldier, who kicked the shed door shut behind him. Mari stared into him, eye to eye, taking the measure of the man. She saw his swirling disgust, his thoughts turning feral. Her perceived insult had him losing control. Would he murder her? Try to rape her? She didn't know. Even *he* didn't know. All he knew was that he was stronger, and she weaker.

Except she wasn't. Her blood was boiling, but unlike his wild anger, her fury was perfectly controlled. She gave not a hint to that leashed fire, just stood there and faced him, unblinking.

"Get out," the soldier said, and he pointed at her. "Right now, or I'll kill you after I'm done killing him. This is your only chance for mercy, you get it?"

Spoken in the imperial tongue. Did he think she could understand? Or did he speak only for himself, a justification for the abuse he planned to inflict? A slight smile crept at the edges of Mari's lips. As her anger grew, she felt a familiar presence. The world around her darkened.

Understanding came to her, as brilliant as the dawn. Of what Endarius was. Of what the Lion wanted when he demanded her rage.

"Can you not hear me?" the soldier asked, stepping closer. He pulled his sword an inch from its sheath, his intentions clear. "Get out of here, you cow."

Mari didn't move. Didn't blink. Only smiled. Despite the threat, she was calm for the first time during her three months spent on Thanet. She was a god-whisperer, and at long last, she had been received.

The soldier reached for her hand, and only then did she react. Her legs pulsed with strength far beyond their normal limits. She slammed against him, toppling him onto his back. Her hands latched on to his wrists. Her knees dug into his upper thighs, locking him down. The soldier stared up at her, shocked silent by her sudden ferocity.

Mari smiled sweetly down at him. Claws stretched from her fingers and sank into his skin. Her elbows jerked as the hinges reshaped. Her chest flattened as fat became muscle. Gray fur sprouted across her bare skin, tearing apart her dress.

"Not cow," she whispered in imperial so he would understand her before he died. The bones beneath her skin broke and reformed. "*Lioness.*"

She opened her mouth, and in response, her upper and lower jaw extended. Gray fur coated her body. Sharp, hungry teeth replaced her own. Mari tore into the soldier's neck, seeking blood and finding it. A single jerk of her head and the man's spine snapped. The taste of warm flesh on her tongue sent shivers through her changing body. Endarius's strength flowed within her, reshaping her, but she did not re-create herself with the same vibrant luster he'd once possessed in life. The Lion was slain, his physical body lost, and her new form would showcase that deathly nature.

Bone plates serving as armor ripped through her gray fur at her hips and shoulders, as well as thick protrusions along her forehead and jawline. Her knees bent backward, snapping audibly as she stood on all fours like a proper feline hunter. She bore no mane as a lioness, but she did possess wings that stretched from her spine, thin skeletal protrusions without feather or decoration. Just sharp, jagged bones eager to cut.

A withered hand stroked her side. She turned to find the priest kneeling beside her. Tears flowed down the sides of his wrinkled face. He could not speak, not with his mouth mangled from the sword slice, but his adoration was clear. Mari nuzzled him with her flat nose, and he flung his arms about her neck. His sobs grew louder. He might be a priest of Lycaena, but the gods had ruled together for hundreds of years, and there was no man or woman on Thanet who went untouched by Endarius's sacrifice.

Mari breathed warm air across his face. The people's faith in Endarius empowered her as well, and with it came the divine right of miracles. Small miracles, perhaps, but miracles nonetheless as the wound within the priest's mouth closed, and torn flesh healed.

"Endarius...you return to us," the man said amid his sobs once his mouth was healed.

"Your god is but a piece of me," she said, trying to explain the conjoining in a way he might understand. Her current feline tongue could not form such words, but it didn't matter. The shimmering word-lace was still around her neck, and it translated her soft growl into words the elderly man could understand. "His presence, his power, guides me, and I shall honor him how I know best. With tooth and claw, I will protect Lycaena from the executioners' blades. I swear it, priest. I swear it upon my life and death."

The priest crossed his arms and carefully bowed low to show his appreciation. Mari dipped her head in return, then turned toward the door. A growl emanated from her throat. She smelled the presence of the three other soldiers outside. Her tail flicked from side to side. In one country, she had been a falcon, and the thrill of the hunt had pounded through her heart before every dive. This was different. Hunter she may be, but not one for stealth and surprise.

To hunt meant to give in to pure, absolute rage.

Mari blasted through the door with a howling roar. The two nearest soldiers offered no defense, they were too stunned, too horrified by her arrival. She swiped her claws across the first's face and neck, opening massive gashes that cut to the bone. The second soldier crumpled beneath her weight. Her wings knifed downward to punch their sharpened tips through his shoulders and into the stone street, pinning him in place. Mari's claws raked his armor, and the metal crunched and folded like paper.

The final soldier fled, but Mari caught her in two quick leaps and closed her wings about her neck. Her armor separated with a shriek of metal matched in volume only by the soldier's scream. The wings' serrated edges sank in and then pulled, ripping apart the soft flesh of her throat in a tremendous spray of blood. Mari sank her teeth into that neck, tasting the crimson flow, drinking the manifest reward of her fury. The kills only heightened her need. She snapped the woman's head off completely and then leaped to the nearby rooftop.

A flick of teeth and the decapitated head flew to the confused and fearful onlookers. Mari stretched out before them on the rooftop's edge, flexing every inch of her muscular frame. Sunlight reflected off the bone plate armor. Blood dripped across her teeth and fur. None could doubt her divine inspiration, but Mari roared it out to them nonetheless. It was her promise to the city of Vallessau, to her people, and to her dying faithful.

So long as the Lioness hunted, Endarius lived. When the Uplifted Church attempted to execute the goddess Lycaena tomorrow, she would be there, and she would bring her fury.

CHAPTER 3

CYRUS

For two years, Cyrus lived as their obedient prisoner. He watched as a regent was assigned by the empire to rule Thanet in his stead. He listened for scattered bits of chatter about the resistance as Thanet's various cities fell one by one and the four lords of Thanet either were killed or had bent the knee in surrender. All the while he held on to hope that his family would be avenged. That the resistance would succeed.

That fleeting hope withered the moment he heard of Lycaena's capture. The empire's paragons had scoured the island in a never-ending hunt, and at last they had brought her low. Without the goddess to aid them, the resistance was nothing. Today it would die completely, for Cyrus stood atop a gigantic wooden platform built in the western fields beyond Vallessau, forced to witness the goddess's execution. Over ten thousand people gathered in attendance. Lines of soldiers blocked off the crowd from the platform, and smaller groups patrolled the edges, checking newcomers for weapons and turning away those they deemed troublemakers.

A lone soldier stood behind Cyrus, his mailed hand resting atop Cyrus's shoulder. The soldier was there to keep an eye on him should he attempt to cause a scene. His grip tightened as Thanet's regent left the center of the platform to speak with him at the platform's edge.

"Stand tall," the regent, Gordian Goldleaf, told him as he gave a once-over to Cyrus's elegant violet shirt and black velvet trousers. "It will do Thanet's people good to see their prince give his approval to the ceremony."

"Prince," Gordian called him, though by all rights Cyrus should now be king. It was how the empire still referred to him in all official proclamations. It gave a vague hint that things might one day return to normal, that the empire's regent was a temporary measure. A lie, of course, one few believed. Gordian may be regent, but Cyrus knew the name most people called him in the streets, a name Gordian had actually mocked one day at the dinner table, he was so amused by it: the Usurper King.

"I'll give no such approval," Cyrus said.

Gordian flashed him his brightest smile. He was a handsome man, muscular, bright-eyed, with his blond hair perfectly shaped beneath a golden crown.

"If you don't, then we shall have two executions on this stage, not one."

Gordian returned to the side of his wife, Katrin. The Usurper Queen. She wore a dress that matched Gordian's royal garb: long, shining waves of silver broken up with deep streaks of red. Fiery-haired, with eyes greener than emeralds and a smattering of freckles upon her cheeks, she was a portrait of beauty just like her husband was handsome. From what Cyrus had learned over his two years, she loved him not a wit. She loved the power that came from the marriage, and that was apparently enough to earn her fierce loyalty. The two shared a false smile as they resumed speaking with the numerous church representatives. Between them stood their little son, Uriah, in a silken suit brought all the way from distant Gadir. He clutched his mother's hand tightly. The boy was barely four. That he would witness the execution at such a young age seemed perverse to Cyrus, but what should he expect from such a twisted empire?

"Back them off," Imperator Magus of Eldrid shouted to his soldiers from where he stood upon the stage. The thousands were growing restless, either seeking the blood they came to witness, or permission to leave the ceremony that had been declared mandatory to attend by the regent. The paragon lifted his shield. "Or I'll do it for you, and it won't be gentle."

Cyrus cast a glance to the center of the platform. Six magistrates were in attendance, influential members of the Uplifted Church and leaders of various congregations. Those six gathered around the Anointed One, handpicked by the God-Incarnate to lead the island's religious conversion. Cyrus knew this young woman was special even among the Anointed, for she was one of God-Incarnate Lucavi's many children he had sired throughout his current six-hundred-year reign. Her name was Sinshei vin Lucavi, and she stood in the center of the platform addressing the gathered crowd. The crimson of her dress was so deep and vibrant, it befuddled the eye. Her black hair was tied into a braid that hung all the way down to her ankles, its weaves interlaced with gold thread. The hair was so long, so extravagant, Cyrus wondered if it was even real.

Braying trumpets signaled the start of the ceremony. The people atop the stage shuffled into place, and Cyrus obediently followed. He stood next to little Uriah. Katrin held his hand, the pair a step behind the Usurper King. Next were the many priests and magistrates in their robes. Upon hearing the trumpets, Magus took his own position ahead of the magistrates, with his sword and shield at the ready. Last, and closest to the crowd, stood the Anointed One, she of the God-Incarnate's own blood.

Read left to right from the crowd, it conveyed the proper order of all things as decreed by the Uplifted Church: child, woman, man, priest, paragon, and God-Incarnate.

The only ones without a place were the heretical gods, hence the three golden knives strapped to the Anointed One's waist.

"My children, be not afraid of the coming change," Sinshei said. The word-lace wrapped about her throat shimmered with blue light as the sapphire embedded in its center flared with magic. Her words shifted from the imperial tongue to Thanese, and they boomed with volume far beyond the capabilities of human lungs. "For centuries, you were deceived. For centuries, you walked in darkness, and crafted idols of your own making. On this day, we end the falsehoods that chained your souls. Be not mournful or afraid. This is a sacred day. A glorious day. It is *your* day, the day you walk free."

She motioned behind her, sending paragons into motion. A hush fell over the crowd of thousands. Fear and awe swelled in Cyrus's throat. There she was, the goddess Lycaena. Two paragons escorted her from the hastily constructed wood prison behind the platform, each one holding her by an arm. Her hands were linked together with steel chains that looped up to her neck. Her dress and wings dragged as they climbed the steps behind the platform. Sickness swirled in Cyrus's gut upon realizing the priests had hacked off the goddess's multicolored hair. Was sacrificing her not enough? Must they humiliate her first? Murmurs spread through the crowd at the sight of her. How many were prayers? How many groaned with disgust at the empire's cruelty? Cyrus hoped it was most, if not all.

"Citizens of the Everlorn Empire!" Sinshei continued. "I extend my heart to you, and hope that you will join me in this holy worship. What I do in the flesh, you may do with your own hearts. Sever the lifeline of heresy that beats between the weak, sinful, and prideful, and this object of idolatry. Today, it ends. Today, I come wielding the knife."

The paragons forced Lycaena to her knees. Sinshei withdrew the three curved knives with golden handles from her leather belt. She handed one to the Usurper King, and then one to his wife. The last she kept for herself.

"Do not weep for this loss," the Anointed One continued. "Do not view this as an end, but instead a new beginning. Let us rejoice in this freedom. Let your hearts be light as you are uplifted by the truth. You need not worship these objects of heresy. You need not bow your heads to a lie. My father, the God-Incarnate of all creation, stands ready to forgive your ignorance and accept your prayers. Let him be your truth. Let him be your righteousness."

Her excitement reached a fevered pitch. She held the knife aloft, and she called out to the throng with a feverish faith glowing from her gleaming smile.

"Will you join me?" she asked. "Will you pray with me? Will you partake?"

A tremendous roar marked the people's answer, and so began the last desperate attempt to save the life of the goddess. Cyrus's eyes widened at the sight of an enormous lioness leaping from the heart of the crowd into the thick lines of soldiers protecting the platform. The resemblance to Endarius was uncanny, only she was a picture of death instead of life, with bones for armor and pale gray fur instead of a lively gold. Her wings were weapons that tore into her foes like bony fingers. The soldiers tightened together, relying on sheer numbers to keep their foe at bay.

Then came the paladins of both Endarius and Lycaena. They rushed the stage with a song on their lips and holy light sparkling off their weapons. Cyrus dared feel hope. The people had not abandoned him, nor had they abandoned Lycaena. A brave few threw stones or fired arrows at the Anointed, but the magistrates surrounding her lifted their hands in prayer. Steady chants rose from their throats, forming a translucent shield to protect them. Arrows snapped in half. Stones bounced off as if against steel. As much as Cyrus would love to see them killed, he trusted the surging forces in the crowd. They would win, he told himself. This was clearly planned and well organized.

Except…except the surge forward wasn't reaching the platform. The scattered members of Thanet's rebellion weren't merging together to form a solid line to join the fight near the front. He watched, trying to make sense of the absolute chaos. Soldiers fell, and the trampled earth was soon bathed in blood, but the imperials held their ground as those uninvolved in the fight fled for the city. Amid the steadily thinning numbers, Cyrus understood what had happened.

Yes, the resistance had seeded hundreds of loyal followers of Lycaena and Endarius throughout the crowd, but so, too, had the Everlorn Empire secreted its paragons. They lacked their usual armor and extravagant weapons, but even without them they were ferocious warriors few could hope to match. Perhaps Endarius's and Lycaena's paladins could, but they were outnumbered, fighting against wall upon wall of soldiers separating the crowd from the raised platform. With each second that passed, more soldiers stationed throughout the outer ring of the crowd closed in, further isolating pathways toward the platform.

The end result was inevitable to Cyrus's eyes. It wasn't enough. Magus of Eldrid had leaped into the fight, anchoring the line of soldiers before the platform. He was a rock the imperials could rely upon as they overcame the surprise of the attack and beat back the rows of paladins. As those first frantic moments passed, Sinshei visibly calmed, her initial fear replaced with disgust. The multiple magistrates surrounding her continued their chant as she lifted her dagger skyward.

"Like newborns, you squabble and fight against what is best," she shouted. The sapphire at her throat shone with brilliant light, projecting her voice above the chaos. "And like newborns, you will be born amid blood and pain."

The paladins surged forward with one last, desperate attack. The Lioness bit and clawed and tore apart all foes. They were so close to breaking through, so close, but it wasn't enough. The Anointed One put her knife to Lycaena's breast. Cyrus broke from the soldier who held him and sprinted across the platform. He couldn't stand and watch. He wouldn't cower while hundreds of others bled and died to save their island, to save their goddess. He ran, extending a hand despite knowing there was nothing he could do. He was too slow. Too weak. Too late.

Just like his parents.

Lycaena lifted her head, and for the first time she addressed the roaring crowd.

"Beauty in all things."

The knife sank into her heart. The shriek that followed rocked Cyrus to his knees. The Usurper King and Queen had their own knives, and they knew their designated role. The screams of the goddess continued. Knives plunged into her perfectly smooth midnight skin. Cut her wings. Tore apart her body. Cyrus had never been one to worship, but he felt something had been irrevocably stolen as he sobbed.

Sinshei noticed his kneeling presence as light swelled across the bleeding body of the goddess, and she lifted a startled hand.

"Get back, you fool," she shouted.

The power within the dying body of the goddess exploded outward, as it had when Endarius fell upon the battlefield. The magistrates protected the Anointed and the usurpers with their prayers, but no such protection extended to Cyrus. Power washed over him, real and tangible like a fiery wind. Thoughts assailed his mind, visions from sparks of time beyond his understanding. He was flying, that he knew, his meager body sailing overhead the chaos. The sky and ground danced, changed places, and then he landed atop some hapless man or woman and rolled.

It was all chaos and blood, with people running every which way and imperial soldiers hacking down bodies at random. Despite his station, despite his birth, he meant nothing to the crowd surrounding him. The fight was over, and every single person fled for their lives. Legs kicked him. Feet trampled him. Heels and knees bruised and battered his body. Breathing was difficult. He couldn't stand. He'd die there, lost amid the crowd. An ignoble death, yet deserved for one so worthless as he.

A hand grabbed his wrist. A single strong pull sent him lurching back to a stand. He looked up into the face of his protector, saw short snow white hair, and a terrible mixture of hope and fear stirred within his chest.

"I pray you stay with me this time," Rayan said. He spread his brown cloak wide to hide Cyrus from sight. "Quickly, remove your shirt."

Cyrus ripped off his violet shirt and dropped it. When done, Rayan grabbed dirt from the trampled earth and smeared some across Cyrus's face and chest. Next he took off his cloak and wrapped it about Cyrus's naked shoulders. Out came a knife. Without a word he hacked off portions of Cyrus's dark hair, leaving it disheveled and uneven.

"This will have to do," the paladin said. "Keep your head down and your cloak up."

"Thank you," Cyrus said. His mind was numb, his senses overloaded by the screams and the memories of a jagged knife plunging into the breast of the goddess.

"Thank me when we are safe and sound," Rayan said. He put an arm around Cyrus's shoulders. "Now run, and never stop to look back."

CHAPTER 4

STASIA

I didn't think you'd come," Clarissa said. A smile lit up the woman's small, round face. "It isn't safe, but I should have known that wouldn't stop you."

The Underhill Tavern was Stasia's and Clarissa's favorite spot to unwind at after a long day. It was dimly lit and sparsely attended, the exact reasons they loved it. Their table was an uneven rectangular slab of wood shoved into a corner, and Stasia sat on the bench beside Clarissa, close enough that their thighs touched. Normally the little red-haired woman would have sunk into Stasia's arms, but affection was dangerous, especially given the three imperial soldiers by the bar. The soldiers laughed and hollered with one another at such volume, it seemed they wanted the entire tavern to hear their crass jokes.

"After today, the last thing I want is to sulk alone at home," Stasia said, risking a kiss on Clarissa's dimpled cheek after checking that no one was watching. The other woman's smile faded.

"It's all anyone can talk about. Was it as bad as I've heard?"

That singular moment when the knife plunged into Lycaena's breast flashed through Stasia's mind. Despite the blood she had shed with her axes, she and her fellow members of the resistance could not breach the line of soldiers. They could not save the goddess from the knives of the empire.

"Worse," she said.

"Did Mari, did she at least—"

"Yes," Stasia interrupted. "She's fine. I'd probably have been captured, too, if not for her. She carried me on her back like a damn horse...cat...thing."

She was frustrated and incoherent. The bartender thankfully arrived carrying food and drink despite never having been asked, a welcome enough excuse for Stasia to shut her mouth. Both women were regulars, and the kindly man with a curled mustache and eye patch knew exactly what they'd want. He carried two metal cups of ale along with a wooden plate stacked with cheese and bread.

"Only the finest for my most loyal customers," the bartender said, a tubby man named Gilbi. His voice lowered. "What a sad day. Consider this on me tonight, Stasia, for what you and your family've done for our island."

He left so they might have their privacy. Stasia tore into the cheese; food was one of her unfortunate vices when something troubled her.

"Leave some for me," Clarissa said as she gently elbowed Stasia in the side. Clarissa used the motion to sink her weight farther into her, and one of her hands vanished underneath the table to settle atop Stasia's upper thigh. Stasia kissed the woman's forehead despite her mouthful of cheese so that she'd know she approved.

"So what happens now?" Clarissa asked after they'd eaten. Stasia drained a third of her ale, then stomped a foot to hold back a cough. Yes, it might be Gilbi's finest, but that still didn't mean it was high quality. They didn't go to Underhill Tavern for the ale, but instead the knowledge that the owner was a loyal friend to the resistance.

"Now? I'm worried my father will ask us to leave Thanet."

"Has he given up on us?"

"It always happens," Stasia said, trying not to sound bitter. "We come, we bleed for a nation, and then we move on when it's not enough. It's never enough. Fuck if I know why we keep trying. But there's no way to dress up what happened today. Our resistance is crushed. Saving Lycaena was our last best hope to keep the people inspired and instead... instead..."

She trailed off, unable to vocalize the thought. Instead they had thrown away countless lives in the attempt. Despite all the money, time, and training her father had poured into Thanet's resistance, it had ended in spectacular failure. Lycaena had been publicly executed, and the last surviving member of the royal family, Prince Cyrus, was presumed dead. Just like all the other nations that the Everlorn Empire invaded, the populace would be converted to worshiping the God-Incarnate. Their customs, their beliefs, even their native language, would be steadily buried and replaced.

The raucous crowd near the bar continued to grow. The three imperial soldiers were lifting their cups above their heads while singing a song most certainly not native to Thanet. Stasia did her best to hide her glare. The bastards were celebrating Lycaena's death, as if killing a divine being were worthy of praise instead of horror.

"Stasia...have you considered not going with him if he does leave?" Clarissa asked. Her body pressed tighter against her. "You don't have to keep fighting his personal war. All the gods and goddesses know you've given your father more than enough of your life."

Stasia leaned her cheek atop her lover's red hair.

"I don't regret fighting," she said. "I just...I want to feel like there's still hope. Otherwise, what's the point?"

"You could always stop fighting."

Bitter laughter bubbled up from her stomach, or perhaps it was the ale and cheese hitting her stomach hard.

"Of all the things in my future, that's the least likely, I'd say."

She wasn't ready for the hurt that flashed across Clarissa's round, puppy-dog face.

"You don't have to laugh at me so." She shifted on the bench, finally breaking their physical contact. "We're so far away from the mainland, they can't possibly rule over us like they do elsewhere. What if we kept silent, kept our heads down, and continued on with our lives in secret?"

Stasia couldn't believe what her ears were hearing. When the Ahlai family had arrived on Thanet, they'd met with the remaining supporters of the resistance that had endured after Vallessau's collapse and the defeat of the island's four lords. Clarissa had caught Stasia's attention at the very first meeting, a mousy little woman with bright eyes and a mind for numbers. Despite two years of subjugation, she had fought back in her own way.

Vallessau's trio of city clerks had been disbanded upon the empire's arrival, replaced with three underlings the church thought more easily controllable. Clarissa had been one such underling, and she used her position to manipulate properties, smuggle and store supplies where patrols would not check, and create safehouses for those who could no longer show their faces in public. She lamented the loss of Endarius and offered prayers for the slaughtered royal family. When times were dark, Clarissa was Stasia's light.

"You don't mean this," Stasia said. She reached for Clarissa's hand upon the table, and for a brief moment she feared the other woman would pull away. Thankfully she kept still, and when Stasia's fingers intertwined with hers, there was still love and tenderness within them.

"Do you know what I do every sunrise?" Clarissa asked. Her blue eyes remained locked on the table. "I walk past the Dead Flags and look upon the faces of every single person swinging from a rope. I look for *you*, Stasia. Every morning, I steel myself to see you hanging with a noose about your neck, and every morning I offer Lycaena a prayer of gratitude that you aren't one of the dead. Every morning, Stasia. Every morning."

She was crying. Damn it all, Stasia wanted to scream. Was she even capable of doing one single thing right?

"I don't know how much longer I can do this," Clarissa continued. "I can't keep going to sleep at night thinking the next morning will be the one I have to say goodbye. The life the empire would leave us, it is wretched, but it is still a life... isn't it?"

Stasia wanted to shrink down into nothing within her voluminous coat. She wanted to pull her hat down so low over her head that nothing of her face remained visible. While she gripped Clarissa's hand with tenderness, her free hand clawed splinters free of the table with her fingernails. These doubts, they came over anyone struggling against so overwhelming a foe. But this confession, so soon after the prince's death and Lycaena's execution...

"I forgot how much the Butterfly goddess meant to you," Stasia said, mentally screaming at herself for her obliviousness. For fuck's sake, Clarissa's father had hung at the Dead Flags for his faith in Lycaena, she knew that, she *knew* it, yet she focused so much on her own hurt that she neglected Clarissa's. "I'm sorry. I'm moping and angry, and yet I should be the one here for you."

"You're always here for me," Clarissa said, and she dried her face. "I'm just scared one day you won't be."

The three imperial soldiers were badgering the men on either side of them to join in their song, something raunchy about a Miquoan prostitute and her lover. Stasia took her now-empty glass and hammered it atop her table.

"For gods' sake," she shouted. "Shut. The fuck. Up."

Her words were a cold iron thrust into the heart of the tavern. Tense silence followed in its wake, not long, a heartbeat of wonder at the repercussions for such impudence before nervous laughter and conversations resumed. The imperials, however, would not let her go so easily.

"Well, well, well, the kitty has claws," said one who wandered over from the bar. A heavy scar ran from one cheek, across the bridge of his nose, and to the other. His words were playful, but his smile was vicious. Stasia noticed that despite coming in for a drink, the man still wore his chainmail and gray tunic. Still officially on patrol, by her guess.

"No claws," Stasia said, already regretting her outburst. "I just want to eat without having to endure awful songs."

"If you don't want awful songs, then don't go to taverns when the moon is high!" The imperial laughed. His lips spread into a toothy smile. "And lighten up. We're all having a good time, aren't we, boys? Today's a day of celebration!"

The other two lifted their glasses, and a few sycophants sitting beside them did likewise. It soured Stasia's stomach.

"Sorry, forgive my outburst," she said. "It's been a long day. I'll do better to hold my tongue."

But it seemed the imperial would not leave her be. He sat on the bench opposite theirs, and he leaned in close as if he were to share a secret.

"Your eyes...you're from Miquo, aren't you?"

Stasia's worry only grew. The people of the forested nation of Miquo were famous for their red eyes. The God-Incarnate had grown enamored with their color and vibrancy upon invading Miquo thirty years ago, and he had briefly taken a Miquoan bride as his fifteenth wife. Rumors abounded of courtesans and minstrels using magistrate magic to change their irises to match, at least until the marriage soured, and the Miquoan woman was executed for unnamed, and likely untrue, acts of sedition.

"I am," Stasia said, hoping he'd drop it.

"Well, aren't you far from home," the soldier said. "I actually fought in Miquo. My elders called it the fiercest and most ruthless rebellion the empire's ever had to put down, and I believe it. Your people were savage, the God-Incarnate as my witness, just completely savage. No man dared walk alone at night, not on the roads, and definitely not through those awful forest-cities. I tell you, it makes Thanet seem like paradise after fighting over there."

Stasia's teeth ached from clenching her jaw so tightly.

"I'm glad you think so highly of my people," she said. She started to stand but he slammed a hand on the table to stop her.

"*Spread thy love to the four corners, and may thy children be faithful and plentiful,*" the man said, suddenly reciting one of the core tenants of the Uplifted. "A simple command, yeah? So perhaps you two can answer me a riddle. How does a woman bear children when all she has bedding her is another woman?"

Clarissa and Stasia froze. Their hands. They were still holding hands, and not even attempting to hide it. Stasia's sour stomach turned thoroughly rotten. He couldn't punish her for it, not until the Joining Laws were enacted here as they were throughout the rest of the empire, but he could bait her into reacting. Given the anger surging through her, it might even work.

"Please, we meant no offense," Clarissa said, her pleading words agony in Stasia's ears. "We'll buy you and your friends drinks."

"I've got plenty of drink," the scarred soldier said. "What say you, though? Are you faithful women of the church?" He winked. "Do you need some help with the whole 'sire children' thing? Not sure how I'd feel with a son of mine sporting the red eyes of a freak, but I'd wager I could accept that to spread the faith."

Stasia stood, but not to her full height. Let him think her smaller, weaker. Her entire body tensed beneath her thick coat. Her twin axes rattled at her hips, but so far the soldier had not noticed them, they were so well hidden by her coat. The arrogant man would see nothing of her honed muscle, her sharpened weapons, or her rage growing within her breast. All he'd see was a woman bending before him, neck bowed, eyes low. Willing. Submissive. As the Uplifted Church would demand it.

"Your friends await you," she said through clenched teeth. "Perhaps another time, when duty does not threaten to interfere?"

Sure enough, the other two soldiers stood by the door, and they were pulling their cloaks off nearby rungs and clasping them about their necks. Whatever time they'd wasted drinking and eating, they'd run out and needed to resume their patrols. The scarred soldier glanced over his shoulder, then let out an exaggerated sigh.

"Yes, yes, my lovely Miquoan," he said. "Another time. I'll keep my eye out for you." He winked at Clarissa. "And you as well. I'd hate for either of you to fail in your duty to the church."

He pushed his bench aside and stood. Before he left, he reached out a mailed hand and touched the metal of his fingertips to Stasia's cheek. When she did not move, he slapped her. Not hard. Not even with any real animosity. Just enough to let her know how little she meant to him.

"Pleasant nights and sweet dreams, you two perverts."

The soldier left, and he laughed with his two waiting friends as if he'd told the greatest joke in the world. Pain flushed Stasia's face as her cheek swelled. Perhaps he had.

"Stasia," Clarissa warned, and she grabbed at Stasia's wrist. "Please, don't."

"I have to," Stasia said. Her red eyes locked on the three men as they exited the tavern. "I'm sorry, Clarissa. I have to."

There were two separate doors to the tavern. While the soldiers exited the front, Stasia ducked out the back to the cramped alley between it and the neighboring home. The moment the door shut behind her, she pulled her two axes free of their hip holsters. The two axes, while usable separate, were actually two opposite-facing halves of a larger weapon. Stasia slammed their backs together, connecting barely perceptible grooves and hooks. Her father's intricate designs worked perfectly as ever, the twin axes locking into a singular great-ax. Next she pulled out a metal pole hidden in a secret side pocket of her coat. The pole was a little over two feet, with one end flat, the other sharpened into a spike. A shove and a twist later, the pole slid into a waiting slot at the base of the ax and locked tight, granting her a much longer reach.

Now she had her great-ax assembled and ready, Stasia ripped her coat off and tossed it upon the thin layer of snow that powdered the alley from winter's last gasp prior to spring. Everywhere she went, she hid her true size beneath coats, dresses, robes, or whatever else fit the fashion of the invaded nation. Anything to disguise the muscles of her arms and tightly corded abdomen. Beneath was a simple pair of trousers and a dark sweater, both bought cheap at a local market. Let her be anyone and everyone, her only singularly distinguishable characteristic that of the finely polished steel of her ax. As for armor, she wore hidden shin guards and metal vambraces, and dared not risk anything more that could lessen her speed or sap her strength. Her fighting style was one of merciless aggression, her battles fought in the chaos of street ambushes instead of organized warfare upon open fields.

Stasia reached into a pocket of her coat and pulled out a long black cloth. It was her only possession that once belonged to her blood-mother, a mask with a roaring panther skull sewn across its center. Her shaking fingers lovingly touched the saber-toothed bones arranged into a snarl. Within her, a rage fed by helplessness and fear stoked a fire hot enough to burn Vallessau to the ground.

"You fear the day you find me hanging," she whispered, Clarissa's words ringing in her ears. "I fear the day they drag us apart with whips in hand and holy screeds on their tongues."

Stasia tied the mask over her face. Last, she touched her word-lace and activated its special magic unique only to hers and Mari's. A brief tingle alerted her it had taken effect. A spell came over her eyes, fading their red irises to a dull brown so that none would recognize her as

Miquoan. She hated disguising herself in such a manner, but this was the price she paid to be the warrior her father had carefully crafted over decades since Miquo's collapse. Everywhere they went, the resistance one day failed. If they were to keep traveling, and keep trying, she could not be identified.

Stasia lifted her great-ax. The touch of cold steel beneath her fingers gave a pathway for her fire to flow.

The life the empire would leave us, it is wretched, but it is still a life . . . isn't it?

Could she exist within Everlorn's rule? Perhaps. But it wouldn't be a free life. It wouldn't be real. It'd be a cruel joke. It'd be as joyful and permanent as the swelling bruise on her cheek.

The corner of the tavern had a small ladder installed for the chimney sweepers, and Stasia dashed up the rungs to the rooftop. From there she sprinted, her powerful legs easily vaulting the narrow gaps between buildings. The boisterous laughter of the soldiers attracted her like a beacon, and she caught up to them when they stopped at another alleyway. Two stood at the entrance while a third loosened his belt and pulled down his pants so he could piss.

"Couldn't you have done that inside?" one of the two at the entrance muttered.

"I didn't need to then," the pissing man shouted back.

Stasia crouched at the rooftop edge. The world tinted red, colored by the stubborn tears in her eyes and painted with a hateful brush. She lifted her ax. An ambush would have been smarter, but she didn't want victory. She wanted a fight. She wanted blood.

"Am I interrupting?" she asked.

The pissing man heard her growl and looked drunkenly toward the sky.

"What the—"

His statement abruptly ended with her ax smashing directly into his open mouth. The edge sank down to his shoulder, so when she ripped it free, his jaw and clavicle tore with it. Blood splashed across Stasia's hands, and it was a warm pleasure against the night's biting cold. She kicked the dying man away and greeted the other two soldiers with the saber-toothed grin of her mask.

"Bloody hell," said the scarred man. The other took the lead, his sword gleaming in the reflection of the moon. Stasia blocked his downward swing with the handle of her ax, and as the sound of metal on metal rang in her ears, she shoved the ax upward, swiped sideways to earn herself needed space, and then slipped past.

It was madness, putting herself directly between two opponents, but she wanted the scarred man first. Let them surround her, she thought, let them try. A scream was bellowing from her throat, one she did not remember starting. She blocked a chop, ducked underneath a swing from behind her, and came up and around while thrusting the sharpened spike at the bottom of her ax handle. It punched below the breastplate and sank several inches in the direction of his lungs. The man screamed, wet and weak. Not the scarred man. Not her desired prey. She ripped the spike free and twirled.

A sword thrust greeted her, but she parried it aside. Her elbow struck the scarred man's neck. He gagged, punched her stomach, and tried to step away. She gave him no reprieve. Her ax came up and around, and when he blocked, his legs quivered from the impact. Stasia brought a second blow down upon him, then a third. Her muscles strained with every swing, but he suffered worse. On the fourth blow his sword snapped in half, and her ax smashed his collarbone. It didn't break through his armor, but it didn't need to. The ax crunched the man's own pauldron into a jagged weapon, and it pierced his gambeson to tear at the skin beneath.

The scarred man's scream was a song to her ears. The bones of his shoulder and arm broke like twigs. It wasn't enough. She swung again, easily batting aside his parry attempt. Her ax tore a gap in his chest plate and sank a full foot into his rib cage. Another scream, weaker. He doubled over, blood splashing across the snow. Hatred seethed in his dying eyes. Did he recognize her despite her mask? She hoped so. She needed it so. She almost ripped off the cloth to show him the welt upon her cheek, but she heard worried cries before she could.

Three more soldiers sprinted down the street, attracted by the sounds of violence and the cries of the dead. Stasia lifted her ax and steadied her breathing.

"More!" she screamed at them. "Bring me more!"

Her father would insist she plan her attack, but Stasia had drifted away from his teachings over the years. Instinct ruled now. She dashed directly into the center of all three, her legs twisting, her ax spinning, its gore-soaked edges the leader of the macabre dance. She blocked one swing, a second, then caught a thrust with a twist of her ax head. She leaped over another swing, using the force of their interlocked weaponry to propel herself farther. Her metal shin guards struck the side of the soldier's head. His eyes crossed. Upon landing, she yanked her weapon free, the force staggering the soldier.

Except he wasn't a soldier anymore. To her, he wasn't even human. Her ax cut him in half, not a living foe, but the personification of the scarred man's leering stare at her and Clarissa's intertwined fingers.

The final soldier's retreat was doomed before she took a single step. Stasia bore down upon her with the long reach of her ax. Off went the woman's ankle above the heel. Off went her shins at the knee. Off went her leg at the hip. Again and again Stasia lifted her ax and then brought it crashing back down. Gore warmed her body. The furious scream bellowing from her throat gave her strength. The tears pouring down her face gave her life.

"Fuck you," she screamed as she pounded the mess in the snow that no longer resembled anything human. Hardly even bones remained to resist her ax's finely honed edge. She was carving cracks into the cobblestones. "Fuck you, fuck you, fuck all of you, damn it, fuck . . . fuck . . ."

A hand grabbed her shoulder. Stasia lashed out, and her fist found purchase. Regret immediately followed. Through the red, she saw Clarissa clutching at her swelling cheek and cut lip, yet her lover did not pull away.

"Clarissa," Stasia said. A thousand words formed and died upon her tongue. "I-I'm, I—"

Clarissa pulled Stasia close and forced her into a kiss. The rage seeped away, and in its shadow remained only emptiness and exhaustion. Stasia tasted blood on her lips, and it was her own fault. Her own sin. What apology could she offer to wipe that guilt away?

"Let's get you home," Clarissa whispered. She carried Stasia's oversized coat, and she gently slipped it over her shoulders. As it covered her body, the last of her fury dwindled. The fire left nothing in its wake. She could barely lift her arms, let alone her great-ax. She leaned against the smaller woman, this person who was so much better than she deserved, and whose love she would sacrifice all the world to protect.

Stasia paused at the door to her house. Now that her blood had cooled, and Clarissa was safely home, she had spent her walk debating her future. She was not done fighting the empire, that much was clear, but neither would she leave the island of Thanet. So what option did that leave her? When her father and sister embarked for a new rebellion, a new nation facing the conquering wrath of the empire, what might she do? To stay was to abandon her family. To go was to abandon Clarissa. Neither was acceptable.

Mood sour, future bleak, she paused at the front door to her home. Soft voices leaked through, and faint candlelight shone in the window.

"Hello?" Stasia asked as she slid the door open. "Have we guests?"

The well-furnished entry room was surprisingly crowded. By the fire stood her father, Thorda, alert and stern as ever despite wearing a purple bed-robe. With him was an older, muscular man she recognized as the paladin, Rayan Vayisa, who had been their closest confidant in planning Vallessau's liberation. The two older men conversed, drinks in hand. Her sister, Mari, tired and ragged from her time as the Lioness, smiled at her from her chair. Most unexpected of all was a third man sleeping on the couch. He was young, and she didn't recognize him.

At least, not at first.

"Impossible," she said as she stood in the doorway, unable to take another step inside. Her eyes locked on that cherubic face, and she remembered him now, remembered his panicked scream atop the wooden platform as the goddess died.

"Far from impossible," said her father, and there was no denying the excitement in his voice. "Shut the door so we might talk. The dead prince lives, and so lives our final chance to save the people of Thanet."

CHAPTER 5

CYRUS

When Cyrus awoke, he discovered he had been moved from the couch he had fallen asleep on, and carried to a small but well-furnished room with a far more comfortable bed. A fresh set of clean clothes lay folded at the foot of it, and he silently dressed. He found himself moving as if in a dream. After two years of living in fearful servitude within the castle, it was surreal to be alone and free of the empire's forces.

Once dressed, he sat on the bed and pondered his fate. Endarius, killed upon the empire's arrival. Lycaena, executed at the Anointed One's ceremony. With both gods slain, he saw no hope for a free nation of Thanet, nor any chance he might one day retake his throne. The regent would claim it for himself; of that much, Cyrus was certain. It had been his in all but name, anyway. Why else had they gone to such lengths to always refer to Cyrus as a prince instead of a king?

A trio of knocks brought his attention to the door.

"I pray you are awake," said a man before opening the door. He was in his early sixties by Cyrus's guess, his brown hair frosted with gray. His tanned skin might have been starting to wrinkle, but there was no hint of age or fading to his red eyes. They carried the fanaticism of a much younger man, and they made Cyrus want to shrink into himself and stare at the carpeted floor. The man's clothes were expensive, and in an elegant, flowing style not native to the island. He carried a wooden tray with buttered bread and two glasses of water, sliced clementines floating in each.

"I was already awake," Cyrus said, and he gestured to his clothes. The trousers were brown, finely pressed, and the buttoned shirt a mute but pleasant orange. They were the expensive-yet-unassuming clothes he'd expect his servants to have worn in the castle. "Thank you for these."

The man waved the gratitude away like a bothersome fly.

"My name is Thorda Ahlai. I do not expect you to have heard of me. Since my homeland of Miquo was invaded, I have spent my time, and my considerable fortune, funding insurrections against the Everlorn Empire and teaching their soldiers how to fight against their better-equipped and better-trained foes."

Magus and the Usurper King had often grumbled with each other over the resistance's stubborn ability to survive, as well as its remarkable coordination. It seemed the explanation stood before Cyrus, and it amused him greatly.

"Then I have you to thank for my escape," he said.

"Perhaps indirectly," Thorda said. "Rayan deserves all of the credit. The only credit I deserve is failing to ascertain the number of paragons the empire would prepare for today's ceremony. It is a mistake that cost Thanet the life of a goddess, and a shame I will carry with me to my grave."

The reference to that awful ceremony sent an unwelcome shiver through Cyrus's body. He shook his head, trying to banish the unpleasant memories.

"Will anyone come looking for me?" he asked.

"Unlikely," Thorda said. "Regent Goldleaf has sent criers shouting throughout the city declaring your death. Trampled during the aftermath of Lycaena's execution, I believe is the stated method. More so, he has pinned all responsibility on the rebels who attempted to disrupt the ceremony."

"That sounds like him," Cyrus grumbled.

"With Lycaena's death and my resistance's utter defeat, your worth as a political prisoner lost much of its value. I suspect the regent would have soon ordered your execution or exile. Consider yourself lucky Rayan was able to rescue you and bring you to me."

"Lucky," Cyrus said, his stomach so sick he wanted to grab the nearby plate and throw it at a wall. "You would call me lucky after everything that has happened?"

"I would," Thorda said. "Shall I drag you to the Dead Flags and show you the fates of those I consider *unlucky*?"

Cyrus bowed his head as heat rose in his cheeks. As cruel as his life may be, he knew it foolish to complain when the Everlorn Empire had killed hundreds, if not thousands, of Thanese citizens in its campaign to eradicate all semblance of Thanet's prior order.

"I'm sorry," he said. "I do not mean to sound ungrateful."

"I don't want you grateful," Thorda said. "I want you motivated, so spare me your apologies. It is good to see disgust and anger yet remain after two years of imprisonment. My fear was that they had beaten the spine out of you and left behind the gutless putty of a prince."

They had tried, Cyrus thought, god and goddess help him, they had tried. Any errant word could lead to a beating on his thighs, ribs, or other places that would show no bruises when he was occasionally trotted out on display to prove to the island he still lived. The slightest hint of protest could cost him weeks of isolation in his bedroom. No meal was ever guaranteed. Throughout it all, overheard complaints about the resistance, Thorda's resistance, had allowed him to endure. So long as others fought for his kingdom's freedom, he had promised himself to lurk, and listen, and pray for a chance to escape.

Now it seemed his prayers had been answered. Before him was the architect, and so Cyrus pulled back his shoulders and stood as tall and proud as he was capable of.

"I owe you much," he said. "And I will repay it as best I can. What would you ask of me? Is it to use my family name? My status?"

The older man crossed his arms and stared at Cyrus with those red eyes for an uncomfortably long time. What was he searching for? Or was he measuring him up, and judging him? Cyrus refused to break before that stare, and he waited until Thorda suddenly resumed speaking.

"I have partaken in seven different resistance movements over the past twenty-five years. The empire dreads my influence, though they know me only by lies and pseudonyms. Their soldiers have learned to fear the arrival of my daughters, the bloody Ax of Lahareed and whatever new form Mari assumes with the land's slain deities. We fight, we kill, and we make the empire suffer. And even when we lose, the seeds of rebellion are sown, and they will sprout again, and again, until Everlorn crumbles underneath the weight of an entire continent."

"Has any nation won their freedom?" Cyrus asked, daring to feel hope that Thanet may be the next. Thorda's face darkened briefly.

"No, Cyrus. Not completely. Eventually the furious empire sends its armies and paragons to overwhelm my rebellions. Every single time, I make them regret the sheer blood and cost it requires. The Everlorn Empire is a tremendous monster, and it will not die to a single blow, but instead bleed out from a dozen gashes. Given the current circumstances, I am hoping Thanet will draw out that fatal drop."

"Us?" Cyrus asked. "What's so special about Thanet?"

"Thanet is months from the nearest mainland port of Garlea," Thorda explained. "Reinforcements will take obscene amounts of time to arrive. Communications from Everlorn and with the Uplifted Church shall carry tremendous delays. Above all, feeding an army is expensive, and vastly more so when forced onto ships for months. All this will strain at the imperial presence. By outmaneuvering the distant, lumbering empire, I do believe we can reestablish your seat upon the throne."

The older man hesitated.

"But all that said, there is no way to overstate the catastrophic damage we suffered yesterday. There are three key losses that are irrevocably linked together. They will wound the hearts and minds of Thanet, and unless we heal them, our chances of recovery are nonexistent."

Thorda held up a fist, and he raised a finger for each of his three points.

"Lycaena's execution, the resistance's defeat, and the end of the Lythan family line. If we are to inspire a populace to war, we must undo this defeat, but how?"

Down went one finger.

"I cannot convince the people a defeat was not a defeat. So instead, we must heal the other two wounds in hopes of overcoming this damning one."

Down went the second finger.

"Your paladin friend, Rayan Vayisa, will do his best to preach Lycaena's message, and convince the people the Butterfly goddess remains a lingering presence on this island. My daughter, Mari, shall continue revealing herself as the Lioness, a physical incarnation of Endarius. It is a tall task, though I believe the pair are up to it."

Now the third finger clenched back into the fist.

"But it is this last point we can use to our advantage. Lycaena is dead, and my rebellion currently broken, but the Lythan family lives. As it is our strongest weapon, we must polish it to an absolute shine and ensure its edge sharp enough to pierce right through the heart of the empire's presence here in Vallessau."

Thorda withdrew an object from within the folds of his robe and held it for Cyrus to see. It was a wooden mask shaped and painted like a skull and with a thin leather cord tied around its back. The way the bones curled around the eyes, it was almost as if the skull were grinning, and that grin possessed far too many teeth.

"This belonged to my husband, Rhodes, a hero known to the people of Miquo as the Skull-Amid-the-Trees. He refused to engage the imperials on equal terms. He slaughtered their leaders. He ambushed their patrols. With kill after kill, he made everyone loyal to the Everlorn Empire terrified to set foot within the city he called his home. People for thousands of miles heard tales of his exploits, a rare enemy the empire truly feared. He taught me the power one man can wield if he makes himself more than a single foe, but the embodiment of the people's fury."

Cyrus picked at the bread on his plate, yet he had no appetite whatsoever.

"What does your husband have to do with me?" he asked.

"I want to train you. No one else but you, every day and every night, until I believe you are ready."

"Ready for what?"

In answer, Thorda tossed him the skull mask. Cyrus caught it and cradled it in his lap as the other man spoke.

"To wear that new face. To become a heroic killer stalking the streets of Vallessau. You will be a rumor at first, one we will seed with whispers in the right ears in the right places. You'll fight alongside my chosen elite as their figurehead leader, and receive all the glory for your combined exploits. Together, you will challenge even paragons. With every kill, you will make real the rumors that we have sown. And then our whispers will change. Who might this killer be? What identity does the cloak and skull hide?"

Thorda grinned, and it took years off his face. His excitement was infectious. His confidence was unparalleled.

"It is a story told and retold all across Gadir, and I trust it will resonate here on Thanet. A beloved royal family, destroyed by an evil invader. Their child, claimed to be dead but secreted away to survive. A mysterious hero, come to right the wrongs of the past. Let us ignite the people's imagination, Cyrus! We will tell a story of Thanet's vagrant prince, miraculously returned from the dead, who would kill all who oppose him and who would stop at nothing to retake his crown. And all the while, I shall be using my wealth and connections to build you an army, one that shall swear allegiance to the Lythan family. When the time is right, you shall cast aside your mask, reveal your survival to the entire populace, and capture Vallessau to mark the start of your rebellion."

Cyrus brushed his fingers across the grinning skull. Could he resurrect the war his parents had lost in a single evening? Could he hide behind a mask, and become some phantom killer to inspire the populace? The logistics of it left him baffled. Where would he learn to wield a sword? What would be his targets? And who all made up this elite group Thorda said he would be the figurehead for?

"What would I have to do?" he asked, trying to wrap his head around any of it.

"Accept my tutelage," Thorda said. "I will teach you to fight. I will show you how to become, not a mere mortal, but a mysterious and legendary killer the people will love and embrace. It will not be easy, nor will it happen in mere months. Are you willing to swear everything to this cause, Cyrus? Are you willing to forfeit any semblance of a normal life for one bathed in blood?"

Cyrus imagined that mask covering his face. Mere days ago he was a hostage, convinced only of his inevitable death as his island was slowly rebuilt in Everlorn's image and the last of their two gods was publicly executed. Now there was hope, however grim and fleeting.

"This hero you would have me imitate," he said. "The Skull-Amid-the-Trees. What happened to him?"

Thorda leaned back and crossed his arms.

"They hung my husband, still breathing, from the gates of the capital. It took him three days to die. The resistance there died with him. The same fate may await you, if not worse. You must be stronger, and faster. My chosen elite will fight alongside you, and protect you as best they can, but they can only do so much in the heat of battle. The hopes of your nation will live and die by your hand. What say you, Cyrus?"

Memories flashed unbidden through his mind. Magus of Eldrid, cutting down his parents. His mother's scream. The dying cries of Lycaena, cut apart by the God-Incarnate's daughter. Despite how much it frightened him, it was no choice at all.

"Vagrant," he said. "Not Cyrus. The prince is dead, remember?"

Thorda's smile stretched ear to ear.

"To the dead prince," he said. "And to his inevitable return."

CHAPTER 6

CYRUS

At last, after fourteen long hours of bumpy carriage rides, Cyrus arrived at the countryside mansion. He stared out the window, stunned despite having been told they traveled to a wealthy estate where they could train far from the eyes of the Uplifted Church in Vallessau. The mansion was built atop a hill, two stories tall, with multiple wings spanning either side of the towering front doors. It reminded Cyrus of the summer home his parents owned, but they were King and Queen of Thanet, whereas Thorda was...

Well. He didn't exactly know *what* Thorda Ahlai was, but his estimation of the older man's wealth and influence was growing by the second.

"I have not lived here for more than a few days at a time, but my brief stays have found this to be one of the more pleasant mansions I own," Thorda said as Cyrus took in the beautiful flower gardens that lined both sides of the gravel pathway, each swarming with butterflies. The two were alone within the carriage, with Stasia riding up front with the driver outside. Mari, the other sister he'd met briefly, remained behind in Vallessau, though Cyrus had not been given nor overheard an explanation as to why. "Even for a child of royalty, I expect you will feel pampered and welcome within. Consider it a needed reprieve from the necessary cruelty of your training you will receive outside of it."

"You own more than one mansion?" Cyrus asked after whipping his head back around.

"I own several dozen properties all throughout the mainland of Gadir. Given the nature of our work, I wanted to ensure my abode in Vallessau was humble and easy to enter and exit without notice. Out here in the countryside there is no need to spare us any pleasantries."

Cyrus was hardly a stranger to wealth as a prince of Thanet, but this home alone was one of the finest he had ever seen. Its size, and the acreage about it, dwarfed even the summer home his family visited in Red Glade. Already it took several minutes for their carriage to roll down the gravel path between the outer gate entrance to the mansion's front steps. For Thorda to have the resources to build...

A chill ran through Cyrus. But of course Thorda didn't build this mansion. Even if he had arrived with the Everlorn Empire, it had only been two years. That enormous, weathered building had existed for decades, if not centuries.

"Who did this place belong to before your arrival?" he asked softly.

The older man nodded, his faint smile showing his approval.

"Now you ask the proper question. Imperator Magus executed dozens of your nation's nobility in an effort to quell the uprisings, and he claimed their lands and titles as his own. Of Thanet's four realms and their lords, three were deposed, with only Lord Mosau maintaining both his life and his rule, through what trickery or show of loyalty, I have not yet surmised. When I arrived on Thanet, Magus's retainers were all too happy to sell the empty property to a citizen of the Everlorn Empire. I've rehired much of the staff, for the previous owner was fiercely loyal to Thanet, and would be proud to know his estate now helps us in our own rebellion."

Cyrus hardly considered himself brilliant on matters of accounting, but he knew such a purchase couldn't have been cheap, or easy. Did he bring gold and silver with him across the Crystal Sea? And even if he did, surely he'd risk running out between funding the rebellion and snapping up properties both inside and outside Vallessau?

"How do you afford all this?" he asked.

Thorda's smile faded, however briefly.

"I make and sell weapons, Cyrus. The term 'Ahlai-made' carries significant weight throughout Gadir, but that is not all. Through either my company, or others I have purchased in secret, I control the only organization large enough to sate the hunger of the Everlorn Empire. I funnel the money they pay me right back into the insurrections I cause. And when those rebellions and crises force the empire to recruit and expand?" He shrugged. "As I told you, be it by blood or coin, I make them hurt. For my haste and their high demand, I make them pay. Exorbitantly."

"Then it seems you fare well off the rebellions you incite."

Cyrus hadn't meant it to be so accusatory, but from the moment those words left his lips, he realized how vicious they were. He had accused the man secretly funding and organizing Thanet's only resistance of doing so solely for profit. The older man steepled his fingers, and his jaw quivered. He wasn't just angry. He was furious, yet somehow he kept his voice firm, and controlled, so only the faintest hint of that fury behind it dared show.

"The Everlorn Empire burned half my nation to the ground as punishment for the resistance my husband championed. The ruination of our forests, the burning of our shrines, the brutal sacrifice of our entire pantheon, it was all a message to the rest of Gadir. They made a *symbol* out of us. If I wanted coin, I would not have spent months in a cramped bunk sailing out here on the meager hope the people of Thanet can accomplish miracles. I have wealth enough to last me a dozen lifetimes. I want *vengeance*, boy. For a home stolen from me. For a people taken from me. If they would make a symbol out of Miquo, then a survivor of Miquo shall be another symbol, one they fear, one that will bring a knife to their throat and bleed them out into the annals of history so we might salvage what religions yet remain beyond their wretched God-Incarnate."

Cyrus weathered the storm, for it was one he deserved. Thorda caught himself, and he looked away to the window. His temper cooled. His eyes closed. When he spoke next, it wasn't rage. It was a confession.

"For their blood, their gifts, and their loves, my daughters are not safe in the world the Everlorn Empire would create. I wish to give them a future, Cyrus. A mountain of gold weighs nothing on the scales when compared to them." He briefly smiled, just a flutter of kindness. "And if it makes you feel any better, you would be surprised how *often* shipments of my weapons are intercepted by the rebels they are meant to be used against."

It didn't, but Cyrus was focused on something else entirely. Thorda's rant had clarified something for him that he hadn't fully appreciated until now.

"I'm to be that symbol," he said. "A symbol of not just Thanet's vengeance, but Miquo's."

Thorda returned his gaze, and there was no hiding how proud he was of Cyrus for reaching such a conclusion.

"My husband left behind a legacy, and I would not see it fade away, but instead be fulfilled. I hope you understand what it means to me, to trust you in such a way. A child of Thanet must be Thanet's savior, and with your bloodline and your family legacy, I know of no better choice."

The carriage rolled to a halt. They'd reached the mansion entrance. Stasia hopped down from the outside seat and thumped a hand excitedly on the carriage door.

"Come on out," she said, oblivious to the seriousness of the conversation she interrupted. "It's time for the grand tour!"

She didn't wait for him before dashing through the front door, needing to weave her way through the servants rushing out. They descended upon the carriage, offering greetings to Thorda, some asking if he had any requests while others grabbed the luggage stacked to the back of the carriage. Thorda tipped his head to them upon exiting, told them to prepare him tea and a bath for later, and then turned his attention to Cyrus.

"There will be plenty of time to unpack and prepare," he said. "As for me, I must tend to the forge."

Torn between chasing after Stasia and sticking with Thorda, Cyrus reluctantly stayed with his master, at least until he was given explicit permission to wander the mansion freely. Arms crossed over his chest, he endured the guarded stares the serving staff attempted to hide. Did they know who he was, who he truly was, or did they think him some orphan the wealthy man had adopted and brought back to the mansion?

Neck flushing red from the scrutiny, Cyrus tried to push it out of mind and followed Thorda around the eastern corner of the mansion. While the building might be hundreds of years old, the open-faced forge beside it was clearly of newer construction. The wooden beams holding up the high rooftop had barely even weathered. The bricks were bright, the bellows built of stained wood that was surprisingly ornate and almost immaculate in its preservation. Dozens of tools lined a hanging shelf on the lone wall, and their metal was so bright and polished, they appeared unused.

Watching Thorda reignite the forge was mesmerizing. The entire trip from Vallessau, the older man had been quiet and reserved. He seemed a man always on guard, and his every word was carefully chosen. Rarely did Cyrus believe he spoke the complete truth. Here in the heat of the forge? He glistened with sweat and honesty as he prepared the coke heart of the furnace. All of his focus shifted to the fire, the stones, the levers and pumps to blow in air to get the rings of coals burning. Callused fingers brushed rows of tools hanging from hooks pounded into a wall shelf. Cyrus couldn't even guess what purposes most of those hammers, chisels, and tongs served, but Thorda greeted them like long-lost children. Last, he put his bare hands upon the anvil's surface. His eyes closed, and he inhaled as if communing with the enormous iron construct.

"Is there...can I help somehow?" Cyrus asked, feeling awkward standing there.

"I have no need nor want of it," Thorda said. He lifted a hammer and twirled it in his fingers. "Forgive an older man's obsession with what brings him comfort."

"You're not that old," Cyrus said, and he grinned. "Your hair isn't fully white, yet you talk like you're a grandfather."

Thorda laughed, loud and hearty. He set the hammer back upon the shelf.

"Of course, of course. But I feel like I have lived a dozen lives, given all I have seen and the wars I have waged. This forge is my true home, child. I never feel like my roots are in place until it is properly lit. But smelting the ore, heating the steel, pounding out its imperfections to shape it into something beautiful and deadly...there's a purity to it the rest of the world rarely allows."

Cyrus suddenly felt, not just awkward, but unwanted. This was a moment of privacy for his master, and he was intruding upon it. He kicked the grass and muttered something about how he should go check on how Stasia was doing.

"Worry not for my daughter," Thorda said. "It is time you focused upon yourself. You've spent two years held in the empire's cage. Tonight, you sleep free. Go inside and choose one of the many available rooms on the second floor to be your own. For the foreseeable future, this is now your home."

The next morning, before Cyrus was allowed to eat his breakfast, Stasia brought him out for laps around the mansion estate. Despite the cool morning, she wore a pair of loose trousers and a shirt with both its sleeves and the lower half cut off so it exposed her arms and abdomen. Stretches came first, and she ran him through a quick set to warm up his muscles and chase away the lingering sleep in his limbs.

"How far is the run?" he asked her at the start. The woman glanced at him, and she corrected his attempt at touching his toes before answering.

"Yours, or mine?"

"Will we not run the same amount?"

Her laughter should have been a dead giveaway to the horrors awaiting him, but he did not yet understand.

"For you, we'll start with just a mile," she said. "Worry about keeping up with me once you can handle that."

Stasia lapped him twice before he finished his first mile, and multiple times he slowed to a walk to catch his breath. It was a dire sign of things to come.

"Everything you do, I do also," she told him when it was time for her physical training. They met behind the mansion, in a patch of soft grass. A few needed supplies lay on a blanket nearby. "When you get angry with me, and you will, remember that. This training may be hard, it may be cruel, but at least when I instruct you, it is *fair*."

They started easily enough, basic push-ups to strengthen his arms. He caught Stasia doing hers with one hand behind her back, and when she wasn't looking, he attempted the same (the result was him nearly planting his face into the dirt). What followed after this was much more unexpected.

"Your orders are simple," Stasia said, having placed two separate pairs of burlap sacks filled with dirt about thirty yards apart. He noted hers were filled with more, but pretended not to notice. "Pick up one sack, carry it over to the other sack, and then drop it. Then bring the second back to drop where you got the first. Don't worry, I'll show you how to lift it so you don't ruin your lower back."

Cyrus grunted when lifting his, and he swore it was mostly rock, not dirt, given how much it weighed. He was sweating, and his arms shaking, by the time he reached the other. Stasia, meanwhile, hardly appeared bothered beyond a little bit of redness in her face and neck.

"How many times?" he asked, dreading the answer.

"I usually do twenty. For you, let's start with . . . ten."

Cyrus's pride pushed him to lift and walk beyond when it hurt, to carry it even when it felt like his entire body vibrated.

He still barely reached five.

"Come on," she said, smacking him on the back as he heaved in air. "Let's give your arms a rest. Sprints next."

She marked two trees at the nearby forest's edge. All he had to do was sprint from one to the other, back and forth, like a deranged dog trapped behind a fence.

"Remember," she said. "I'm right here, with you all the while. We're doing this fair."

He walked the last few she demanded of him. Stasia zipped on past during her own laps, and with each one, she elbowed or nudged him in an attempt to get him to run. Next came a tree with a sturdy low branch. Stasia showed him how to tuck his hands around it to lift, then found a different, slightly higher branch for herself to leap up and catch.

"How many?" Cyrus asked. The question had begun to terrify him.

"I usually go until I can't anymore," Stasia said as she bobbed up and down. The muscles in her exposed abdomen tightened, and slick sweat trickled down her arms and neck. Cyrus had not appreciated how strong she was until this morning. He doubted there was a single spot on her body that wasn't pure muscle.

Twenty-five years, Thorda had said he led rebellions against the empire. Did that mean Stasia had been working and perfecting this routine for twenty-five years? If so, how long would it take until he could do a fraction of it?

Cyrus lifted and dropped until his arms gave out. Stasia laughed and picked him up as if it were all a cheerful game.

"Come on," she said. "I cut a few trees for us to leap from stump to stump, which should help keep you flexible and balanced. The fighting style my father will teach you is heavily reliant on speed. You can't just be a big hunk of muscle like a lot of paragons."

He missed several jumps, the worst cracking his shin against the side of the stump hard enough for it to bleed. Cyrus refused to let a limp show. He feared it might only encourage Stasia to push him even harder somehow, as punishment for the error. At least his balance seemed decent, which he discovered after she had him try a few stances on one leg. Most of his issues came from his tired legs feeling wooden and weak.

"Not bad," she said. "Now, I know I said you need speed, but you do also need some muscle, and a lot more than what you currently have."

A little outdoor shelf next to the mansion stored whatever things Stasia kept for her workouts, and she retrieved the newest set now: two vaguely circular lumps of metal he assumed she'd taken from Thorda's forge.

"Lift those up above your head, then lower them, like this," she said, demonstrating. "I want you to do that, and only that, while we walk a single lap around the mansion. Up and down, that's it, you can do up and down, can't you? And they're not so heavy, right? Yours are much lighter than mine, even!"

Cyrus tentatively lifted them up over his head, then back down so his elbows touched his hips.

"Not so terrible," he said, and even risked a smile.

And they weren't so terrible, nor so heavy, the first ten or so times. But as he walked, and the motion repeated, it seemed they grew in weight as his arms tired. What started as an easy lift above his head soon topped at his shoulders, then barely into the air at all.

With the end of each exercise, he prayed for a break, but never received it. Next was a return to the sacks of dirt, which, after having Cyrus lie on his back, she set one atop his legs.

"Lift it," she said, as if it were that easy, as if his legs weren't made of jelly after the morning run and the sprints and the leaping from logs. The entire lower half of his body shook as if he were trapped in an earthquake.

Stasia showed him no pity, nor remorse.

"Higher," she said. "You got this, little prince, now again, and higher."

Cyrus had no idea so many different exercises existed, but Stasia knew them all. Hour after hour passed, broken only by occasional rests and breaks for water.

"I can't," he said at one point, perhaps an hour in, perhaps a lifetime. Time had grown untrustworthy. No matter how hard he tried, he couldn't catch his breath. Currently she had restarted him on pushups, and he lay on his stomach, heaving, the grass tickling his nose and lips. Stasia continued with her own set, counting up to twenty before acknowledging his failure.

"Not yet you can, but you will," she said, and then winked. "Hopefully."

At last she took pity on him and called a break for lunch. Cyrus collapsed onto his back and lay there, debating if the effort to walk to the mansion was worth the food. It was, but only just, and only after he gave himself ten minutes to recover. He covered his face with an arm, hiding from the sunlight.

In at least one thing, though, Stasia had lied, and the constant reminder of it burned at his pride like fire. She did not do everything he did as was promised.

She did more.

After eating a simple lunch, a collection of greens, cheese, and freshly caught salmon he assumed bought from some nearby market, it was time for his sword training with Thorda. Part of him dreaded it, for merely walking set off a dozen flares throughout his sore body, but the idea of swordplay gave him a burst of energy. Clashing steel against steel sounded much more exciting than the torture Stasia had subjected him to.

Yet the only steel in sight was that at Thorda's nearby forge as the two of them met in a small, cleared-out circle on the eastern side of the mansion. Thorda had replaced the robes he wore around the house for one almost akin to a dress in its thin gray fabric, tied tightly with a white sash around his waist. His sandals he swapped for black leather boots overtop trousers made of similar gray fabric. His long hair he tied behind his head with a string. The change, while seemingly minor, gave the older man an even more severe appearance.

"Have you had any training with a sword?" Thorda asked. Cyrus nodded. When he was twelve, the paladin Rayan Vayisa had been assigned as his instructor. The man was as patient as he was skillful, and Cyrus had always looked forward to their weekly sessions.

"About two years' worth," he said. "But not any since…"

He need not say it. The Usurper King certainly bore no need to teach Cyrus how to defend himself with a blade.

"Good. You should be familiar with the weight, and have some basics, but nothing deeply ingrained enough that it will interfere with my own instruction."

Thorda talked as he retrieved three wooden poles he'd brought with him and set on the stool from his forge. The longer one was for him, the two shorter ones for Cyrus.

"Because of our narrow mountain paths and dense godwoods, our nation did not battle like other nations. Our armies did not meet in wide fields with ten-man-deep formations. Our wars were fought in skirmishes, nightly raids, and a thousand instances of one-against-one atop rope bridges and inside deep caves. The fighting style of our greatest warriors matched the need, and I was blessed to have a truly exemplary master as my teacher."

"The Skull-Amid-the-Trees," Cyrus said, remembering the story.

"Indeed, a legendary killer the Everlorn Empire learned to fear, for we eschew any concept of fairness or honor that hinders certain other nations in Gadir. I will teach you that same ruthlessness. Our foes will be paragons wielding weapons heavier than most men alive. They will be priests and magistrates whose prayers summon golden blades of light, the perfect manifestation of the empire's cruel faith. Their forces outnumber us by a thousandfold. A fair fight is a dead fight, and so we will attempt no such thing."

Cyrus accepted the two wooden poles that would represent his future weapons. The bottoms were wrapped in soft leather, and felt good in his hands.

"Given the skirmishing nature of Miquoan war, your greatest enemy is rigidity. I will teach you to analyze a foe's weaknesses, and then exploit them. If they are stronger than you, then you will be faster. If they are faster, then you will be trickier. If they are trickier, then you will overwhelm their feints and bluffs with savage fury."

"Why two?" Cyrus asked as he swung the poles about, enjoying the feel.

"Your off-hand will be heavier, and shorter. You will use it more like a shield, with an emphasis on blocks and parries. However, if the need arises, you may attack with both in tandem. Defensive, or offensive, as the situation dictates."

So much emphasis on reactionary changes. He tried to wrap his mind around it, but struggled.

"I always thought sword fighting was more focused," he said. "You swing, and I block it. If I'm slow, I die. If I'm faster, I can swing back, making you block. Again, you fail, you die. I know that's putting it simply, but...what you're describing makes it feel much more loose and confusing. There's a right way and a wrong way to defend a hit, isn't there?"

Thorda did not answer immediately. Instead he used his free hand to position Cyrus's.

"Do not move," he said. Cyrus obeyed. His master stood before him, using exaggerated slowness to lift his sword in an overhead chop and then bring it down toward Cyrus's head. A foot away he halted it in the air.

"What do you do?" he asked.

"I block it," Cyrus answered.

"Which sword? Left, right, or both?"

He hesitated.

"Right," he said. He brought the sword up, and Thorda tapped the wooden poles together. A flex of his arms, and the sudden power flung Cyrus's sword away. The pretend blade continued to lightly tap Cyrus on the forehead.

"What if I am too strong? There is no standing toe-to-toe against a paragon's might."

Cyrus had seen the enormous weaponry and armor the paragons wielded. Sure enough, trying to halt one of their gigantic weapons would be foolish.

"Then I dodge."

"Which direction? Backward? To the shield side? To the sword side? How far, Cyrus? One step? Two? Three?"

Cyrus hopped left, just enough to avoid the hit. Thorda continued the pole's movement downward, as if the swing had gone unabated.

"One swing, numerous decisions," his master explained. "You cannot withstand a paragon's might, but you can scurry and dodge until they bleed out from a hundred wounds. You cannot tire or disarm a magistrate whose weapon is a gleaming blade of faith, but you can overwhelm them, your parries and cuts meant only to close the distance between so you might score a quick, lethal blow. Now return to your first stance."

Cyrus did as ordered. Thorda lifted up his sword, the hit clearly signaled in advance.

"Reactions will not be enough," he said. "Even knowing what is coming, and believing your actions the wisest, may not suffice. The battle will be over before you blink."

Down came the sword. Cyrus dashed left, moving far faster than their first example, but Thorda's blade curled on its downward slope. The pole cracked into his knee, then swept the leg upward. He cried out at the pain. He never even saw the second hit, only felt wood bash his ribs, toppling him. He landed on his rear in the dirt. His master stood over him, calm as ever. It was as if he had not even moved.

"I will show you the movements," Thorda said. "You will memorize the stances, each with their own purposes and their own consequences in how they shape the battle and dictate your next actions. You will learn when to use which, and how they flow into one another. For a time, you will be slow. You will think on what is proper, and that delay will cost you. This will frustrate you, but you will persevere. Your thoughts will grow silent. Your decisions will become instincts. You will not shift from stance to stance, but instead flow through them like water. It will be a deathly dance, and you will know it better than most alive. You are not there yet. You will not be near it tomorrow, either. But step by step, day by day, you will grow ever closer to that goal."

Cyrus's eager excitement dwindled and died in the face of harsh reality. The entire day felt like one long, lengthy session explaining how weak, slow, and pitiful he was in his current state.

"How long will that take?" Cyrus asked. "Until I am ready?"

Thorda crossed his arms, and he did not soften the blow.

"Three days of solid training, one day at half measures for your body to recover. That will be the rhythm of your life." He hesitated. "For the next few years."

"Years?" he asked. Could he wait that long? Could Thanet? He wasn't even through his first day, and already his muscles were raw and weak, and he could not make himself stand up. The wooden poles quivered in his touch. Thorda noticed, of course he noticed, but Cyrus was learning quickly the man was not one for soft words.

"There is no way to put this lightly, Cyrus, so I should speak it plain. You will face men and women older than you, with years if not decades more training. You will face paragons who have conquered more cities than you have fought battles. The gap between your foes and the skill you possess now is a gulf wider than the Crystal Sea."

Cyrus leaned his forehead across his arms as he slumped farther.

"So it's hopeless," he said.

"It does not mean it is hopeless," Thorda said. "It means you must try even harder. One day of your training will involve more than most soldiers experience in five. 'Competence' will be the dirt far beneath you as we drag you to the stars. We will push your mind and body to become something far greater than you thought possible. Through Stasia's drills, and my training, you will achieve miracles. You must believe that, Cyrus, or all else means naught."

His master knelt beside him. His callused hand cupped Cyrus's cheek. Their eyes met.

"It will require extraordinary effort on your part. It means enduring trials that would break the weak-willed, and countless moments of finding the strength to drag yourself up from the dirt to try again. I will push you to the edge of your body's limitations. Will you endure, Prince Lythan? Or will you break?"

Cyrus could not look away. It wasn't only the honesty in the words that captivated him. In those eyes he saw something he himself desperately needed.

He saw hope.

"I'll manage," he said. "Somehow. I won't let you and Stasia get the best of me, even if it kills me."

A faint smile tugged at his master's lips.

"Good. On your feet. We go again."

The sun descended, a faint white hint of the moon marking the night's approach, yet still his training was not finished. Cyrus followed Stasia to the edge of the woods that surrounded the mansion. He limped slightly, the result of a bad twist while trying to properly imitate one of Thorda's million different stances. They'd spent the entire afternoon on just those stances. Most were awkward to perform, and pulled at his arms and waist in uncomfortable ways. The light wood of the poles became heavier than stone to his drooping limbs. Each and every stance had a name, and Thorda called them out incessantly. Sometimes they took breaks to focus on his footwork, easily the worst of the lot. It felt less like battle and more like learning a strange, old-fashioned dance. Yet Thorda insisted it just as important, if not more so, than the placement of his hands. It might be important, but it made his ankles and thighs ache like mad, and multiple times he collapsed to the ground, unable to maintain the stance on his shaking legs.

"On your feet," Thorda would say, the same words each and every time Cyrus found himself in the dirt. "Try again."

Some six hours or so of this, and Cyrus's mind was numb, barely able to process any of the commands given to him. His errors compounded, until at last Thorda declared them done for the evening. Thinking his training over, Cyrus could barely contain his relief.

"Not quite," Thorda had explained. "Stasia has one last skill set for you to improve upon."

And so the pair trudged to the woods. For reasons he could not guess, Stasia carried a chair she'd retrieved from the kitchen, and he was too tired to ask. He'd be told eventually, of that he was certain, so best to find out in time. Anything beyond that would involve thinking, and thinking was hard. Concentration was an impossibility. He was so exhausted, he'd begun fantasizing about curling up in the grass and falling asleep right then and there.

"This'll do," Stasia said, putting the chair down outside the line of trees. She sat in it, back to the woods, and groaned with satisfaction while stretching her arms and neck. "Consider this the least taxing portion of your training. Stealth and sneakiness are not what I would consider my strengths, so I'll use the same methods my father used to teach me. The rules are simple. You start thirty paces deep into the woods. While my back is turned, you must tap my shoulder without me hearing your approach."

"That's it?"

She winked.

"The ground is uneven, full of twigs and leaves, and we're still a good hour before the crickets really get to singing. I may not be good at stealth, but I assure you, Cyrus, my ears work damn well. Reach me, and you finally get your dinner. Whether it's warm or cold depends on you."

It couldn't be that hard, could it? Cyrus didn't think so, but with how hard everything *else* had been that day, he feared otherwise. He counted out the thirty paces, weaving through the dogwoods, and then turned around. Her back was to him, and she gave no signal to start. Shrugging, he began to tiptoe forward. He made it only two steps before Stasia waved over her head and laughed.

"You want to be a mouse at night, not an elephant. Try again."

Cyrus didn't know what an "elephant" was, but he presumed the comparison was not a compliment. Biting his tongue, he returned to his starting spot. He breathed in and out, centering himself. He could do this. Traversing a forest in silence couldn't possibly be that difficult.

A leaf crunched beneath his foot on his fourth step.

"Try again."

Back to roughly same position. He took it slower, fully convinced a careful approach would be enough. On his ninth step, she called out, the rustle of grass somehow discernible to her sharp ears.

"Heard that. Try again."

"Gods damn it," he muttered.

"Heard that, too."

Another try, slower still. Failed. The next was ruined by a sneeze, so he mentally argued that didn't count. The one after, where he kicked a leaf with the front of his boot, most certainly did.

"Check your footing," she said. "You want a light step, toes first, not heel."

"Your advice isn't all that helpful."

She exaggerated her shrug so he would see it from afar.

"I told you I wasn't good at this. Don't worry. You've hundreds of nights to practice ahead of you. It's inevitable you get better at this. Hopefully."

"Your faith in me is so great, it may move mountains," he grumbled as he retreated those thirty paces back among the dogwood trees.

"Wait until your first fight with a paragon. It's going to feel like you're trying to move mountains, too."

Two more attempts, one halfway there, one a third, both ended with lazy callouts of "Try again." The dim light was on purpose, he was quickly realizing. It made it hard for him to pick out potential obstacles and instead focus on the shift of his weight amid his movements. This knowledge did not, however, make it easier when yet another "Try again" sent him back to the start.

The tediousness was getting to Stasia, too, though in a very different way. She slid deeper into the chair, and she cocked her elbow and rested her head on her fist.

"Falling asleep on me?" Cyrus called out.

"You better hope I do, little prince. It's the only way you're getting dinner tonight."

A snapped twig. Try again. A rustle of leaves. Try again. A rustle of his trousers against a bush. Try again. Those two words became the bane of his existence. As his frustration grew, he attempted to catch her cheating. He stood perfectly still, barely breathing, and let a full minute pass. If she blamed a bird or a gentle gust of wind for his own movements then he could claim the exercise pointless. Yet her silence matched his own. If anything, it only made it worse when the first step he took, accompanied by a frustrated sigh, immediately caught her attention.

"Try again, and do it faster, would you? I'm getting hungry myself."

Exhaustion kept his frustrations in check. Try again. Try again. Try again.

He slumped to the ground, his back against a tree, as Stasia gave some sort of advice about footwork. The words weren't making sense anymore. His stomach hurt. No, *everything* hurt. Tired and drained, he shed tears that made him feel ashamed and angry in equal measure. The ground was cold, but it felt so good to sit still. His knees curled closer to his chest for warmth. He could start another attempt after a minute. He just needed to gather himself. One moment. That's all. One breather. When the tears were gone, he would be ready.

Arms lifted him. His feet moved, walking of their own accord.

"Stasia?" he asked, confused and groggy. The stars were out. The woods were pitch black.

"Come along, little prince," she said, her shoulder tucked under his arm, his weight so heavily leaned upon her, she might as well have carried him. "It's been a long day. Let's get you to a proper bed."

CHAPTER 7

CYRUS

Cyrus awoke to ships burning. He bolted upright, hands clutching the front of his thin shirt hard enough that his fingers ached. Sweat poured down his face. The world around him was red and black, flame and ash, and in the distance he heard the screams of dying soldiers and the clash of metal. Piercing all of it was his mother's anguished, pain-filled shriek as Magus...

His surroundings darkened as he returned to the waking world. No. No screams, no metal. No smoke or ash. Just a dream, the same dream that had haunted him for years now.

"It's fine," he whispered into the cool night air. "You're fine."

Cyrus was alone in the dark room he had chosen. The red hue of fire was only a small candle softly burning within its glass jar on his nightstand. He should go back to bed, he knew. Tomorrow would be another long day of training, and he needed the rest. Sleep, however, was not coming. He lay there, eyes wide as he stared at the ceiling. Faint shadows danced from the light of his candle. It was raining, he realized belatedly. Soft pings hit the glass of his window. He'd not even noticed. The rain...He'd thought it the crackling fire of burning ships, the sound so normal to him, so constant, it receded into the background.

A groan slipped out of his lips. Everything hurt. His limbs were wood. His neck ached. His right knee in particular pulsed with pain from when Thorda had struck it at the start of practice. Blisters wept from across his palms and between his thumbs and forefingers. Nothing in the world sounded better than sleep, yet he could not. His heart pounded. The muscles in his neck tightened, and breathing turned difficult. Panic. His entire body was locked in panic.

"Damn it."

He flung the sheets off. He didn't know where he was going, and he didn't care. Every instinct said run, and so wearing only his soft bed shirt and bottoms, he slipped out into the main hall. The dream, the memories, they would not leave. His mother's dying scream chased him down the green carpet that burned his bare feet. Candles flickered within their candelabras, lighting the hallway. He saw closed doors, and a distant staircase. Cyrus ran toward it, feet quietly thumping atop the carpet. He didn't dare question why he ran, to where, or what from. Just down the stairs. Into the main foyer. To the front door. If he stopped for even a moment, he might realize where he was going, and what he was doing.

He might acknowledge he was a frightened coward, and that he was running to the front door to leave and never return.

A shadowed figure sat on a tall chair directly before the door, interrupting such plans. Cyrus skidded to a halt upon the tile. He couldn't see his face, but Cyrus immediately knew who it was by the voice that quietly rumbled in greeting.

"Good evening," Thorda said. "Trouble sleeping?"

Shame fought with Cyrus's deep panic. His intense desire to run increased tenfold. No, not run. Escape.

Escape from what? he wondered. He didn't know. He didn't want to know. Shame and embarrassment warred within his head, and it paralyzed him. He wanted to answer, yet couldn't, so he turned away. Maybe his master would be kind, say nothing, and let him retreat to his room. Maybe the dreams wouldn't return. Maybe when the next day came, and the day after that, and the day after that, the training would not break him like it had that first day.

"Sorry," he muttered, as close to an answer as he could give Thorda. He turned for the stairs, managing a mere three steps before Thorda's words struck him and held him in place. In the quiet, they were a thunder, somehow given power by the wide space and empty darkness.

"Be still."

Cyrus halted at the foot of the stairs. His jaw clenched so tightly shut, he feared he might crack his teeth, all to hold back the tears that were building up unwanted in his eyes.

"Yes, Thorda?" he asked, still not turning around.

"You will address me as 'master,' child. Now look at me."

Child? He was sixteen, but perhaps "child" was fitting, given his behavior. Cyrus slowly spun on his heels. In that brief pause, he discovered Thorda had somehow lit a candle, and he set it beside his chair in a small tin carrier. His red eyes glinted within its glow. He said nothing, only gestured for Cyrus to come close. Cyrus did, his every step feeling like approaching an executioner. Such a foolish thought, but one he could not force out of his head. His master sized him up and down, his face so perfectly still, it was an unreadable mask.

"Kneel with me," he said at last. "Close your eyes, and let us pray."

"Pray to who?" Cyrus asked.

"To each of us our own."

Thorda put his hands atop Cyrus's shoulders, and he leaned forward until their foreheads touched. Cyrus smelled the forge on him, lingering sweat, a hint of coal, and worst of all, a forever stain of smoke. His attempt to focus, to pray, faltered.

"But I have no god to pray to," he said. Visions flashed before his closed eyes. A spear piercing the Lion's side. Daggers tearing into black flesh and ripping apart wings. "Lycaena...Endarius...they died."

"Gods do not fade away in death, not like humans do. They can linger, their presence hovering about their faithful, eager to return should that faith remain strong enough across the years. But you need not pray if you do not wish. Think on your hurt, if you would, and allow me my own prayer."

They were so close, forehead to forehead, and it made Cyrus feel small compared to the older man. He squirmed. Think on his hurt? Why? Hadn't that been his entire existence for the past two years? Locked up in a castle that no longer belonged to his family, occasionally paraded about to remind the populace that the Everlorn Empire held him hostage as they worked to erase every shred of Thanet's religion and culture. Ordered to put on a smile and offer a brave face to a beleaguered populace.

Eyes closed, he knew what best represented that hurt. It wasn't a prayer, not in any way he understood it, but it was a memory. His mother and father, smiling and happy as they ate a meal together in the royal garden. He remembered the way the light made his mother's brown hair sparkle. He remembered, not the joke itself, but that his father had said something amusing now lost to time, and it had sent young Cyrus rolling with laughter atop the recently cut grass. The happiness of it was a knife across his raw mind, but it was the truest version of his hurt, and the world he lamented, forever lost.

"I was right, you aren't broken," Thorda whispered. Cyrus opened his eyes, but his master's were still closed. Even his breath somehow smelled of the forge, and made Cyrus think of melting steel. "But you are wounded, child. So deeply wounded. There is a part of you that you refuse to acknowledge. A part of yourself that frightens you. It rots your soul. It denies you peace. My training will break you, and one night you will slip out when I am not here to stop you. So look inside, Cyrus. Face your truth, and give it a voice. I am listening. I, and I alone."

Cyrus pulled away from the older man, and he pushed himself to his feet. His emotions roiled within him, bubbling, scraping at the edges of his mind. What was in him? What had he suppressed during those two years of imprisonment?

But of course he knew. He knew it when he had been dragged through the halls of the castle by the Usurper King. He knew it by his nightmares.

"I'm scared," he said. "I'm so scared, and if I'm this scared, I can't be...there isn't any way. I can't be the hero you need, or this island needs. How could I be?"

Thorda leaned closer, and he shook his head.

"No, Cyrus. You're not scared. You only believe it is fear, for you were never allowed to act on it. You let it swallow you in your helplessness. But you aren't helpless anymore. Think again. Live it again. What is it you truly feel?"

What else could it be? It swallowed him each day. It choked his stomach. He felt sick, rarely ate, and every night came the nightmares. He saw the burning ships. He heard the ringing of metal, heard the echoing scream of his mother, cut down but not yet dead. Screaming in pain. Magus, raising the sword. He didn't want to see it, he didn't want to relive it, and surely that meant he was a coward, he was afraid, he was a broken child...

You're not scared.

The moment he dared think it, it was like tearing a hole in a dam. The primal cry he could never voice, not once for fear of servants and soldiers loyal to the Usurper King, roared within his skull. But there were no conquerors here. His emotions came bursting out, his voice challenging the rainswept quiet of the night.

"Anger," he screamed. "They took everything from me! My...my mom, my dad, I saw it. I watched it. I can't sleep. Barely eat. All I want is to hurt Gordian, hurt Magus, hurt everyone responsible."

"Good," his master said. "Anger is good. It is useful."

Cyrus's entire body shook as if he had caught a fever. How could that be true? How could this consuming fury be anything other than a curse?

"My mother, she said anger is a fire," he said, trying to make sense of things. If only he could remember what wisdom his parents offered him before their murders. "And if I let it, it would burn me up and leave me hollow."

"Your mother was wise," Thorda said. "And your mother is dead."

Cyrus swung a fist for his master's face. The older man barely moved, and he didn't even blink. His left hand caught Cyrus's wrist, and he pulled them closer together, forcing their gazes to meet. Those red eyes, glinting in the candlelight, became Cyrus's whole world.

"But she was right," his master said, his voice suddenly intense. "Anger is a fire, it does destroy, but it can do so much more. Fire fuels my forges. It melts steel and crafts weapons. I do not want your anger ended. I want it to flare so brightly, it lights the entire island aflame. I want your fire to consume the banners of empire, to char the priests of the Uplifted Church, and to set free an entire nation. Do not deny it. Do not hold it back. Let that fire grow, Cyrus. Let it *burn*."

Two years of submission. Two years of crying alone in his bedroom. Two years dreaming of a flame-swept harbor. Could this anger truly be enough? Cyrus yanked his hand free, and he staggered several steps backward when Thorda released it without a struggle.

"And if it leaves me hollow?" he asked.

The older man leaned back in his chair. His face was as hard as any piece of ore he smelted.

"You are a prince, Thanet your kingdom, and her people your wards. What price is too high for your vengeance, or their freedom?" He lurched to his feet, grabbed the door handle, and shoved it open a foot. Cold wind swirled into the mansion, and the distant patter of rain took on a starker, clearer quality.

"There is your escape if you believe that price beyond what you can pay. The life awaiting you is of a vagabond in hiding. At best, you will accomplish nothing beyond your own survival. At worst, you will be captured and executed. I will not deny you the choice. I do not want a prisoner. I have no need of a slave. I want a weapon. I want a god of death the empire one day fears. Is that you?"

Thorda put a hand on Cyrus's shoulder. Despite the hardness of his words, his touch was gentle and comforting.

"I asked you this when I first rescued you, but that was cruel of me to make such a demand when you were still vulnerable and confused. You were in ignorance of the task before you, and of the trials your mind and body must endure. So I give you that choice now. May you have pleasant nights, Cyrus Lythan, be they under the roof of this mansion or in the rain-soaked hills beyond."

The older man climbed the stairs and disappeared around the corner. Cyrus watched him go, then turned. He stared at the open door. Rain fell, lit by the faint shred of moonlight capable of piercing the clouds. His panic returned. His heart thundered like the storm. He thought of waking the next morning, and the morning after, and the one after that, each time enduring the training, the bruises, and the exhaustion. Not for days. Not for weeks. Years.

Without realizing he'd made a decision, he burst out the door and into the night. He ran across the gravel path leading toward the dirt road at the far end of the property. He ran, his thin clothes no protection from the rain and the cold and the chill seeping into his bones. He ran until his weary legs gave out and he collapsed to his knees. The gate to the property was within reach. He could touch its bars if he wished.

Cyrus crumpled into himself, elbows pushing into his stomach and his hands balled into fists. Something sharp and jagged cut loose from the center of him, and it tore out his throat. Amid that downpour, he howled. Let the raindrops drown the two words he repeated, two words that defined the paralysis crippling him. Let only the storm clouds hear his confession.

"I can't," he screamed. "I can't. I can't. I can't."

It didn't matter how the thought of murdering his former captors put a pleasure in his heart so powerful it terrified him. It didn't matter that every single shred of him pleaded incessantly to flee unknown into the country night. At least here, he had a purpose. He had someone to provide him with a means for revenge. But to train under Thorda, to become someone new and entirely different than the boy who had suffered two long years of imprisonment...could he even do it? Was it even possible to become so ruthless a killer? His foes were paragons, elite warriors who slew *gods*. How could he ever compare?

Too frightened to stay, too frightened to leave. The rain fell. The mud gathered beneath his knees.

Never give in to your anger, his parents had told him, but Thorda was right. They were dead. Anger was all Cyrus had. Anger, and revenge. He could run from neither, no matter how far his feet carried him. There was no distance he could cross that would prevent the burning ships from following in his wake. Better to hold out hope for something better. Better a meaningful death over a shameful life in hiding.

Cyrus rose from the mud. He walked the gravel path to the mansion entrance. It was a black specter upon a hill, and instilled none of the same awe or curiosity as when he'd first ridden the carriage to its steps. He slipped into the main foyer, dripping wet and caked with dirt.

Again someone waited for him in the shadows. But instead of Thorda, it was Stasia Ahlai leaning against the stairway banister. She held a folded towel in one hand and a tin cup candle in the other. She wore a loose bed shirt and leggings quite similar to his own, but if she was recently roused from sleep, she seemed remarkably alert. The woman tossed him the towel as he shut the door.

"I knew you would come back," Stasia said. She shot him a crooked smile that seemed all the more mischievous in the poor lighting. "Even when you ran out into the rain, I knew."

"How?" Cyrus asked softly. He padded his face dry as an excuse not to look at her. It seemed her red eyes were glowing embers in the faint candlelight.

"Because I know what it's like to have nothing left. To know that, no matter where you run, you will never have a home, not the one you want. Not the one that was stolen from you. To be honest, I'd have thought less of you if you didn't doubt my father. It's good you're willing to question your superiors."

Cyrus couldn't tell if she was being honest, or merely trying to cheer him up, but he appreciated it nonetheless. He wiped what mud he could off his clothes and onto the towel.

"So you've doubted it, too?" he asked.

That cocky smile faltered for the briefest moment.

"More times than I can count, Cyrus. It's a path of blood, but for whatever comfort it offers, know that I will walk it with you."

CHAPTER 8

CYRUS

First it had been a mile, one single mile Cyrus had to run before he was allowed to eat breakfast. Stasia mocked him incessantly every moment he tried to slow down or rest. "It's just a mile," she'd say, as if running laps through the trees lining the estate boundary were easier than breathing. As the weeks passed and his stamina improved, that lone mile became one and a half, then two, two and a half, until Cyrus awoke knowing three miles of jogging stood between him and a decent meal to start the day.

"It's just three miles," he muttered as he huffed and puffed along the worn dirt path. Over the months he'd flattened a nice groove through the dogwood trees. He knew each little bump and visible root like the back of his hand. Coming up was a favorite patch, where instead of trees, a small field of flowers awaited him, always awash with butterflies, which scattered when the pair came running.

"It's still less than the twelve miles I do on a good day," Stasia said, overhearing his complaint. They had only started their run, and she had yet to leave him in her dust. "I usually don't feel like I'm hitting my true form until the fifth."

"Yes, but you're not human," he shot back.

"Then what am I?"

"I don't know. A monster? A cruel, evil taskmaster meant to punish hapless princes."

Stasia laughed at that, her pace quickening as the path sloped upward to crest the minor hill at the back of the estate. This part of the run was always the most brutal stretch of each lap. She called after him, all grins and laughter to encourage him to press on, even if fueled only by stubbornness and spite.

"Run, run, little prince, your princess is escaping and the wolves are at your heels."

Thankfully their running path led them past a stone well dug into the field along the western side of the estate. Cyrus paused for a moment to draw himself a drink. The mansion grounds were large enough that a single trip around it was three quarters of a mile, and he was about to finish his third lap. Close, so close to done. He drank half the water in the bucket, dumped the other half atop his head to shock himself fully awake, and then resumed his run.

Exhausting as it might be, at least the view was worth it. The dogwood trees were beautiful as their leaves bloomed with the arrival of spring. The surrounding area was mostly hills and forests, but the mansion had been built atop the highest elevation in the area. One stretch behind it in particular offered a stunning view seemingly to the horizon of the forest clustered atop the rolling hills. Sometimes robins took flight in tremendous flocks, and there was a dreamlike quality to their emergence from the morning fog. Each morning he'd catch wisps of smoke from homes built underneath the canopy of trees, and he idly wondered who lived there, and what their lives were like.

Most likely they were getting more sleep than he was, Cyrus thought with a bitter frown. Every week, the same. Three days of brutal training, one day off for study and greater emphasis on swordplay drills. The runs never stopped, though. Perhaps they wouldn't until he was dead.

Thorda taught Cyrus to study his opponent, to learn their moves and anticipate how they might think and react. In swordplay, that meant tracking feet placement, hand movements, and eye contact. In the war against the Everlorn Empire, it meant learning its history of conquest and territorial expansion. Thankfully Thorda was equally armed on this front, for his mansion was privately stocked with a library of books brought along with him from Gadir. After the running, the exercises, and the painful spars that left Cyrus's body covered in bruises, he limped his way to the library for his favorite way to end the day. He would collapse into an overstuffed chair in the corner, grab a book, and read while his body recovered. Sometimes he'd read deep into the night prior to retreating to his bedroom. Sometimes he didn't make it that far, and fell asleep in the chair, book still in hand.

For perhaps the first time in his life, he was thankful that Regent Gordian had forced him to learn the imperial tongue. It was in that language that all of Thorda's books were written. His grasp of it was still weak, but it quickly improved over the passing days. He slowly tweaked and shifted the contents of the library like a bird adjusting a nest to make it better accommodate his presence. Favorite books were stacked atop an unused writing desk. On a little square table beside his chair, he piled up books he would read next. No matter how hard he tried, that pile never seemed to shrink. He was always finding new tomes, books he'd originally skimmed over, thinking them worthless, only to later realize their value. When Thorda had called the library his treasure, Cyrus could understand why.

"Children's tales?" Stasia asked him once when coming to inform him that dinner was prepared. As if to mock him, she'd even tapped him on the shoulder before he noticed she had entered the room.

"I found it interesting," he said defensively.

She snagged the picture book from his grasp and flipped through the pages.

"What's interesting about pictures of animals?"

He grabbed it back and set it on the table beside him.

"This," he said, after finding the proper page. On it was a pencil drawing of a pack of lions hunting through tall grass. Above it was the name of where it supposedly depicted, an area known as the Highlands.

"Oh, I've been there," Stasia said. "The grass stretches on for miles. You should see when the wind ripples through it in waves, almost like an ocean."

"And are there lions? Regular lions, without feathers for manes, as this picture shows?"

She'd laughed long and loud at that, her amusement a reminder of how ignorant he was of the lands beyond his island.

"I forgot, you know them only through Endarius. Yes, little prince, there are lions in the Highlands, hundreds of them, and if you aren't careful, they will eat you for dinner. Speaking of dinner, come eat yours before I carry you out of this library over my shoulder. I swear, you push the limits of what is healthy when it comes to reading..."

Instead Cyrus buried himself deeper into the books, determined to remove the ignorance wrapped about his worldly understanding, starting with his ultimate foe. From what he pieced together, the Everlorn Empire had started out as a tiny city-state known as Eldrid some three thousand years ago. The history was thin, and notably overwhelmed with fanciful tales of epic battles and betrayal. At some point the king of Eldrid had declared himself God-Incarnate and crushed an invasion of a neighboring country so utterly, their name was no longer permitted to be written. Through the might of the God-Incarnate, and his chosen warriors known as paragons, Everlorn had first conquered its invaders, then set its eyes hungrily on its neighbors. A lone city-state became a nation, and a nation soon became an empire.

His most shocking discovery had come a month later. Drawn in the exact center of a history book was a map showcasing the boundaries of the Everlorn Empire. It offered little in terms of geography, barely more than a faint scratch of lines for major rivers and mountains. The map's interest was explicitly on national boundaries, of which there were depressingly few not listed as either part of the Everlorn Empire or existing as vassal states. The map tickled Cyrus's brain, something about it that didn't feel quite right.

"Is this map correct?" he asked Thorda, who sometimes accompanied him during his library excursions, content to quietly read in a corner in case Cyrus had any questions. His master left his chair, crossed the crimson carpet, and peered over his shoulder.

"About a century or so outdated, actually." He pointed across the map, highlighting tiny little spaces of clear white that had not fallen under the slanted fill lines marking imperial territory. "Antiev, Onleda, Noth-Wall, Aethenwald, Lahareed, and Miquo have all been taken since."

"Miquo," Cyrus said. "That's...that's your home, isn't it?"

Thorda hesitated.

"It was," he said softly. He tapped his finger upon the little sliver along the southeastern portion of the map that somehow remained without lines despite being swallowed on all sides by imperial territory. "Tucked deep into the mountains and built beneath towering godwood trees so tall, no building of human construction can reach half their height. Those mountains and trees protected us better than any wall, which is why they waited centuries to even try."

Cyrus could tell he was opening old wounds, but his curiosity ached to know the story.

"Why did Miquo fall?" he asked. "Is the empire truly so strong?"

"Do you see this nation right here?" Thorda said, pointing to a similar bit of unconquered land labeled ANTIEV. "There are only two entrances into Miquo. One is through the Vermell Mountains along the south. We rigged countless portions of the path so that we could trigger avalanches. The empire's first attempt at an invasion died before it even began, for we cut off the army from their supplies. No army can fight long on empty bellies. And so the empire turned to the second entrance..."

He tapped Antiev.

"It took them years, for Antiev was covered with trees akin to our own godwoods, but it finally fell. The Everlorn Empire gained an entrance far less dangerous than our mountain paths. War came at last to our home. Over a decade we fought hard, we bled, and we died. The gods of Miquo fell. The Everlorn Empire planted another flag."

Silence fell over them both. Cyrus stared at the map, trying to imagine what that war had looked like. He'd had but a taste of a potential invasion. As much as it wounded his pride, he knew Thanet had offered a meager resistance. Miquo had fought for years. Vallessau, Thanet's capital, had fallen in mere hours. Cyrus skimmed the map and the outlying coastline, then flipped through the book from where he'd found it.

"Is there a map of Thanet in here as well?" he asked.

"Doubtful. Thanet is already on the map, and I suspect it contains what little information the designer possessed."

But that made no sense. He turned back, and at his hesitation, Thorda indicated a tiny little island nearly disappeared off the fraying edges of the paper.

"I suspect the distances are inaccurate, and its overall shape is an educated guess, but this here is Thanet."

Cyrus stared at the map, and it felt like his whole world had been betrayed. If Gadir were the size of his two hands laid side by side, Thanet was represented by a stretch of land no larger than a fingernail. How could such an enormous place exist? Thanet was a little over one hundred leagues from tip to tip, and thirty leagues at its widest. Gadir must be over a thousand leagues wide, and another five hundred leagues tall.

"I don't understand," he said. "The maps in our castle always showed Gadir as not much larger than Thanet, maybe twice its size at most."

Thorda gently put a hand on Cyrus's shoulder and squeezed.

"I suspect a great many things you know are lies and exaggerations. Every nation wishes to believe itself the strongest, the wisest, and the hardest working. Their gods are the true gods. Their kings, councils, and presidents are benevolent rulers laboring against cruel foreign despots. Sometimes it is true. More often, it is a comforting lie."

"And what of you, and your stories of the Everlorn Empire's crimes? Are they lies, too?"

"You've seen their cruelty with your own eyes," his teacher said. "You need only imagine it performed again and again, upon a hundred different Thanets all across Gadir."

Thorda left him to stew over what he'd learned. After a moment of debate, Cyrus ripped the map out of the book, located a hammer and some nails by Thorda's forge, and then returned to the library. He pinned the map to the wall, directly above his preferred reading spot. Every day, it would be a reminder to the sheer size of his enemy. Every day, a reminder at how hard he must train to overcome such a foe.

CHAPTER 9

RAYAN

Rayan Vayisa gently folded his hands upon the old woman's chest and flattened his palms against the ridges of her rib cage. He could feel the faint heartbeat within, but it was strong compared to the rattle of her lungs.

"Close your eyes, Alliya," he said. "And repeat my words."

He'd performed this exact same ritual weekly over the past few months, yet still he instructed the elderly woman at every step. The repetition calmed him, and it gave him strength when he may not have any left.

"Amidst our troubles you guide us," they spoke in unison, Rayan's voice aged and strong, Alliya's wet and wilting. "Amidst our sorrows you comfort us. Grant us healing, Lycaena, we pray. May your brilliance and light chase away sorrows, precious goddess above all."

There was a time, in those blessed years before the Everlorn Empire invaded, he'd have seen shimmering white magic flow from his hands and into the sick woman's chest. Now he saw not a spark, and he heard only the faintest ringing of distant bells. Rayan closed his eyes, feeling ashamed of his doubts. Before he could attempt the prayer again, Alliya put her hand on his shoulder and swung her legs off her bed.

"Lycaena bless you," she said, barely able to get the words out before a coughing fit took her. Rayan bent down and slid his shoulder underneath her arm so she might lean her weight against him. Her lungs hadn't been right for months, and without his healing prayer, she could not find the strength to leave her bed. Day after day, her condition worsened. That, or his prayers weakened. Neither thought was a comforting one.

"You don't need to travel to the market on your own," Rayan suggested. "I'm sure there are a few bored youngsters who would shop for you if I asked."

Alliya waved him away.

"If I can't leave my bed, or leave my house, or buy my own food, what reasons have I to carry on?"

The old woman currently wore a long shift coupled with wool breeches. Rayan helped her layer more on for the weather, then looped a scarf about her neck and put a knitted bonnet atop her gray hair.

"You carry on because people love you and would miss you terribly," he said, and he gave her his best smile.

"Poppycock," she said, dismissing him with a practiced wave of her hand, the sharp motion honed over five decades of teaching in Vallessau's schools. "Never had kids of my own, and my parents are long gone to join Lycaena in her green fields. No one's left to love me."

"Then I love you, Alliya."

"Hah! Your hair may be gray as mine, but I have too many years on you. There's still hope you find yourself a nice husband or wife. The only man waiting for me is holding a shovel next to an empty grave."

The deep ringing of a bell dampened their conversation. It was the dismissal of congregations from the nine different churches throughout the city that had been converted into service for the God-Incarnate. Attendance twice a week was all but mandatory, for soldiers would harass anyone seen on the streets once the bells rang. There was good reason Rayan kept inside, and prayed over Alliya, during such an hour.

"Had my neighbors ask if I would come with last week," Alliya said as the ringing of the bell faded. "Told me things were better now, since Lycaena's death and the forsaking ceremony. They tore down the Dead Flags, didn't they? Damn fools. They were lucky I didn't spit at their feet."

Rayan offered her his arm.

"Try not to judge them too harshly," he said. "They're frightened, that's all."

"Then let them be frightened of *me*, and not coming knocking on my door while I'm trying to rest."

Together they exited the three-room home built at the end of a cul-de-sac that had rapidly grown in wealth as the demographics of Vallessau shifted with the inevitable changes of time. No doubt there were plenty of investors ready to purchase her home the moment she passed. They wouldn't move in, though, oh no. They'd tear down the spackled bricks and weathered shingles so they could build some multistory mansion matching those of her neighbors. Alliya walked with a cane, and even if Rayan had offered her his arm, she'd have waved him off. Anytime Rayan pondered berating her for her pride, he reminded himself that her pride was likely why she'd lived past the age of ninety in the first place.

They separated at the next fork, each making for their own destination. Once his morning prayer for Alliya was finished, Rayan's next stop was his story session for children at the Midtown market. He slipped a colorful scarf out from his pocket and tied it around his neck as he walked. Symbols of Lycaena were expressly forbidden, but the people of Thanet had slowly pushed the limits of what slipped past the laws and censors. Some might not get the reference, but others would see the color splashed against the rest of his white outfit and remember the way the long, colorful cloaks of Lycaena's paladins had contrasted with their brilliant armor.

"Aya, Aya!" a little girl shouted upon seeing him, and others quickly joined in, the play on his name making them all sound frightened by his arrival.

"You're all cruel as ever," Rayan said as he sat upon a little stool set in a shaded corner of the market. Shoppers bustled about, but two men in particular kept watch at the edges of nearby stalls. They were both parents to a few of the dozen children assembled for story time. Should imperial soldiers, or goddess forbid, a member of the Uplifted Church make their way near, the parents would alert Rayan so he might scatter the children and pretend he was a tired man seeking rest.

"What story this time?" a little seven-year-old with brilliant emerald eyes asked him. Some children didn't care much for his stories, and attended only because their parents forced their participation, but this little one always listened with rapt attention. It helped that he was often the first Rayan gave honey-glazed almonds to when Rayan had some coin to spare.

"A new one," Rayan said, trying to push Alliya and her sick lungs out of his mind. "It's about when Lycaena had to come rescue Endarius, for the Lion god had gotten himself stuck at the bottom of a dark ravine leading to the Heldeep..."

For the next half hour he told stories to the children in an attempt to counter whatever nonsense the Uplifted Church had filled their heads with during their mandatory lessons. Some had simple points about being kind to others, remaining true to your inner selves, and refusing the ugly behaviors of the prideful and cruel. Others gave examples of Lycaena's mercy, or Endarius's stubbornness. Rayan did his best to keep the telling lively, raising his voice for Lycaena and deepening it to a nearly unintelligible growl for Endarius. He even took on a sinister tone when speaking as Dagon, the weak-hearted coward who ruled the Heldeep at the farthest pit of the ocean where the evil and unrepentant were punished.

The hour ended, and the younger children scattered to their waiting parents, who chatted with shopkeepers that lingered at the doors to their shops. The older ones returned home unattended, though three remained, speaking in hushed tones as they debated what to spend their small allotment of copper crowns on. Rayan wished life could be as simple as children often saw it. There were right actions and wrong actions. You strove to choose the right actions while forgiving yourself and others when performing the wrong ones. These children didn't yet know the sting of impossibility. They didn't know the dread of the unrepentant and the determined ugliness of the Uplifted. They would, in time. When they did, Rayan prayed his stories of hope and forgiveness might bring them comfort.

Normally lunch was a slice of rye bread with a generous helping of butter and honey, but today he felt like something different. He'd heard one restaurant in particular had gotten their hands on an extremely spicy powder made of crushed violet peppers, and he was eager to discover if the sauce they made for their breads was as hot as they claimed. He hummed an outlawed song as he walked, stopping only at an angry cry to his right.

"Leave me alone, all of you, just leave!"

Three men had cornered a crossed-woman in front of a hat stall. She held one of its soft leather hats in hand, its cyan ribbon matching the pale blue of her dress and sea green of her heeled shoes. That outfit no doubt cost a small fortune, and the crossed-woman wore it with pride. It seemed that pride, however, had earned her some detractors.

"Look, we're saying that Leonard here makes some mighty fine hats," the biggest of the three men said, and he gestured to the stall's owner. "And it'd be a shame to have someone so ugly be seen wearing one of them fancy Leonard hats. That's reasonable, ain't it?"

The stall owner stood with his arms behind his back and his gaze burrowing into the street with unmatched focus. Whether he agreed or disagreed, he offered hints to neither, which was enough of an answer in Rayan's eyes.

"There's nothing reasonable about threatening a woman," he said, stepping toward the group.

"Woman?" the balding man on the left snorted. "Check your eyes, I just see me a pervert in a dress."

Rayan's hands bunched into fists.

"My eyes see three brutes up to no good. Now leave her be, lest things come to violence."

The crossed-woman tried to step past the three harassers.

"It's fine," she muttered to no one in particular. "I'm going, it's fine."

"Oh no, you're not." One of the three grabbed her by the hair and pulled with such viciousness, it'd have broken her neck if the hair weren't a wig. The woman screamed and turned, and despite her smaller size, she heaved her weight against him and reached for the wig. A split lip from a backhand was her reward.

Rayan stepped closer, and the practiced, polite smile left his face. Others nearby were watching, but none intervened. The indifference was a fuel upon the fire growing in his chest. Not long ago, such disgusting violence would have had the trio chased out of the market. Now it was ignored.

"I didn't seek blood," he said. "But you've spilled it first, so allow me to spill it last."

Rayan lacked a sword and shield, but certain fundamentals of combat remained the same. His fighting style had been passed down through generations of paladins, supposedly from the first men and women to take up service in Lycaena's honor. Quick, steady movements, like the opening and closing of the wings of a butterfly. Step into a stance, arms positioned in a block, attack, or parry. Step out, avoiding a hit, blocking a blow, or merely stealing a quick breath to steady oneself for the fight ahead. These men were big, but weight didn't mean muscle. They outnumbered Rayan, but that didn't mean proper coordination.

Rayan had crossed blades with paragons. Three ignorant blowhards were like children compared to them.

He stepped into their center, his left arm up as if he wore a shield, his right punching in a mimicry of a thrust. It struck the gut of the nearest man, and his gasp confirmed him unprepared for actual combat. The tallest of the three swung for Rayan's head, but it was clumsy and high, and Rayan's steady slide backward made it an easy dodge. Back in, an elbow to a man's throat, a punch to the face. Out, avoiding a frantic tackle. In, both fists together to crack across a man's nose. He wasn't fast, but he moved through them with ease, sensing their attacks before they made them and responding in a way that left them always grasping at nothing.

"Pig shit!" one screamed as Rayan smashed his forehead into the man's face. Blood exploded from his broken nose. The other two punched and kicked with the wild recklessness of those who fought only in bars and workplace scuffles. Blows struck the paladin's sides, but he could ignore them. No fight would go perfectly. All that mattered was that his foes suffered far worse. Rayan shifted his feet, braced his legs so he had a firm foundation, and then struck again. That he took a punch to the cheek was irrelevant. A facial bruise meant little compared to a kidney strike that nearly crippled his foe.

Back out, reassessing, his hands coming up to defend both his sides. Back in, arms carrying strength many knuckle-ring fighters would envy. Ribs shuddered beneath his blows. Pained whimpers escaped grimaced mouths. Rayan could hear his heartbeat in his ears, but his mind remained calm, almost placid. These three meant nothing to him, less than nothing, and he feared not a single blow they could make. He was a paladin of Lycaena. It would take far, far more than three thugs to bring him low.

Not that they'd have the chance. The commotion had finally summoned a patrol of imperial soldiers from the opposite side of the market, and they came running with their weapons drawn.

"Enough!" the lead soldier screamed. "I said enough!"

The three backed away, and they looked more than happy for an excuse to cancel the fight. Rayan remained perfectly still, carefully watching lest any make one last cowardly attempt. None did, and once the imperial soldiers arrived, they acted as if they'd not been in a fight at all.

"You come just in time," Rayan said. "Those three sought to beat us bloody."

The soldiers merely glared. They barely spoke any Thanese, Rayan realized, and it seemed none had one of the word-laces the paragons and magistrates wore that translated speech with imperial magic. The lengthy stare at the crossed-woman, and the crumpled wig, seemed to spell out what had happened well enough for them to understand.

"Go home all. Home. Now."

"And what of them?" Rayan asked, pointing to the three brutes.

"They problem," the lead soldier said in stuttering Thanese. He gestured to the crossed-woman. "He problem. Fair is fair."

And then he walked away.

Rayan bit his tongue to hold back his retort. The crossed and twice-born were not explicitly outlawed, although Thorda warned that was coming with the inevitable introduction of what he called the Joining Laws. The Uplifted Church, however, made it abundantly clear their opinion on such "sinful deviances." Rayan knelt beside the crossed-woman to help her to her feet.

"I'm sorry," he whispered. "The Uplifted Church's influence has sunken deep into the cruel-hearted."

"As if I don't already know." She tried to smooth out wrinkles in her dress, and she winced at the flecks of blood that stained the blue fabric. A bitter curse slipped from her lips. "Why bother with this wig and paint and squeeze myself into a dress if this is all it gets me?"

The woman reached for her wig, and Rayan settled his hand atop hers before she could withdraw it.

"Because Lycaena asks it of us," he said. "We walk a world flooded with color, and sing in joy at the cornucopia Thanet offers. My brethren and I cherish beauty, and see it in every blade of grass and every painted smile. I see that same beauty in you, too. This world is cruel, I know that, but we cannot surrender to it. We cannot let Thanet wither to ash and dust so all that remains is a sea of gray. That's worth fighting for."

His words had meant to inspire her, and comfort her, but they had the exact opposite effect.

"I bleed so you get your colorful world." The crossed-woman shoved her wig into the interior of her coat. "Damn you, paladin. What good are you, then?"

She left behind her sea green shoes with raised heels. Rayan knelt down and retrieved one of them. His fingers caressed the shoe absently, and he wished he knew better words, and possessed a stronger faith to believe them, when he spoke.

A bored-looking man waited for Rayan at his house, a dock worker based on his clothes and the plentiful mud upon them.

"Fisher brought this by boat," he said as explanation when Rayan asked his purpose for a visit. From one of his deep pockets he pulled out a tightly folded scrap of paper. "It's for your eyes only, paladin."

Rayan accepted the scrap and wished him well. Once inside, he sat in his favorite chair, and with a cup of boiled tea, he unfolded it. He expected a note from Thorda Ahlai, who had exited Vallessau three months ago to begin training the young prince. Instead, he found it addressed to him by a distant aunt, one who had retreated to the farthest northern reaches of the island when the royal family fell.

Dearest Rayan, every lifelong servant knows secrets of the castle, it began. *But mine was greater still, afforded by my friendship with then-princess Berniss. There are more ways into the castle than the front gates . . .*

Rayan read the note four times, committing every detail to memory, and then tossed it upon the fire. It was too dangerous to keep on his person, and the guards at the city gates were known to perform random searches.

"Well, Cyrus," he said, planning the trip in his mind. Such information must be given to Thorda, and in person. "Perhaps it is time I see how your training fares."

CHAPTER 10

RAYAN

Two women joined Rayan for the painfully long carriage ride from Vallessau to the distant estate. Rayan was good friends with Mari Ahlai, and had worked often with her as the Lioness over the past months. Nothing too drastic, and not always focused on killing. Merely keeping her presence known to the people was vital if faith in Endarius were to endure. When Rayan proposed a visit to her father, she had readily agreed, and paid for the carriage herself.

The other woman was Clarissa Greene, one of Vallessau's city clerks. He met her on occasion, always in the secret meetings organized in the deep of night with those still fighting against the imperial takeover. Rayan assumed she had business with Thorda regarding her occupation, but he did not ask. Her business was not his own. This charming woman remained faithful to Lycaena, so instead, he casually chatted about matters of faith and history with her as they crossed the fourteen hours of winding dirt roads, through gradually higher hills, and several forest highways to the Ahlai mansion. His assumption was immediately proven wrong upon their arrival, when Stasia swept Clarissa up into her arms and covered her face with kisses.

What once was open must now be hidden, he thought, the excitement of their arrival now tinged with bitterness.

"I'm surprised you could get away," Stasia said when they separated.

"Sometimes even we hard workers need a brief reprieve," Clarissa explained. "That, and my mother is likely telling everyone I'm deathly ill even as we speak."

Mari rushed past them while laughing, making a beeline toward her father. Rayan stayed beside the carriage, pretending not to be anxious. Between the two years of absence during the prince's imprisonment, and now the months spent training with Thorda, Rayan had worried there would be a distance between him and Cyrus that would not be easily crossed. The young man's slow approach only added to that worry. Whereas Clarissa and Mari received immediate joy, Cyrus kept himself measured. He walked with head stiff and spine straight, as if the paladin were a foreign dignitary. His head dipped low in greeting.

"It's good to see you, old man."

Just like that, all of Rayan's worries melted away. He beamed a grin and opened his arms.

"So says the little boy."

They embraced, years parting, Rayan once more the close protector and teacher, Cyrus his student and friend. Meanwhile Stasia set Clarissa back to her feet, keeping her close, her tiny body fully wrapped in her arms. Her attention briefly turned Rayan's way.

"Fair warning, the prince is getting a mouth on him now that he's had a few months of training."

"Getting?" Rayan ruffled Cyrus's hair. Even on the day the empire invaded, the prince had poked fun of his age when prodding him to join the battle. "No, he has always been like that. It just hid for a while."

He sized the young man up. His face and arms were bruised, his hands blistered. His left wrist was wrapped in a splint. A lifetime of practice allowed Rayan to easily hide his worry with a warm, welcoming smile.

"How goes your training?" he asked. "I'd love to see what all Master Ahlai has you perform in a day."

Stasia finished burying Clarissa in kisses, then gestured to her father.

"I'm done with him for the day, but I doubt you wanted to watch me and Cyrus run exercises for two hours anyway. I'm sure you'll find Thorda's training much more informative. You might even learn a few things yourself."

Rayan did indeed learn two things within minutes of Thorda's instruction. One, that the combined attention to detail and imparted skill were of incomparable value for Cyrus.

Two, that Thorda was an absolutely ruthless master.

"Try again," the older man said as Cyrus crouched on his knees. He'd tried, and failed, to properly block as Thorda demanded. His reward had been a strike to his shoulder by the master's wooden pole. When Cyrus had tried to catch his weight on his splinted arm, it had crumpled, and he'd whimpered in pain.

As much as it killed him, Rayan waited to react. To do so now would make his reasons obvious. Patiently, he watched as the young prince settled back into a stance. Down came the hit, and finally Cyrus blocked it exactly as desired. Thorda chopped twice more in rapid succession, ensuring his student fully memorized the lesson, then stepped back. The momentary relief, and at a moment of accomplishment, gave Rayan his desired opening.

"You've grown so much since I first put a sword in your hand," he said, leaning heavily on the nostalgia to disguise his true purpose. He entered the training circle, and stood between Cyrus and Thorda. "And to use two blades instead of one? Surely more difficult than I with my shield. If you would indulge me, I would love to see some examples of the core tenets of Miquoan fighting."

Thorda fell silent to observe. Rayan pretended he wasn't there, and he nodded his head supportively as Cyrus began talking. The young man started slow, careful to put minimal pressure on his splinted arm. He began with what appeared to be the basics, a few key initial stances that the rest of his actions would spiral out of. The more he talked, the looser he grew, and the easier he smiled. His explanations became more animated, his movements sharper. It hurt him to use that arm, that much was certain, but less than before, for he was relaxed and in control.

"I suppose you have trained enough, and it would be cruel to keep you from your guests," Thorda said after a time. "I will await you inside."

Mari passed him on the gravel walkway to join them, and she briefly stopped to greet him before continuing.

"Done practicing already?" she said, clearly disappointed. "But I just came out to watch."

"There's not much practice to watch," Rayan said, and he gestured to Cyrus's splinted arm. Thorda might be reluctant to acknowledge it, but he wouldn't. "One can only do so much when injured."

"You're injured?" she asked.

"It's nothing," Cyrus said, embarrassed by the attention. "Stasia says it's only a sprain."

"Then it will be that much easier for me to heal."

Mari took his bandaged wrist into her hands and closed her eyes. Rayan winced as if struck. Such healing magic should be available to him as well...but then again, his struggles with Alliya lingered on his mind. If Mari could do so with Endarius's gifted magic, then let her. There was no reason to risk ruining his mood with his own potential failure.

Whispered prayers floated from her lips, too quiet for Rayan to hear. The two men stood respectfully silent and still. A soft breeze blew against them, carrying the scent of tall grass. Faint rainbow light shimmered across her fingers, so quick and brief it might have been his imagination.

"I'll need to pray on it more," she said, opening her eyes and letting go. "But for now, does it feel better?"

Cyrus lifted his arm and gently twisted it one direction, then the other.

"Yeah," he said. "I think it does."

"Wonderful!" she said, tugging his good arm toward the mansion. "Now come inside, and find yourself a comfy chair. Give me a few hours of prayer, and by tomorrow, you'll be a brand-new you."

"Impossible," Cyrus insisted.

"It's true," Rayan said. The group gathered in a large den, with a ridiculously huge fireplace roaring on one side. Mari sat next to Cyrus in a padded chair, cradling his splinted arm. She'd not left his side since dinner, and every few moments she stopped to offer it another prayer. Thorda lingered by the fire, occasionally prodding it with a poker, while Stasia and Clarissa cuddled on a sofa. Empty ale cups and wineglasses lay about, loosening their tongues as they chatted the evening hours away.

"But I saw the Lioness fighting at Lycaena's execution," Cyrus said. "The way she ripped and tore apart those soldiers? You can't possibly be her. You're so ... nice."

"I cannot decide if I should be flattered or insulted."

"Probably a bit of both," Stasia said. "Want me to flick his ears for you?"

"I'm perfectly capable of defending myself, thank you."

Before Cyrus could ask what she meant, Mari squeezed his injured arm hard enough that his eyes bulged.

"See?" she said, the pressure of her fingers relenting. "Even us nice people can be cruel. We just don't enjoy it."

"Seemed to enjoy that just fine," Cyrus muttered.

"You caught me." Mari yawned. "I must surrender to bed. Between the carriage ride and Cyrus's arm, I'm completely beat."

"Need me to carry you?" Stasia asked.

"Seems like your hands are already full to me."

It was not often Rayan saw Stasia blush, but her cheeks burned a bright red. Leave it to sisters to know exactly where and how to poke at each other. Before the door had even closed from Mari's exit, Stasia lurched to her feet. She hoisted Clarissa up with her, easily cradling her in her arms.

"Mari may joke, but she wasn't wrong, and at this point I feel like accepting it as a challenge."

Clarissa waved at them while feigning helplessness.

"I guess this is good night," she said, her giggles made all the louder by the amount of ale she had consumed. Rayan wished them well, and he found mild amusement in the blush that came over Cyrus's face. Ah, to be so young and easily embarrassed. Meanwhile, Thorda vanished into the adjoining room and returned holding a tall glass of white wine. He sipped it while settling more comfortably into his chair beside the roaring fire.

"Forgive the directness, Rayan," he said. "But you have failed to broach the subject at your own discretion, and my curiosity gets the better of me. Why have you come? The ride here is too long, and your need in Vallessau too great, for you to arrive without a reason. The night is deep, and the fire warm. Share it."

Rayan took a moment to recollect the contents of the note.

"I've a distant aunt who retreated to North Cape after the island's invasion," he began. "But she had retired from her service in the castle many years before then. It took time for me to find her, but once I did, I asked her if she might have knowledge that might benefit our resistance, knowledge perhaps forgotten or hidden. Her answer arrived in a letter, and it was more than I could have hoped for. There's a secret entrance into the castle, meant to be an escape tunnel should it be besieged."

Both Thorda and Cyrus snapped to attention.

"Tell me," Thorda said. "Spare not a single detail."

Rayan did so, starting with the location of a home with a secret door within its cellar. Thorda slowly pinched his lip as he listened, his eyes glazed and thoughtful. When Rayan was finished, Thorda had him repeat the instructions so he might fully commit them to memory.

"Are you certain this entrance exists?" he asked finally. "Her mind has not withered in age?"

"If you could read the writing, you'd know her mind is sharp as ever. I believe the passage real."

Cyrus burst up from his chair to his feet.

"Then we have to attack," he said. "We can assassinate the Usurper King!"

"Absolutely not," Thorda said. "Not until the time is right."

"The time is right? What do you mean? How could we possibly afford to wait?"

Rayan crossed his arms. His thoughts had matched Cyrus's at first, but during the carriage ride to the mansion, he'd had plenty of time to reconsider.

"Killing the Usurper King doesn't accomplish anything meaningful," he explained. "His son will simply be declared regent-in-waiting, his widow will assume most duties, and all else will continue as normal.

It would be a victory, yes, but its impact would mostly be symbolic. If there is nothing prepared to take advantage, then it means little in the long run."

"Which is why it must be accompanied by additional actions," Thorda said, nodding in agreement. "We have in our hands a deadly blade, but it will break after a single strike. Once the empire knows of the secret entrance's existence, they will scour the castle until they find it. Let me think on this and best forge a scenario for its use. If we are to kill Gordian Goldleaf, let it be accompanied by the corpses of priests and magistrates. Let it be when his city is aflame, his soldiers are hunted, and you may be there to take full credit as the Vagrant assassin."

"Those reasons all sound like excuses," Cyrus argued. "Gordian is awful. I know. I was with him each and every day. I don't give a shit who kills him. He's a monster. Put him in the ground. Isn't that what your resistance is supposed to do?"

Thorda rose up, shoulders widening, eyes narrowing. He seemed larger somehow, older, and much more dangerous. The fire cast his shadow across the room, a burning silhouette.

"I will hear no more of this prattle. Bite your tongue, boy. My decisions are not to be questioned."

The way Cyrus shrank before his master, all his smiles and jokes and anger gone so he might become small and obedient, soured Rayan's mood. Silence lingered, heavy and uncomfortable. His gaze flicked to the splint on the boy's arm. He would not let this go unaddressed.

"Leave us," he told Cyrus. "I would have a word with your master."

The young prince reluctantly obeyed. Rayan waited until he was gone, and took the time to organize his thoughts. As much as he understood the imperative need, he could not reconcile the damage it was inflicting upon the boy.

Thorda sat back in his chair and smoothed out his robes.

"What is it that bothers you?" he asked.

"You're working him too hard."

"I work him as hard as I must."

"I observed the training regimen you put him through, and spoke with Stasia about her own part in it. There are professional soldiers who would call it cruel. Sunrise to sunset, with barely a moment to eat. His young body is tearing apart. The bruises and the splint prove it."

The wealthy master crossed his arms and looked to the fire.

"Spare me your concerns. The training is acceptable, and the trials endurable. The boy will not break."

"How do you know?"

"Because it did not break Stasia!"

Thorda glared in his direction, but Rayan matched it intensity for intensity.

"Yet Mari did not undergo the same training when she later came of age. I wonder why?"

A long, dangerous pause followed. Thorda slowly stood, his hands clenched into fists at his sides.

"You stumble blindly, and know nothing of what you speak. My tutelage is necessary if Cyrus is to become what Thanet needs. The Everlorn Empire is cruel and merciless. We must be the same if we are to achieve victory."

"Then you admit you are cruel to him?"

Thorda slammed a fist to the wall. Perhaps it was a reflection from the fire, but the flames burning in his red eyes, they seemed so real.

"Enough. You are not the only one who cares for the boy!"

Awkward silence overcame them. Rayan leaned back in his seat, debating priorities. His sermons and lectures in Vallessau and the surrounding countryside were vital to maintaining belief in Lycaena. But he had also sworn an oath to the Lythan family. Here in this mansion was the last of that family. How did one balance such responsibilities?

"Let me train him," he said, breaking the silence.

"Absolutely not. You will be a fine test for him, but only when his skill set is firmly established."

"My duty is to the royal family," Rayan insisted. "And you yourself will readily admit I am capable with a sword. Why would you deny my involvement?"

The Miquoan man smoothed out his robe, and he appeared embarrassed by his prior outburst.

"Twice before I have attempted to give conquered people a new champion. Both times I chose the greatest fighters the nation may offer. In Aethenwald it was a priestess raised from birth to be a master wielder of their spears. In Noth-Wall, a knight who won dozens of their prize-tournaments. Neither survived, for they knew not how to fight against paragons, and their training clashed with my own, often in ways I failed to predict. I cannot scour habits and instincts I am unaware of. But with Cyrus? He is dedicated, focused, and will know only that which I teach him. He can become everything Rhodes sought to create. I failed my husband, but I will not fail Cyrus. We will succeed. I know it. I *feel* it, Rayan, feel it deep in my bones. Here, upon this jewel of the Crystal Sea, we shall accomplish miracles."

There was a possessiveness here that Rayan deeply distrusted. Thorda's dedication was unmatched; of that, the paladin had no doubt. But what he was doing with Cyrus, it felt desperate. It went beyond training. Was it the connection to this rarely mentioned Rhodes Ahlai?

"You won't fail him," he asked slowly, carefully. "How did you fail your husband?"

The vulnerability left Thorda. Hardness replaced it, and he glared at Rayan for broaching such a topic.

"I need a year, perhaps two, before Cyrus is ready to fight alongside my daughters," he said, ignoring the question. "His growth over these past three months has been extraordinary. Hold faith in him, paladin. Is that not what you are meant for?"

"I hold faith in my goddess alone."

"And how fares the goddess's faith in Vallessau? You attack my part in our plans, yet what of the responsibilities you shoulder?"

It was Rayan's turn to stand. He would retreat from no challenge, no matter who offered it. Alliya's sickly cough echoed in his ears as he spoke, and he did his best to ignore it.

"The Lioness inspires faith in Endarius. My prayers and teachings keep alive hope in Lycaena. Yet we both preach belief in dead gods, while the priests of the Uplifted Church spread the message of a living God-Incarnate. It is a losing battle, and will be until we can banish the empire from our shores."

"Then it is good Cyrus's training progresses so well."

Rayan closed the distance between them. He couldn't make an enemy of Thorda, not when the man's coin and connections were so vital. And as much as he hated to admit it, he could not neglect the spiritual nature of his calling by remaining here in the mansion as Cyrus's trainer. Thorda would get his chosen fighter, molded exactly in his desired image. That didn't mean he had to like it, nor that he would leave without one last warning.

"My family has served the Lythan family for centuries," he said. "We have fought, bled, and died protecting their honor. The last of that bloodline resides under your roof while I serve my goddess in Vallessau. Train him. Better him. But do not ruin him. You would craft a weapon. I would return to find a prince."

"They can be one and the same," Thorda said softly.

"You forget which one matters more."

"And which one is that, paladin? What do the people cry out for when their land is conquered, a crown, or a killer?"

"They cry out for salvation," Rayan answered.

"And salvation is what I shall give them, but it must come at the bloody edge of a blade."

The effects of Mari's prayers were already showing on Cyrus when Rayan hugged him goodbye early the next morning. The splint was gone, replaced with a tight cloth wrapping.

"Stay strong," Rayan said as they broke their embrace. "Whatever Thorda throws at you, I have full confidence you can rise above it. Make this old man proud."

Cyrus grinned at him.

"This little boy will do his best not to disappoint."

Rayan took his seat beside Mari. On the opposite side of the carriage, Stasia and Clarissa finished their goodbyes, and the tiny red-haired woman climbed in to join them.

"Fourteen hours each way for a single night together," she said, shaking her head. "I'm not sure why I agreed."

"Was it not worth it?" Mari asked.

Clarissa blushed slightly.

"It might have been, but it's still inappropriate for you to ask."

A crack of the whip and the carriage rumbled into motion. Mari slumped down in her seat, getting comfortable for the many, many hours back.

"I agree, though. It's a shame we couldn't stay longer."

Rayan stared out the window as the mansion receded into the distance. An image of Thorda standing before the fire, anger burning in his red eyes, haunted his memory.

"A shame indeed," he said.

He told himself the young prince was in good hands, and Thorda would raise him well. He told himself the future was bright, and his faith strong enough to keep Lycaena alive in the hearts and minds of Vallessau's people. He told himself lots of things, enough that he did not know what he believed, and what was a lie.

Rayan knocked to enter Alliya's home his first morning back in Vallessau. No response. A refusal to believe the worst kept him from panicking. He hadn't been gone long, he told himself. Not long at all. He put his ear to the door. Not a sound within.

"No," he whispered. "Please no."

He broke the door open with his shoulder, splintering the simple wood lock. The smell hit him immediately. Tears built in his eyes as he approached the bed. He need not examine Alliya when he found her underneath her blankets. Her eyes were open and dry. Her mouth was slightly ajar. No movements to her chest. No soft, uneven flow of air in and out of her sickly lungs.

"I'm sorry, Alliya," he said as he crumpled to his knees beside the bed. He stared at her wrinkled hands. Her fingers linked together with the strength of death, clutched as if she'd died in the midst of prayer. Three months of weekly morning rituals, and he'd not rid her of the illness that plagued her. Three months, and his faith had meant nothing.

Rayan placed his hands over hers, skin against wrinkled skin, and wondered how much longer until his own body shriveled.

"Is this the reward awaiting us?" he asked the dead silence. "Futile prayers met with death in isolation? Did the knives of the imperials cut deeper than I believed?"

Rayan had been mere feet away when the first of the ritual blades sank into the flesh of the magnificent Lycaena. More had followed, but that first knife had been the worst. His beloved goddess had screamed in pain he'd never known she could feel. Despite the sharpness of his sword and the strength of his shield, he could not protect her. He could not save her. Yet for the past months he had clung to hope. He had believed his goddess a survivor. The faith of her followers would keep her strong, no matter the damning words of the Everlorn Empire's Anointed One.

Or perhaps it had all been a self-serving lie. He'd fooled no one but himself as he wrapped his colorful cloak about his shoulders and prayed to a god as dead as the royal family he'd failed to protect.

Damn you, paladin. What good are you, then?

"Is this...is this it?" Rayan asked. He pressed his forehead to his clenched fists. He let his tears flow unimpeded. "Is this what's left to us, goddess? Do emptiness and silence await instead of eternal green fields? Do you hear me, Lycaena? Did you *ever* hear me?"

Questions, questions, always questions, never answers. Fury bubbled in his stomach. Despair lashed his soul with open wounds.

"Or are we alone?" he whispered. "Has this world abandoned us with the same cruelty that took the life from your splendid body?"

In his nightmares he still saw the sacrifice. Curved knives cutting holes into her black flesh. Brutal hands ripping the rainbow wings from her back. The Usurper King had cut and carved her like a butchered pig. Anointed Sinshei vin Lucavi had flung what was left of her ruby and emerald hair to the crowd like trophies. Together, they'd splashed blue blood across the faces of an imprisoned crowd, and they'd done so while singing a song of worship on their tongues and proclaiming glory from the deepest depths of their hearts.

Alone. The answer was the only viable one. How could he pretend otherwise as he held the hands of a dead woman he lacked the strength to save?

"I'm sorry," he whispered to Alliya. "I'm so sorry. I could have helped you, once."

What did his devotion matter if he could not save the lives of those who needed him? What use was beauty to a world whose masters would burn it with purifying torches? Thorda placed the burden of Vallessau's faith in Lycaena upon his shoulders. He was to keep it alive, a bulwark against the hate the Uplifted Church would spread. Yet how could he maintain the people's faith in Lycaena when his own faith was brittle and crumbling?

Silence. The only answer to greet his prayers.

"You deserved better," Rayan said as he rose to his feet. He let go of Alliya's hands and carefully lowered her eyelids.

Alone. The way she had lived the remainder of her life. The way she had died. The way her soul would pass on without Lycaena to take her upon brilliant wings. His broken heart could handle no other truth.

Alone.

Alone.

Alliya's mouth trembled.

Rayan stepped back. Horror seized him. He dared not move as Alliya's lips vibrated as if touched by the faintest of winds. His mind failed to understand. The dead woman's lips were parting. Not to release sound, but because something crawled from within. It was small, so small, its body soft and bathed with fuzz. A butterfly, he first thought, but no, not a butterfly. A moth, pale and slipping free of her mouth so it might stretch its wings.

"Lycaena?" Rayan whispered.

Another moth curled around the underside of her left ear. It climbed to her hair and stopped to stretch its wings in a similar manner as the first. Rayan took a step back. Drums hammered within his rib cage. A third moth fluttered in through a crack in the nearby window to land atop her blanket. A fourth, a fifth, fluttering from underneath the pillow, the half-open curtain to the closet. They gathered upon the body and waited with their wings opening and closing. Waiting, but for what?

And then he saw the truth. In his greatest despair, he had believed a lie. Alliya had not died alone. Her fingers parted, her hands opening to release a hundred moths from her sheltered grasp. They swirled like a funnel, surrounding him, enveloping him with a ceaseless flutter and a whirlwind of gray. Rayan stood with his eyes turned heavenward as the moths kissed his skin with the soft touch of their wings. The whisper of the air was a promise. The number of moths grew, hundreds, thousands, a count beyond measure. The physical bounds of Alliya's room meant nothing. The swirl of moths held him in a vital embrace, comforting him, and within their fluttering song he heard the voice of his goddess.

No. Not alone. His legs went weak, and he openly wept within the embrace. Never alone, not even when the moths scattered, the song ceased, and only an empty physical shell remained upon the bed before him. Never alone, for even now, his goddess would grant him strength to inspire amid the gray.

CHAPTER 11

CYRUS

To mark the end of six long, grueling months, Thorda summoned Cyrus to the forge.

"As with all art, there are times when the needed effort meets only the barest minimum," his master explained as he pumped the pedal that pushed air into the forge. "But there are times when I put a piece of my soul into the work. Times when the work is vital, and necessary, and the care and effort must rise to meet that need. Today, I craft you your weapons, Cyrus. They will be a part of me, and they will become a part of you. You will know them like you know your own fingers. They will connect to you as your own bones. Watch silently, young man. I ask only that you bear witness to the art, so you might appreciate its beauty when I gift you these blades. But first..."

He reached into the deep pockets of his apron and pulled out two sword hilts. They gleamed with silver, and their expertise was immediately apparent. Cyrus accepted them graciously, eager for a closer look. They were wrapped in soft black leather, and somehow they seemed perfectly crafted for his fingers. While their cross guards were similar, their bases were not. One was cut into the head of a roaring lion, while the other, the unfolded wings of a butterfly. Their details were formed of little indents and swirls cut into the metal, and Cyrus wondered how he'd never seen his master working on the two hilts before when they clearly had taken countless hours to make.

"They...they're better than I deserve."

"And yet exactly what you need," Thorda said, and he gently took them back. "Find yourself a seat. While I seek to instruct in all things, in this I must apologize. This task is beyond your capabilities. Whatever questions you have, save them for the dinner table. Until then, do not break my concentration. Do not speak. Observe, and appreciate the art."

Cyrus bobbed his head up and down.

"Yes, master," he said, beyond eager to witness the man at his forge.

The folding of the steel took hours of sweaty, back-breaking labor, yet Thorda showed not a hint of exhaustion. Amid that forge he was as tireless as the march of seasons. Cyrus watched without saying a word, for he could feel something special happening, a magic far beyond his understanding. These swords...Thorda hadn't been exaggerating. A piece of his soul was going into these weapons. His concentration never broke for an instant. Come nightfall, he set the worked steel aside and spoke for the first time in hours.

"We finish tomorrow."

The next day, and an additional ten hours later, he declared the swords complete. For the final cooling, he poured a mixture of oils and petals into the water trough. "Trade secret," he said, as if sensing Cyrus's unspoken curiosity. The hiss of heat and steam was deafening in the twilight hour.

"Give them their time," Thorda said, and he hung the pair upon the wall rack, their brilliant, shining steel captivating Cyrus's eyes and filling him with excitement. "Tomorrow, I promise. You wield them tomorrow."

Tomorrow took an eternity to arrive, but a quick dinner and a fitful sleep later, he ran his laps around the mansion grounds with renewed enthusiasm. No more practice swords. No wooden replicas or exaggerated weights. At last he would wield real blades. His master, though, was in no hurry, and it was only after finishing his breakfast that he finally agreed to join him at the forge.

After the ceremony involved in crafting them, Cyrus was surprised how nonchalantly his teacher gifted the finished weapons. No speeches or promises, merely a single word as he handed both over.

"Careful."

Cyrus held the sister swords up to the light. The hilts had been meticulously designed with his exact grip in mind. The blades themselves were both unlike any he'd seen on Thanet. The right-hand sword bore the lion hilt of Endarius, and was the longer of the two. Its upper half was thick and straight, but it thinned as it progressed. At its midpoint it didn't curve so much as bend downward at an angle. From that bend onward, both sides of the blade were impossibly sharp, and it ended at a curving tip that looked powerful enough to thrust through chainmail.

The butterfly hilt of Lycaena belonged to the off-hand blade, and it was exactly as heavy as the other despite being a full foot shorter. It was also straight, and sharp only one on side, the other thick and reinforced so it could endure Thorda's fighting style. That off-hand blade was mostly used for blocking and parrying, and Cyrus would wield it in a reverse grip as much as he did in a traditional hold. Even the hilt guard was wider and reinforced to protect the hand.

Cyrus swung them through the air, a thrill shooting through his body. The weapons *sang* as they sliced and danced. Nothing in Thanet's armory had ever compared to the expertise on display. Simply holding them made Cyrus want to practice from dawn to dusk so he might be worthy of their craftsmanship. Last but not least, Thorda presented him with a sword belt, a traditional sheath for the Lycaena blade, and a unique leather half sheath for the upper half of the Endarius blade on the opposite hip. Cyrus handed the swords to a watchful Stasia while he buckled the belt about his waist and adjusted the tightness.

"Some damn fine work," Stasia said as she admired the weapons. "They're almost as nice as my axes. Maybe we should find ourselves a proper swordsman to put them to use."

"A proper swordsman already has them," Cyrus said, grinning at her. Gods and goddesses help him, simply holding the fine weapons inspired confidence.

"We shall see," Thorda said. "Stasia, retrieve the sparring poles from that shelf. I want Cyrus to feel what it is like to use them in true combat."

Cyrus's excitement grew. He'd never dueled Stasia before, only seen her occasionally practicing with her axes. Sure, she performed drills with him, but it was Thorda who taught him forms and stances, and who tested his reflexes. While Stasia grabbed the poles, Thorda dragged his stool he kept at the forge out to the flat, worn space used for training beyond it. He sat, legs and arms crossed, and prepared.

Stasia returned with two wooden poles of approximate length to her axes. She twirled them in her grasp, showing the easy familiarity of someone practically born with a weapon in hand. Cyrus almost replicated the motions with his own weapons but thought better of it. If he slipped and cut off his own fingers, he'd spend the rest of his life drowning in humiliation.

"Shouldn't you have armor in case I hit you?" Cyrus asked, worried he might hurt her with the blisteringly sharp edges of his swords.

"Don't worry," Stasia said. "You won't."

"Someone's cocky."

"Someone's about to get destroyed and doesn't know it yet."

Cyrus swung his swords to limber up as well as get a feel for their weight. They were drastically lighter than any of his practice weapons, and it made him feel quicker, more dangerous. His eagerness grew as Thorda lifted his arm above his head. Sitting on that stool, he looked like a professional judge for one of the tournaments Cyrus had watched with his father in the grand courtyard. The same courtyard they'd been executed in.

The sudden memory poisoned his mood. Cyrus forced a smile to his face and pretended all was well. He clanged the weapons together, using that clear ringing to bury the painful emotions deep, deep down. Thorda dropped his hand, calling out the start of their duel.

"Begin!"

Stasia dashed at him, both poles swung together in a downward slash. Wood hit steel, but Cyrus's pride at properly blocking lasted all but the span of a heartbeat. One pole shoved his longer sword aside, the other thrust for his exposed belly. Training kept his feet moving, and he retreated out of harm's way. He found no reprieve, for in came another dual slash. Cyrus crossed his swords into an X to block, and he grunted at the painful jolt that traveled up his elbows to his shoulders.

Of course Stasia needn't worry about being hit, he realized. His opponent solely held the offensive, for it took all his concentration to properly block. With each movement he had a half second to decide his next position, his next stance, so that he could deflect whatever follow-up Stasia unleashed. Yet as his panic eased, a rhythm established between them. The less he fretted over moves, the more his instincts took over. Raw and untested as they may be, they were still expertly honed by his master. Stasia clacked a pole against his leg once, and jabbed him in the stomach thirty seconds later, but by the time Thorda ordered a halt, those two hits were the only ones he'd suffered.

Cyrus wiped sweat off his forehead with his sleeve. He flashed Stasia a smile, proud at how well he had done. His master, however, seemed completely unimpressed.

"Fight him at your best," Thorda told his daughter. Stasia glanced his way, the wooden poles twirling in her agile fingers.

"Are you certain?" she asked.

"I am. He must learn the scope of his deficiencies."

Cyrus lowered into a stance, and his foe did likewise. Something changed in her, something subtle he couldn't see but could absolutely feel. Her muscles were tensed more tightly, her red eyes sharp, her cocky smile fading away into concentration. No longer did he feel like a partner, or an equal. He felt like a deer before a panther. Pride kept his stance firm, and he swore he would hold his own no matter how skillfully Stasia fought.

Thorda's voice was a whip cracking the air.

"Begin."

The distance between them vanished. She opened with the same dual slash, and he blocked it as he had before. The difference this time, though, was that Stasia held nothing back. Her poles slammed into him, catching him retreating instead of properly setting his feet. The uneven footing robbed his defense of strength, and she batted aside his block as if it were nothing. As if *he* were nothing. One pole hit his shoulder, the other curled inward to strike his ribs. Cyrus swept his left hand in an arc, trying to brush both weapons aside as he'd been taught when fighting in such close proximity. Stasia's right pole was already dropping in anticipation of the move, its flat tip smashing atop his knuckles. The pain and shock of it made him release the hilt, and his frantic mind was dimly aware how horrific a mistake that would be in real battle.

Still exposed, Cyrus tried to bring his other sword up to parry. Stasia's elbow struck his chest in reward. He gasped at the spike of pain that followed. His parry attempt came up weak. She smashed that sword aside with both her poles, then hit the underside of his wrist. Out came the sword. He reached for it, flailing, as her leg swept through the backs of his knees, toppling him. Her poles twirled in the air, twirling, twirling, until their flat ends jammed straight down into his exposed stomach as he landed helpless on his back. A whimper escaped his lips as his insides twisted.

"Enough," called Thorda.

Cyrus lay in the dirt, beaten, bruised, and struggling to breathe. His hands stung. Everything ached. His swords lay beside him, and in an attempt to hide his humiliation, he grabbed them both and jammed them into the sheaths buckled to his hips. His teacher waited, the silent seconds dragging interminably, before he spoke.

"Now do you understand how much left you have to grow?"

"I didn't know she'd elbow me," Cyrus snapped. He immediately regretted those words. They sounded so whiny and childlike. Such excuses would never work with Thorda. His master hopped off his stool and crossed the distance. Cyrus tried to stare at the older man's boots instead of his disapproving face. Even that was denied him. Thorda's fingers hooked underneath his chin, dragging his gaze upward so they might stare eye to eye.

"I am not training you to win sanctioned duels, Cyrus. You will not fight in an arena with fair odds, equal numbers, and rules of engagement. You will kill men and women who want you dead. It will be brutal, chaotic, and make a mockery of your sense of time. Some moments will last an eternity. Other decisions you will make so rapidly, you won't know you are making them. Every swing, every block, every parry, and every dodge must be *perfect*. Anything less is death. Thanet's resistance has clung to life by its fingertips after Lycaena's execution. I will not build you up just so you may hang from the Dead Flags, the slain prince whose corpse marks the end of the rebellion. You will be a phantom killer. A merciless shadow. A god among mortal men. Do we understand one another?"

A stubborn, childish part of Cyrus withered and died as he met the gaze of one who had watched thousands of men and women fall while fighting for their homelands. He would not be another. Thanet would be different. It would be free.

"Yes," he said. "I understand clearly."

Thorda released his chin. Cyrus shivered, a breath he didn't know he'd been holding leaking out his nostrils. There was something so intense about the older man, something raw and dangerous beneath the controlling veneer, that left Cyrus deeply unsettled. Thorda headed into his forge, and he spoke while his back was turned.

"I will not send you back to Vallessau, and put into motion our entire plan, until you are ready."

"So how will I know when am I ready?" Cyrus asked from his spot in the dirt. "When I can beat Stasia?"

His master laughed.

"I've been training her for twenty years. I doubt you will ever surpass her."

Cyrus's cheeks flushed. Stasia offered him a hand, and he took it. When she pulled him up, their bodies bumped into each other, and she used the opportunity to lean in close for a whisper.

"Don't listen to him. Keep at it. You'll beat me yet."

He wiped at his trousers, head bobbing up and down slightly.

"Hopefully," he said, and grinned to show his pride was not so terribly wounded. His attention turned to his master. "If not Stasia, then who is my final test?"

Instead of immediately answering, Thorda returned from his forge carrying two long metal poles that would be his own swords for the upcoming practice session.

"Your former tutor, Rayan Vayisa," his teacher said. He clacked the metal together and slowly tensed into a crouch. Despite Cyrus's many bruises, the day's training had only begun. "Your daily spars with Stasia and myself will build a familiarity too intimate for fair judgment. Instead I would have you test your strength against a foe blessed with divine strength akin to a paragon. Hold your own with a paladin of Lycaena, and I shall deem you ready to become the hero of Thanet."

CHAPTER 12

CYRUS

Has it really only been a year?" Rayan asked as he stepped out of the mud-covered carriage. Cyrus stood tall and puffed out his chest as the paladin got a good look at him. They'd not seen each other since his lone visit a few months into the start of Cyrus's training. He was stronger now, and brimming with confidence after his daily sparring with Thorda.

"A year and six months," Cyrus said. "But who is counting?"

"All of Thanet is," Rayan said, and he smiled. "You're taller, I see. If you take after your father, it won't be long before you tower over me as well."

The casual familiarity pricked a tiny welt of pain in Cyrus's chest. Rayan had been friends with his father, and had known the man far longer than Cyrus did. That realization hit him with a sense of loss painfully fresh despite the years that had passed since the island's invasion.

"Cyrus!" Mari Ahlai shouted. She exited the other side of the carriage, a ball of happiness bouncing toward him. Face blushing slightly, he bent down to accept her excited hug.

"It's good to see you, too," he said.

"Gods, Rayan is right, you *are* taller. Stop aging this instant. You're starting to make me feel old."

Cyrus laughed, and in response he squeezed her harder. Mari Ahlai visited the mansion every few months, and her arrival always bright-ened everyone's mood. Sadly her duties in Vallessau as Endarius's voice and presence kept her from staying long. Cyrus still struggled to believe the short, chubby woman with a mile-wide smile was the Lioness who had torn through dozens of soldiers during Lycaena's execution. He'd watched for signs of falsehood in her laugh, or a potential hard edge in her voice when describing life in Vallessau. He never saw or heard any such sign. Despite the daunting trials she faced alongside the rebellion, and the murderous role she played as the Lioness, her optimism and joy appeared genuine.

For some reason, that made Cyrus the tiniest bit frightened of her.

"Need me to carry anything?" he asked the pair after separating from Mari's embrace.

Rayan gestured toward the top of the carriage.

"If you'll spare an old man the labor, you may carry my armor to wherever it is we will duel."

Cyrus's heart leaped at the word. Their duel. The deciding factor on whether or not Cyrus was ready to return to Vallessau and set into motion everything Thorda planned. His master had spent the passing year building Thanet's insurgence from scratch, with Rayan and Mari doing their best to keep faith alive in their respective deities during the absence. All of it was mere preparation, laying down a framework for a resurgent rebellion. Kindling, for the spark that would be Cyrus and his Vagrant persona.

"I'd be happy to," he said. The many pieces of well-oiled and padded plate and chain were stored in two large sacks and tied to the carriage roof. It took two trips, but Cyrus hefted them both to the dueling circle on the far side of the mansion.

To call it a "circle" was a bit generous, for the area had no official limits or markings. It was merely a wide, vaguely round patch of earth beaten underfoot by countless hours of training. Thorda hammered away in the nearby forge, as he often did during his spare time. He set down his hammer upon Mari's arrival, a rare smile crossing his leathery face as he embraced his younger daughter. Cyrus meanwhile joined Sta-sia in the dueling circle, each of them holding their respective weapons, he his swords, she her twin axes. The two of them flowed through rigid formations meant to stretch the body and build muscle memory, not actually contest each other. The sound of steel on steel rang out amid Mari's bubbling laughter.

"You're distracted," Stasia said after one of her swings nearly cut his arm. His expected routine block had come much too late.

"Sorry," he said, and he shook his head as if he could shove his distractions out his ears.

"Nervous?"

A year and a half of training under Thorda was about to be put to the test, his worthiness as a symbol for rebellion judged. If he succeeded, his time as the Vagrant would begin, with actual bloodshed and battle against real opponents. If he failed...he wasn't even sure. More training? Different training? Or might they give up on him entirely?

"Yeah," he said, voicing none of that. "I probably am a tiny bit nervous."

Stasia put her axes aside and ventured into the forge. After a brief pause to greet Rayan and her sister, she returned carrying four long wooden poles.

"Here," she said, tossing him two. "If you're distracted, then let's up the tempo so you have to focus...but let's also do it with weapons that won't cut my fingers off when you do something clumsy and stupid."

He laughed, both insulted and grateful. It was a combination Stasia somehow accomplished with ease. They sparred for a bit, gradually upping the intensity. It still wasn't a true battle, nothing like the onslaught Stasia had unleashed the day he was given his swords, but it did work up a sweat. Cyrus's tensions eased, as Stasia had predicted. There was comfort in the rhythm, in play and counterplay when dueling with mock swords. If only all problems in life could be solved so easily.

They paused to catch their breath, and for Stasia to fetch them both water to drink. Cyrus stood awkwardly in the dueling circle, watching the forge from the corner of his eye. Mari and Rayan were chatting away within the shade of the forge, while Thorda listened and interjected occasionally while he tended the furnace. The kinship among them was as tangible as the clouds above. Was it the time spent together during the first two years of rebellion? Or was it because they had battled side by side, relying upon one another while risking life and limb?

Cyrus didn't know the answer, but it left him feeling like an outsider to the small group despite them having never shown him anything but kindness. He was relieved when Stasia returned, two enormous wooden cups in hand. It was only with her that he felt truly comfortable. Daily jogs and workouts certainly helped with that, as did their training. He spent similar time with Thorda, but no such bond had formed. There was always a feeling of distance between them, an invisible curtain that never once parted.

Cyrus accepted the enormous wooden cup and drank down half of the well water. The rest he dumped over his head, the cool shock sending a welcome shiver down his spine. As he recovered his breath, he again looked to the forge, where Mari was laughing with her father. A certain curiosity pushed at his mind. Though the two were sisters, and their faces almost mirror images of each other, Stasia was a good foot taller than Mari, and seemingly pure muscle. Cyrus voiced his question, but did it with his best attempt at tact.

"My training regiment, it's the same your father gave you, right?" he asked.

"Mostly. I've tweaked it plenty over the years as I've learned what does and doesn't work best for my body. Why?"

Cyrus watched Mari cheerfully poke her father's side as he tried, and failed, to return to his smithing work.

"Did Mari not have to train like that, too?"

Cyrus had always known Stasia to be cocky and charismatic, as much confidence as muscle, but her mood darkened and her lingering smile was far from genuine. There was hurt here, hurt he didn't understand and would likely never be privileged to. He immediately regretted his clumsy attempt for an answer to a question he had no right to ask.

"Father has always made it clear our blood differs," she said. "Mari inherited the gift of a god-whisperer. I didn't. So we both make do with what fate granted us."

Cyrus flushed and dropped his gaze.

"I'm sorry," he said. "I shouldn't have—"

"I think you're warmed up enough," she interrupted. "Let's see if Rayan is ready to put you to a real test."

She returned to the forge and said something to Thorda and Rayan. Cyrus wisely decided not to follow, and instead retrieved his two swords from where he'd set them aside.

"If a certain overeager young man insists," Rayan said with exaggerated volume, and he knelt over the two sacks containing his armor.

Cyrus studied his opponent preparing for their duel. His well-oiled platemail was still painted pristine white, but that was the only part unchanged from before the empire's invasion. When Rayan strapped on his cloak, Cyrus noted it was as gray as a springtime cloud, and split down the middle so that the two sides vaguely resembled wings. Once attached, he belted his sword to his waist and lifted his shield. Its original rainbow surface was painted over with a cascading mixture of white, black, and numerous shades of gray. Had he abandoned his faith in Lycaena? That didn't feel correct. Perhaps merely hiding the colors so he might travel more freely through the occupied lands?

Such curiosities could wait. Cyrus bounced on his heels, getting his blood back to pumping. His swords twirled in his fingers. He knew Rayan well, for he had been a constant presence at the castle throughout his childhood. The man had ever been a loyal retainer and protector of the throne, as had his entire family line for countless generations. But his actual combat prowess? Their training sessions when he was younger were but child's play compared to real battle. Cyrus had only faded memories of duels the paladin had fought during the springtime Fisherman's Festival. He may not have always won, but Rayan was a constant favorite, and Cyrus's father placed his friendly wagers on him when betting with other members of the court.

"I see you over there, eager and impatient," Rayan said as he stepped into the dueling circle. Instead of his own sword, he wielded a blunted blade borrowed from Thorda's workshop. "Give an old man time to stretch. Those tedious hours on the ride here did me no favors."

"Can you blame me?" Cyrus asked. He tried not to feel insulted that Rayan expected no blunted blades on Cyrus's behalf. Did he trust his platemail? Or did he have zero fear that Cyrus would score a hit? "I've suffered through all this training, and the only ones I may showcase the results to are Stasia, who will tell me to run some laps around the mansion, and Thorda, who has never given a compliment in his life."

"Truly your life is one of struggle and misery," Rayan said with a wink. They both looked to Thorda, who lifted an arm into the air to make their duel feel more official, then dropped it.

"Begin."

With the Ahlai family, each battle was a sort of dance. Stasia might be more aggressive, Thorda more methodical, but it was a rhythm of give and take. Weapons intertwined, defenses tested, openings sought and taken advantage of. Cyrus didn't appreciate how much he had grown accustomed to that style of combat until engaging an opponent who deviated from it so severely.

Fighting Rayan was like trying to crack a boulder with a spoon. Even worse, there was no interplay. No dance. When Cyrus would slash in with his right hand, the paladin smashed the attack away with his shield, then returned to his stance. His footing was solid, his movements perfectly calculated. Cyrus thrust with both swords, trying to bait out a counter, but Rayan would not have it. His shield barely had to shift to slide both weapons harmlessly aside. Upping the tempo accomplished nothing. The quicker he swung, and the less accurate his hits, the more savage Rayan's retaliations were when he smacked aside the swords or rammed into him with his shield.

There was, however, a rhythm to their exchanges. One-two, every single time. One, a block with his shield or sword. Two, a dismissive shove to send Cyrus staggering backward. That was it. One-two. One-two. It was maddening. Worse than the inability to score a hit, or engage Rayan in a true whirlwind exchange of steel, was the creeping disappointment growing on the paladin's face.

"Will you only stay defensive?" Cyrus asked, trying hard to disguise his frustration with a deep layer of sarcasm. "I want to fight, not wail at a training dummy."

Cyrus's sister swords hammered the gray surface of Rayan's shield. He shifted closer, hoping to angle around the shield's edge with a follow-up thrust, but the paladin retreated two steps in anticipation of the maneuver. His sword swept wide, parrying the thrust.

"If you believe yourself ready for it, child."

To be called "child" added flame to an already burning mood. Cyrus abandoned all pretense of self-defense as he weaved his weapons into a barrage of hits upon both sword and shield. He would force the paladin into a real duel. Once he was no longer on the defensive, there would be ways to use his sister swords to their fullest. His greater speed would win out over the heavily armored man in platemail.

At least, that's what Cyrus told himself.

Rayan disabused him of this notion within seconds. When Cyrus dual-slashed downward, Rayan blocked both with his shield and then stepped forward to add strength to his shove. Only this time, he did not retreat back into his defensive stance. He pushed forward, his shield a battering ram. Forward, forward, quick steps each time the gray metal battered Cyrus's body. He tried to force the man back with his swords, but they were too close, the weapons long and awkward at that distance against the brutal simplicity of the shield. At last he tried to roll off its surface, feet spinning beneath him for a wide slash above the shield for Rayan's head.

A single swift kick to Cyrus's leg ended the move before it began. He dropped to his knees. A flash of light shimmered from the corner of his eye as the tip of Rayan's sword hovered an inch from his throat.

"Dead," Rayan said simply.

"Another round," Cyrus pleaded as he hopped up to his feet. The first inklings of panic surfaced in his tightening chest. "I don't have much experience fighting against a shield."

Rayan glanced over to Thorda, who calmly watched from his seat. The old master shrugged.

"He's not wrong. An oversight I shall correct, I assure you."

The paladin returned his gaze, and he settled back into a stance, shield forward, sword back and at the ready.

"Very well," he said. "Bring your swords to bear, Cyrus. Let me see how well you think on your feet. Show me flexibility, and not excuses."

Thorda's arm rose and then dropped.

"Begin."

Cyrus paced before Rayan, slow steps that made the paladin shift on his heels to follow. He needed to study his foe. Respect his greater skill. Thorda constantly preached that there would be differences between opponents, and Cyrus's responsibility was to take advantage of his opponent's weaknesses and nullify their strengths. Speed, Cyrus decided. His advantage had to be speed and maneuverability.

One-two remained the exchange, and so Cyrus tested it. Prodded it. Several times he danced out of the way of a retaliatory swing after Rayan blocked an experimental thrust. Still Cyrus kept circling. He was the hunting panther, Rayan the prey. Keep control. Keep the battle on his terms. Perhaps he imagined it, but he swore he saw some of Rayan's disappointment melt into concentration.

Faster now, he'd dance in, swing for an arm or leg knowing full well the paladin would block, and then dance out. Rayan was a turtle. That was how Cyrus viewed him now, a turtle that needed to be forced out of his shell if he was to be beaten. If he could only get one counterthrust or swing made in error. One mistake, that was it, one mistake and he would prove Thorda's training worth it. Instead of being frustrated by the shield, he tried to take amusement in the constant hammering of his swords against its surface, as if he were a drummer and the shield his instrument.

"Are you ready?" he asked, needing the false bravado to keep his spirits up against this maddeningly difficult foe.

"For what?" Rayan asked.

"To lose."

He feinted an attack, baiting out a counterthrust. Finally, an opening! He twisted his body to avoid the thrust, then kicked off with his left leg to send the two into a collision. His shoulder hit the shield. His shorter off-hand blade kept the sword wide and out of position. Cyrus was younger, stronger. He pushed, hoping to topple the older man, or at the least knock him off balance so he could strike with the Endarius blade. His legs tensed, teeth clenched, muscles screaming.

Every bit of his momentum broke. Rayan was the boulder. Cyrus was the harmless wave. Panic hit him fully upon realizing this, and he tried to redouble his efforts while the paladin's sword was still locked out of position . . . except Rayan sensed the attempt and reacted accordingly.

He stepped aside, angling his shield so Cyrus, shoving forward without anything to resist him, slid across its shining surface. Cyrus tried to bring a blade up to block while he staggered unevenly on his feet. Rayan batted it aside with ease, punched the hilt of his blunted training sword into Cyrus's gut, and then battered his head with his shield hard enough that Cyrus's vision flooded with lights. His footing failed, the world flipped, and he landed on his ass.

The silence of the training circle was worse than any condemnation.

"Another round," Cyrus said. Despite his swimming vision, he clambered back to an unsteady stand.

"It will change nothing."

"Please, one more, I feel like I'm already improving."

"My mind is set," Rayan insisted. "I am sorry, Cyrus, but the outcome speaks for itself. You are not ready. You are not prepared. Should I have been an imperial paragon, there would be no second or third rounds. You would be dead, and our hopes extinguished."

Cyrus retreated to his room after dinner under claims of exhaustion, but truth be told, he was frustrated and ashamed. Being around others was the last thing he wanted. He lay wide awake on his bed, staring at the ceiling. Every moment of his duel with Rayan replayed itself in his mind. At times he remembered proper parries and blocks, the moments he'd read the fight and reacted correctly. More often, he focused on his failures. The missed parries. The improper footing, and the cost to his balance. The many instances he wrongly anticipated Rayan's attacks.

The final hit that knocked him on his ass haunted him in particular. Where had he gone wrong? What misstep led to getting clocked by a shield to his face? The humiliation had sent him all the way back through time, to when he was twelve and fumbling to properly hold a sword.

"Damn it, just grow up," he told himself. Sulking in his room would not make him a better fighter. Both Rayan and Thorda were dedicated to his instruction. Going downstairs and *asking* his betters; that was how he would improve. Cyrus shoved off the bed, exited his room, and started down the stairs. His pace slowed halfway down, for he heard the unmistakable sound of an argument coming from the nearby den.

"... cannot afford to wait," Rayan was insisting. "The death of Lycaena weighs heavily on every heart, no matter how many prayers I offer in clandestine sermons. Each and every month, more boats arrive from Gadir. The imperial tongue steadily replaces Thanese. Delay is no longer feasible."

"I only ask for patience, paladin," Thorda's deep voice argued back. "My chosen apprentice has already shown tremendous improvement. I need six months, perhaps a year at most."

"Then choose another, for we don't have six months to a year. Cyrus is not capable. Your 'test' proved as much. If he accompanied me on a raid, he would perish against his first skilled opponent."

"You exaggerate his defeat. Losing to you is no source of shame. Few alive could beat you in a straight match."

They were talking about him, and his failure. Cyrus pressed his back against the wall, ear turned toward the half-open door, and quietly listened. Despite knowing he was playing with fire, he was desperate to hear what his master truly thought of his abilities. Thorda was so rare with praise, and so vicious with criticism, it often felt like Cyrus wasn't improving at all.

"I didn't just beat him," said Rayan. "He's quick, I'll give him that, but that wasn't nearly as difficult as I was promised. For the role you want him to play, his skill is not at the needed heights. He can't fight at our level, not with me, nor Stasia, nor Mari. Given what you've told me of that heretic Arn you're bringing over from Gadir, I doubt he's equal to him, either."

Cyrus bit his tongue to remain silent. His face burned a deep red with shame at such a casual dismissal. And who was this heretic, Arn, that Rayan referred to? Did Thorda think Cyrus needed even more help?

However deeply wounded his pride, what came next was so much worse.

"He doesn't *need* to be equal," Thorda insisted. "He isn't you or Stasia or Mari. He's the Vagrant Prince of Thanet. With his name, and his bloodline, he merely needs to be good enough. Carry him if you must. Once the tale of his valiant return spreads throughout the island, he can retake his throne amid a surge of popular support."

"But how many years will it be until he is ready to retake that throne?" Rayan asked. "And can Thanet afford the wait? Every day, the Uplifted Church spreads its hateful faith. You may unleash a savior upon an island that no longer wishes to be saved."

"Arn will arrive within nine months, perhaps a year at most. That delay will benefit everyone involved, and allow Cyrus significant growth while we accumulate more soldiers in the island's outskirts. As I said, I don't need to achieve perfection, only acceptable—"

Cyrus pushed the door and stepped inside. He could listen no more. Rayan and Thorda stood opposing each other before a roaring hearth, and they fell silent at his entrance. Cyrus stared at the blue carpet, unable to meet their gaze. Instead he closed his eyes and focused his mind inward, needing that confidence, that focus, to force out the words he must say. His innards were a cacophony of humiliation, shame, and wounded pride.

"I wish to apologize for my failure today. I promise to double my efforts so that next time I will perform better. I will succeed in the test given to me." He paused for emphasis. "However long it takes."

He left without another word. When he returned to his bed, he again lay wide awake staring at the ceiling, but it was for far different reasons.

Cyrus was waiting for Stasia at the start of their looping track come the next morning.

"Someone's up bright and early," she said cheerfully.

"I want you to know, however far you run this morning, I'm running that far, too."

Stasia lifted an eyebrow as she worked her arms and legs in a stretch.

"Your best ever is six miles, Cyrus. I try to never do less than eight."

Cyrus hopped up and down to get his blood flowing and fight off the chill air.

"Don't care. Still doing it."

She stared at him, and he sensed an inner debate he was not privy to, but it ended as rapidly as it began.

"All right," she said. "Let's do this, then. No mercy. I won't wait for you when you fall behind."

Not "if," but "when." Cyrus used those words to fuel his stubbornness. He let Thorda's words ignite his rage at his own feebleness.

He merely needs to be good enough.

"The last thing I want is mercy," he said. "And if you slow down for me, I swear, I *will* be angry with you."

"Have no worries, little prince. I slow down for no one."

Cyrus managed seven miles before he collapsed to his knees and vomited bile and air upon the dirt. True to her word, Stasia did not wait, and did not slow. Still, Cyrus was encouraged. As awful as he felt, he clung to one simple, undeniable fact: Seven was better than six.

CHAPTER 13

MARI

Mari paced the midnight halls of her father's countryside mansion, debating a return to her bed for an unlikely sleep, when she passed by the cracked door of the library. Candlelight flickered from within, catching her eye.

"Trouble sleeping?" she asked as she stepped inside. Cyrus was slumped sideways on a padded chair in a manner most unlordlike. He wore loose trousers and a bed shirt, and his hair was a mess. A candle was lit on either side of him, and he held a book high to catch their faint light. She thought he'd be startled by her entrance, but he barely flinched.

"I read when I have trouble sleeping," he said.

"It seems to me that you're often reading."

"I often have trouble sleeping, too. Funny how that works." He smiled to show his barb was only due to tiredness. He swung his legs around to sit properly in the chair. "Why are *you* awake right now? Had a few nightmares of your own?"

"Not quite." She crossed the library to the tiny fireplace. Cyrus had let the fire within die down to faint embers, and she began the rekindling process. It was good to have a task to occupy her hands. "The Lioness has become a part of me, a blessing I would never disparage, but there are the occasional inconveniences. One such inconvenience is that the Lion prefers to hunt at night."

"The forests around us are full of game. Go grab yourself a rabbit."

For a brief instant, Mari imagined one between her teeth, and the sensation was so strong, it was like a forgotten memory. Fur parting between sharp teeth. Blood dripping across her tongue.

"Perhaps," she said. "But you misunderstand the desired prey. While it benefits your training to be so far out, it does leave precious few imperial soldiers to hunt."

Embers became flames became a roaring fire. Mari took a seat opposite Cyrus. The young man had set aside his book, and he slumped in the chair. He looked so tired, the poor thing. Even in the dim light she could spot a dozen new bruises blooming on his body, and his eyes were horribly bloodshot. It had been six months since Rayan's test of his competence. That failure had clearly changed him. During this recent visit she'd watched him fling himself at his training like a man possessed. There was no denying the results, either. He was practically all muscle, and his sparring matches with Stasia were beautiful and savage in equal measure.

"Do you care to talk, or would you prefer I leave you to your reading?" she asked him. "There's always time for another lesson."

"I would be a poor student at this dismal an hour."

Mari smiled at him. She had begun visiting the mansion every few weeks, a chance to both visit her father and spend time with Cyrus. Thorda, always uncomfortable when it came to spiritual matters, had requested she teach some rudimentary concepts and lessons from Gadir. The young man's understanding, limited to Lycaena and Endarius, had left him woefully ignorant. And so she taught him of the various pantheons, some living, some lost to the empire's expansion. Of gods who could change shapes, who looked like humans, who resembled wild animals so completely, they rarely communicated beyond chirps and growls. Cyrus, bright and curious, always listened and always learned.

"So I should leave you to your book then?" she asked.

"My hope in reading is that I'll fall asleep during it, so please stay and talk away. You're as comforting as a book, honestly."

"I see someone's been developing a silver tongue."

"Don't be mean," he said, and blushed. "It's way too late for that."

The playful exchange did not hide how exhausted Cyrus looked.

"When was the last time you had a good night's sleep?" she pressed. Cyrus tapped his lips.

"Let me think. The Everlorn Empire invaded, what, almost four years ago? So four years. Now I see that look on your face. Don't worry. I'd say I'm quite due for a good night's sleep, wouldn't you?"

He was joking to avoid acknowledging how deeply seeded his trauma was. Four years, thought Mari. Four long years of nightmares and doubts and fears for his future. She knew it all too well.

"I was eight when we had to flee my home of Miquo," she said. "I barely remember it, but I do remember waking up crying. It was a nightly ritual between me and Stasia. I'd cry, she'd leave her bed to come to mine, and then I'd listen to her sing until I fell back asleep."

"Stasia? Singing?" Cyrus shook his head. "That hardly sounds like the brutal taskmaster I know."

"I thought you said it was way too late to be mean, little prince?"

The rebuke did not have the intended effect. His grin stretched ear to ear.

"Stasia called me that when we were first training," he said. "Sometimes you two seem so different, and then sometimes, so very similar."

Mari thought of those simple nursery rhymes her older sister had sung, arms wrapped about her quivering body, warm breath blowing against her neck as the songs calmly flowed. Those early years following Miquo's collapse were so dark, so clouded with fear and confusion her young mind could not understand, but there had been good among them. There had been peace, however fleeting. Could such a moment ever be recaptured? Stasia was now the fabled Ax of Lahareed, and Mari a god-whisperer. They had built legacies of death and bloodshed over these past two decades.

To go back to singing nursery rhymes. To be that innocent again. An impossible dream.

"Forgive me," Cyrus said softly. "It seems I have a gift for reopening old wounds through ignorance."

"It's not your fault," she said. "They're good memories, mostly. Consider it the dangers of talking truthfully at so late an hour. People say it is in the daylight that things are laid bare, but I've found truths are best revealed when the moon is high."

Cyrus was not convinced. He sat up in his chair and then leaned closer. His eyes focused on the carpet. Mari recognized this look, this posture. She embodied gods and goddesses, and she had been at the receiving end of many quiet, heartfelt confessions.

"It's always the same dream," Cyrus said. "I'm back on the balcony, watching our boats burn. Rayan isn't with me, either. I'm alone. I don't see the fight. I don't see Endarius die. It's just Magus, my parents, and me. He's calling for me, demanding I show myself, otherwise my parents will suffer. I try to shout out, but I can't move. I can't speak. I see my parents kneel. I see the sword lift."

His eyes filled with tears, only Mari wasn't sure if he realized it. He looked so distant.

"'I'm here,' I shout. 'I'm here.' But the sword has already fallen."

No more words came, for the final image could not be spoken aloud. He was lost in the mixture of dream and memory, one confused and malformed, the other stark and vivid. Mari recognized it well. She had helped others through such trauma. She had lived it herself.

"You've been given no time to heal," she said. "Held prisoner, without a proper funeral or chance to grieve over what you lost. Once free, you were dragged here, to be shaped and molded. The pain you feel, it is normal, Cyrus. It is cruel, and sharp, but it will one day fade. Until then, you must be strong."

"Strong," he bitterly echoed. He snapped back to the present, and his wounds bled into his voice. His words were sharp, his eyes weeping. "Strong? Like you? Like Stasia? I try. I always try. I want nothing more than to be what your father asks. Then I fall asleep, and I'm a helpless boy watching his parents die. Who in any god's name am I to be Thanet's savior?"

Mari stood from her chair. At least in this, she felt confident. She was a god-whisperer. Though much of her gifts now involved killing, that had not been her first purpose. Her kind were meant to remember, and to heal. She knelt before Cyrus, and she offered her hands to him.

"Do you trust me?" she asked.

He met her gaze, and Mari's heart broke. There was such a kind boy locked inside this shell her father had crafted, someone intelligent and forgiving, who wanted to read and learn and tell jokes with friends. His soul was as bruised as his body, and she feared the day it perfectly molded with the killer he needed to become. Would that kind boy be lost forever, lost like the Stasia who sang nursery rhymes, or the frightened little Mari who needed them so desperately to sleep?

"I'm scared to trust anyone," he said. "But I will try, Mari. For you, I will try."

"Then close your eyes."

Mari took Cyrus's hands into hers. She clutched them tightly, her own eyes closed, and silently spoke to the divine presence that had coexisted within her for the past two years.

Your prince needs you.

The change struck immediately. The essence of the slain deity gathered inside her, dwelling within the offered vessel that was her body. A need to hunt and kill struck her, brief but savage. The rage of the Lion. The fury of one whose chosen people lay with their necks crushed beneath the bootheel of an empire.

"The stench of doubt hovers over you," Mari spoke. Her voice was deeper, and not her own. The words came of their own accord, and she need only relinquish control to allow them passage. She opened her eyes, the dark library now brightly lit to her changing pupils. She smelled grass, and felt a wind that should not have touched her through the building's walls.

"If you know the path set before me, then you know why I doubt," Cyrus said, stammering in his defense. "How could I not?"

"You are of Lythan blood. You are my anointed, my caretakers, my chosen heirs."

"And look how we have fallen."

"That failure weighs heavily upon me. I weep for your father. I weep for your mother. And I weep for you."

"Me?" Cyrus asked. "Why me? I lived."

The roof above them vanished. The smell of grass grew stronger. Mari felt dirt beneath her knees despite the carpet of the library.

She dimly recognized these hunting fields. They were the highlands believed to be the eternal paradise awaiting Endarius's faithful. A sea of grass. A sky full of stars.

"I weep, for I know what you must become. And become it you will. You are strong. You are mighty."

"So were my parents."

Endarius's presence burned hotter within Mari's breast. To possess so much of it in her human form, without transforming fully into a resemblance of the god, caused her physical pain. Compassion kept her fully human. She wanted Cyrus's hands in hers. She wanted to be there for him, and to share in the moment, so he did not feel alone in the presence of a god.

"Indeed they were," said the Lion. "And a cruel world took them all the same. Will you be stronger, Cyrus Lythan? Will you carry their legacy?"

Cyrus's entire body was shaking. His hair blew in the wind. Grass had risen all the way to his chest, threatening to swallow him completely. Still he kept his eyes closed.

"And if I cannot?"

Mari feared the Lion would show contempt, for he was a mighty beast, not known for mercy. Instead she felt sympathy, and kindness. A Lion, but also a father. A hunter, but also a protector. The fireplace snuffed out. The walls of the library faded completely. The horizon stretched eternal.

"Then I will await you in my green fields, beloved child. I see your wounded heart, and the courage it yet possesses. Walk your path. Walk it, for I cannot."

The wind blew harder. Mari's chest tightened, and exhaustion grew throughout her limbs. The grass paled and turned ashen. Stars faded, one by one, as the divine receded back into the mundane.

"Wait," Cyrus said, and at last he opened his eyes in a panic. "My parents, are they with you? Are they?"

The library was dark and quiet. No wind, no grass, just flickering candles in place of a field of stars.

"Too late," he whispered. "Of course too late. I am always too late."

What began as a few tears became a river. What succor he might have felt melted into despair. He collapsed into himself, wordless, broken. Mari leaned closer, and she lifted his hands so that she might kiss his fingers. He didn't know. He didn't understand. Mari was the Lioness. Until she relinquished that power, or the people's faith in Endarius faded away completely, she would *always* be the Lioness.

"Yes, dear child," she said, two voices spoken with one mouth. "They are with me. And they love you."

Cyrus shook. His lips trembled. He could barely force out the words through the silent sobs.

"Can you tell them? Tell them I miss them? That I love them?"

Mari's own tears were falling, but she would not let them halt her tongue.

"They know, child. They know."

Cyrus crumpled into the chair and wept. The presence of Endarius eased away until Mari felt fully herself. She released the young man's hands, then leaned to either side to blow out the candles. When finished, Mari climbed into the chair without a care for the tight fit. She wrapped her arms around him, and despite all his muscle, he seemed so small. He sank into her, and it felt like surrender. His hair scattered across her forehead as her lips hovered at the back of his neck. Her eyes closed. She traveled a world away, to a different time, in a cherished place of memory.

"*I once knew a bird, a blue little bird,*" she began to sing. "*And every morning, I would watch it fly, fly, fly . . .*"

CHAPTER 14

CYRUS

A year after their first major clash, Cyrus and Rayan stood in the same circular patch of dirt, wielded the same set of arms, and fought under the same set of rules, but they were not the same fighters. Cyrus would make that clear the moment their swords connected.

"Begin," Thorda shouted.

Fighting Rayan the first time had felt like trying to chip away at a boulder. This time, he took a page from Stasia's book. How did one break a boulder? By smashing it to pieces. He lunged at Rayan with every bit of wild fury Stasia had shown that first day he received his finely crafted swords. His eyes peeled wide, instincts taking in every reaction by the paladin. Just because he was vicious didn't mean he would fight carelessly. He watched for openings, places where the other man's shield would struggle to block. One after another, he thrust and stabbed, his feet a shifting blur beneath him so he could constantly change the angles of his thrusts without robbing them of power.

Rayan was clearly caught off guard by the aggression. He retreated several steps, his shield swaying side to side to block the blows. Cyrus gave him no chance to properly set his stance. Surprise was everything now. With every lunge he swayed a little bit to his left, which meant the paladin had to keep shifting his feet to reset the angle of his shield. Hit after hit battered its dark gray surface. Rayan refused to retaliate, but it was coming. Cyrus was expecting it. Needing it, for every bit of this exhausting assault was a trap.

At last Rayan attempted to punish Cyrus's aggression. He blocked a hit, stepped close, and thrust his longsword. Cyrus twisted his body so it missed wide, then slashed with the Endarius blade, aiming for the edge of the shield. His sword slid across it, then caught in the sharp hook midway down the blade, granting him increased leverage. A shove, and the entire shield flung out of the way, leaving Rayan completely exposed. Cyrus dashed to close the distance, his off-hand elbow catching Rayan's arm so his sword could not come back for a block. Up came the other blade, its edge resting a hair's width away from the black skin of the paladin's exposed neck. There they froze, the duel ended lest either come to actual harm.

Cyrus refused to pull the sword away. He gasped in breaths as sweat dripped down his face. He met the older man's gaze. What thoughts swirled behind those amber eyes? Meanwhile Stasia and Mari cheered and clapped from their seats beside their father.

"So am I capable?" Cyrus asked, unable to keep the bite out of his words. That overheard conversation between Thorda and Rayan had driven him the past twelve months, pushing him to reach new heights of skill and speed for this inevitable rematch.

"Most capable," Rayan said. His tone was even, giving away nothing. He retreated so there would be adequate distance between them and then lifted his sword. His head bowed, and he closed his eyes. "Let us see how capable."

The paladin whispered a prayer to his goddess. Light shimmered across his blade like a divine fog latched upon the steel. He swung the sword twice, each swing leaving an afterimage that burned into Cyrus's eyes, and then Rayan settled into a stance with his shield at the ready.

"I do not suggest you try a similar tactic," he warned.

"No holding back, Cyrus," Stasia called out. "I've trained you as much as my father has. Show him how well an Ahlai can fight."

"That's right," Mari added. "This is family pride. Beat him senseless."

Despite the seriousness, despite the stakes, Cyrus laughed, and Rayan shared with him a playful smile. Their amusement faded back to determination as Thorda's hand raised.

"Begin."

Cyrus took the offensive despite the paladin's warning. Given his weapons, the fighting style he had been taught, and the temperaments of his teachers, it was too deeply ingrained in him to do anything otherwise. He would set the pace. Countless hours dueling Stasia had shown him how dangerous it was to let an opponent dictate the terms of a fight. His swords beat against the shield, three quick hits, but this time Rayan's feet were set. He weathered the storm, then slashed with his sword toward Cyrus's waist. His off-hand shot low to block.

The moment those blades touched, Cyrus realized his error. Holy light flared across the steel. He had a better chance of stopping a charging bear with a twig. The swing continued, pushing Cyrus's sword along with it, trapping the flat edge against his side. The impact jolted pain throughout his waist, and no doubt it would leave a mighty bruise. His right leg went limp, allowing his body to pitch sideways to remove a bit of sting from the hit. Momentum continued him into a tumble, and he came out of it swinging.

No blocking, he thought. *Got it.*

Rayan blocked the first swing, then sidestepped to parry the second. He seemed surprised, but pleased, that Cyrus still fought. Cyrus gritted his teeth and tried the same trick as before, using the curve of his sword to slide the sword in and then jam aside the shield. He would not cower before Rayan's divinely gifted strength. His ultimate enemies were paragons of the empire, inhuman soldiers with power unmatched. If he could battle them, then he could battle a paladin of Lycaena. Thorda had given him the training. Time to use it.

The trick failed the second time, with Rayan ramming his shield against the sword so strength countered strength. His glowing sword thrust, and this time Cyrus committed to dodging. The paladin took the offensive, chasing with steady swing after swing. Cyrus used both weapons each time in his parries, needing the combined strength to force the attacks aside. Never blocking. Never testing their strength directly against each other if he could help it. He needed to be faster than Rayan, more nimble, and quicker to react.

Cyrus shoved aside a downward chop, then stepped closer so he could slash with his off-hand. Up came the shield, already anticipating the attack. Steel hit steel, feet shifted, and in came another thrust. This became the new dance. Parry, dodge, then counter. They read it in each other, a mutual understanding that Cyrus had only started to grasp over the recent few months. No longer did he focus solely on re-creating the moves taught to him. Reading his opponent, and understanding decisions they would make, was what separated the common brawlers from true masters. Every fundamental had to be perfect, for a single missed parry meant a lost limb, or worse.

Such constant defensiveness eventually paid its price. Cyrus's foot scraped along the dirt, just enough to twist his knee at an awkward angle. Rayan's sword crashed down for his head. Cyrus crossed his swords into an X and blocked despite knowing how terrible an idea it was. The impact, and the horrid pain in his elbows and arms, confirmed the folly. His swords bowed inward, then fell. The glowing blade sank down, halting an inch away from Cyrus's nose. He stared at the sword, knowing if this had been a real battle, and Rayan an imperial paragon, then his skull would have been cleaved in half. All those years of training would mean nothing.

His frustration and anger bubbled out in a single, calmly spoken word.

"Shit."

Rayan laughed as he pulled back. Once both sword and shield were stowed away, he offered Cyrus a hand to help him back to his feet. The paladin was all smiles and excitement, the exact opposite of how he'd been at the close of their first duel.

"A far cry from the boy I first taught to swing a sword," Rayan said to all gathered. "And a good deal better than our last duel, too. In my opinion, he passes my test. What say you, Thorda?"

Cyrus looked to his master sitting upon his stool. The older man tapped his fingers together, and Cyrus swore he was dragging out the silence on purpose.

"I say we pack our belongings," he said. "Tomorrow morning we leave for Vallessau."

CHAPTER 15

ARN

It had been a long two months for Arn Bastell, sharing cramped quarters on the caravel, and he still had another month to go until he reached the shores of Thanet and docked in its capital of Vallessau. One more long, awful month. If only he could avoid murdering someone until then.

"Praise and glory to the holiest of holies," prayed Jarvis, one of the acolytes. The men and women in matching white robes gathered in a circle on the center of the deck, holding hands and tilting their heads so the sunlight washed over their faces. Their eyes remained closed as they prayed. "Watch over us, Lucavi, grace of the heavens, incarnate of the divine, god above all gods."

"Our god of gods," echoed the others in the circle. Arn leaned over the railing, his back to the circle, and rolled his eyes. No matter how dramatic the need Thorda had insisted in his letters, Arn found himself questioning the time and torment it had taken to cross the Crystal Sea.

"Do the faithful bother you, Meffrit?" a man asked as he joined him at the railing. "I caught that eye roll."

Arn was his real name, but Meffrit was the lie he'd used to secure passage to Thanet, and thankfully he'd grown accustomed to it quickly during the trip.

"They're decent enough folk," he said. "I've never been much for prayer."

"Bold to tell a paragon as much."

Arn glanced over at the blond man. Like all paragons, he was a mountain of muscle, and he towered over everyone on the ship. Everyone but Arn.

"I've known a few paragons in my life, and they never seemed the type to care about little things like that. Crushing armies, breaking gods, that was their lot. Who cares if a stupid builder like me says his daily devotions, you know?"

The acolytes began singing a hymn, some nonsense about how the God-Incarnate loved and protected all of his faithful children.

"I daresay you belittle us. Would we fight so ardently to defeat heretical gods if we didn't care for the salvation of the common folk they lead astray?"

A dozen bloody memories came unbidden to Arn. His hand lowered to his side, and he patted the charm hidden in his front pocket. Its comforting presence chased away the memories. It countered the all-too-familiar song of the acolytes.

"I don't pretend to know why a man fights," he said. "I just know their prayers don't help my seasickness."

The paragon laughed and slapped Arn across the back. His jaw was square, his skin smooth and pale, and his flowing hair bound in two intervals given its reach down to his waist. His name was Lendsy, and Arn hated his guts.

"We're almost to Thanet, so hold on a bit longer. I fear your poor stomach may not find refuge once ashore. I've heard rumors Thanese food is fouler than shit, and better to eat raw fish than risk what their spices will do to your innards."

"No worries there," Arn said. "My guts may be weak when it comes to the sea, but they're strong as iron when holding in food and liquor. This is my first time at sea. I've had a whole lot more practice at the latter."

Another laugh. Another slap. The paragon considered "Meffrit" a friend, or at least a pleasant acquaintance. It was Arn's own fault, really. Ever since he boarded the boat under the false name of Meffrit Mason, he had worked to endear himself to the boat's crew. Given his impressive girth, remaining inconspicuous wasn't an option, so he found it better to work odd jobs and help with lifting supplies and pulling ropes so that if the sailors would not forget him, they would consider him a friend. That also meant making nice with the lone paragon and his group of acolytes come to spread the true word of the Uplifted Church to the Thanese people.

"A shame you have such an incurious mind," Lendsy said. "I bet you could be a fine soldier for the empire. Man like you, with arms like that? You might have made a name for yourself."

"Sorry," Arn said, and he exited for the lower decks. "That life ain't for me. I break bricks better than I break skulls."

Arn slipped the charm into the box he kept in his cramped bunkroom. It was foolish to bring it out, especially so close to Thanet, but he'd been feeling nervous without it over the past few weeks. Yet it wasn't safe in his pocket. One simple error, and he might give up the whole game.

"Meffrit, are you in here?"

Arn slammed the chest shut and kicked it underneath his bed.

"Yeah?" he asked, spinning about to sit on the edge of his bunk. Lendsy entered the cabin.

"The crew is hauling in nets, and they want your help."

"Sure thing," he said, and grinned as if he weren't nervous in the slightest. Together they returned to the deck. Given their lengthy voyage, the caravel dragged fishing nets daily for fresh catch to feed the passengers and crew. Despite the aid of the pullies, lifting the nets was a laborious process under normal circumstances. But with Arn's help? Or with the help of an imperial paragon?

"Slow it down, you two, or you'll fling the net over the damn mast and off the other side!" one of the sailors called out, and laughed.

"Don't blame me, Lendsy's doing all the work," Arn lied.

Several men leaned over the edge, grasping at the soggy net squirming with fish to guide it in. Arn pretended he was straining more than he was, and let out an exaggerated sigh when one of the sailors opened the bottom of the net to dump the contents across the main deck.

"Fine work," Lendsy said, and he clapped Arn across the shoulder.

"No need for compliments. I'll be eating some of that fish myself."

They stood side by side, watching the flurry of activity as fish were grabbed and gutted, parts dumped into barrels, waste to the sea. To an outsider, it would be chaos, but to the sailors, an organized process, each and every man knowing their place.

"Your comment about the devotions, and paragons," Lendsy said, quietly enough so no one else would overhear. "It means more to me than you think."

Arn attempted to head off the conversation with a dismissive wave.

"Just hot and empty words. Don't put any thought into them. I rarely do."

"But you echo a sentiment I hear all too often." He leaned in, closing the gap between them. "We paragons are meant to inspire the populace! Yes, we are the fist of the God-Incarnate, and this often means we fight at the vanguard of his conquering forces. This is a result of our gifts, but it isn't the *purpose* of them."

Arn raised an eyebrow. A few of the passengers had come to watch the haul, and though they pretended otherwise, they had begun eavesdropping on the conversation.

"Paragons aren't made to fight?" he asked, curious how Lendsy would argue against such an obvious truth.

"We are made to be perfect, Meffrit! With the prayers granted us, and the sacrifices made to empower us, we show that the limits of mortality may be transcended. Does our title not say it all? We are the ultimate form humanity may achieve. We are the pinnacle. The hope. The goal."

Whatever honesty Lendsy was trying to convey was ruined by the increasingly grandstanding nature of his pronouncement. He was aware he had listening ears.

"So you're the pinnacle," Arn dared argue. "That don't mean you'll help those beneath you, no different than a crown on a man's head means he'll help those who prop up his throne."

The paragon put his hands on Arn's shoulders, and he lowered his voice. No, perhaps he read the situation wrong. This part, this truly was heartfelt from the paragon. That only made it that much more horrible.

"If we are to be what humanity strives to attain, then we must cherish those who would walk in our footsteps. We must lead, heads high and hearts full, so others follow. So I care for those in my shadow. I love them, and protect them. What we bring to this world is good, and necessary. I would have you believe that of me, and of us, rather than see us merely as killers."

"You truly believe that?" Arn asked softly. "That paragons bring nothing but good to this world?"

"With all my soul."

Memories of a burning city came unbidden to Arn. He smiled to banish them.

"I'll keep it in mind," he promised.

It wasn't the first time Arn regretted agreeing to come save Thorda's ass, nor would it be the last. He wiped vomit from his lips as he leaned over the railing, cursing any and every god who might listen.

"Whoever you are, the coin isn't enough, and the job ain't good enough, either," he muttered. He'd never met Thorda, only heard of him in rumors as the mysterious plotter and benefactor of some of the severest uprisings the empire ever had to subdue. It had taken two years of fighting, and an offer to sail to Thanet to join a new resistance, before Arn even learned Thorda's true name.

"Has the seasickness come again?" asked Jarvis. The acolyte joined him at the railing, and he rested his arms upon the aged wood. His white robe fluttered in the salty breeze.

"That implies it ever leaves."

"True. Might I pray for your illness? The God-Incarnate urges all to come to him for succor, for struggles both great and small."

Of the world's many, many cruelties, having the bald acolyte pray for him was down near the very bottom Arn wished to endure, right among crotch blisters and being eaten alive by rats.

"Save your prayers for those who would appreciate them," he said. "It's a queasy stomach. I'll endure."

"You need not cling to pride. We are all inferior and weak in our own ways. I promise you, one prayer, and you will feel instantly better."

There was no doubt in Arn's mind this was true. There was also not a chance in the world he would allow it.

"Your kind ain't much for taking no for an answer, are you?" he said, perhaps the greatest understatement in the history of Gadir.

Jarvis smiled. It was a familiar expression to Arn, for he had seen it so often during his training. Priests and priestesses of the God-Incarnate seemed the only people capable of manifesting it so perfectly. The smile was faint, without joy or laughter, and it did not reach the eyes. It was pleasant, meant to seem kind, but there was too much pity in it for there to be comfort. Little more than a mask.

"Dwell in your sickness if you must," Jarvis said. He joined Arn in looking out over the rolling blue sea. The man was likely oblivious to the bitterness in his words. No doubt he thought it a mere statement of fact. "The people of this world often prefer sickness rather than the comfort of our god. It takes a strong man to bend the knee, and humility rare to all but the most faithful."

Try not to puff yourself up too much, Arn thought. Too much more and he'd float off to the clouds.

"I'm hardly humble, but at least I'm strong. Wouldn't be coming to Thanet if I wasn't."

"What does bring you to the distant island?" Jarvis asked. "Especially if sailing delivers you such misery?"

"I'm good with hammers and nails," Arn said, the cover story concocted for his voyage to go along with his false name. "Your priests want someone with proper training to build them a church, and I was the only one foolish enough to say yes."

"It is a good deed you will perform. You should take pride in it, and in all the tribulations you suffer to accomplish it."

"Taking pride in my work I can understand," he said, unable to hold back a biting retort. "But you want me to take pride in puking my guts out into the sea?"

"It is the way of our faith," Jarvis needlessly explained. How could the young man have any clue how much schooling Arn had endured in such matters in his early days? Every scripture, every verse, every song, had long been memorized during his own training. If only he could purge them from his mind like he had that morning's breakfast from his stomach.

"Everything involves your faith," Arn argued. "Waking, eating, shitting, all somehow done in glory to the God-Incarnate way off in Eldrid."

"You mock, but you're not entirely wrong. It is about sacrifice, Meffrit. The greatest any one of us can do is give of ourselves to another. We teach children this through sharing. We teach the commonfolk by their time spent in churches and their offerings given as alms and charity. But the sacrifice goes on and on. Soldiers, spilling their blood on the battlefield. Magistrates and paragons, dedicating years in service to the divine. Through sacrifice, this sinful, chaotic world is forced into a better way. Sacrifice is the splint that will allow the broken bone to mend. If everyone in Gadir engaged in such selflessness and humility, the strife of our world would end in a day."

"Yeah?" Arn asked. "And what great sacrifice have you done? Given up a few meals to pray instead? Read some books in a warm, comfy library while others were busy breaking their backs in fields or sweating away in shops?"

Jarvis pulled back his shoulders and tilted his chin. For all his talk of humility, there was no hiding the pride dripping from his every word.

"Everything, Meffrit. I will one day give everything, all so another might lift their sword high as a loyal paragon of the empire."

The realization hit Arn's gut harder than the waves. He pretended to have another bout of sickness. He didn't dare risk giving away his true shock. Someone on the island was preparing to break all the rules of the Uplifted Church. The acolytes...He should have realized it sooner, given the fervor of their devotion, or how there were ten of them in total. Ten, the exact number for the sacrifice required to create a paragon. They weren't just acolytes. They were the ultimate faithful, the men and women who would cut their own throats with a smile on their faces and a song on their lips.

They were Seeds, come to shed their blood on Thanese soil.

Someone's playing games in the shadows, he wondered as he stared into the distance. *But who?*

Too many questions, to which he could only offer guesses. He would have to wait until arriving at Vallessau for answers.

"Be well," Jarvis said, and he patted a pitying hand on Arn's shoulder. "I shall pray for your health."

"Joy," he muttered.

One month, he thought. *One bloody more month . . .*

CHAPTER 16

CYRUS

The fourteen-hour carriage ride to Vallessau felt interminably longer on the return trip. By the time the city was visible, and only a single mile remained between it and their carriage, the sun had started its lazy descent toward the horizon. Cyrus and Mari sat on one of the two bench seats, with Thorda facing them on the opposite. Stasia rode outside with the driver, as always. Upon seeing the city in the distance, Thorda reached into one of his pockets while snapping his fingers to gain Cyrus's attention. He pulled out an object wrapped in gray cloth and held it a moment, that quiet reflection enough to instill Cyrus with a sense of importance and gravitas.

"It is yours now," Thorda said. "May you embody everything it once represented."

Cyrus accepted it and slowly unwrapped the cloth. Within was the skull mask his master had shown him years ago. He brushed the skull with his fingertips. Though it looked like bone, it was actually carved of wood and painted by an absolute master of the craft. How else did the skull manage that faint illusion of a smile? How else did it possess so many grinning teeth?

"Thank you," Cyrus said. "I will do my best."

"Of course you will!" Mari chirped. "That's all you've done ever since I met you, Cyrus, give us your best. And my father might not convey it well, but I'm sure he's proud of what you've accomplished. Isn't that true?" Thorda's gaze locked on the countryside beyond the window. "I said isn't that true?"

"Perhaps," he muttered through his hand. "We would not be returning to Vallessau otherwise."

Mari winked at Cyrus, and he laughed to show his appreciation. Compliments from Thorda were rare, but by the gods, she'd dragged one out of him. That amusement slowly faded as their carriage crossed the final mile to Vallessau. The gated entrance approached, and he fought against his growing tension. Imperial soldiers inspected all arrivals, slowing entrance to a crawl. His chest tightened, and he glanced between Thorda and Mari to see if they shared any of his worry. They did not.

"Calm yourself," Thorda said. Though his eyes never left the window, it seemed he could sense Cyrus's unease. "I am well known to the Everlorn Empire. As for yourself, we were fortunate to rescue you when we did. I doubt we even needed to grow out your hair. Nearly three years vanished during your most formative years will do much to disguise your appearance, and that is if they even think to compare. The whole island believes you dead."

Easy words to hear, harder to believe. Cyrus remembered his trips to the market with his father. All eyes would be upon them both, even if the crowds pretended not to notice the royal family while they bartered and bargained. He was taller now, older, his skin tanned from countless hours outside with Stasia and his hair grown long to help hide his face. Could those years truly make so much of a difference? He slipped his mask underneath his shirt and vowed to be ready in case they didn't.

When the carriage rolled to a halt, Thorda offered a scrap of paper he pulled out from a pocket of his robe. The guard who approached took it, read for a few seconds, and then handed it back with a bow of his head.

"Enjoy your time in Vallessau," the soldier said in the imperial tongue. That was it. No other inspections. The armored man didn't even peer through the window to check the other passengers. The carriage rolled through the gate, passing underneath an archway built of faded white stone along the base, the upper half cut from painted pine. Where once hung a plaque containing the Lion and the Butterfly in dance now hung a gray flag bearing the two red hands clenched in prayer that symbolized the Everlorn Empire.

Cyrus watched the city roll past him outside his window. He tried to believe he was coming home, a liberator to his people. If he were honest with himself, he felt neither. No, what he felt was strangely alien to a city in which he had spent the first sixteen years of his life. Even the language they spoke suddenly seemed awkward. Thanese, of course. They were speaking Thanese, whereas he had spent the last two and a half years reading and conversing with Thorda in the imperial tongue. Was that all it took to feel estranged from his former life? A mere few years?

"Don't be nervous," Mari said. "We're all here with you. We'll make sure things go off without a hitch, I promise!"

Carry him if you must.

"Thanks," he said, wishing he shared her optimism.

The carriage arrived at the home he had woken up within all those years ago, when Rayan had smuggled him out of chaos following Lycaena's execution. It was two stories, and even from the outside one could tell it would be cozy and well furnished. The donkeys pulling the carriage slowed to a halt, and both Stasia and the driver hopped off the outside seat to begin unloading luggage. Cyrus exited, gathered his own meager belongings packed into a single sack cloth, and carried them inside. Stasia cheerfully told him which room would be his, and so he climbed the stairs, passed the first door, and entered at the second.

Bare walls. A white bed. An empty dresser. He set his belongings down (mostly books he'd brought from the library with Thorda's permission) and stood awkwardly in the doorway.

"I'm home," he said, and he wished he didn't sound so bitter. Didn't sound so broken.

Downstairs was a flurry of joyful activity, none of which Cyrus felt appropriate to join in. Stasia was tearing through the pantries, checking out the fruits and vegetables purchased by their servants in advance of their arrival. Mari was busy opening up windows to let in fresh air while also lighting candles to ward off the coming dark. Thorda, as was his want, knelt before the hearth, steadily building up the fire to his liking.

"I'll be going out for a bit," Cyrus told them.

"An excellent idea," Thorda said. He nudged the core of the flames with a metal poker. "Get a feel for the city. Study its many pathways, both the obvious and the secret. That familiarity may one day save your life."

Hardly what he had in mind, but he nodded as if that were his reason. In truth, Cyrus wanted out. He wanted to wander, and forget himself for however long that might be. His nerves were fraying every second he remained close to Thorda. His teacher was a constant reminder of the mission they would soon undertake, an assassination attempt on one of the Uplifted Church's magistrates. His first big reveal to the populace, and the first step in crafting the Vagrant persona Thorda believed would lead to Thanet's salvation.

The weather was cold. That was why he took a long-hooded cloak with him when he departed. It wasn't to hide his face as he wandered the streets. After all, who would recognize him with his more mature face, longer hair, and faint shadow of stubble around his lips and chin? It couldn't be because he was afraid, for that would mean Cyrus was a coward, and a coward couldn't succeed at the impossible task Thorda set before the Vagrant.

For the first time in years, Cyrus walked the streets of Vallessau. Everywhere he looked, he saw evidence of change. Old signs torn down and replaced with the buildings' names rewritten in the imperial tongue. Symbols of butterflies and lions, once as common as the rain, were painted over or scraped off doorways, signposts, and windows. The sun set, and with the rising darkness he felt more at home. More than anything, Cyrus wished to go unseen. He wished to convince himself he could be like the men and women he passed, who were so deeply vital to the city, no one gave them a second thought. No one immediately thought them an outsider. The imperials were the outsiders, not him.

So then why did the few imperial soldiers he saw seem so much more comfortable within the city than Cyrus?

Head down, he walked faster, jaw clenched and mind awhirl. His wandering took him to an old bell tower at a wide intersection used for temporary markets and festivals. A need to escape somewhere high up overlooking the city claimed him. The door was locked, but that would be no bother. The walls were uneven stone bricks, and it was child's play to climb through one of the windows. Cyrus slipped inside, feet setting down upon the winding steps leading to the belfry. He gave his eyes a moment to adjust to the dim light, then carefully climbed one stair at a time. The darkness eased as he neared the top, until he stepped out into starlight shining down atop the bell tower. He reached up to touch the brass bell. Faint impressions of both Lycaena and Endarius were carved into its sides. Had the Uplifted Church missed it during their sweeping purges of Vallessau? Or did they consider the bell so distant from the citizens that it didn't matter?

Cyrus turned from the bell to the waist-high wall that formed a protective barrier along the tower's edge. He sat atop it and, from that perch, took in the wondrous view of the city. *His city*, if Thorda were to be believed. He was their rightful king, born to rule by his royal blood.

"My city," he whispered into the night. He waited for it to mean something. He stared at sprawling rooftops and scattered windows lit with lanterns and candles. He drank in a hundred dark wisps of smoke from chimney fires.

"My city."

No thrill. No heavy sense of responsibility. But wasn't it his city? Those words, they were true. They were the beating heart of his entire quest for vengeance.

Except they weren't. His father's body collapsing in twain. His mother's pained, dying shriek. That spurred him on. This city, this crowded collection of homes and buildings squeezed together about the massive docks…it could not compare to those memories. He felt no attachment. No connection. No kinship. What was Vallessau to him but a strange land he had known only fleeting glimpses of in his childhood? To call himself their king felt like a sick joke. It felt like calling a woman his dearest wife despite having never seen her face.

Time passed, and he could not bring himself to leave. Perhaps he would stay there forever, a monster in the belfry. Not a prince. Not a hero. Just a shy, weird creature trained to kill.

Despite how soft her footsteps, Cyrus still heard Mari's approach up the staircase to join him atop the tower. She'd changed from her earlier gown to a much thicker, warmer cotton dress dyed a faint blue, and she'd covered her neck with a checkered scarf.

"How'd you get up here?" he asked.

"I have my ways," she said. He raised an eyebrow her direction. "All right, I picked the lock. Some of us who can't swing big scary weapons have to learn other useful skills."

Cyrus chuckled, but the mirth was forced. He turned back to the view. Mari was a beacon of joy, and it made him feel that much more awkward and dismal by comparison. To share his doubts with someone so kind was unfair, but that never seemed to stop her from prying.

"Are you all right, Cyrus?" she asked, her hand gently settling on his shoulder. "Something has troubled you ever since we arrived in Vallessau."

"Is that why you followed me here?"

"Because I'm worried about you? Yes. That is my reason. I think it's a pretty good reason, don't you?"

It was a stupid thing to argue about, so instead he gestured for her to take a seat on the belfry's edge beside him.

"Sorry," he said. "I don't mean to be rude. And if I'm honest, I fear I am not ready for this."

"I'd be surprised if you weren't at least a little nervous," Mari said as she sat. Her elbow playfully jabbed his side. "But I've seen the training my family's put you through. Sure, you may not have *beaten* Rayan in your duel, but you gave him a solid fight, and that's more than most any-one can say here on Thanet. You'll pull this off, and you'll do it with us at your side."

Cyrus stared at the castle atop the hill. Candles lit every window, and torches burned from braziers built into the outer walls so that the castle could be viewed at all times from all angles of the city. For two years he had lived inside it as a prisoner, separate from the people of Vallessau. A hostage for an entire nation.

"That isn't actually what I meant," he said, struggling to put into words his mess of complicated feelings. "If your father says I'm ready, then I'm ready. No one's a harsher judge than him. I more meant that I'm not ready to be king. These people here in Vallessau, and across Thanet, they're my subjects. So shouldn't I feel... something? If this city is mine to rule, and to protect, shouldn't I hold an attachment to it in some way? My father, he...he referred to Vallessau as his child. I was his son, and Vallessau his daughter, and he said he would raise and teach both to the best of his abilities. So why don't I feel that way? When I look out at the shining beacon of Thanet, why do I feel nothing?"

Mari clasped her hands before her, her legs swinging freely over the tower's edge. While he took in the view, she only stared into her lap so she might focus while she spoke.

"Cyrus, what is your purpose as king?"

He frowned.

"I don't understand."

"I've traveled all across Gadir, and every nation with a crown has a justification for their king's rule. What is Thanet's?"

The reason was one offered Cyrus since he was but a babe in a cradle, and he recited it like a student in class.

"Four hundred years ago, refugees from Gadir fled here from the Everlorn Empire, and the empire embargoed our island in retaliation. Our struggling realms turned on one another, beginning the War of Tides. Endarius declared such bloodshed unacceptable, and pledged allegiance to the Lythan family to unify Thanet under a single crown. With the Lion on our side, we ended the war, and ever since have ensured peace and prosperity for all generations."

"It is a noble purpose," Mari said. "But that's not what drives you, is it?"

Cyrus chewed on his lower lip. How did he explain when he didn't understand it himself?

"The thing is, while the four lords rule their minor realms, Vallessau was always ours. This city was special, to my family, to my line, to my own parents. I should want nothing more than to take it back from the empire, shouldn't I? They stole it from me. Stole my throne. My crown. And yet...and yet..."

How else to explain it? Crowns and thrones meant so little to him.

All he wanted was vengeance against the empire that hurt him. Such a confession made him sound ruthless and vile, even to his own ears. What kind of king cared so little for his people, and sought only personal revenge?

Mari reached out and put her hand on his. She hesitated to make sure he didn't flinch, and then wrapped their fingers together and squeezed.

"You're thinking of the city as a thing to own," she said. "You're thinking of it as a collection of buildings, towers, and piers. My father has a saying sometimes. 'Twigs are not what make a nest.' It's the eggs laid within it that do. It's the people within a city that make it worth protecting. The young and the old and the wise and the feeble and the destitute. Must you own them to care about them, Cyrus? Must you possess them to wish them a kind fate?"

"No," Cyrus said. "I don't believe so."

Their fingers disentangled. Mari rotated until she could slide off and set foot in the belfry.

"Then let that be enough," she said. "Being the throne's heir is useful to my father's plan, but you need not be a king to make things better for others. You need not be of the same blood to wish someone a better life. A noble purpose is enough."

"Is that how you justify it?" he asked her. "All the killing and murder as the Lioness?"

The woman put a hand on the brass bell, her fingers curling across the carved outline of Lycaena. A wistful look crossed her face. Moonlight shone off her brown hair, and she was so regal, so beautiful in its glow.

"When I hunt, there is pleasure in the blood upon my tongue," she said softly. "War makes monsters of us all, but that is why I become the Lioness. I hunt so no one else must be a monster. I hunt so others may know peace, and love, and live in the joy of their gods and the beauty of their rituals. For me, that is enough to grant my soul peace. What will it take for yours, Cyrus?"

She descended the stairs. Cyrus turned his attention to the castle illuminated in the distance. He could not see the courtyard hidden behind the surrounding castle walls, but he could envision it. The gently sloping grass hill. The cobblestone walkway. The giant crack pounded open by Imperator Magus of Eldrid's shield, a deep chasm into which the blood of his parents had flowed. What he could see clearly were the gray banners hanging over the walls of the castle, red hands clasped in prayer in their center. Those banners proudly declared to every citizen of Vallessau that the Everlorn Empire ruled supreme.

Did his soul even want peace?

Cyrus pulled out the skull mask Thorda had gifted him on their trip back into Vallessau. He slipped it over his face and tightened the leather cord's knot. A calmness passed over him as he felt himself becoming something different. Something new. This path meant inheriting the legacy of the killer who came before, the Skull-Amid-the-Trees, but wasn't that the nature of his life? The inheritance of legacies, and the struggle to make them his own? With this new face he beheld the castle and its gray banners.

Will you be stronger, Cyrus Lythan? the Lion had asked. There was only one answer he could give.

"You took from me everything I loved," he whispered. He spoke his promise to Magus, to Sinshei, to the Usurper King, and to the distant God-Incarnate who ruled the Everlorn Empire. "My parents. My kingdom. Even my gods. I can't unmake the loss, but I can make you hurt. I can make you afraid."

He pulled his beautiful sister swords free of their sheaths and held them up to the moonlight as he spoke his promise. Cyrus Lythan was dead, but a new man would take his place, one to fight alongside the Lioness. One who could make such a bold promise, and believe it.

"And you will fear me, monsters of empire. You will fear the Vagrant Prince when he comes to reclaim his crown."

He lowered his swords. A smile cracked his stern expression to match the one on his mask. He laughed to himself, his mood unable to remain so serious for so long.

"Hopefully."

CHAPTER 17

CYRUS

Everyone's in position," the young boy said, his hands clutching the outside windowsill so he could peek into the house. "Paladin says to wait for the whistle."

"Thank you," Cyrus said, and he flicked the boy a copper crown. Cyrus hated that Thorda involved kids so young in Thanet's rebellion, but there was no denying that children could sneak about the city of Vallessau unnoticed and undetected.

"Are you nervous about making your vaunted debut?" Stasia asked, the woman leaning against the far wall of the dilapidated home. The pair both wore matching gray shirts, trousers, and gloves, though she lacked his long cloak. Her short brown hair was tied into a stiff knot to keep it away from her eyes. Daylight reflected off her freshly sharpened axes belted to her hips.

"Shouldn't I be nervous?" he asked. "So much can go wrong. I wish Thorda had chosen an easier task to reveal my presence to the city."

"The point is to inspire," Stasia said as she glared out the window. "No one's going to be impressed with a few dead soldiers."

"Well, thank the gods and goddesses you're here. You can drag me to safety when I fall."

The woman shot him a wink.

"You fall, you're on your own, prince. I haven't survived so many battles by taking pity on the incompetent."

"I see why Thorda wants *me* to inspire the populace instead of you."

The shrill whistle outside stirred them both from their banter.

"Secret names from here on out, Vagrant," Stasia said as she tied her cloth mask over her face.

"Of course. Stay safe, Ax, and don't get too crazy. You're meant to funnel the guards, not defeat them single-handedly."

"I'll consider it."

Together they stepped out into the streets of Vallessau. Stasia veered right at the first turn, while Cyrus continued on ahead. A crowd of a hundred people or so formed a wall around a painted carriage. From his distance Cyrus could not see much of it, nor the soldiers standing guard, but he could see Magistrate Marthalos atop a little wooden dais attached to the back. The elderly man was rambling something about the duties of the faithful and the great power of the Uplifted Church. Lies of the God-Incarnate's beneficial deeds for the island of Thanet slid easily from his tongue.

"We among the Uplifted are not deaf to your fears!" the magistrate shouted to the crowd. "We know that peace has not yet settled like a blanket upon your weary bodies. But it is not the church preventing this peace! Far too many of Thanet cling to dead gods and forgotten rituals. Far too many seek absolution from heretical beings that can grant no forgiveness. Listen to our words. Look upon the might and glory of the Everlorn Empire! Is it not obvious, is it not clear, who are the righteous and who are the fools?"

Three barrels were stacked side by side along the edge of the next home, just out of sight of the magistrate. Cyrus withdrew his sword belt and looped it about his waist. He fumbled once with the buckle despite attempting to don it in a smooth, practiced motion. Nerves were making his hands jitter. This was it. No turning back.

Last he retrieved his mask, the same mask of the Skull-Amid-the-Trees, only with one key change. The skull was now nailed to a silver crown, and Cyrus slid that crown over his forehead to secure it upon his face. Once settled, he pulled his cloak's hood up and over his head, hiding every bit of his pale skin and dark hair. Only his eyes were visible, and in them his foes would see their doom. They would see rage, and fury, and the retribution of a dozen nations conquered and a pantheon of beloved gods slain.

"I'll make you proud," he whispered to the memory of his mother and father.

He drew his weapons, taking comfort from their hilts, both the roaring lion and the folded butterfly. His boots thudded upon the cobbles. Seeing his approach, a planted resistance member put two fingers to his mouth and whistled. The crowd parted, and through the sudden gap Cyrus dashed, swords already pulled back for a thrust. His weapons crossed the throat of the nearest baffled soldier. Cyrus kicked his chest, tumbling him into the carriage's side. The screech of metal and the rustling of the tarp were deafening in the temporary silence.

"For Lythan blood!" another planted resistance member screamed from a nearby window. A barrage of arrows fired from all directions, but the arrows shattered as the magistrate dropped to his knees and lifted his arms. An invisible shield formed about him as the power of the God-Incarnate flowed from his glowing palms. All part of the plan. Cyrus needed the magistrate focused on defending himself so he might kill unabated.

Soldiers rushed Cyrus, determined to fling their bodies between him and the magistrate. Time slowed. While others in Thorda's elite would participate, they were stationed strategically throughout the city. The initial attack would be his alone, the spark others would witness and remember. This was his moment, his first step in banishing the empire that had stolen his nation and slaughtered his people. Years of effort and training now came to this. His nerves faded. His uncertainty vanished. Beneath that grinning skull mask, he felt reborn. Thorda Ahlai had molded him mercilessly, and it was time to prove it.

The soldiers thought to surround and overwhelm him, but he would allow no such simple tactic to succeed. He flung himself at the nearest soldier, his shortsword shoving aside a clumsy thrust. The defenders thought they had numbers, and therefore the offensive. Cyrus robbed them of that delusion. His shortsword shifted an overeager thrust aside, his body twisted sideways, and the two collided into each other. Cyrus's other sword cut above the shield, and its curved tip punched through the chain and sank into his foe's lung. Instead of losing momentum, Cyrus rebounded off the shield, body twirling, his dark cloak masking his movements. He sank the shortsword into a man's neck, batted aside a panicked thrust, and then rammed his sword straight through another soldier's mouth.

Blood splashed across his blades as he cut down a foe too slow to block in time. The crimson gifted Cyrus with confidence. These soldiers, they moved so slowly, and they spent so much time reacting instead of controlling the flow of battle. They paled compared to Thorda's speed. They lacked Rayan's strength. They could not touch Stasia's ferocity. Coordination was their only hope, but the surprise of the attack denied them that.

Another volley of arrows thudded into the carriage's side, and two found purchase in the driver's side.

"Go, go, go," the driver shouted weakly as he slapped the reins. Half the escort stayed to fight while the other half kept with the fleeing magistrate. Those who remained were of two minds on how to react. Some attacked, while others tried to back away with their weapons up defensively. Cyrus's grin matched that of his mask as he stalked them, but that joy went no farther than his lips. These men and women, these soldiers of the Everlorn Empire, were not responsible for the cruel acts of their masters. These were not the Anointed of Eldrid dictating church doctrine. They were not the God-Incarnate sitting upon his gilded throne. They were mere mortals, some devout in their faith, some needing coin, and others merely enjoying the chance to be cruel. Cyrus brought them down one by one, and he let his rage wash away the guilt for their broken bones and spilled blood.

At last they scattered. Cyrus remained in place but a moment as Thorda had instructed. Most of the people who initially gathered to hear the magistrate speak had fled, but a good many remained at the edges of the fight, and they gawked at Cyrus, his mask, his cloak, and his blood-soaked weapons. Cyrus lifted the swords and clanged them together, spilling blood, imperial blood, to the ground. Once all had seen his grinning skull, he turned and chased after the fleeing carriage. The thoroughfare would be the quickest route the carriage could take, which was why

Mari and Stasia had set up there in preparation. Cyrus expected a massacre when he arrived, and he was not disappointed.

Stasia ripped and tore through a scattered line of soldiers with her dual-wielded namesake weapons. Nothing held her back. When a soldier tried to feint or hold her at bay, she'd ignore it completely. Her hefty axes punched through steel like cloth. Her only armor were the metal vambraces atop her wrists and shins, and she used them to bash and shove the occasional errant strike harmlessly aside. Gore coated her cloth mask, that of a saber-toothed panther skull.

"The magistrate!" Stasia shouted over the din. A thin line of soldiers surrounded her, keeping her from chasing the fleeing carriage. "We have this, Vagrant. Get the magistrate!"

The guards who cornered her might have thought otherwise, but that was before the Lioness leaped upon them from the nearby rooftop. It was the first time Cyrus had witnessed Mari in her full two hundred and fifty pounds of glory, barring a distant glimpse of her during the chaos of Lycaena's execution. Her gray fur was torn at the shoulders, flank, and face, making way for stark white bone plates grown as armor. Unlike Endarius, her wings bore no feathers, but the long bones that grew from her shoulder blades were frighteningly sharp and serrated. Mari wielded them like a second pair of arms, stabbing underneath breastplates and slicing exposed flesh as she pounced from foe to foe. Together, the sisters fought like gods themselves, and none could survive their combined fury.

Cyrus chased after the carriage, cries of the dying and the roar of the Lioness heavy in his ears. With the two sisters having blocked the main thoroughfare, Magistrate Marthalos's carriage had turned onto a much thinner side road. The last member of Thorda's elite waited there in ambush, and by the looks of it, he'd succeeded in halting the carriage completely by cutting the horse free of its straps. A half-dozen soldiers lay dead at his feet, but the fight was far from over.

"Where have you been, Vagrant?" Rayan, secret-named Paladin, shouted. His gray hair and beard were hidden behind his plate helmet, which bore a T-shaped opening across the front. A half skull was nailed to its interior to cover everything below the man's eyes. Though paladins of Lycaena traditionally wore colorful cloaks and shields, he wore the new ones he'd adopted since first visiting Cyrus back at the mansion, which were a mixture of white, black, and waves of gray.

"Busy," he called back. "Is the magistrate insi—"

The back of the carriage exploded outward as a towering man in brilliant gold platemail exited it. He appeared to be a red-haired monster, his plate weighing at least one hundred pounds. He casually carried a two-handed sword across his right shoulder, and he grinned at Rayan with smug confidence. This man was a mountain that had never been conquered. He was a storm that had lost no fury upon exiting warm ocean breezes and crashing ashore.

"Wonderful," Cyrus said. "Bloody wonderful."

"This farce ends here," the paragon said as he approached Rayan.

"Get the magistrate," Rayan said as he lifted his shield in challenge. "I'll handle this bastard."

No matter how strong he was, no lone paladin could defeat a paragon one-on-one. However, neither could they win with the magistrate's magic aiding in the fight. Cyrus rushed the carriage while watching the fight from the corner of his eye. The paragon lifted his sword in both hands, and when Rayan refused to move, he brought it crashing down in a direct challenge of Rayan's raised shield.

Any normal fighter would have crumpled, but Rayan was a paladin of Lycaena. Though his goddess may be dead, her power remained, and it sparked a rainbow of light from the center of his gray shield. The metal held, as did the man behind the metal.

"Surprising," the paragon said, and he followed it up with a second swing that rocked Rayan back several inches on his heels. "You'll still die, but consider me impressed."

Cyrus couldn't spare the fight further attention, so he offered a silent prayer that his friend would endure. He grabbed the door to the carriage, which still sported several arrows embedded into its side. Blinding light greeted its opening.

Stupid, he thought as he staggered backward, his eyes stinging. The magistrate might be hiding, but he wasn't helpless. Cyrus leaped left, for he knew standing still meant death. A crystalline ringing filled his ears as he rolled across the ground. Three spears of pure golden light struck the street, one after another, sinking a foot into the stone before dissolving away like mist. He slid up to his knees, his heart a pounding drum in his chest.

"Not quick enough," he said. Cyrus dashed back to the door, this time cautious of another magical attack. No attack came. The opposite door was open, and the magistrate's red robes fluttered in the distance as he fled. Cyrus noted the direction and did not bother to give chase. The man fled toward Ax and Lioness. He would find no safety there. Instead Cyrus rushed to aid Rayan in his battle against the paragon. Yet again the enormous two-handed sword had crashed down upon his shield. That the older man's bones hadn't shattered was a miracle in and of itself.

"About time, Vagrant," Rayan shouted. He tried to lift his shield, but Cyrus noted the sluggish movement, caught the wince of pain in the older man's eyes. Enduring another hit was not within him.

"You would torment your elders?" Cyrus shouted to the paragon as he approached. "I expected better from the Uplifted Church's finest."

The paragon hesitated, and when Rayan retreated away, he turned fully to face Cyrus's charge.

"That man stood with the power of a god. What hope have you, stranger?"

"Hope is irrelevant. I have more than enough anger."

"Anger?" The paragon looped his two-handed sword for an overhead blow that could fell a tree. "Is that it?"

"It's all I need."

Cyrus sidestepped the swing, and when the paragon tried to cut it back up in a V-pattern, he parried it aside. Twice he slapped his swords across the armored man's chest, hits meant to do nothing more than annoy him. Back around came the two-handed blade. The air whistled with its passage. Cyrus dropped beneath it, dented the giant man's boot with a chop, and then pirouetted away.

"Stand and fight," the giant man demanded.

"Fight? I'm not here to fight. I'm here to dance. Care to be my partner, paragon?"

Weapon matched weapon, blow matched blow, until Cyrus's sweat-soaked hair clung to the outside of his mask and the paragon's armor rattled with his every labored breath. At no point did he try to block, a tactic Thorda had drilled into Cyrus's head by having him spar with Stasia and her great-ax. The strength of a paragon was unmatched, which meant constantly parrying thrusts and swings. Use the momentum and weight of his enormous weapon against him. Take advantage of smaller size and speed. His foe was a lumbering giant, and Cyrus would frustrate him, exhaust him, until even his expert training faltered. Paragons were meant to dominate entire battlefields. They weren't meant to fight singular, elusive prey.

"What in god's name are you?" the paragon asked after yet another thrust failed to find its mark.

"No names, not for us," Cyrus said. He grinned, the challenge thrilling him beyond anything he could have anticipated. After two years of captivity, and another two and a half of isolated training, finally releasing his rage behind a mask felt divine. "If you must address your better, call me Vagrant."

The paragon launched into another offensive. Swing echoed swing, each one strong enough to cleave a man in half, and each movement faster than should have been possible with such a heavy weapon. Cyrus remained the faster. He ducked underneath slashes, sidestepped thrusts, even leaped over them if need be. His swords rattled off the paragon's golden armor, not once drawing blood. It didn't matter. His foe was exerting himself to a staggering degree despite his inhuman strength. His frustrations led to even clumsier swings. Cyrus found himself predicting them with ease, his grin growing, his confidence total.

And then the paragon revealed it for a lie. Cyrus drifted inward, thinking he had the measure of the man and his next move. Instead he found the paragon's movements suddenly faster, and instead of a thrust, he punched with his off-hand. The fist connected with Cyrus's chest, and it felt like being kicked by a horse. His footing slipped. His breath faltered in his lungs. Savage glee sparkled in the paragon's eyes as he lifted his sword in the other hand and sent it whistling through the air.

Too cocky, Cyrus thought. *Cost you your damn life.*

Stasia crashed in before the sword could claim Cyrus's head. Her two axes hooked the sword with their lower edges and drove it to the ground. The sword carved a groove through the cobblestones, but it was low enough that Cyrus could leap over it, then dance several steps away to gather himself. The paragon wrenched his sword free, then swung a fist in Stasia's direction. She retreated to join Cyrus as together they faced their foe.

"Thanks, Ax," he said, his voice hoarse. "The magistrate?"

"Lioness has him. Go right. I'll take left."

The exhausted paragon lifted his sword and braced his legs.

"Try it," he said. "You'll all hang by this day's end."

Cyrus took two steps, feinted a thrust, and then dashed aside to grant Stasia her opening. Her axes battered at the paragon, blow after blow so he couldn't dare try to counter. Cyrus weaved in the opposite direction, positioning himself toward the paragon's back. Even then it seemed they might not possess the needed advantage. Now on the defensive, the paragon became a veritable wall of armor and steel. What he could not block, he deflected with his expertly crafted armor. His movements slowed yet again, this time with exhaustion Cyrus believed was real.

Then two foes became three, and Cyrus knew victory was theirs.

"Holy be the light of Lycaena," Rayan called as he returned to the battle. His glowing sword cut through the golden armor, scoring a deep gash across the paragon's side. Blood flowed, and the paragon hollered out in panicked fury. No matter his strength, no matter his training, he could not endure when assaulted on all sides by such skilled opponents. One slipup, that was all Cyrus needed, one tiny slipup.

The paragon rammed his elbow into Stasia's chest, and when she staggered backward, he swung his two-handed sword at Rayan, convinced he had a proper opening. Rayan blocked, and as sword met shield, the paladin screamed in pain. The shield dented inward, sparks of light showering the ground. The paragon had thought it would break him, and that his sword would continue, but both paladin and shield held strong. Caught in the metal, he held no defense against Cyrus's blades. The Lycaenan shortsword jammed up through the man's armpit, while his other sword sliced straight down through the neck, clipped the spine, and buried to the hilt through his ribs and in his heart. The paragon gasped once, blood spewing from his lips, and then dropped lifeless.

"Are you all right?" Cyrus asked after ripping his weapons free. Stasia knelt on one knee, still trying to recover her breath, but she nodded in affirmative. Rayan looked even worse, his shield arm hanging limp at his side.

"Been better," Rayan said. "But my heart still beats. For now, that's good enough."

A snarl turned their attention down the road. Mari arrived carrying Magistrate Marthalos in her mouth. Blood dripped from bitemarks across his face and neck, but the thicker trail flowed from the severed tendons in his wrists. They were cut, denying the magistrate access to the divine magic granted to him through his faith in the God-Incarnate. Mari dropped the man at Cyrus's feet like a cat delivering a mouse.

"This won't stand," Marthalos said. His eyes were unfocused and his speech slurred from the loss of blood. "Thanet will...will suffer."

Cyrus knelt before the older man. His wounds were already fatal if untreated, but one significant goal for the day remained. An unease settled in his chest that he found distinctly unwelcome. The Vagrant's legacy was to be one without mercy or remorse. None of the empire may live.

"The people must know this death was at your hands," Stasia said, for she, too, understood Cyrus's hesitation.

"I know," Cyrus said softly. "Thorda has already spoken with me of such a need."

He grabbed Marthalos by the jaw and lifted him up so they looked eye to eye. There was no recognition, not with Cyrus's face hidden behind the skull mask. He adjusted his hood to ensure the magistrate saw the silver crown that looped about his forehead.

"Your church stole from us our gods. Your soldiers stole from us our kingdom. You stole my crown, magistrate, and so I give you the only crown I deem you worthy to bear."

He pressed the shortsword to the magistrate's forehead and cut him temple, forehead, to temple, and dropped him to die. The others watched but said nothing. Silently he strode to the dead paragon and gifted him a similar crown. A magistrate and a paragon. They couldn't have hoped for a better start.

Bells sounded in the distance, the rest of the city finally alerted to the ambush.

"Let us hurry," Rayan said, and he clasped Cyrus about the shoulder with his healthy arm. "It would be a sad end to Vagrant's story if he were captured due to laziness."

Waiting on the other side of the alley was a covered wagon, the driver a burly man with a long beard and complete indifference to the growing clamor from afar.

"Was worried my shipment would be late," he said upon seeing the four come running. Cyrus saluted him with two fingers, then joined the rest in climbing into the back. The group sat amid piles of cabbages as the carriage rumbled across the cobblestone with a clop of hoofbeats. Mari sat before her sister, who took a prepared blanket and laid it across her lioness form.

"A fine victory to remember," Rayan said as he set his helmet aside.

"The church will indeed remember," Stasia said. She yanked off the cloth mask that covered her face. "To lose both a magistrate and a paragon will anger and humiliate them. They will respond. They must."

A soft crack of bone followed by ripping skin delayed further conversation. The body beneath the thick blanket twisted and changed, arms and legs extending, wings retracting, and thick, corded muscle and armor-plating bone relaxing into fat and tissue. When finished, a naked Mari sat up with the blanket wrapped about her body.

"Everyone's so dour," she said, and she beamed a smile at the group. "We succeeded in Cyrus's first real mission! And I must say, it certainly could have gone worse."

"It certainly could have," Cyrus said. He coughed, trying to work up the nerve to say something both emotional and embarrassing. "Thank you, all of you. For helping me. For getting me this far. I couldn't have done any of this without you."

"Damn right," Stasia said. Her smile lit up the wagon. "As much as

I'd hate to admit it, you did pretty good yourself. I daresay we might be able to pull this off."

Cyrus laughed.

"We just might," he said as the wagon rolled on, and alarm bells rang throughout Vallessau the news of the magistrate's death.

CHAPTER 18

SINSHEI

Sinshei vin Lucavi took her seat at the council table deep in the heart of the Vallessau castle. Like most of Thanet's architecture, it was of finely carved pine, the trees far easier to obtain than the limestone that made up most of the castle keep's base. Little swirls and grooves were faintly chiseled along the surface of the table so that additional varnish gathered within them during its final layer of application. This caused the markings to be various darker shades depending on the depth, resulting in a shockingly detailed map of Thanet in the table's center. Boats sailed across exaggerated waves in the surrounding Crystal Sea. Little serpent heads peered from below the surface. A masterpiece of craft and detail.

"About time you arrived," Gordian Goldleaf said, his legs crossed and his boots resting atop the table's surface.

"I had prayers I must attend," Sinshei told the island's regent. There were only three chairs, so her paragon bodyguard, Soma Ordiae, positioned himself beside the door. His arms crossed over his blue platemail, his spear rattling as he leaned against the wall to observe the meeting in silence. A picture of absolute boredom covered his fair-skinned, handsome face. He hated these meetings, a sentiment Sinshei equally shared.

"Perhaps we should have left you to your prayers," Magus of Eldrid said, the occupant of the third seat. "God-Incarnate knows the faith of the populace is thimble deep."

Sinshei glared at the Imperator. Any remarks about the island's faithfulness were a direct critique of her as the Anointed One of Thanet. That he came armed and wore his golden platemail to a simple meeting irked her. Did he hope to intimidate her and Gordian? Her hands clenched into fists, holding back a spark of divine flame. Let him showcase his physical strength. She had the magic of her prayers. At least he wasn't wearing his damn bull helmet, so she could read the reactions in his silver eyes.

"Their faith is thin because you hasten the process the Uplifted Church has perfected over centuries," she said. "You never should have implemented the Joining Laws early."

"Except I didn't implement them," Magus said. "They are but half measures per yours and Gordian's requests. We see how well that worked. The population still protests, and will wail like babes when we go the necessary additional steps to better prepare their souls. I may well have to rebuild the Dead Flags given the fits they are throwing."

The Imperator referred to an argument that had raged for weeks between the three key leaders of the invasion. The Joining Laws were a strict set of measures meant to reshape conquered societies so they might better acclimate into the Everlorn Empire, as well as prepare the people's hearts and minds for proper worship of the God-Incarnate. Depending on the land, the people could easily transition into these laws, or face terrible hardships. From what she learned of Thanet, and the religion preached by their god and goddess, she had correctly guessed this would be one of the more difficult transitions.

"Perhaps the people would be more willing to listen if it had not taken so long to kill the people's heretical gods," Gordian chipped in. Gordian Goldleaf was Thanet's regent, the appointed political figurehead meant to replace whatever structure existed prior with a new royal court properly loyal to the empire. Sinshei was Thanet's Anointed One, in charge of coordinating the Uplifted Church's efforts to erase all memory of prior gods and convert the populace to the worship of the God-Incarnate. Magus held the title of Imperator, which meant he commanded the Everlorn Empire's military Legion, made up of both soldiers and paragons. Together, they were the Three Pillars of Conversion. Every imperial conquest, great or small, was led by the same key figures.

Theoretically, the Court, the Legion, and the Church would work together to accomplish their goals. It rarely went so smoothly in practice. Each held significant influence and power, but the final say belonged to the Imperator. The plotting and carrying out of an invasion ultimately fell on their shoulders. Gordian and Sinshei could make life miserable for Magus, but whatever he demanded, he was given, and three months ago he decreed a watered-down version of the Joining Laws be put in place despite church doctrine recommending doing so only after a minimum of ten years' preparation.

"You would blame my soldiers for the failures of your priests and magistrates?" Magus said, sounding almost bored by the attempt. "Spare me. It is your fault the people are reluctant to release their faith in their dead gods. They are, after all, dead, and that accomplishment belongs to my paragons."

With Thanet's timeline behind schedule, Magus would need someone to blame. That he went after Sinshei instead of Gordian did not surprise her. Even children of the God-Incarnate were not immune to the consequences of failure.

Especially the daughters of concubines.

"Perhaps the people would not be so reluctant to release their faith in their dead gods if members of the church weren't being slain in cold blood," she said. "Two years ago you declared the resistance crushed and disbanded. Now a paragon and a magistrate are murdered. Care to explain yourself?"

Gordian slid his feet off the table and sat upright. The attack was the reason for their hurried meeting. The conversion of Thanet's people was under an incredibly strict timetable, and while they had made great strides since Lycaena's execution, any rebel resurgence could undo years of work. The people's faith was proving maddeningly stubborn, and Sinshei suspected the vast distance between Gadir and Thanet was partly to blame. It certainly didn't help that they couldn't flood the island with a sudden influx in wealth and trade as was normal procedure, which helped immensely in buying the loyalty of the upper strata.

"I'm also curious what to make of this attack," Gordian said. "These rebels called out the name of the Lythan family, which while annoying, is predictable. Let them cling to memories of a slain royalty. But I hear stories already of a new hero among their ranks, a man who supposedly killed a paragon in solo combat."

"Vagrant," Magus said. He growled out the word as if it hurt to speak it. "And those stories are lies. The assassin had multiple people helping him, several of whom I've been aware of for years."

"Aware of, and yet not captured or killed," Sinshei noted.

"Try not to gloat too loudly, Sinshei," the Imperator said. "No one has whispered their locations to your priests in their confessionals, either. If resistance remains upon Thanet, it is because they hold no love for the God-Incarnate."

"But why would they love him?" Soma asked from beside the door. All three at the table looked his way, their expressions varying degrees of surprise. Soma might be a paragon, and a well respected one at that, but he was certainly out of line to speak at a meeting of the Three Pillars.

"Have things reached such a low on Thanet that even a paragon would speak blasphemy?" Gordian asked.

"I merely speculate on the lack of faith you all freely acknowledge," Soma said. Amusement sparkled in eyes that perfectly matched the blue of his plate armor. Despite their glares, he remained perfectly relaxed in his lean upon the wall. "I was there when we finally conquered Miquo, and I assure you, its populace was far more vicious and deadly than anything we've encountered here on Thanet. Yet when matters calmed, and its capital fell, God-Incarnate Lucavi proudly marched its streets amid dozens of parades. He blessed Miquo's regent. He prayed with her Anointed. He laid hands upon the orphans of Miquo and healed their wounds. In doing so, he gave the people a reason to believe in his deific nature. Yet what have you offered Thanet other than stories and badly chiseled statues?"

Sinshei cast a glance to Magus, conversation passing unspoken between them. No, her father had not come to Thanet. Not yet. But when he did, would he be greeted with the prayers of a faithful populace . . . or would he find lurking assassins and unchecked rebellion?

"The task may be difficult," Magus said carefully. "But I trust the stories and sermons of the Uplifted Church to convince the people that their salvation comes through faith in the God-Incarnate. A difficult task, but a worthy one, am I right?"

He was trying to extend a cooperative hand to the church, Sinshei sensed. As Imperator, no matter how much he might argue, the fault of a dead paragon and magistrate ultimately fell upon his shoulders.

"A task that would be made easier if my magistrates and priests might lecture without fear for their lives," she added.

The Imperator rose from his seat, and he clasped both hands across his chest.

"I vow upon my honor, in full witness of the Three Pillars and the God-Incarnate who watches over us, that I shall find and slay the insurgent known as Vagrant. His blood shall flow across my blade. His head shall hang above the gates of Vallessau. I swear it, and I shall make it so."

Sinshei caught Soma smirking from the corner of her eye, and she hoped Magus did not notice such a disrespectful reaction. The Imperator was an absolute beast in battle, and he commanded the loyalty of the empire's troops like no other, but he was painfully straightforward in his approach to everything. If a thing worked once, then it would work again. If a thing was good and proper, why wait to make it so? He knew only how to beat a soldier to the dust and break him physically. He didn't understand the subtlety needed to truly seduce a heretic's heart.

God-Incarnate help her, she could not wait for the Seeds to arrive on their boat. Her plan of ridding herself of the Imperator forever relied upon them and their gifted power.

"I hold full faith in your ability to do so," Gordian said. The regent stood from his chair. "Though I must admit I hoped you would come to this meeting knowing *anything* about this Vagrant person. I trust it will be only a matter of time until you do. Good luck in your hunting, Imperator. Let me know if there is anything I can do to help. My city guard are not as skilled or well armed as your soldiers and paragons, but their patrols take them to many deep corners your own men and women do not go."

"I do have something in mind," Magus said. "If you would, wait for me at the castle armory so we may discuss the matter further."

"If you wish," Gordian said. He dipped his head to the Imperator, then offered a more elegant bow to Sinshei. The difference in respect was both sincere, as well as meant to prick at Magus's pride. Sinshei smiled sweetly at him and acknowledged the bow with a curling gesture of her hand. Worms of doubt squiggled in her stomach, though she let not a hint of that show on her face. Magus didn't want her privy to the details of whatever he was planning. Not a good sign.

"Come, Soma," she said, rising from her own seat now that Gordian was gone. "Rumors spread like wildfire of the heroic nature of this murderous Vagrant. We must meet with the other magistrates across Thanet. Our sermons must cast his actions as insidious instead of heroic."

The blue-armored paragon bowed low and then held the door open for her.

"Another productive meeting," he whispered as she exited.

"I've suffered through worse."

Before they could leave, Magus called out to them from the other side of the table.

"Hold," he said, but not to Sinshei. "I would speak with you a moment, paragon."

Soma glanced at Sinshei and then lifted an eyebrow.

"Meet me in my room," she said as answer to his unspoken question. "I would know what the Imperator is plotting."

CHAPTER 19

SOMA

The Anointed One exited, leaving the two paragons alone in the council room. Soma crossed his arms and leaned against the wall, the tip of his spear clacking against the weathered stone. He waited for Magus to speak, but the giant man seemed in no hurry. Instead he put his hands on his hips and sized Soma up and down. It was a feeling Soma was well familiar with. Magus was deciding if he could defeat Soma in a battle. It took all his effort to keep his smirk hidden.

"I've heard about you," Magus said. "Less of *you*, I suppose, and more of your Ordiae heritage. A family of god-killers? You've inherited quite a legacy."

"A legacy well earned."

"And one you honored here in Thanet. It was your spear that claimed Endarius's life, was it not?"

Now this was a smile Soma need not hide.

"Indeed, it was. I will cherish that memory for as long as I live. My only sorrow is that I could not partake in Lycaena's death as well, but I suppose the knives of the Anointed and her magistrates must suffice."

The Imperator crossed his arms. Intelligence sparkled in those silver eyes of his. A ruthless man, Soma knew, one who rose to prominence not due to family connections or inherited wealth, but brutal efficiency in command. Magus had taken over the war in Noth-Wall after its first disastrous decade, and was largely credited with destroying its resistance so the Everlorn Empire could turn its efforts to Miquo and Antiev. It was this accomplishment that convinced God-Incarnate Lucavi to appoint Magus as Imperator of Thanet's invasion force.

"I lack the libraries of the Anointed to research as I would prefer," Magus continued, "but I do remember hearing stories of your campaign in Aethenwald. You were ruthless, a true hero of the empire, and slayer of Anyx and Cathun. For a single paragon to fell three gods borders on the unbelievable."

"Do you doubt the tales?" Soma asked. "Or the eyes of witnesses? Perhaps you deem me an opportunist, striking when a god is dying? It wouldn't be the first time I and my family have heard such claims."

The Imperator leaned closer, his arms unfolding in a clatter of plate-mail to rest atop the table between them.

"I doubt not your deeds, but your motives," he said. "Three gods slain, but you seek no promotion beyond your paragon station. Rare is a man who kills even one god, let alone three, and that privilege is often enough to ascend to paragon praefect. Mighty deeds, a respected name, and the backing of one of the God-Incarnate's children? You could make a viable claim for an Imperator position. And yet..."

He pushed off the table, his silver eyes boring into Soma's blue as if he might dig out every one of his secrets.

"And yet you remain a mere paragon, content to be Sinshei's obedi-ent lapdog."

"There is no such thing as a 'mere' paragon," Soma argued. "Not we who walk as heroes among men. But I am where I want to be, Impera-tor. I seek no additional responsibilities, nor do I wish to be a prae-fect and command my brethren. Give me gods to slay, and I shall be content."

"And when there are no more gods left to slay?"

"Then there will be no need of paragons, praefects, and imperators. The heavens spare us such a horrid fate."

Soma could tell the Imperator was losing patience. Good. Anything to end this dull meeting sooner.

"Sinshei claimed you as a bodyguard, and removed you from your praefect's command." Magus shook his head. "I do not believe you without ambition, Soma Ordiae. I suspect you hope to find it at Sinshei's side instead of with your own command."

There it was. Finally Soma knew where Magus's questioning led. Truthfully, it bored him to tears.

"You guess at motives and ascensions, yet give me no reason as to why you even care, Imperator."

"Then I shall abandon subtlety. I fear your loyalties lie to Sinshei, and it will be her orders you follow instead of mine. Sinshei may be of divine blood, and an Anointed One of the Uplifted Church, but *I* am Imperator. She is but the daughter of a disgraced concubine, not even in line as an heir. My will is the will of the God-Incarnate. I would hear from your lips an assurance that you will always obey, and commit no heresy or treason against the empire."

Soma uncrossed his arms. His right hand floated downward, his fingers brushing the long handle of his spear.

"If you fear I will commit treason, then you anticipate Sinshei ordering me to commit treason. A dangerous accusation to make against an Anointed, let alone the daughter of the God-Incarnate." Soma's grin widened. "Surely I am mistaken in what I heard?"

His fingers tightened around the handle of his spear. Magus's platemail rattled as he reached for the sword sheathed upon his back.

"Thanet is a long way from Gadir," said the Imperator.

Soma ripped the spear off his back, twirled it thrice above his head, and then slammed it upon the table between them, the razor-sharp tip pointed directly at Magus. The table cracked, splitting the re-creation of Thanet in half as its center bowed. The Imperator never flinched.

"You speak to a slayer of gods," Soma said. He yanked the spear off the table. "Save your threats for someone who would fear them. Good day to you, Magus of Eldrid. I do believe Sinshei is waiting for me."

"And she will continue to wait," Magus said. "I have a task for you, a simple one given your level of . . . expertise. A paragon and a magistrate are dead. Retaliation must be swift, and public. I know the location of a resistance cell, and I would have you expunge it from Vallessau."

"And why did you not share this information earlier during our talks?"

"Because I do not trust Sinshei, and I do not trust you."

Soma laughed despite the tension. At least Magus was painfully honest when it came to these little dances of intrigue.

"You decry games and hidden ambitions and yet rope me into your own. I do not appreciate the hypocrisy."

The floor shook with the weight of Magus's shield hitting the ground. His arm slid through the twin interior leather loops to grab the metal handhold. His sword remained sheathed, but his hand was on the hilt, ready to draw it free.

"I have given you an order, paragon," he rumbled. "Will you obey, or will you defy?"

Soma twirled his spear twice, enjoying the sound of it cutting through the air, and then returned it to the clasps fashioned into the back of his armor.

"I am ever loyal to the empire," he said. "So tell me where to go, Imperator, and who I am to kill. While the wretched, intolerable children of Vallessau watch, I will give them a glorious and bloody show."

CHAPTER 20

STASIA

Stasia and Clarissa lay intertwined on the bed, their tangled sheets soaked with sweat. It had been three months between Clarissa's last visit and Stasia's return to Vallessau, and they had spent the past week working hard to make up for such lost time. After Cyrus's first successful mission, Stasia had practically broken down the door to her lover's two-story home in her eagerness to celebrate. Daylight spilled across them through the slats of the shuttered window, the warmth wonderful on Stasia's naked skin. The only thing she wore was her word-lace. Given Stasia's limited knowledge of Thanese and Clarissa's of the imperial tongue, it kept things simple and clear between them.

"You'll be staying for a while now, right?" Clarissa asked. "As much fun as your whirlwind weekends are, it's not exactly the settled-down life I imagined when I was a little girl."

"Well, what did you imagine?" Stasia asked, sidestepping her initial question. Clarissa rolled onto her back, arms stretching long above her head as she stared at the ceiling. Her red hair splayed out underneath her like a crimson curtain. A tingle shot all the way down Stasia's spine. Gods, the woman was beautiful.

"Everyone makes fun of it, but I always wanted a traditional Lycaenean wedding on the beach, just like my parents had."

A little bubble of laughter escaped Stasia's best attempts to remain silent.

"You mean where you're wrapped together in ribbons and then have to squirm around to escape, all while people throw paint on you?"

"Like a chrysalis! Lycaena's chrysalis, now stop laughing, it's not that weird. You emerge together as a butterfly, colorful and unique and, most importantly, together. And that's just the fun part at the beginning, when everyone's getting liquored up for the dancing and singing that follows. You can't tell me Miquo didn't have its own weird little traditions."

"Oh, we had plenty, and all of them involved trees. I suppose that was our thing, trees. Planting them, climbing them, getting married in the shade of the oldest, most tilted, most rotted boughs imaginable as if it would bestow wisdom from its bark. I suppose we could merge the traditions. We'll be buried together in a hole, then have to dig our way out like a sprout."

Clarissa's blushing was almost as red as her hair.

"I knew I shouldn't have told you. Of course you'd make fun of me."

"I'm sorry, I'm sorry, I like to tease. I've been all over Gadir, and I swear, a Vallessau wedding isn't even in the top ten strangest things I've encountered. Much of it really does sound quite beautiful. Though I'll admit, becoming a butterfly doesn't exactly appeal to *me*..."

Clarissa tossed a pillow at her. Stasia caught it and hugged it to her chest, flashing her lover a grin she knew would melt her insides.

"No one would ever mistake me for a romantic," Stasia said. "But I guess it has been almost four years. Shall I drag you to the city lawhouse and demand they tie us together in wedlock?"

"We couldn't even if we wanted to," Clarissa said. Whatever amusement she'd shown at the idea faded. "They've put a halt to any marriages unsanctioned by the Uplifted Church, remember?"

Stasia's blood ran cold. Her joy mere moments ago in Clarissa's arms peeled away like burnt skin.

"They've done what?"

"Oh. I thought, what with your father, that you'd have surely heard. Regent Gordian announced them alongside Anointed Sinshei and Imperator Magus about three months ago. It's not the Joining Laws, not as you've described them to me, but they seem similar. Marriages have to be church-sanctioned, all property sales are subject to magistrate approval, and all adoptions must be to parents of adequate wealth and proper social standing."

Stasia hugged her pillow tighter. She tried to tell herself she had known this was coming, even if it'd been years sooner than anticipated. She tried to tell herself every nation across the Everlorn Empire eventually implemented the Joining Laws, and still people resisted. They still loved whom they loved, even if it must be clandestine. Hollow, wretched comfort.

"It's parts of it, all right," she said. "But not all of it. The full laws are worse. So much worse."

Clarissa shrank before her. Her gaze seemed to recede within her skull. Stasia so often viewed her as soft and round and delicate, but as her body curled into itself, she revealed something harder. Something battle worn and very nearly broken.

"The Usurper King says it is temporary, but we know," she said softly. "There were protests for weeks, Stasia. Many turned into riots. It just made them promise to do worse. They . . . they've arrested so many of my friends. Stolen their children. Beaten us. Hung us in public, even whispering they might rebuild the Dead Flags if we don't submit."

Stasia wanted to rage, but Clarissa was bleeding before her, and she didn't need anger right now, she needed comfort. Stasia pulled her close and held her naked body against hers. She whispered soft promises that everything would be all right. Her fingers brushed through red hair. As warm tears trickled down her shoulder, Stasia glared into nowhere and imagined a thousand curses to shout at her father. A prelude to the Joining Laws enacted, and riots ignited all throughout Vallessau, yet Thorda kept her in the dark in their countryside mansion. Gods and goddesses forbid something interfere with precious Cyrus's training.

"I didn't know," Stasia said. "I swear, I didn't know. I'd have been right here with you, with all of you. I'd have helped you burn down the city if that's what it took."

Clarissa rubbed her face across Stasia's shoulder, wiping away the tears as she tried to gather herself.

"It didn't matter," she said. The defeat in her tone was heartbreaking.

"Will it ever matter? Nothing changed. We set our fires and spilled our blood, and each night our numbers grew thinner. Their Anointed, Sinshei…she prayed for us. While we demanded to be treated like equals, she stood before her soldiers and prayed for our salvation. She begged for us to hear the words of her glorious God-Incarnate. Grace would save us. Redemption would purify us. And when we wouldn't listen, the swords of her soldiers spoke real damn loudly for her."

Stasia was glad to see anger replace her despair. Fury was always preferable to surrender. None of what she heard was new, but that didn't lessen the sting. The empire had come to Thanet, and brought with it every sick tenet and law of the Uplifted Church. The God-Incarnate was the ideal. All were to live in his image, obey his precepts, and strive to replicate his own life. God-Incarnate Lucavi had taken over two dozen wives across his six hundred years of reign, but how dare Stasia take a woman of her own.

"I know it's hard, but it's not too late," Stasia said. She put her hands on Clarissa's shoulders and forced her to lean back and meet her gaze. "We've finally begun to strike back. My father's plan, it seems crazy, but I truly believe it will work. We've already killed a paragon and a magistrate. Vallessau will have its hero. The people of Thanet will rise up in rebellion. Please, don't give up hope. Don't give up on us." She gently brushed her fingers across Clarissa's perfect round face. "On me."

Clarissa sniffled and wiped her eyes.

"I try, you know," she said. "I'm not a fighter like you or your family. I'm just little, quiet me, but I do try to use my position as a city clerk to help. People know to come to me if they need a home away from prying eyes. The members of our resistance, or those the empire has condemned, I find them places to stay. I sneak them into neighborhoods where the Uplifted Church has made no inroads. 'Do what you can, Clarissa, and together we'll change the island for the better.' That's what I tell myself. But I've seen the maps. The Everlorn Empire has conquered all the world. We're a speck of dirt in the ocean. Our surrender, it's only—"

"No!" Stasia snapped. "Don't speak like that. Don't think it. Don't believe it. Empires crumble. They grow and swell and conquer, and with each gluttonous mile they swallow down, they come that much closer to bursting. Their foundation is rot. It trembles beneath them as they climb for the sky. Let Thanet be the breaking point."

Clarissa slid from the bed, and she turned her back to Stasia as she peered out the thin, fogged window to the early daytime city. Her hand touched the dirty glass.

"Stasia," she started, and it seemed her every word caused her pain. "My mother is always pleading for me to leave Vallessau for safer lands. Maybe we should—"

Her entire body froze. Her spine went rigid. It was like a rabbit discovering the presence of a hunter.

"Clarissa?" Stasia asked.

The smaller woman looked over her shoulders. Fear dominated her every feature.

"Soldiers."

Stasia was off the bed and across the room in a heartbeat. She pressed her forehead to the glass and squinted. A squad of imperial soldiers blocked the crossroad five houses down, and when she tilted her head to peer in the other direction, she found a similar squad. Her dread grew. She knew these tactics. They'd been refined over millennia of conquest and subjugation. Already smaller groups were bashing down doors and forcing occupants to gather in the street. Many would be brought to prisons for questioning. Few would ever see the light of day again.

"No, no, no," she said. "Is there a resistance home nearby?"

"Across the street. I set it up myself."

"*Fuck!*" Someone had leaked word, initiating the sweep. The block was already sealed. Any hope of a clean, unnoticed escape was long gone. Stasia's mind underwent a shift, all fear and emotion replaced with orders and strategy. Their survival depended upon it.

"Get dressed," she said, and pointed to their pile of clothes. "We have to flee."

Stasia flung her trousers on, then her boots. A touch at the word-lace around her neck, and the magic enacted, changing the color of her eyes from red to brown. A glance over her shoulder to check on Clarissa showed the tiny woman having wrapped her skirt around her waist and reaching for a shirt.

"No, not yours," Stasia said. "Mine."

Lessons of a dozen rebellions screamed loud and clear in her mind: Do not be identified, and do not get caught. Her heart thundered inside her chest cavity as she ripped open a wardrobe. Clarissa's style was significantly higher class, her shirts more colorful and bearing the frills along the neck and sleeves currently popular throughout Thanet. It almost hurt to rip the sleeves off one when she put it on so it wouldn't restrict her movements come the inevitable battle.

"Tie your hair back, quick."

Stasia dropped to her knees and reached underneath the bed. There awaited the objects she never went without: her twin axes and her cloth mask. Stasia positioned the skull of a roaring panther over her face, taking comfort from its presence, comfort she needed to remain calm when she heard banging on the door downstairs. She put one ax on the bed, then used the other to cut a slit into a second shirt from the wardrobe. That done, she slid the shirt over Clarissa's face, the slit settling over her eyes, and then tied a knot around the back of the neck. Face covered, hair hidden, and body clothed in Stasia's baggy shirt...it'd be enough. It had to be enough. If Clarissa was seen during their escape, and identified...

"We won't hang," she said, retrieving her other ax. She pressed the two heads together, then locked them tight after sliding in the connecting handle so she might hold the great-ax with one hand. "You hear me, Clarissa? We're going to escape. No matter what happens, no matter who I have to kill, you don't stop running. You are going to run, and run, until you're on the gods-damned other side of Vallessau. Am I clear?"

Clarissa nodded in answer. The knocking on the door intensified. Angry shouts accompanied it. They'd bring a sledgehammer soon. Every building must be checked, every person must be identified, otherwise the sweep would not be ruled complete. Stasia stared into the blue eyes of the woman she loved and vowed to burn Thanet to the ground if that was what it took to keep her safe.

"We use the back door," she said.

"Won't they be ready?"

"Not for me."

One hand for her great-ax, one for Clarissa. Stasia led them down the stairs, through the tiny den, past the fireplace, and to the rickety back door. She didn't bother pressing her ear to it or sneaking a glance through the keyhole. She knew the tactics of a sweep. When they started sledging open the front door, they'd also check the back for inevitable runners. But unlike the front, in clear view of the street and the other squads barging into the nearby homes, there would be only one or two soldiers hidden in the back.

Stasia carefully unlocked the door, let go of Clarissa, and then tensed with the ax gripped tightly in both hands. She waited, every muscle primed for explosion. A soft, startled cry escaped Clarissa's lips when a loud smash marked the sledge hitting the front door. Stasia never even flinched, only imagined the scene in her mind. The soldier pulling back the sledgehammer, hoisting it up and over his shoulder for another swing, and then sweeping it back down.

That second hit masked the sound of Stasia's shoulder ramming open the back door. She burst into the alley with her ax already raised. As she anticipated, a soldier waited on either side. Her ax buried into the ribs of the man to her right, the sharp edge punching through his chainmail and into the vulnerable meat and bone underneath. Instead of trying to pull the weapon free, she powered her swing through, every muscle in her body tensing as she dragged the dying soldier around. The hapless man found himself between her and his partner, his body a shield that absorbed the frantic thrust meant to skewer Stasia through the back.

Stasia relinquished her ax, a decision her remaining foe foolishly did not replicate. As the other soldier tried to pull his sword free, Stasia shot over the body and collided with the man. Her hands found his throat. His windpipe crumpled beneath her grip. The momentum carried them both backward. He tried to swing at her, but it was wild and desperate. She leaned in closer, her elbow catching his wrist so the weapon flailed ineffectually behind her. Her right hand flipped the helmet off his head, then pulled back into a fist. Three times she bashed his face, smashing cartilage until it barely resembled a nose, all the while holding him upright with a vise grip about his throat.

She dropped him, a sputtering, gagging, bleeding mess. Whether or not the wounds were fatal, she didn't know, but it didn't matter. A single, hard pull freed her ax from the first dead soldier. Now rearmed, she offered her bloody hand to Clarissa.

"We must run," she said as the front door shattered.

They locked hands. Together they ran, Stasia guiding them while tracking their locations in her mind. Thank all the gods for her midnight trips to Clarissa's home. Doing so had taught her all the various alleyways and street corners. Despite their years safely together, she had not once forgotten this was a possibility. Since she was twelve years old, her entire life had been a war against the empire. One did not simply forget, and so she'd planned her potential escape from a sweep. The soldiers would guard all major crossroads, and they'd form a perimeter to box in the entire district, but there were a few thin alleyways connecting it to the next. They'd be guarded, of course, but nothing like the main streets. Reinforcements would come in time, which was why they had to outrun the wind.

A left here. Right there. Wending between homes, through alleyways, and only once dipping into the main street. Her grip on Clarissa's hand tightened, and when she started to fall behind, Stasia pulled her along. They couldn't linger, not if they were to escape. Their best hope was amid the initial chaos. Every which way, they heard shouts of soldiers, crying children, and frightened families herded out to the street for questioning.

Another turn. The lone major intersection was ahead of her, and three soldiers rushed toward them while shouting for reinforcements. Stasia let go of Clarissa's hand and charged. Savagery was her finest weapon. Her foes saw her muscles, her face hidden behind a roaring skull, and her gore-soaked ax, and suddenly halted their chase. Instead they lifted their shields and braced for her assault. The hesitation amused her, and it was while sporting a grin she whirled into the three of them.

Her first hit dented the shield and sent her foe staggering. The opening wasn't much, just a half step backward, but it was enough for her to shift sideways and slide across its surface on her back while positioning the length of her ax shaft to block a sword swing. Momentum carried her past the three, and they frantically spun to face her. Armored and wielding long swords and heavy shields, they moved so clumsily and slow when matched against her rage. Her left heel dug into the ground, granting power to her swing as her ax buried into the nearest soldier's neck. Warm blood splashed across her in a wild spray.

Two swords plunged toward her, one a thrust, another a high slash at her exposed chest. Wisdom said to retreat from them, force the two soldiers to overextend when she could take them out one by one. Limited time demanded otherwise. She ducked underneath the slash while batting aside the thrust with her ax handle. Her knees scraped across the hard stone, tearing skin. The pain mixed with her panic to fuel her rage. Up came her ax, denting yet again that same shield. The frightened soldier retreated, thinking she would continue the assault, but Stasia bounced right off to swing at the other man. The damn fool tried to block it. His sword snapped in half. The ax continued unabated, chopping off his arm before burying into his chest underneath his armpit.

A mindless, savage cry of victory marked the tearing of her ax free. Warmth splattered across her face, neck, and hair. The final soldier rushed her with his shield leading, thinking he might overpower her. She doubted it, but even if he could, she didn't bother trying. She smacked his dented shield with her ax to throw off his charge, then stepped aside, her foot swinging for his ankles. He tripped, his landing awkward due to the shield strapped to his left arm. Stasia pounded the ax one final time to the cobblestone, cleaving the last soldier's head from his neck. She brushed gore-soaked hair away from her face, regretting not tying it back in a ponytail prior to their escape. Returning her ax to her right hand, she once more offered her left to Clarissa. Even more blood coated her, but Clarissa never hesitated to lock fingers and hold on tight.

Almost there, Stasia thought as they crossed the intersection into another long alley. At its far end, they'd pop out into one of the main thoroughfares through Vallessau. It was always crowded, and would especially be so at midday. Within that teeming mass, they could escape the imperials and find refuge back at her father's home.

Escape would not come so easily. A man landed from the rooftops before her to halt their flight. A drop from such a height, and while wearing heavy blue platemail, should have shattered his kneecaps. Instead he sprang lightly to his feet, practically bouncing with giddiness. He'd pulled the visor of his helmet up, exposing blue eyes that matched the color of his armor and pale blond hair that clung to the sides of his face with sweat. Stasia skidded to a halt, and she released Clarissa's hand to ready her ax. Nothing could possibly be worse than this.

"Out of the way, paragon," she said. "Can't you see we're in a hurry?"

The towering man in blue plate removed his spear from his back and twirled it before him as if it weighed less than nothing.

"Such poor manners. Do strangers not introduce themselves on Thanet? I am Soma Ordiae, Paragon of Spears." He flipped the spear to point its tip at her. "I pray you know how to use that fine-looking great-ax?"

"It's only my namesake," Stasia said.

A grin spread across the man's face, flashing pearl white teeth.

"My, my, I believe I've heard of you before. The Ax of Lahareed, am I right? You've been stirring up trouble for years now. I wonder, how worthy are you of your reputation? Or can any woman with an ax and a mask pretend to be you?"

Lahareed was ten years ago, yet another nation brought to heel by the empire. Stasia had thrown herself into its resistance, still young enough to believe she alone could be the difference between victory and defeat. She had slain hundreds, yet it mattered not. Her reputation, and the fear she inspired, had been but a stumbling block as the priests taught their faith, the native language warped, and the old gods faded away in death.

"There's only one of me," Stasia said. "And if you're doubting, come find out."

Much of it was bluster. A singular duel against a paragon was a death wish. Soma lowered his spear, and his body coiled.

"If you so politely insist."

Clarissa's scream marked the attack, for the man moved so fast, he was but a sapphire blur. Stasia swept her ax sideways, a defense against the chest-thrust her gut said he would make. Metal hit metal, her guess correct. Her ax bashed the tip of the spear aside. She twisted her body, legs bracing, and then smashed into him with her shoulder. Pain spiked throughout her body. He was armored, and stronger. The best she did was tilt him slightly onto his heels. Experience said to close the gap against the spear wielder, though, and so she tried. Her elbow shot for his face and missed. Her ax came back up and around, yet he easily parried the attack aside. His boot found her stomach, and she staggered.

Soma did not chase despite her vulnerability. Instead he twirled the spear and laughed while she retched for air.

"If this is the best you can muster, it says poor things about the quality of our soldiers you killed in Lahareed."

Stasia exploded back into motion, hoping to catch him off guard. He dodged her first two wild swings, showing an agile grace unusual for one decked out in heavy plate. On the third, he caught her face with the butt of his spear. She cried out, using pain and anger to push forward. The paragon had shifted positions from the dodging, and at last she had the man where she wanted him. Planting her feet, she swung a long, looping arc aimed for his waist.

Her ax struck the shaft of the spear, yet it made not a dent, for beneath the black leather wrapping was a layer of steel instead of wood. It should have made the weapon unbearably heavy, but the strength of paragons made a mockery of such normal limitations. She pushed harder into him nonetheless, keeping their weapons locked. There would be no defeating the paragon who clearly outmatched her, but that was not her primary concern. Stasia now directly faced Soma, with Clarissa's path toward freedom unblocked. There may be no escape for Stasia, but at least Clarissa might live.

"*Run!*" she screamed.

Clarissa hesitated but a half second before breaking into a sprint. Soma pressed his spear shaft harder against her ax, his grin insufferable, his blue eyes stunning in both their beauty and the depths of absolute disgust swimming within them.

"Clever," he said. "But pointless. I want you to suffer, Ax, and the best way to do it is damn obvious."

His knee shot upward, and she realized her error the moment she disengaged. He wasn't attacking her, only buying himself space. The paragon retreated, his spear swirling in his grasp as if it were impossible for him to hold it still. He bent his legs and then vaulted, the divine strength gifted to him as a paragon carrying him halfway up the building, which he kicked off to send himself soaring ever higher. Stasia swung her ax at him, but he was too high, too fast. He landed on the rooftops, rolled to preserve his momentum, and then leaped once more.

All time slowed. A wordless scream tore from Stasia's throat. The paragon descended, his spear leading, its impossibly sharp point aimed straight for Clarissa's spine. Light sparkled off his sapphire plate. The image burned into Stasia's mind, carved deep with horror. No words, no time for thoughts, only terror that this frozen moment would scar so deeply, she might never recover. She screamed, and screamed, waiting for the spear to pierce through her lover's back and emerge from her chest. One more precious person taken from her. One more joyful light snuffed out by the damnable empire.

A blur of bone and fur flashed overhead, colliding with the paragon with such force, metal shrieked. Mari flipped in place, all her momentum transferred into her foe. The paragon flew aside, limbs hanging limp as he smashed headfirst through the window of the nearby home amid a shower of glass and wood.

"On me!" Mari ordered, her snarl translated by the word-lace she wore. Clarissa climbed atop the Lioness, legs wrapping about her sides and her arms locking together about her neck. Stasia's relief was so great, she could almost cry, but they weren't safe yet. There would be time later to collapse in Clarissa's arms and bathe her with tears and kisses. For now, they must run.

Mari led the way to safety, none alive who could keep pace with her bounding lioness form. Stasia followed at a growing distance, legs pumping, lungs burning, and heart thankful for every single mile she'd run around their countryside estate. She looked back only once. The blue-armored paragon had climbed out the broken window and stood in the center of the street, spear twirling lazily in his hands. She could not see, not at such distance, but she knew with absolute certainty that the bastard was smiling.

CHAPTER 21

CYRUS

Cyrus watched the hanged bodies sway. Each had a hand outstretched to the other, bound together with rope, and then bolted palm to palm with a long, single nail.

Why didn't you tell me they enacted parts of the Joining Laws?

Stasia had screamed it at Thorda when she and her sister returned home earlier that day. Cyrus had caught only a glimpse of her before she stormed into her father's room. Blood had been splashed across her clothes, and bruises covered her body. The thin walls had offered no protection against her anger.

"The Joining Laws?" Cyrus had asked Mari upon her transformation back to her human body. And so Mari told him of the rules governing marriage, property ownership, and adoption that were implemented throughout the empire. They required mandatory religious service attendance, changed inheritance laws, and outlawed the print and distribution of anything deemed critical of the God-Incarnate. All of it was under the guise of establishing the proper order of the world, the hierarchy from child to god that guided all their principles.

"They're normally enacted ten to twenty years after a nation is conquered," she'd explained. "But Regent Goldleaf declared them law here in Vallessau a few months ago, while you were still training at my father's mansion." She'd glanced at the door to Thorda's room, and the argument roaring within. "I meant to tell Stasia, I really did."

Afterward, Cyrus had come alone to stare at the swaying bodies, the pair hung in the middle of the street where the Dead Flags used to stand. He imagined Stasia's body hung by the neck. He imagined her hand bolted to Clarissa's. The pit in his stomach swelled and grew.

"It's been months?" he'd asked Mari, horrified by the details she so calmly explained. "Why haven't we done anything?"

"But we have," Mari had argued. "Every day, every mission, every kill, we fight back. Nation after nation, rebellion after rebellion, that's what we do. Why would you think we've ever stopped, Cyrus?"

Except that answer wasn't good enough for Cyrus. Gordian had been the one to announce the laws, and so Gordian should be the one to pay. Thanet would not be forced into a mirrored reflection of the empire's cruelty. Yet what had Thorda said when Cyrus demanded action?

Patience. Always patience.

"To the Heldeep with patience." Thorda had trained him to be Thanet's heroic murderer. Why were they starting with magistrates? Why undertake assassinations on lowly people without true power or influence? Why not make a kill that would mean something?

The bloated lips and swollen tongue of the corpse became Gordian Goldleaf's.

"For two years you held me prisoner," Cyrus whispered. "But I'm not that boy anymore."

Two soldiers clad in gold armor patrolled the walled hill which the Vallessau castle was built upon. They held long halberds with the handles braced firmly against the sides of their hips so as not to interfere with their march. Fading sunlight sparkled off the curved metal of the halberds' ax heads. Little red ribbons fluttered from the sharpened spear at the top. Cyrus hid on a nearby rooftop, his body wrapped in his deep gray cloak. He slid his skull mask over his face and drew his swords.

"Just two," he whispered. "No one will miss them."

Once he dragged their dead bodies safely into hiding, Cyrus dashed to the wall surrounding the castle. His destination was burned into his mind, and had been ever since Rayan had given its details to Thorda nearly two years ago. A nearby home directly adjacent to the wall had an outdoor cellar in its backyard. Nothing about it stood out, and as Cyrus crouched before it, he wondered if even the owners knew of its secret.

The cellar was locked, but said lock was old and simple, more meant to keep out kids and drunkards than someone with nimble fingers like Cyrus. Lockpicking had not been a particular emphasis of Thorda's, but he'd spent a few weeks teaching Cyrus the basics during the off-hours while he recovered from the physical exertion of his training. Prepared for once, Cyrus withdrew two long, thin picks from a pocket and set to work. The lock clicked open, Cyrus tossed it to the grass, and then descended into the dark.

The twin shelves within were bare and cobwebbed. Had the owners even survived the tumultuous years of imperial invasion? Cyrus pinched his lip in thought. While the walls appeared stone, one of them was false, with the stone fastened to a wooden door on a hinge. But which one?

After moving both shelves, he found it behind the second. Faint grooves in the stone that happened to fit his fingers. It took some prying, but at last he forced open the hidden doorway. Before him waited a two-foot-high tunnel. Cyrus climbed in and then closed the false wall, enveloping himself in darkness. At the start of the crawl his hands brushed a wooden box. Within he found a stash of candles and some flint to light them with. Cyrus took one, lit it, and then began crouch-walking forward. It didn't take long for his back to protest, so when the tunnel squeezed tighter, he was almost relieved to drop to his hands and knees for a crawl.

Time passed weirdly down there in the candlelit dark, but if he were to guess, it was only ten minutes before the tunnel began to expand. The dirt around him gave way to carved stone and the occasional wooden support. Soon he was crouch-walking again, and then walking with only a slight stoop. The size of the passage, and its tight integration into the building's construction, sparked his curiosity. How many other tunnels might be hidden throughout the castle grounds? If only he had known about them during his days of imprisonment at the hands of the Usurper King. Not that he'd have known where to go once out of the castle. Perhaps, as begrudging as he was to admit it, things had gone as best they could, with his rescue by Rayan and delivery into Thorda's hands.

Cyrus suspected himself reaching the end of the tunnel, given the sudden, sloping rise of the floor. Sure enough, the dark passage came to an abrupt halt. He set the candle down to check the wall. A rope hung overhead, with a round bit of metal tied at the end to give it a handle. Presumably this would allow him entrance, but first, to make sure his infiltration didn't end the moment it began by stumbling headfirst into guards or servants, he put his ear to the wall and listened for several long, painful minutes. Only silence.

Here goes nothing.

He pulled the handle. A thin line of light sliced into the dark as the wall opened slightly. Cyrus pressed his hands to it and pushed, rolling it open a foot. When he slid through, he emerged from the slender gap into a well-furnished parlor. As his ears had predicted, it was empty. He slid the false wall shut, and as he did, an adjacent candelabra clicked upward in place. The sight put a grim smile on Cyrus's face. Just like something out of the stories he'd devoured as a child. Now he lived them.

"So where are you hiding, Usurper King?"

The hour was late with twilight approaching. Cyrus tried to remember Gordian's daily schedule from his years under house arrest. He'd have finished eating his dinner. What then? Relaxing by a hearth? Spending time with his wife? It'd been too long, and Cyrus hadn't paid attention to such matters like he should have. Still, if his presence went unnoticed, he could be patient. Gordian's bedroom was on the third floor of the castle. Cyrus didn't need to be flashy with this kill. A knife in the dark was an excellent way to announce the Vagrant's prowess to the nation.

Cyrus's insides slowly turned cold as he climbed the stairs and walked the carpeted hall. Everywhere he looked awakened memories. Most of the paintings of former kings and queens were gone, but the landscapes remained. He remembered his father's lectures, describing the painted locations and where they fell within their realm. He passed a table scuffed on one leg from where he'd accidentally hit it while play-fighting with Rayan. Even the sounds of the servants humming their songs while he hid behind a curtain threatened to drag him into a past where he'd known only happiness and ignorance.

He passed room by room, careful of guards as he wound his way to the bedrooms. An open door caught his attention, and he glanced through to ensure no servants within might notice his passage. His stomach flipped the instant he realized where he was. The door opened out to a balcony, smaller than most and decorated with a cast of gargoyles scattered about the ornate pillared balustrade. They hung from the edges, clung upside down with their clawed feet, and floated on tiny wings much too small for their chubby bodies. Cyrus stepped out onto the balcony despite the urgency of his task.

From up on high, he overlooked the castle grounds. A wide paved road led up the hill to the castle entrance below, either side flanked by tall cedars grown and trimmed so their branches formed a wave pattern. His heart skipped a beat as memories flooded out from the suppressed corners of his mind: the distant docks aflame, and the road not empty but instead filled with imperial soldiers armed to the teeth.

It was on this balcony he had watched his kingdom crumble. From up high, he had watched Endarius die. Cyrus stared at the gash in the stone the Imperator had made with his shield. No one had ever repaired the damage. Instead, the Usurper King had declared that spot the designated killing ground for all executions made in the ensuing months as Thanet was steadily brought to heel. The stones were stained red, and what had been an empty crack was now a depository of skulls left to rot after a beheading. Such privilege was reserved only for the wealthy and political elite, of course. Commoners and heretics executed during the early purges were hung at the Dead Flags, made an example for the other lowborn in the city. It was only visitors to the castle who would smell the stench of old blood and see the garish pile of jawbones, cracked skulls, and scattered teeth. After all, not all beheadings were kind, nor quick.

"S–sir?"

Cyrus turned to find a small boy staring at him with his head tilted. The door to the balcony remained open behind him. Cyrus recognized him and immediately dashed past. A solid kick slammed the door shut. The boy startled, but he didn't panic, not at first.

"Sorry," Cyrus said. "It's rude to leave doors open like that. It lets in a draft."

The words were barbs on his tongue. He'd been told the same thing a dozen times in his childhood by various servants brave enough to chastise him. He had never listened.

"Um, all right," the boy said. "Why are you here? And what's with your face?"

A grim smile spread behind Cyrus's mask. Here, alone, was Uriah Goldleaf, the only child of the Usurper King. He had gained a few inches in the years since Cyrus last saw him, his cheeks a bit chubbier, his hair longer and tied in a clumsy braid at the neck. That Cyrus noticed these things, that he reminded himself the boy was barely seven years old, sparked a doubt he tried to ignore.

"The balcony is quiet, good for solitude and silence," Cyrus explained as if everything were calm and normal. "As for the mask, my face is quite hideous, and I hide behind it in turn. Pay it no mind. Pray tell, why are *you* here, child?"

Uriah kicked the ground, unsatisfied with the answer but also young and nervous enough that he was unwilling to press the issue.

"I like the gargoyles. And sometimes when…when Mom and Dad are yelling, I go out so I can't hear them anymore."

"Then let me tell you a secret. I used to come here as a kid, and I know something that's really neat to try. Come. I'll show you."

He walked to the balustrade, and after a brief hesitation, the boy followed. Cyrus knelt beside its pillars, then gestured for the boy to do the same.

"Put your legs around each one," he said. "And then scoot as closely as you can so that you hug the pillar."

The boy did so. Cyrus pretended to do likewise, and then demon-strated what he wanted him to do next.

"Duck your head underneath and then slide a little bit to the side," he said. "Once you're holding on tight, very tightly now, look down."

By holding on to the pillar with arms and legs wrapped around it, the boy could hang out over the entire drop somewhat safely. Cyrus had done it dozens of times, and the exhilaration was always worth it. By the gasp the boy made, he agreed. Cyrus remained sitting beside him, his hands resting on his knees. Only a tremendous amount of self-control kept them from shaking.

"Is it not amazing?" he asked.

"It is!" Prince Uriah said, and for a brief moment he sounded unwor-ried and unafraid. Cyrus watched him hang suspended over the air. His attention shifted to the black ring about the boy's forefinger, bits of cloth helping fill it out so it sat comfortably above the joint. Should the ring be forcibly removed, or his mother or father don the matching ring, they would activate its magic, killing Uriah instantly and without pain. When one is the Usurper King to a newly conquered nation of the Everlorn Empire, such measures were necessary to prevent the capture and torture of one's children.

But no one knew the boy was in danger. No guards. No warnings. A more perfect time to kill would never come.

"I'm Uriah," the boy said after he pulled back, though his arms and legs remained wrapped around the balustrade pillar.

"People call me Vagrant," Cyrus said. "It's nice to meet you, Uriah."

Uriah smiled, but it was forced. His nervousness was growing. He might panic and call for help soon, if not distracted...

"Look there," Cyrus said, and he pointed to a distant glow of torches. "If you squint, I bet you can see the animals drawn in fire by the Bel-haven Tavern. They use torches to do it, little dots close together to cre-ate shapes. Some say you can see it for miles."

Cyrus stepped back from the edge as Uriah made a good show of looking. He pulled the hood up and over his head. He drew one sword, then the other. Each action was slow, methodical, and meant to delay what he knew must be done.

With a single slice of a sword, he could sever vital arteries. With a push of his boot, he could send the child tumbling to the ground below. If there were justice in the world, the little boy's body would bounce and roll until it came to a stop within the bloody executioner's crack Magus of Eldrid had pounded into the stone. All the pain, all the torment heaped upon him since he was fourteen years old, Cyrus could inflict back in return. So simple, this act. So easy to take the life of a child, if one could bear it.

Cyrus's hands finally shook. He observed the way Uriah peered at the city bathed in twilight. Did he know of the actions of his father? Of course not. He was six years old, not even halfway to seven. This was a world beyond him, far more than it'd been beyond Cyrus when he watched his fleet burn and the imperial ships disembark their troops. But how many thousands had died by his parents' hands? How many lives had been snuffed out for resisting the Everlorn Empire's insatiable desire for more nations, more worshipers, more exultant voices to sing the praises of the Uplifted Church and their God-Incarnate?

In time, Uriah would grow up to be like his father. He'd serve the Everlorn Empire faithfully. There was no difference in killing him, Cyrus told himself. It didn't matter his age, or that the boy had always been kind to him during Cyrus's years of imprisonment. The Usurper King had taken everything from him, *everything*. Was it truly so wrong to take a single life in return? Cyrus had pledged his entire existence to revenge and rebellion. Did one little boy's life matter when compared to that?

A soft, smothered cry pulled him from his thoughts. Uriah had buried his face against the pillar. His eyes were closed as he sobbed.

"Please don't kill me," he said, his words muffled by the stone. "Please, please, I'm sorry, don't—don't—don't kill me."

Cyrus looked to the swords in his hands. Saw the tremble of their blades.

What price is too high for your vengeance, or their freedom? Thorda had asked that first night spent in his mansion. Cyrus returned his attention to the young boy, and the black ring upon his finger.

Perhaps his hate and anger were not so vast as he believed, for there were some prices he was still unwilling to pay.

He sheathed his sword, grabbed Uriah by the scruff of his neck, and flung him toward the door. A horrified wail escaped the boy's throat as he rolled. Within seconds the door burst open. Cyrus expected imperial soldiers, but instead Gordian himself stepped onto the balcony, dressed in the loose, crimson silks he slept in. His bare feet skidded to a halt upon the cold stone. His son's name died on his throat as he realized his predicament. He bore no weapon, no armor, no protection of any kind.

Cyrus grinned behind his skull mask.

"Greetings, Usurper King," he said. "The Vagrant has come to say hello."

He sprinted for Gordian, his arms extended, his twin thrusts eager for blood. They should have impaled the man in the gut, but a hand reached from outside the doorway to grab the regent's shoulder. A single tug and he fell backward. Magus of Eldrid took his place, his enormous shield filling up the entire doorway. Cyrus's thrusts struck the metal and scraped harmlessly aside.

"You've also come to die, Vagrant," the Imperator growled from behind his shield.

Cyrus quickly danced away from the paragon. At such a close distance and narrow space, overcoming the advantage of his shield would be impossible. Worse, Gordian was safely off the balcony, no doubt in the arms of more soldiers frantically approaching due to the shouts of intruders. Whatever hope he had of successfully assassinating him died. All that mattered now was escape. Cyrus spun as he retreated, disguising his movements with a flourish of his cloak. His movements ended with his curved sword pressed against Uriah's neck.

"Easy now," Cyrus said as he circled toward the balcony edge, careful to keep the weapon close while not drawing blood. He twisted the sword so the flat edge lined Uriah's throat, guiding him so the two could approach the balustrade. "I came for the king, not the brat."

"Touch either and I will break every damn bone in your body," said Magus.

Cold stone bumped against the backs of Cyrus's legs. He grinned behind his mask, preferring amusement over the feeling of panic threatening to overtake him.

"You'd have to catch me first."

Directly beneath them was a second balcony, and he'd sometimes wondered if, given the way several of the gargoyles hung from the balustrade's edges, he could use them to safely descend from one to the other. It seemed his childish curiosity was about to be confirmed. Cyrus jammed both his swords into their sheaths and then leaped off the balcony. Surprised shouts followed him as he dropped. His right hand caught the foot of the nearest gargoyle, and he used it to swing closer toward the castle, aiming for the balcony below while also peeling away a bit of his momentum.

Damn, that hurts, he thought as he rolled to lessen the impact of his landing. His knees throbbed, and his legs wobbled unseemly his first few steps, but at least he was down and moving. He burst through the balcony door, surprise his greatest weapon. All the soldiers were rushing for the stairs to the higher floors. The secret passageway in the parlor was unknown to them. A young soldier spun about upon hearing the door open. Cyrus cut his throat before he could even draw his sword. Two servants in a nearby room screamed at the spray of blood.

"Out!" Cyrus screamed, and he pointed his sword eastward down the hall. They fled, which was all he needed, for the next room west was the parlor. He pulled the lever disguised as a candelabra and slid into the crack in the wall. Voices shouted after him, but he would be faster than any chasing guard. They'd find the tunnel eventually; he was sure of that. Nothing else would explain his disappearance, and after having a sword put to Uriah's throat, Gordian would tear the whole castle apart to ensure his son's safety. But that would take time, and by then Cyrus was long gone.

Cyrus took the long way home. He told himself it was because he needed cold air on his now-unmasked face, and that the walk would be calming as the excitement of battle slowly faded from his body. It certainly had nothing to do with using the secret access Thorda had hoarded close to his chest for some unknown perfect timing. It wasn't because he feared the ire of the ice-blooded teacher.

Over an hour later, he returned to find Thorda waiting in the entry foyer of his home, sitting on a lone stool like he did so many days of training back at the mansion. There was no sign of either of his daughters, nor Clarissa, who had been crying in Stasia's room when Cyrus left to exact his revenge.

"I would hear it from your own lips first," Thorda said.

"I see word travels fast around Vallessau," Cyrus said, purposefully stalling.

"There are many within the castle who send me their whispers in exchange for a glint of silver. After tonight's debacle, they came running. But whispers can be wrong. They can be incomplete. Explain yourself, Cyrus. Let me hear where the blood on your mask came from."

Cyrus puffed up his chest and pulled back his shoulders.

"I made an attempt on the Usurper King's life," he said, purposefully leaving out his encounter with Gordian's son. "If not for the untimely arrival of Imperator Magus, I'd have been successful."

"And yet you failed."

"I nearly took his life."

"An assassination is either successful or it isn't, Cyrus. If Gordian Goldleaf still breathes, then you failed, and failed miserably. You damn fool. No plan. No hope for success. Worse, you've revealed our ability to enter the castle at will. They'll be on guard now, and likely find the hidden tunnel. A secret weapon, wasted, all because you have the patience of a toddler."

The older man struck the wall with his fist. Wood broke beneath strength that shaped metal. Cyrus had never seen Thorda like this before, not even half this angry all throughout his training. It terrified him.

"Three years! Three years, we invested in you. We built you from nothing, molded you, trained you, all while planting the earliest whispers of your return. Yet you could not afford us similar courtesy before striking out on your own? Damn it, we are so close, so very close to a meaningful victory. The people's faith in you is but a seed, and it will blossom, but not if you die alone on a fool's errand! Everything about you, from your appearance to your weapons, has been carefully chosen. I sought to bequeath you a reputation of invincibility, an air of undeniable death. Yet tonight you tried to assassinate Thanet's regent, *and you failed.*"

"I regret that I failed," Cyrus said, unable to endure such an assault in silence. "But would you rather I do nothing? How could I not after Stasia's and Clarissa's lives were in danger?"

"Our lives are *always* in danger," Thorda seethed. "Since she was twelve, Stasia has fought against the Everlorn Empire's cruelty. Do you think her a stranger to these risks? Do you deem her incapable of seeking her own vengeance? You murdered a magistrate and a paragon. Are you so dense as to believe the empire would not retaliate?"

"Of course, but to do nothing—"

"Is not the same as being patient!"

It was Cyrus's turn to lash out in frustration. He turned and kicked the closed door behind him, rattling the wood.

"Patient?" he asked. "Patient, while people are suffering and dying? You trained me to kill, gave me these swords, and told me to unleash my rage upon the empire, and so I did! How can I focus on anything other than the unspeakable things being done to my people? We have to retaliate. We have to act."

His master stepped close, and his voice dropped to a dangerously slow and steady cant.

"I will explain this once, boy. These horrors that are so new to you? They are a lifetime to us. They are the world Stasia has known since she was twelve, and Mari since she was eight. You panic and thrash about, demanding we act, but are blind to the wisdom that *everything* I have done these past decades is exactly that. Every dead magistrate, every slain paragon, every torched building and emptied prison, is a step toward salvation. You see only one step before you. I see the many steps ahead, and the thousands behind. If you wish for any hope of victory, you shall listen to the wisdom of your betters. *Is that understood?*"

Cyrus's face was flushed solidly red, the heat reaching all the way to his ears. What little wisdom he still possessed shouted within his skull to swallow his pride and admit his error.

"Understood," he said. "And for what little it means, I truly am sorry. I will do better. I swear."

Thorda crossed his arms and looked away, instead staring into nowhere. What he thought of such a vow, Cyrus could only guess, for he did not mention it when he spoke next.

"I believe I can portray this as a warning, and not a true assassination attempt. On his part, Gordian will seek to downplay the danger to his life, so as to not appear weak. This will actually lend credence to the idea you were delivering a message. Yes, I believe I can make this work." He shook his head, and his anger vanished behind a mask of calm Cyrus trusted not a wit. "At least you returned in time. I feared we'd have to cancel completely, but if we hurry, we should make it within a reasonable hour."

"Make it where?"

"To the party you are already late for."

"Late?" Cyrus asked. "For a party I didn't know about? Why didn't you tell me?"

"I sought to avoid making you nervous," Thorda said. "I see now my worries were displaced. I should have feared you running loose like a fool and getting executed. Three years. Stars have mercy."

Cyrus's ears burned red with shame.

"I'm sorry. It won't happen again, I swear."

"Make sure that it doesn't." Thorda put his hands on his hips and scanned Cyrus up and down. "At least you're already dressed. Come with me. It's time you experience the less savory side of fostering a resistance."

"Less savory than the killing?"

His master grabbed his coat from a hook by the front door.

"There is a simple truth to fighting, young Cyrus. Tonight, you'll discover a far more distasteful battle—dining among the wealthy and political."

CHAPTER 22

CYRUS

"This cannot be safe," Cyrus told Thorda. The pair stood in a white pine gazebo built in the heart of a garden belonging to a mansion in the wealthy northwestern corner of Vallessau, amid the rows of houses built onto lips carved across the surrounding Emberfall Mountains. Rosebushes surrounded an empty pedestal behind them, and judging from the small chunk of broken stone atop it, there had once been a statue of either Endarius or Lycaena positioned there before imperial decree demanded its removal.

"Nothing we do is safe," Thorda said. His hands brushed across Cyrus's outfit, straightening the cloak and picking off stray hairs and bits of dust. He scratched his thumb at Cyrus's mask, then changed his mind. "Leave the dried blood. It will impress."

"And what am I to do? Walk around? Make speeches?"

"You are a prince of Thanet," his master said, and he stepped back and crossed his arms. "Surely you have attended more than a few formal gatherings and were taught some rudimentary dances."

Of course he had. He was a prince, after all. But most had been when he was a child, content to laugh and joke with family friends while eating far too many sweets coated in honey. As for his more recent attendances...

"Gordian paraded me around to remind the nobility I was still alive and in their custody," Cyrus said. "There wasn't much care that I knew how to dance."

Thorda retrieved Cyrus's swords and belt from where he'd placed them atop a bench.

"You need not speak a word if you desire," he said as he handed the weapons over. "Rayan and Clarissa are currently inside spreading tales of your assassination attempt, preparing them for your momentous arrival. Let the people in attendance look upon you. Let them see your grinning skull and your silver crown. You must be real to them. That is all that currently matters."

Cyrus buckled his swords to his waist and choked down a sigh.

"Will you be in there, too?"

A faint image of candlelight shone through the blurry glass carved into the back door, followed by a knock.

"In a manner," Thorda said. He turned and opened the door. A stranger stood there, an older man based on his build. His clothes were garish, colorful, and no doubt ludicrously expensive. A red-and-green cloth mask covered much of his face, clashing hard with his blue trousers and finely fitted yellow vest.

"While within, you will address this man as the Coin," Thorda explained. "And so far as any in attendance knows, this man is the true financier and mastermind of our rebellion."

"Charmed to meet you," the stranger said, and he bowed low to Cyrus. "You are as frightening and deadly looking as advertised, Vagrant."

"I don't understand," Cyrus said, glancing at his master. "Will you not attend? Or is this imposter meant to go in your place?"

"Imposter?" The Coin flailed his hands about with the skill of a man who had spent a lifetime in theater. "You mock the brilliant financier of our rebellion. I assure you I am no imposter, and I pray you are not stupid enough to say so in the presence of others."

"Of course, forgive me." He vowed to learn the real name of the Coin once the evening was over, if only so he might properly carry a grudge for being called stupid. It made sense, of course. If Thorda were to fund and plan insurgencies all across the empire, he couldn't afford to be named or identified. It was the same logic that had Stasia disguising her eyes when she fought.

"I will await you at home," Thorda said. He put a hand on Cyrus's shoulder and squeezed in a rare moment of emotion. "Do me proud."

The old man faded into the starlight and vanished amid rows of roses. The counterfeit Coin put his hands on his hips and gestured to the back door with a tilt of his head.

"Now that we've made acquaintances, are you ready to make your grand reveal?"

Cyrus's hands fell to his sword hilts, and absurdly, he was more nervous now than prior to his recent battles.

"As I'll ever be," he said, and followed the imposter Thorda inside the mansion. The Coin chatted as they walked through the kitchen, washrooms, and quarters dedicated to the servants. His movements remained exaggerated, but his tone lowered, and a bit of seriousness crept in almost unbidden.

"I pray you are everything we have hoped for. Thorda has a habit of promising much more than he can deliver. Remaining patient over these last few years has been..." He sighed, greatly exaggerated, while twirling his right hand. "Difficult."

"Have you been with the resistance long?"

"From the very beginning. The empire took from me someone I loved dearly, and it seems even an actor in a mummer's troupe must play their part in a rebellion."

"You went from a performer of mummeries to impersonating Thorda to help lead a resistance? That's a bit of a journey."

The Coin laughed behind his mask.

"Not so much as one might think."

The carpet shifted color, from a rugged brown to a much more flamboyant red. Painted portraits decorated the walls, and in the distance, Cyrus heard the deep hum of conversation. The Coin turned a corner, leading them into a short walkway and halting before a set of double doors painted white and lined with gold. Faint music played within, intermixing with the murmurs. A lone servant stood before them as a greeter, looking sharp in traditional Thanese finery, a sweeping, long-sleeved green outfit that opened up near the legs like a robe to expose his tight black trousers and emerald-studded belt.

"The guests are ready for your arrival," the greeter said. "Would you prefer introductions?"

"No introductions," the Coin said. "Our presence will be noticed quite readily on its own." He lowered his voice, peering at Cyrus over his mask. "Walk tall, Vagrant. Thanet needs you, now more than ever."

Cyrus straightened his posture, crossed his arms, uncrossed them, and then signaled he was ready despite feeling anything but. The greeter flung open the double doors, and the pair strode through them into the mansion's opulent ballroom. It paled compared to the hall Cyrus had played in while growing up in the castle, but it was a fine attempt at recreating the white walls, gold-chiseled pillars, and array of paintings across the ceiling showcasing the beautiful countryside of Thanet.

Though music played, no one danced, the dozens of people within busy whispering and drinking from tall glasses. Their eyes turned his way. Discussions ceased, as if everyone present held their breath. Fear froze Cyrus in place. He wasn't a highly trained killer anymore. He was fourteen, eyes red with tears, being forced into a dancing hall.

Behave, the Usurper King had ordered. His clothes were the finest silk, his blond hair braided with silver and gold. *Smile. Show them how greatly we care for you.*

When Cyrus refused, the man had grabbed him by the neck and dragged him into attendance. All eyes had been upon him, just as they were now. They'd been full of pity then. What did they see in him now? His skull mask felt paper-thin. His mouth dried out. Should he draw his swords and prance about? Give a speech? He didn't know. He wasn't trained for this. He wasn't ready. Give him a blade and let him kill, anything but this. The stares. The whispers. They were getting louder, less subtle.

"Follow me," the Coin whispered, tugging on his sleeve. The command pierced Cyrus's paralysis. Relieved to have even the simplest of orders to follow, he did as asked. The flamboyant man kept his voice low so no one could overhear amid the hum of the party. "Walk about, mingling, and say nothing. You are best when a mystery. I will be near, and help when I can, but this part you have to manage on your own. I must appear deferential to you, not the other way around."

They parted. Cyrus stood in the center of the crowd, lost like a piece of driftwood in the ocean. What had begun as fascination suddenly turned into everyone ignoring his presence. No one approached him. Were they frightened of him? Or unimpressed? Gods help him, he would strangle Thorda for this.

Desperately seeking refuge, he scanned the crowd and was relieved to find Rayan, dashing in a white suit with long coattails, idling among the guests. Black ribbons were tied around his wrists and about his neck, the faintest symbolic hint of mourning for his deceased goddess. The familiar face drew Cyrus like flame to a moth. Maybe his nerves would cease if around someone he knew instead of all these strangers.

A young woman conversed with Rayan, their appearances similar enough that Cyrus wondered if there was a family relation. Her flowing dress was black and laced with seemingly dozens of thin gold strands. Her hair was tied in braids, and it, too, glinted a hint of gold. The brooch about her neck bore a faint outline of a butterfly. Easily the most striking was the paint across her face, a colorful splash of red and orange meant to mimic Lycaena's spread wings.

"Welcome to the party, Vagrant," Rayan said. He shook Cyrus's hand. "Glad you could join us."

Even that simple contact, of a handshake among friends, did wonders to peel away the fear and stress stacked heavily on Cyrus's mind.

"You look nice," he said in return. "I didn't know paladins could wear something other than armored plate."

"Most days, we would lecture and visit instead of battle. May we soon return to those times."

"But there is no returning," the woman at his side said. "Not with the goddess slain."

Rayan's practiced smile denied any of his true feelings, but Cyrus could feel the weight of his words when he spoke.

"I daresay the two of you have not been introduced. Vagrant, I would like you to meet my first cousin once removed, Keles Lyon."

"I find 'niece' and 'uncle' far easier, and preferable," the stunning woman said while offering her hand. Cyrus accepted it into his and then froze. Respectable behavior dictated he kiss the fingers during a bow, but what in blazes was he supposed to do while wearing his skull mask? His hesitation drifted into awkwardness, and he quickly dropped his head into a clumsy bow while forgoing the kiss. All the while, Keles's fingers tingled through his glove as if her skin were electric.

"A pleasure to meet you," he said, forcing the words out much faster than intended.

"Likewise," she said. She did not withdraw her hand. It seemed she was perfectly fine dragging out his embarrassment. "Rumors claim you are a ruthless killer, yet I swear you are blushing behind that mask, Vagrant."

He released her hand and straightened his posture. Gods damn it, she was probably right if the heat building in his neck was any indication.

"Even the coldest of hearts can be melted by the strongest of beauties," Rayan said, bailing him out. Still, Cyrus did not like the man's faint smile. It was too...amused.

"Forgive my hesitation," he said, trying to explain himself. "I would show proper manners, but I doubt you would appreciate the touch of this mask."

"I would indeed not," Keles said. "There's fresh blood on it."

But of course. Despite that seeming an impossibility, he now felt even more foolish. At the same time, it was nice how little she cared for his outward persona. The people around him seemed on edge at the mask and his swords. The same could not be said for Rayan and Keles. Cyrus remained with the pair as his nerves slowly eased. Rayan was a pleasure to be around as always, but Cyrus's attention shifted constantly to Keles. She studied him without bothering to hide it, and her tongue was sharp as she poked and prodded him throughout their conversation. Out of everyone present, she seemed the least impressed with his mask, crown, and macabre garb.

"I suppose I should go mingle with others," she said after a few minutes. "As with my uncle, Thorda has requested I spread rumors of your failed assassination attempt on the regent."

"You mean his message," Rayan said. "The Vagrant did not fail."

"Of course not," she said, and her smile was playful and mocking in equal measure. "What was I thinking?"

The paladin and his niece both bade Cyrus farewell, once more abandoning him to the crowd. Thankfully this time he need not search for another familiar face. With Thorda remaining absent, Cyrus had thought the same would go for his daughters, but he was wrong. Stasia sought him out, her hair tied back in a ponytail and her face hidden behind her panther skull mask. She wore her wrist and shin guards, polished to a shine. Her twin axes hung from clips attached to her belt. Unlike all the finery around her, she wore plain trousers and a dark gray shirt with its sleeves cut at the shoulder, granting a fine display of every rippling muscle when she moved her arms.

A man and woman accompanied her, and they bowed in greeting. Though he had met her only twice, Cyrus recognized the red-haired woman, Clarissa. Unlike Stasia, she very much belonged, wearing a tight green gown that left little to the imagination. The other person, gray-haired and wearing a black-and-violet suit, was wholly new to him.

"I'll let you three discuss in private," Clarissa said upon the four gathering, and she kissed Stasia on the cheek. She winked in Cyrus's direction before vanishing into the crowd, and for a brief moment he feared she had noticed his wandering eyes.

"It is good to meet you at last, Vagrant," Stasia said, the lie easy on her tongue. "Allow me to introduce you to a vital member of our resistance, Commander Pilus Arenthan."

Cyrus took measure of the man. He was gray haired and golden complexioned. A little fat around the waist and cheeks, but a hint of muscle remained when he offered his hand in greeting. His face and hands were covered in scars, and though he wore his suit well, it did not erase the military air that hovered about his stiff and straight posture. His smile was good-natured, and Cyrus found himself immediately warming to the man.

"Commander, she says." Pilus laughed. "I was master at arms for the good king and queen, but long retired before the dark days that followed." He shook his head. "Most of my friends in military leadership lost their lives, so I suppose there are benefits to old age."

"Yet he is retired no longer," Stasia said. "The soldiers of resistance need their commander, and so now we have one. Pilus trains those who are willing, and should Thanet have an army one day, it will all be because of this good man right here."

"I do not know if I would call myself a good man, but I am a dedicated one." He dipped his head in respect to Stasia. "I hear rumors of the Coin's elite, and I know I am but a small part in the greater battle. It is people like you, and Vagrant, who will inspire hope in the populace that my few soldiers cannot."

More praise, so much of it unearned. They had killed a magistrate and a paragon, but he had been one among many, his achievements no more special than Mari's, Rayan's, or Stasia's. Why did this bother him so? Why the doubt?

Carry him if you must.

After a few more minutes of idle banter, Stasia gestured for Cyrus to follow her. Once separate, she leaned close, her voice dropping low.

"I heard what you did for me and Clarissa," she said. "I'm flattered, but I assure you, I'm quite capable of scoring vengeance on my own."

"Yeah, your father gave me an earful of similar," he said. "For what it's worth, I'm sorry."

"And for what it's worth, when I do try for that vengeance, I'll make sure to invite you to tag along."

She flashed a smile, beautiful and deadly, and Cyrus knew he was lucky to have met someone like her. She playfully punched his shoulder, then gestured toward the distant minstrel stage at one end of the ballroom.

"Well, I believe everyone's gotten a glimpse of you. It's time I summon the entertainment. Good luck!"

Cyrus returned to Pilus after she hurried away. The older man glanced over Cyrus's shoulder.

"Where does the Ax run off to?" he asked. Cyrus shrugged.

"I suppose we will find out together."

Yet it wasn't Stasia who began the proceedings, but a handsome man in his forties, his coat crimson and his red hair powdered white. He clapped his hands above his head to gather everyone's attention as he stood atop the minstrel stage, having banished the four-piece band playing there with a wave of his hand.

"Who is that?" Cyrus asked.

"The owner of this fine mansion, Ludwig Ariti," Pilus explained. "A good friend of mine, and loyal to Thanet all the way down to his bones."

"Greetings, friends," Ludwig said once all were silent. "We risk much in gathering, and so I would thank you for your trust. Though we talk freely here, I remind you to keep your lips sealed once we leave our grand party, for the empire has ears everywhere, and not all native hearts upon our island are resistant to bribes or whips."

Solemn heads bobbed up and down in agreement.

"Now enough of my speech, for we have a special guest. To mark this momentous occasion, I present to you the Ax of Lahareed."

Stasia climbed atop the platform as Ludwig descended, and she addressed the crowd with a powerful charisma that Cyrus only wished he could match.

"The Coin promised entertainment, and he didn't mean music and dance," she shouted. "To the squeamish, I warn you to leave now. This won't be pretty."

A pit of dread grew in Cyrus's stomach. Stasia vanished into an off-stage room hidden behind curtains, then returned dragging a prisoner. His mouth was gagged, his feet tied, and his hands bound behind his back. By his uniform, Cyrus marked him as an officer in the imperial army. Stasia flung him to the center of the stage. He rolled twice, then settled on his knees. His face was freshly battered and bruised. How long ago had they captured him? Had it been during yesterday's attack? Tonight? And why had no one told him?

"Come, Vagrant," Stasia called. "Show the people your work."

Cyrus's feet remained firmly planted in place. His skin itched as if it were on fire. So many eyes were upon on him. Held breaths. Cravings for vengeance. These people had maintained power even after the original resistance was crushed. No doubt pragmatism had led to surrenders and concessions otherwise hated. This execution, it would be revenge by proxy. It was both theater and a promise. Stasia hopped down from the stage, and she swaggered toward Cyrus as if this were part of the theatrics.

"What sick joke is this?" he hissed once she was close enough that he could whisper. He was furious such a morbid act would be forced upon him, with neither choice nor warning given.

"Did you think you would save Thanet without dirtying your hands?" Stasia whispered back.

"You didn't tell me I would need to kill for their entertainment."

"And you didn't tell us you'd try to kill Regent Goldleaf. Consider it fair trade. Now prove you have the spine to do what must be done."

Cyrus glared at the bound prisoner. There was no turning back from this, not without causing significant damage to the reputation Thorda was building for him. This was a test, it had to be, hence its secrecy. For years, his master had trained him in swordplay, but some things could not be taught.

He easily hopped up to the stage, and he paced before the imperial officer. The man glared up at him despite his condition. Cyrus's distaste grew. He had killed soldiers before. His entire life was sworn to eradicating the Everlorn Empire from his homeland. So why should the slaughter of one officer bother him so? Why would he hesitate at a justified execution?

Little Uriah's face flashed in Cyrus's mind, and he felt shame and guilt for his hesitation. Could he afford such principles if he was to become the killer Thorda painstakingly crafted? Perhaps not, but there had to be some sort of line he could walk. There must be a way to fight for freedom yet not become the monsters they fought. But where was that thin, blood-soaked line?

For the first time that night, he addressed the crowd. The voice that came from behind his mask surprised him with the depth of its anger. It was deeper, too, though he never meant to disguise it in any way. It merely felt natural. It felt like the persona the wide-eyed crowd expected.

"Give him a weapon."

Murmurs rumbled through the crowd. Cyrus ignored them, his attention locked upon the officer. The man was bent over on his knees, but he tilted his head up and locked eyes with him. The man's spirit was unbroken. That made it better, somehow. Fairer. Stasia disappeared into the crowd, then returned holding a golden-hilted sword offered from some merchant or nobleman. A family heirloom, no doubt, and rarely used, given the smoothness of the leather and the perfection of the steel, without a single chip or nick. Stasia tossed it to the stage, where it landed with a clatter of metal.

Cyrus drew his swords. He first cut the prisoner's wrist bindings, then sliced the gag in half alongside his cheek, which also drew a faint line of blood. The murmurs of the crowd deepened. Cyrus sensed their bloodlust. It seemed he could even see it in the air, like a red fog. The officer grabbed the sword before him and sawed at the rope tying his ankles.

"What is this shit?" the man asked once he could stand. His short brown hair fell across his forehead, matted with sweat. He retreated several steps and held the blade out with both hands clutching its golden hilt. "Hoping to give your friends a little show before I'm executed?"

"Not a show," Cyrus said. "A lesson."

The officer licked his lips, and he glanced at the wealthy men and women in attendance.

"Traitors, all of you. You'll hang from the flags."

"No they won't. Attack me. I have a lesson to teach."

Cyrus's confidence was unnerving the man far more than the skull and crown ever could. This officer would be no pushover. He appeared in his forties, and he commanded soldiers of an imperial invasion force. Of course he was comfortable with a blade. Perhaps he had trained his fair share of grunts, too.

"I don't know what you are," the man said. "You can come in dressed like it's a martyr's festival, but it won't matter. I've seen more battles then you have years in your life, yet even I am *nothing* compared to our paragons. Whatever you're doing here, it is a pathetic charade."

Cyrus tilted his head to one side.

"You're not attacking."

Faint titters of laughter from the crowd. The officer's neck flushed red.

"Fine," he said. "I don't care if you cut me down afterward. I'll die knowing I had the pleasure of humiliating you in front of your traitorous ilk."

The officer lashed out, a strong blow but one Cyrus easily blocked. The same went for the next few that followed. At no point did Cyrus attempt to retaliate. In grim amusement, he realized he was doing what Rayan had done in their very first duel. Every single attack, he beat down and ended with ease, then stepped back and prepared for the next. With each passing second, it became that more obvious the disparity of their skill. The officer's attacks turned desperate. He swung harder, wider, not caring if it left him vulnerable. What did it matter if Cyrus never countered?

Cyrus shifted tactics, now engaging the officer in a dance. Was this not a display? Was this not a game for the crowd to watch and cheer? He parried a thrust, batted the steel twice, then swung for the man's neck. Not fast. Not hard. Just enough to force the defense. Their blades weaved between one another, but while the officer was covered with sweat, Cyrus remained relaxed. Whatever effort he did exude, he easily hid it behind his skull mask and flowing cloak.

"Our armies will crush you," the man said, but it was clear he was starting to panic. Twice more he thrust, expert jabs with every movement and muscle extended to maximize their strength. Cyrus danced around them, knowing the destinations and readying parries before the thrusts even extended. With every passing second it seemed the fight grew slower. His heart calmed. The stress of the party eased into a welcome understanding.

Stasia, Thorda, and Rayan: They had been his only comparisons. Throughout his training he'd struggled and pushed himself so he might be worthy of their efforts. But he had been built up from nothing in the image of absolute masters. Year after year, day in, day out, immersed in a level of skill few might ever experience in their entire lives. It had honed him, elevated him, and forced him to be better. He had learned to anticipate unnatural speed. He had faced Stasia's savagery, Rayan's indomitable shield, and Thorda's ever-perfect positioning of both foot and blade.

This officer, he knew how to swing a sword. Against Cyrus? Against the Vagrant? That wasn't good enough.

"Bring me your armies," he said. "Bring me your paragons. I am better than them. I am better than *you*."

Enough. Prolonging the fight further was like a cat playing with a mouse. He slammed the man's sword up and aside. The expected counter, he batted that away, too. The distance between them vanished. His knee rammed the officer's crotch. His fist broke the man's nose.

"I will see my island freed."

Knees weak, the officer dropped. Cyrus pressed the edge of his reverse-gripped sword against the man's forehead.

"All of Thanet will know my crown."

A single, vicious yank was all it took. Blood splattered across the stage as Cyrus carved upon him the mark of the Vagrant. He flipped the hilt and reversed direction, the returning swing cutting a hole in the officer's throat. More blood on the stage. He kicked the corpse away. It crumpled, and the faint thud on the wood could be heard throughout the deathly silent ballroom. Cyrus remained still, refusing to grant the people his attention. A flick of his wrist, and blood flung off his blade, droplets scattering toward the shocked crowd. The spell ended the moment his swords clicked into their sheaths. Murmurs erupted, along with scattered cheers and applause.

Cyrus's already poor mood soured further. The officer deserved to die, of that Cyrus held no doubt, but why must it be in such manipulative circumstances? This was no battle, but a public execution for a party of gawkers dressed in finery. The man was the oppressor, a tiny cog in a machine built to grind Thanet into submission, yet this entire setup felt foul. Part of Cyrus rejected their approval, for it was the applause of those who knew not the sting of death, and saw warfare as only a game.

Part of him, the part at home behind the skull mask, drank it in like a fine wine.

"Enjoy your dance," he told the crowd, though he doubted anyone beyond the first few rows could hear him. He dropped from the stage and made for the exit, retracing his steps through the hall to the distant garden. At one point he passed a servant, and the smartly dressed man flung himself against the far wall as if avoiding the path of a hunting beast. It would have made Cyrus laugh if his mood were not so dour.

He burst out the door and into the garden, thrilled for the cool air. He thought Thorda might be waiting for him, but the gazebo was empty. Cyrus collapsed onto the bench in its center, and he sucked in long, deep breaths to calm his heart.

What he had done was right.

It was just.

It was necessary.

And he still felt like shit.

The door to the mansion opened, and Cyrus glanced up. It wasn't Stasia, come to console him, nor the Coin or even Rayan. To his surprise, Keles walked the cobbled path to the gazebo. Moonlight sparkled off the gold of her dress and the ties of her braids.

"I suspect Thorda would prefer you were still in there prancing about," she said, and she gestured toward the mansion and the faint sound of music playing within. "Perhaps licking the blood off your blades. A real brutal display to open up the coin purses."

"You know of Thorda?" Cyrus asked. He adjusted the hood of his cloak to hide his face as she sat next to him. He was trying very, very hard not to stare at her. He was failing very, very hard, too. He could control his swords like a master, but apparently his eyes were beyond taming. The coloring of her makeup mesmerized him. The red and orange merged on her cheeks, then faded away as it trailed toward her mouth, only to be reapplied on her lips, a deep red mark in their center that streaked orange to yellow.

"My uncle has told me plenty, young prince."

That got his attention off her lips. A flicker of panic danced through his chest, as if he'd been caught committing a crime. He'd relied on anonymity to keep calm amid the crowd. For Keles to know...

"So I take it you're a member of Thorda's resistance, then?"

A faint hint of sadness stole some of the starlight from her dark brown eyes.

"I was. No longer. I laid down my sword and shield when Lycaena died."

Silence grew between them, but it wasn't awkward, only heavy.

"When Lycaena..." he whispered, judging the distance of years. Suddenly he hated his mask, the skull, the hiding of his sincerity. "You had to have been fighting while yet a child."

"Sixteen is old enough to wield a blade, especially when the life of your goddess is at stake. Some of us were not given the privilege of hiding while the Everlorn Empire conquered everything we loved and held dear."

Cyrus quietly accepted the rebuke. He looked to the dirt, his hood falling low over his mask. So many people, suffering and dying, while the years passed during his training. So many people relying on him to justify those sacrifices, to give life to a fading resistance.

Keles's hand settled on his shoulder.

"You haven't seen much of Vallessau, have you?" she asked, then continued without waiting for an answer. "Would you like to leave this grim party behind and see my favorite part of the city?"

He smiled behind his skull.

"Absolutely."

CHAPTER 23

CYRUS

Cyrus and Keles sat atop a tower built into the cliff face overlooking the ocean on the northern end of the docks. The moon rippled imperfectly atop the water, the stars flickering amid the deep black like a second night sky. So high up and alone, Cyrus finally pulled his mask from his face and threw off his hood. He breathed in the salty air, then ran his fingers through his hair a few times to sweep errant strands away from his mouth and eyes. The wind blew, teasing them right back in full disregard of his attempts.

"It's beautiful," he said.

"The mornings are sometimes better," Keles said. "Watching the boats coming and going can be a wonder."

Cyrus glanced at the docks. The sky shimmered red with phantom fire. A bolt shot through his spine, and he turned his gaze back to the stars before he saw burning ships.

"I prefer the night," he said.

"I do, too. It's peaceful. Quiet. Sometimes, when I'm up here, I feel like I can still hear Lycaena's whispers."

Keles loosened the strings of her black-and-gold dress a tiny bit for comfort. That it exposed much of her chest did not escape Cyrus's notice. More heat swelled in his neck. He felt so young and stupid and embarrassed. So much for being the fearsome Vagrant with a grinning skull and a silver crown. His attention turned to her intricate face paint, and its obvious allusions to the Butterfly goddess.

"Are you a paladin like your uncle?" he asked out of curiosity.

"I was deep in training to become one," she said. "But proper procedures and tests are trivial when war begins, and so my uncle declared my lessons complete, and I took up the sword and shield for Thanet. I believed, I truly believed, our god and goddess would protect us. Even after my parents were murdered, I held faith. When Endarius died, I clung to my faith even harder. This was the dark time before the glorious resurrection, I told myself. This was the pit the heroes find themselves in near the end of the stories, the final test of resolve prior to victory. We would charge the stage, save Lycaena, and then destroy the empire with a blaze of fire from her brilliant wings."

She breathed in the salty sea air and then sighed.

"Well. You were up there on that stage. You saw how it went."

That he had. The failed assault, the knives piercing the goddess's flesh, the way she'd screamed in pain and sorrow as the life bled out from her...

"It haunts my dreams still," he said. "And I wasn't close to Lycaena in worship. I can't imagine the pain of one of her paladins. I...I'm sorry, Keles. I'm sorry you ever had to suffer through something like that."

"Bold of you to apologize on behalf of an entire empire."

Cyrus was starting to believe he could never say anything correct when in the woman's presence. Acting on that belief, he fell silent and watched the waves crash far below upon the white sand shore. Perhaps Thorda should have spent a week or two teaching him how to speak and act in various social settings amid his years of training, especially if his master intended to throw him headfirst into these types of parties.

"What happened afterward?" he asked. "Did you keep fighting?"

"Afterward?" Keles laughed, with a bitterness far too heavy for her age. "I was captured trying to escape, and spent a month in a prison cell. Normally I'd have been executed, but with Lycaena's death, the Anointed One made an overture at reconciliation with her grand forsaking ceremony."

Forsaking ceremony? Cyrus had heard of no such thing while safely tucked away in Thorda's mansion. His frustrations with his master grew. First the Joining Laws, now this. What else had been kept from him?

"I'm afraid I don't know what that is," he admitted.

"The Uplifted Church sought to press upon Thanet that the war was over, and a time of healing had commenced. The forsaking ceremony was when any worshiper of Lycaena and Endarius could publicly disavow their faith and swear to never lift arms against the empire. In return, all their crimes would be forgiven. The war was over, and so, too, would its bloodshed be forgotten in a quest for unity."

Keles shook her head.

"What was I to do? Our goddess was dead. And you, the last of the royal bloodline my family swore to protect? I saw you knocked from the platform. I watched you trampled underfoot. You, Lycaena, the rebellion, our freedom; it was all dead. And so I stood before the people of this island and cast aside my faith. I was unchained, and finally free to return home. And in a cruel, twisted joke, who do I find waiting for me there but my uncle Rayan, eager to tell me of the young prince Cyrus's miraculous survival."

A hundred conflicting emotions jumbled together within Cyrus. That she should undergo such trauma, only for *his* survival to be a supposed balm? He felt pity, and guilt, and sorrow, and a formless, shapeless desire to make things better despite having not the slightest clue what the first step might even be.

"I'm sorry," he whispered.

Keles wiped her eyes, carefully with the tips of her fingers so that it would not smear the paint. If she were emotional, she kept it well hidden from her voice.

"I must admit I attended this party with an ulterior motive," she said after a time. "When my uncle told me you'd make an appearance, I knew I had to accompany him. I had to see what kind of man the missing prince had become."

Keles stared at him, and under such fierce study, he withered and looked to the Crystal Sea instead. He didn't know why he even cared, he'd just met this woman, yet he found himself agonizing over every second of her silence.

"I pray I didn't disappoint," he said when it seemed she would offer nothing to put him out of his misery.

Keles winked.

"You almost did."

"Almost?" He laughed. The tension in the air dissolved, and he was beyond thankful. "So how did I save myself? When I stumbled during my introduction? Or when I nearly exposed my face trying to eat one of those grapes the servants were handing out on their platters?"

"When you gave the soldier a sword to defend himself."

Cyrus shrugged, the mood between them darkening. So much for that easing tension.

"Maybe I wanted to humiliate him in battle before I killed him?"

"I don't believe that was the reason, and you don't believe that, either. The war isn't real to the wealthy, not even here on Thanet. Most bowed their heads, bent their knees, and promised allegiance to the Everlorn Empire the second they cut your parents down."

"They're risking their necks now by aiding us," Cyrus argued, not sure why he was defending the strangers he'd met mere hours before.

"My uncle once told me there is knowledge people carry in their heads, and there is knowledge that travels to the heart. In their heads, those lords and nobles know they are at risk. In their hearts, they believe themselves safe. Others will be fighting and dying in a war against the Everlorn Empire. They'll play at this distant game, hand over some coin, and encourage their servants and workers to join instead. That's why Thorda brought you in and gave you a victim to slaughter. It's the closest to a fight any of those spoiled silk-robes will ever see. It'll excite them. Entertain them."

"And I duly obliged," Cyrus said, still not understanding. "So why would this redeem me in your eyes?"

"Because you were angry," she said softly. "It wasn't a game to you, was it? It couldn't be. Not after Imperator Magus cut down your parents." She leaned forward, chin on her hands, and sighed at the sea. "I suppose I should apologize for doubting you. You may be a prince, but you have lost just as much as I have, if not more. You could never be like those in the crowd."

Cyrus thought of the conversation he'd eavesdropped on between

Rayan and Thorda, and of his importance as not necessarily a killer but as a symbol. Executing the enemy soldier on the stage only reinforced that understanding.

"I am exactly like those in the crowd," he said. "And that is why Thorda chose me. The Lythan name has power. I was born at the foot of a throne. My blood is recognized by those whose lives are gold and silver. If I have to play these games to free us from the Uplifted Church and its Joining Laws, then I shall play them. If I must become a monster, than I shall do that, too. I shall be both and one, Prince and Vagrant, so long as it gives the people something to believe in. If they cannot believe in Endarius and Lycaena, then let them believe in me. I accept the mantle no one else may bear."

He felt naked before her, exposed in a way he hadn't been when in the company of Thorda and his daughters. Keles stood from the tower edge. She smoothed out her dress, and he lurched to his feet to join her.

"I will never put my faith in you, Cyrus," she said. The wind blew across her, teasing the braids of her hair. "I put my faith in a goddess once. If she can die, then so can you. My days as a paladin are over, and no skull mask or outrageous promises from Thorda Ahlai will have me believe anew. Thanet belongs to the empire, and so shall it be to the end of my days. I pray I am wrong. I fear I am right."

Cyrus wanted to argue with her. He wanted to draw his swords and make grand proclamations of the imperial lives he'd take and the vengeance he'd unleash upon those who had slaughtered his family. The display would have worked in that ballroom. It would mean nothing here in the light of the stars. So instead Cyrus risked a far bolder move and reached out for her hands. She accepted the touch. He cupped her fingers in his, and it felt like he held fire. He met her gaze, and he spoke to her his honest truth.

"Then I shall hold faith for the both of us," he said. "Thanet will be free, and her people saved."

Keles smiled, and she was so beautiful, and so wounded, that he would give his life to make that smile genuine.

"I pray your faith is not rewarded like mine was, prince. Here on Thanet, far too many faiths end with execution."

CHAPTER 24

CYRUS

Cyrus and Stasia crouched behind a pair of crates stacked earlier in the day by unassuming dock workers loyal to the resistance. Now that the night was deep and the stars were aglow, the crates provided the perfect cover for the two to observe the entrance to the jail, and the lone guard stationed out front.

"This'll be too easy," Stasia whispered. "I hope they have more people inside."

"You could have gone with Paladin," Cyrus offered. "At least then you could burn down a few buildings."

Rayan was several blocks away, accompanied by six soldiers sworn to Commander Pilus. They had torches and swords, and would bring both to bear on one of the language centers the Anointed One set up to teach the imperial tongue. Though the burning would be symbolic, it was also meant to serve as a distraction, ensuring any nearby patrols rushed west and away from the docks and the dockyard prison.

"If there is anything I am not, it is a mere distraction. The fun is here, and so am I."

The moment Cyrus saw smoke float toward the starry sky, they had their signal to begin, but it would not be either of them who started the fight. Above them, dark fur camouflaged into the night, lurked Lioness. She leaped from the rooftops, a perfectly silent hunter. Her weight blasted the outside guard off his feet. Whatever scream he tried to give, it died instantly as her teeth sank into his throat. A single, hard jerk and she ripped it open entirely, spraying blood across the cobblestones.

"Heldeep take me," Cyrus muttered at the gore.

"Figured you'd be used to this by now, Vagrant," Stasia said as she rushed ahead with her twin axes readied.

"Sorry, Ax, not all of us have two decades of warfare to render us heartless killers."

"Eh, you'll get there."

Stasia blasted the door open with her shoulder, and Cyrus followed in her frenzied wake. Four men sat at a round table, scattered dice between them. Stasia went left, and so Cyrus went right, the unspoken plan between them made in an instant. The men scrambled to their feet, reaching for weapons and shouting curses, but it was over before it even began. He slashed open the nearest man's throat, a much cleaner cut than what Lioness had torn. Then he buried his off-hand blade into the next man's belly, pinning him to his chair. He hollered, blood seeping across his waist as he tried to pull it free. A thrust with Cyrus's other blade, right to the heart, put an end to that.

The other two, arguably, fared worse. Stasia buried an ax into the first man's shoulder, sinking it all the way down to crack ribs and have his arm dangle at a stomach-churning angle. While he collapsed and bled out, she faced off the lone weapon managed to be drawn, a slender dagger that couldn't hope to compete against her axes. As if insulted, she pounded him to the bloody floor, hacking open his stomach with chop after chop until he stopped squirming.

"Where are the prisoners?" Cyrus asked. A fog settled over his mind. The blood and innards, while stark and horrifying to his eyes, weren't real to him. He couldn't dwell on those details, not if he wished to keep going. Had to push it deep down and far away. Had to be like the Ax of Lahareed and the Lioness.

"I'm guessing in there," Stasia said, gesturing to the lone door leading farther into the small, squat building. After a quick check of her two kills, she rounded the table and kicked the pinned guard off his chair. The body landed with a splatter of blood. She quickly patted him down, then stood, a twinkle in her eye. No doubt she grinned behind her mask as she dangled a pair of dark iron keys.

"Hurry it up," she said, tossing Cyrus the keys. "Get them marked first, then open the cell. I'll wait for you outside."

No amount of reasoning could completely quell his distaste for the deception. There were four of them in Thorda's band of elites, but it was always the Vagrant who received credit for the work.

"Wouldn't it inspire the people better if they knew there was a group of us working together?" he had asked Thorda after their first few missions. "Maybe even convince them we are the start of an army?"

"I don't want them to trust groups and armies," his master had explained. "I want them to see what one lone man can do, and then imagine what an army with you at the helm might accomplish."

And so despite half the corpses belonging to Stasia's axes, Cyrus walked from body to body, carving a bloody crown across their foreheads. That done, he opened the wooden door to the interior and entered. It was a small jail, built to handle drunkards and the occasional thief. Nine men and five women were crammed within, forced to stand shoulder to shoulder. They startled at his arrival, but their fear and shock did not last long. Something new replaced it, something Cyrus was steadily growing familiar with.

"The Vagrant," a man at the front said. He was missing a hand, and he pressed the stump of his wrist through a gap in the bars. Seeking to touch him. To receive affirmation. "You're real."

"Very real," Cyrus said. He pressed the key into the lock. "And your guards are very dead. Follow me."

A trio of soldiers under Pilus's command waited in the street outside the dockyard jail. They ushered the fourteen to hurry, throwing cloaks and coats over them for both warmth and disguise. Safehouses were already set up for them, but first they had to get there. Cyrus lurked nearby, weapons still drawn. Thorda would like that, he knew. Let the people see the blood on his blades, feel the deadly gaze of the watchful killer.

Only one other member of Thorda's group was allowed to share in the Vagrant's adulation, and she roared from her rooftop perch above the jail and spread wide the jagged bones of her wings.

"Be free," Mari told them through the magic of her word–lace. "Be strong."

Already shaken by the sight of the Vagrant, several burst into tears, and one fell to his knees to prostrate himself before her.

"Up, up, pray later," one of Pilus's soldiers said as he forced the man back to his feet. The group hurried away, following a preplanned path that would take them to a safehouse half a mile away. It was only when they were gone that Stasia emerged from around the corner, her arms crossed and her axes buckled at her hips.

"Dead imperials, and fourteen lives saved from the flags. Not a bad night, I'd say."

"I'll still be happy to crawl into bed," Cyrus said, but to his surprise, she shook her head.

"Got one more task. Sorry. Bedtime will have to wait."

She gestured for him to follow, and he reluctantly did so. Mari bounded over within moments, making hardly a sound on her padded feet.

"I will await you there," her word–lace translated after a growl. She raced ahead, easily outpacing the other two with her feline speed.

"So what now?" he asked.

"This mission's a surprise."

"You and your father love your surprises, don't you?"

Stasia winked at him.

"You'll like this one, I promise."

They traveled deep down into the city, to the poorest stretches located near the docks, where guard patrols were few. Their destination was once a confectionary. Based on the half-broken sign and the boards over the windows, it had been months since it last opened for business. The faintest hint of candlelight shone through gaps in the boards. Stasia pressed against the wall beside the entrance, and she gestured for Cyrus to take the opposite side.

"On your lead," she whispered. Cyrus nodded, lifted his swords, and then smashed in the door with his shoulder leading. He barreled inside to find it well lit with dozens of candles across shelves and tables. Waiting for him at one such table, their faces a mixture of surprise and amusement, sat Thorda and Clarissa. His master wore an expensive green-and-gold robe from his homeland, and Clarissa, though less fanciful than during the clandestine meetings in ballrooms and mansions, was still radiant in a frilled, long-sleeved shirt and crimson skirt.

"Is something amiss?" Cyrus asked as he removed his mask.

"I have been a poor caretaker," Thorda explained. "But tonight we celebrate an occasion I neglected to properly mark the past few years."

Cyrus glanced between him and Clarissa, confused.

"Which is...?"

Mari answered by coming down the stairs, having changed into a simple blue dress. She carried an enormous silver plate in her arms, stacked high with honey cakes.

"Happy nineteenth naming-day!" she called. "I baked these myself."

"And spent a fortune on the jarred honey in the process," Thorda said, but his ire was entirely false.

Cyrus's confusion melted into amusement. Gods help him, they were right. He'd forgotten completely, for the previous two birthdays while training with Thorda had come and gone with nary a mention at the mansion. Stasia smacked him on the shoulder as she followed him inside, her grin so smugly satisfied, it bordered on the profane.

"A party after a jailbreak?" he asked her as the two of them stashed their weapons by the door. "Isn't that a bit, I don't know, morbid?"

Stasia laughed as she swept Clarissa into her arms and set her on her lap as they shared a chair.

"We could have had the party *before* the jailbreak, but I worried you'd be nervous and distracted."

Cyrus took a seat opposite Thorda but had hardly a moment to settle down before the door opened. He turned to find Rayan and Keles come together to join the celebration, the paladin in his platemail, Keles with her hair back and a black dress laced with gold underneath the heavy coat she wore to hide it on her journey there.

"Excellent," Rayan said as he unbuckled his sword belt and rested the weapon beside the door. "I see we are not late for the festivities."

"Just starting, actually," Mari said, and she gently lifted one of the honey cakes. "Come, try, but only after Cyrus tries one first. It's his special day, after all. Or night. Close enough."

The smell of the cakes, and the golden brown layer of honey baked across their surfaces, kicked off a rumble in Cyrus's belly.

"If you insist," he said, and he took one in hand, careful to cup his fingers to catch the falling crumbs. It was as delicious as he could hope for. He offered a silent prayer of gratitude that the pile was so high upon the plate as he tore into them. He had already finished his second before Rayan could cross the room to take his first.

"Spare some room for the drink, too," Thorda said as he fetched glasses and bottles of both wine and beer from a wall cabinet. "You may not be much for it, but others present are."

Everyone gathered at the table, and conversation flowed easily among the group. Mari in particular radiated happiness at how much everyone loved her cooking, to the point of blushing.

"Uh, Mari," Cyrus said, noticing a small red splotch near the left side of her mouth. He pointed at his own to show her. "You've got something on your face."

Mari wiped at it, then shrugged.

"Just blood," she said. "Every now and then some remains on me after I revert."

That she so easily dismissed the lingering blood of a soldier she had torn apart with her teeth only confirmed to Cyrus his long-held suspicion: Appearances and temperament aside, Mari was easily the most terrifying of the Ahlai family.

The alcohol flowed, and the pile of cakes dwindled down to a burnt few Mari had hidden at the bottom of the plate beneath the much more presentable ones. Cyrus stuffed himself, unable to remember the last time he'd had any such dessert. Though he could afford it all and more, Thorda ordered his cooks to provide meals meant to be hearty and filling, but not necessarily sweet to the tooth.

After the food was eaten and the cups ran low, Thorda clapped his hands twice to gain everyone's attention. To Cyrus's shock, he actually looked a little nervous and embarrassed. It was an expression entirely foreign to the older man's face.

"I believe the giving of gifts on a naming-day is also a tradition here," he said. "As such, I have picked one I think you will enjoy."

Thorda lifted up a large book hidden beneath the table. Cyrus accepted it, and his fingers brushed the front cover.

"Fables?" he asked. The book was old leather, and finely embroidered. The pale brown paper crackled as he flipped through the pages, each one dense with writing that moved and shaped itself about dozens of ink illustrations. He saw the island's two gods often among them, but there were others, goats and sheep, foxes in a forest, women with bows atop horses and men with axes fighting curled serpents.

"You have read much of my library," Thorda explained. "But I feel it appropriate you learn more of your own history and culture. You not only fight to protect what the empire would take, but to remember what the priests would have you forget."

Cyrus closed the book, eager to read through the pages but knowing doing so in the middle of his own party was hardly polite.

"You spoil me with gifts and cakes," he told those in attendance. His grin narrowed at nearby Stasia, busy wolfing down the final three cakes like a woman on a mission. "Though it seems you also spoil yourselves, too."

"Damn straight," Stasia said as she crammed the last honey cake into her mouth. "I'd say we deserve it for dragging your ass around."

"I suppose I could make your job easier by leaving entirely. How is that for a plan?"

Stasia socked him in the shoulder.

"Stop acting like you don't deserve some fun. I couldn't get rid of you even if I wanted to. You're the little brother I never wanted."

Cyrus smiled to hide the kick to his gut. He looked across the ramshackle confectionary, to Thorda and Mari, Clarissa and Stasia, Rayan and Keles. They were his comrades in arms, men and women who had trained and molded him in a quest to retake a throne. But over the years, he had seen their time together, however pleasant, as an obligation. He was a goal to achieve, and little more. That they would do so willingly? That they were his friends, and actively desired his companionship beyond the fighting?

That they would consider him family?

"Thank you," he said. He clutched the book of fables to his chest and fought back a sudden wave of emotions. All eyes were upon him, but this was so different from when he was paraded about elegant ball-rooms. His pulse did not race, and his panic did not rise. He wore no mask, and here, he recognized every face. He did not wish to hide from them, for there was nothing at all to hide. "I'm so lucky for each and every one of you."

Mari clapped excitedly, and he was thankful her joy masked over any awkwardness of his emotional gratitude.

"We have the eating and the drinking," she said, turning to Rayan. "But I believe we are missing the third key pillar of a proper gathering, and that is the dancing."

"Did you prepare me a lute as I requested?"

In answer, she pointed to the far corner, where a lute lay unnoticed and untouched atop a chair.

"I am not one to miss a detail," Mari said, and she winked. "Especially when it comes to a gathering of friendly company."

The paladin squeezed Keles's hand, then rose from his chair and crossed the room.

"It has been a few years," he said as he lifted the lute and glanced over the finely made instrument. "I pray my fingers remember their way."

The paladin began to play, scattered and slow at first, but gradually steadying out the rhythm. His hand strummed, and as the deep hum of the strings filled the room, Rayan started to stomp with his right foot, a second instrument in its own right upon the hardwood floor. He did not sing, only hum, a perfect accompaniment.

The music pulled at Cyrus's chest, and he was hardly alone. Stasia was the first on her feet, and she dragged a playfully protesting Clarissa up with her. The two pushed the other table to the wall, clearing up space. It took only a moment of Mari badgering her father to convince him to dance along with her. Cyrus tapped his own feet along to the rhythm, and then Keles stood. His heart skipped, and he immediately chastised himself for making assumptions.

Assumptions that proved true when she offered him her hand.

"Come, prince, I would not have us the only ones seated."

"Me?" Cyrus asked, feeling stupid the moment the word left his mouth.

"Do you see anyone else my age to dance with?"

He took her hand and stood, then accepted her other so they were a foot apart. Her touch sent lightning coursing up his arms. His throat constricted so words became difficult. She swayed softly a moment, watching, until he realized she was waiting for him to take the lead.

"Sorry," he said. "I'm not sure how."

"You know how to kill but not how to dance?"

A bitter retort rose and then died on Cyrus's tongue. He had been learning how, for a young prince was expected to know his way about a ballroom. Such training had halted when the empire arrived. The Usurper King had only needed his obedient presence. There was no need for him to dance, or sing, or enjoy pleasant company.

"Haven't had much time to learn," he said, leaving all else unspoken.

"Your priorities are poor, but what should I expect from our ruthless, otherworldly Vagrant? Follow my lead, then."

She stepped back, hips twisting slightly, and at that pull he shifted closer, mirroring the movement. A quick dip caught him off guard, and her hip bumped his as he failed to turn along with her. Her amusement grew with his frustration. Again her hip bumped into his, this time not an accident. Their fingers tightened. His face flushed red. They were the slowest of the dancers, yet they also best matched the pace of the song, an issue in which Stasia took particular offense.

"Faster, old man," she called to Rayan. "This is a party, not a dirge."

"Mark my words, woman, your bones will be old one day. Let us see how quickly you dance then."

Yet he stomped his foot harder, and his fingers began to rapidly flow across the four strings.

Cyrus recognized neither of the other pairs' dances. Mari and Thorda used simple movements, a back-and-forth that focused on the feet and an up-and-down rotation of the hands. It reminded Cyrus a bit of a dance he'd seen once at a farmyard festival his father had taken him to when he was nine, all the way at the southern tip of Thanet. Stasia and Clarissa, meanwhile, pressed against each other, hips to hips, chest to chest, in a manner that almost felt lewd if not for the sheer joy both expressed at each other's company. As for his own pairing, he and Keles moved in the circular patterns of a ballroom, albeit at a slightly faster tempo.

"You're picking this up quickly," Keles said. "Perhaps you are not so hopeless after all."

"Must you mock me at every turn?" His grin stretched ear to ear. "Give me time. Perhaps I can turn the Vagrant into a god of both killing *and* dancing."

"May the Lion and Butterfly spare Thanet such a dire fate."

Her left hand rose so he might carefully guide her through an exaggeratedly slow twirl. Before he might finish it, Stasia broke from Clarissa and descended upon their duo like a hurricane.

"It's not dancing if you aren't putting effort into it," she said as she slid between him and Keles. She grabbed Cyrus by the hands, her motions jolting instead of gliding, her sway wild yet purposeful. Her laugh was infectious, and he found himself imitating the back-and-forth movement of her hips as best he could.

"You dance exactly as you fight," Cyrus said. "Like a crazy person."

To punish such audacity, she yanked him close enough so they pressed chest to chest. Her arms rose, and they swirled in a circle, noses almost touching, the room a blur, their feet twirling to maintain balance. Her red eyes enveloped him, her mischievous smile a delight.

"Have some confidence," she said, her voice low. "Not all women will wait forever."

Before Cyrus could ask what she meant, Stasia separated with an exaggerated flourish, her arm rising high and extending so that she practically flung him like a top away from her and next into Clarissa's arms.

"I know, she's exhausting," the tiny woman said, expertly catching Cyrus's hands and pulling him into a similar dance as if this were a practiced occurrence. "Even if I love her for it."

"You should train with her sometime if you want to see exhausting," he said, and they shared a laugh. From the corner of his eye he caught Stasia whispering something into Keles's ear, and his curiosity soared to unbearable heights.

"Good luck to the both of us then," Clarissa said, and then twirled him away from her, albeit with far less impressive strength than Stasia. Cyrus went along nonetheless, playful on his feet until returning to Keles's embrace. She caught him and held him until he steadied. They parted, but not quite so far as before. Fingers re-entwined. Without warning she guided his left hand to the small of her back, and her thin shirt meant little to his touch. He felt the smoothness of her skin, and the tightness of her muscles.

"It *is* your birthday, as Stasia so eloquently reminded me," she said, as if she could read his every thought. "Or naming-day, as the Miquoans seem to call it."

Her smile melted his insides. Back and forth, ever closer, her presence lightning, her brown eyes a smoldering fire. His heart firmly lodged itself in his throat.

"I was quite content with just a book," he said.

"Perhaps you were not the one who needed this?" Her forehead leaned upon his chest, and she slowly exhaled. "To dance with a prince. I dreamed of this once."

Cyrus slowed to a gentle sway. In the corner, it seemed Rayan noticed, and despite Stasia's glare, he similarly lessened the tempo of his playing.

"Was the dance hall so drab and poorly lit?" Cyrus asked.

"The floor was white marble, the walls gold, and the set of guests far more dignified." She put her own hand about his waist. "But we make do with what the world gives us."

The song ended, and a new one began. Rayan's boots stomped harder, and it seemed the Ahlai sisters recognized it, for they both loudly sang along. The intimate moment passed, but Cyrus was grateful for it nonetheless. Despite not knowing the words, he attempted to join in, and Keles's grimace at his lack of skill only made him belt it out louder. His joy could not be contained. Years of weight fell off his shoulders, sudden and freeing. In this dark, crowded little confectionary, he would change nothing. The late hours slipped away, each one a gift.

This was perfect. This was home. Here. Now. Eating, laughing, and dancing the night away with the family he entrusted with his life.

CHAPTER 25

MAGUS

Magus of Eldrid stood before the entrance to the jail. Soldiers scoured the premise, but they investigated what Magus had already confirmed. Dead guards. Vanished prisoners. The Imperator lifted the note he'd received earlier that night, somehow smuggled into his bedroom without anyone noticing. He ignored the large, blocky lettering in Thanese to instead read his Signifer's translation.

Come to the dockyard jail. Find it empty. Let this be my proof of trustworthiness. Await my next orders if you would claim the Vagrant's head with your blade.

Magus rested his hand upon the hilt of his sheathed sword, and he drummed his fingers across its gold surface. No evidence remained at the jail, just corpses cut with a far-too-familiar crown of blood. His own informants had unearthed nothing. Sinshei's confessionals heard only the mildest of admiration for the mysterious killer making a name for himself within Vallessau. The bastard had nearly killed Regent Gold-leaf, and could have murdered his son if he'd felt so inclined. He was nothing but trouble, and what Magus wouldn't give for a face-to-face confrontation, and to crush the bastard beneath his shield.

"What game are you playing at, little spy?" he wondered aloud before returning to the castle for a proper night's rest. Until the Vagrant made a mistake, it seemed waiting would be his only recourse.

CHAPTER 26

SINSHEI

The wide courtyard atop the capital hill sported several amenities for the royal family, and it was to its archery range Sinshei traveled in search of Regent Gordian Goldleaf. She arrived just in time to see him loose an arrow, and presumably his aim was perfect, for the arrow sank directly into the eye of an old woman bound to a wooden stake thirty yards out. Two soldiers rushed to untie her dead body, while two more dragged a bound-and-gagged man from a small procession waiting alongside the castle wall out of sight.

"A fine shot," Sinshei said as she stood to his right.

"The movements keep it interesting," Gordian said as he reached into his quiver. "Real targets in battle don't sit still."

He was trying to sound calm, and failing miserably. The attack on his family had unnerved the regent severely. The cynical side of Sinshei wished to remind Gordian he had never fought in battle, and likely never would, given the wealth and prestige of his Goldleaf family name. But she had come to the archery range seeking to make allies, not enemies, so instead she gestured in the direction of the prisoners.

"Who are they?" she asked, as if she didn't already know the answer.

Gordian pulled back the string and sighted another arrow.

"Heretics. Criminals. Maybe the homeless. Does it matter?"

The arrow sank into the old man's chest with a meaty thunk. His body sagged, his pained scream muffled by his gag.

"Only a few such crimes deserve execution," she said.

"I decide what they deserve, and right now, each and every last native of Thanet deserves a coffin at the bottom of the ocean."

A wave of Gordian's hand, and the soldiers rushed about, dragging the corpse to a growing pile while preparing the next target. Sinshei purposefully refused to watch. She found this whole display shameful. Heretics and insurgents these people may be, but their punishments were given for a purpose. Lesser crimes meant chopped fingers, branding tattoos, or the loss of an eye. The worst were given the spectacle of a public hanging. All of it bore the hope that the suffering and loss of the few would lead to the conversion of the many. When it came to the end goal of eternal salvation, no tactic was too cruel. This, however, was nothing more than an elaborate tantrum.

"I heard what happened," she said, hoping conversation would halt the arrows. "I come to offer my sympathies."

"It wasn't your soldiers and paragons that let an assassin slip into my castle."

A point she was pleased to hear him verbalize, not that she'd so casually admit it. The regent pulled back the string as he sighted his current target, a teenaged girl with a darker shade of skin common to families along the northern reaches of the island.

"My son," Gordian seethed. His entire body vibrated with his anger. "That shit-eating masked murderer threatened *my son*. If I hadn't arrived when I did, if I hadn't shown up to give him a better target, then he might...he might..."

His arrow sailed wide. It plinked off the wooden stake the girl was bound to, the arrow shaft splitting in half with an audible snap.

"Piss!" he screamed, and flung aside his bow. Sinshei stood perfectly still, her face as calm as a painting as the regent drew a knife strapped to his hip. He crossed the gap at a brisk pace, his teeth bared from his clenched jaw. The moment he reached his target, he rammed the dagger into her stomach. Blood poured across his hands, and the gag was meaningless against her shriek of pain. Again and again the regent tore into her, punctuating each thrust into her guts with a frustrated curse.

"Lucavi! Damn! Every! One!"

He spat on her when he'd finished, then flung the bloody knife into the dirt.

"Get rid of the rest," he said to his soldiers guarding the waiting line of prisoners. "I'm done with my practice."

Sinshei did not hide her disgust. The girl was still alive, and still screaming in pain.

"God bless and keep me," she prayed, the power of her faith swelling within her breast. She felt it keenly, light and fire and a killing edge to punish the nonbelievers. Her hands rose, palms to the heavens. A divine sword shimmered into existence before her, wielded by her own mind. A single thought, and it swung sideways, opening the bound girl's throat and ending her scream. That matter finished, she dismissed the blade and turned to the tantrum-throwing regent. She failed to drain the venom from her voice when she spoke.

"A regent should show far better restraint when dealing with the difficulties of rule."

"The difficulties of rule?" Gordian picked up his discarded bow and tossed it to a servant patiently waiting nearby. "I am used to the difficulties of rule. I know the people call me usurper and burn effigies, and I'm sure half of Vallessau fantasizes about cutting off my head. What I am not prepared for, and what I refuse to ever accept, is being hunted and attacked in my *own damn castle.*"

Sinshei let the outburst hang a moment in the air before addressing the others nearby.

"All of you, leave. I would have words with Thanet's regent."

Servants and soldiers alike hurried to obey. Leaving the regent unguarded after an assassination attempt might seem unwise, but Sinshei had her magic, and despite the outlandish stories of what this Vagrant could do, she trusted in her abilities to keep them safe.

"Why are you here, Sinshei?" Gordian asked once they were alone in the archery range. "It's not to apologize for Magus's errors; of that, I'm certain. You'd rather burn yourself alive than accept any blame meant for his direction. So what is it?"

Sinshei slowly breathed in and out, disguising the act with a soft smile.

Though Thanet was her first appointment as an Anointed One, it was not her first invasion. Prior to crossing the Crystal Sea, she had helped in the religious conversion of Onleda, and their transition from worshiping their trinity of gods to the God-Incarnate. Twice their regent, a charming man named Arlo, had ventured out into the crowds during full-blown riots to address their concerns. He had worked tirelessly to convince the people of the benefits of imperial rule. Along with faith in the God-Incarnate came an abundance of trade, as well as funds to rebuild Onleda and repair the damages suffered during its conquering.

But the empire had cared about Onleda, and meant to see her prosper upon Gadir for centuries to come. Thanet had no such future. And so Gordian Goldleaf, charming on the outside, rotten on the inside, had come to oversee its conquering instead. She hated the man, but he trusted her, even lusted after her. She saw the way his eyes lingered. She noticed how he had stopped mentioning his wife whenever they were together. Sinshei had fed those desires in return, always little by little, a smile here, a laugh there, a lingering touch of the hand that could mean nothing and could mean everything.

If Sinshei was to wrest control of Thanet from Imperator Magus, she would need a regent in her pocket. At long last, the docks had brought her method of securing that loyalty.

"A new wave of boats arrived from Gadir this morning," she said.

Gordian straightened, and he inhaled sharply.

"The Seeds," he asked. "Are they finally here?"

Her sweet smile grew.

"They are. I have already begun the preparations. You need only commit yourself to the cause, and I can give you the strength and swiftness of our beloved God-Incarnate's most cherished and faithful paragons."

A shadow fell across the regent's face, but there was no denying the excitement in his words, nor the lustful gleam in his eye.

"Are you sure this is wise?" he asked. "I haven't undergone any of the paragon training. What if I do not survive the change?"

Sinshei dared not react beyond a confident smile. Of course Gordian would reveal his doubts now, months after the plan was set in motion.

The wealthy man was used to power being given to him, and never at any cost to himself. Yet the strength, speed, and extended life of a paragon was an overwhelming temptation he could not resist, regardless of the inherent risks. Sinshei slid closer to him, and she burdened him with yet one more temptation to weaken his already soft will.

"I will be there with you each and every step of the way," she purred. "Your life will be in my hands, ever safe and secure."

Gordian swallowed down a heavy knot in his throat. His gaze had grown distant. He was imagining things. Power. Strength. Or perhaps, even her?

"Does Magus know?" he asked.

Sinshei shook her head. Conducting the paragon ritual anywhere other than at the capital of Eldrid, and on someone not approved by the ruling masters of the Bloodstone, was highly unorthodox, if not outright blasphemous. Yet they were so far from Gadir, and she had her blood connection to the God-Incarnate. Rules could be bent. Eyes could look the other way. Besides, if things on Thanet went as planned, it didn't matter what Magus thought. He'd be dead.

"He will know only when it is too late to halt matters lest he risk alienating my magistrates and priests," Sinshei said. "And how will he deny you the right to protect your family after the Vagrant nearly took the life of your son?"

She let her voice dip and her smile vanish. It was only the two of them here, sharing secrets and mutual understandings. Her whisper was full of promises.

"You won't be at their mercy ever again. You'll never need Magus and his paragons to protect you. By your own hands, you will bear the strength to rule Thanet as it must be ruled. For this gift, you need only the courage to open your heart and accept it."

For a long while the handsome man stared at her, no doubt attempting to decipher her true intentions. Sinshei held not a shred of fear he would succeed. She had grown up in the courts of Eldrid as one of the God-Incarnate's daughters. She had walked amid secrets and plots since the moment she took her first steps.

"And once I am a paragon, we won't need to fear anyone," he said, carefully choosing his every word. "We won't need to listen to the Imperator, not after all his failures. The church and the royal court shall hold mutual sway. We will rule Thanet, you and I, together."

Just one word, but a hundred promises within it, and a thousand fantasies the wealthy man had no doubt entertained over the past four years.

"Together," she said.

Gordian lifted his hands, still wet with the blood from the girl he'd butchered.

"I will never be helpless before these wretched people again," he said. "The ritual cannot come soon enough. What must I do, Anointed One?"

"When the moon is at its zenith, you must only accept the sacrifice of the faithful. Have no fear. Come the appointed hour, it shall be my hand that holds the dagger."

CHAPTER 27

ARN

It seemed every single man and woman on that caravel piled onto the deck to gawk at the approaching island and its capital city of Vallessau. Arn kept away, content to let the shorter folks crowd the railing. With his arms crossed and his back leaning against the mast, he took in the distant docks, the houses steadily rising up higher and higher in a vague U-shape around the inlet. Arn was disappointed by how normal it looked. He'd hoped the buildings would be weird and exotic, reminiscent of the stories of far-flung places such as Miquo and Lahareed. Instead, they seemed remarkably commonplace, their lower foundations muddy bricks and their walls cut from pine. Hardly much different than the homes he'd passed by every day of his life back on Gadir.

"Praise the God-Incarnate for such a safe and swift voyage," said Jarvis in front of him, and others echoed his thoughts. Arn felt a need to throw up a little in his mouth. He turned away, a nameless worry scratching at his insides. Everyone was on deck to watch the landing. Everyone, but...

Telling himself it meant nothing, Arn descended the stairs to the lower decks of the massive caravel. He patted his pocket, found it empty. He so badly wished his charm was with him. He usually went nowhere without it, but constant proximity to Lendsy and the acolytes had made him stash it away. Stupid. Should have kept it close.

Arn slowed at the door to his cabin. It was already cracked. He pushed it open the rest of the way, the creak of metal and wood announcing his presence to the trespasser in his room. Paragon Lendsy sat on the bottom bunk, Arn's tiny chest of belongings resting beside him on the bed. Its contents were splayed out atop the sheets, mostly changes in clothes and some silver and bronze imperial coins. His secret charm remained still inside, its purpose apparently unnoticed by the paragon. The danger came from two separate objects: the word-lace lying on the bed and the enormous gauntlets Lendsy cradled in his lap.

"A word-lace for a simple builder?" he asked, not even looking at the silver and sapphire string of magic.

"Family heirloom," Arn lied.

"Is that the same lie you plan to tell about these gauntlets?" Lendsy lifted a gauntlet higher and squinted in the poor light. "Such craftsmanship. Exquisite, truly exquisite. Ahlai-made, is it not?"

"So I've heard," Arn said, pretending at calm. He stood in the doorway, blocking the exit. "Never cared much for such things."

"But you should, and I can confirm the authenticity." The paragon flipped the gauntlet, and he pointed to a small marking carved at the base near the wrist. "This is his symbol, rarely advertised, but always present. It wasn't just his company that made this, but Thorda himself. They'd fetch an exorbitant price at any market, but that isn't their only blessing."

He put the metal to his lips and closed his eyes. Arn tensed the muscles in his legs. He almost attacked then and there, but he couldn't shake the feeling he was being baited.

"I can feel the faith imbued within," Lendsy said. He opened his eyes. "How many hours did our acolytes pray over this pair, I wonder? How many tears did they weep upon the leather? How much blood did they spill upon the iron?"

"You're imagining things," Arn said. "They're a fine pair of gauntlets I bought on the cheap, that's all."

"You are a poor liar," Lendsy said. "I wouldn't believe you even if I didn't sense the prayers of the faithful imbuing the metal with strength beyond measure. No market would dare sell these, not even the underground traders who scurry beneath our noses like rats. These are the weapons of a paragon."

Arn closed his hands into fists. Up above, excited shouts celebrated the approaching docks of Vallessau.

"For your own sake, put them back, and pretend you never saw them," he said. "I'm warning you."

"I knew it from the first moment I met you," Lendsy said, ignoring the threat. "Forget your size and strength, Meffrit, assuming that is your true name. An aura radiates about you. It is the gift of the God-Incarnate, though it is weak. Gray. I tried to pry out the reason, but you kept your heart locked tightly shut. A shame I could not break it open as I did this chest. You abandoned your faith. You lost your way. Now you come to Thanet. Why?"

Lendsy's sword remained on his back. It was much too tight quarters for him to swing it anyway. Arn's heart hammered in his chest. It would be strength against strength. He couldn't hope for better.

"I found a better way," Arn said softly. "A chance to redeem myself from the path I once walked."

"Redeem? Whatever acts you performed in the name of our God-Incarnate, there is no sin among them. There is no need for redemption. Are we not but little reflections of our maker, who share in his perfection?"

"Perfection?" Arn shook his head. "We are far from perfect, and so is he."

Lendsy lowered the gauntlets into the chest and rose from the bed. He showed no anger when he turned to face Arn, only sadness.

"Then you have lost yourself to heresy and doubt. We paragons . . . we may be humanity perfected, but that does not mean the road we walk will be easy. Always, there are trials. Always, there are struggles. But that isn't reason to forgo your faith! Would you insult the lives sacrificed to make you what you are? You've heard the prayers of those acolytes over these past months. You've heard their joy, and their pride in their roles. How can you stand in the presence of that faith and consider yourself anything but the purest—"

To kill a paragon took far more than a regular human. Body blows would never do it. Ruptured organs could heal through the most egregious of wounds. Arn had witnessed a fellow paragon survive a knife to the heart. But one thing always worked, and that was a broken spine. Before Lendsy could move, Arn's biceps were latched about his neck. The muscles in his arms bulged, and his jaw clenched as he steeled every part of his body. Lendsy thrashed as his face turned red. His elbows blasted into Arn's stomach with force to dent platemail. It wouldn't be enough to break that grasp. Arn's arms twisted, back and forth in savage, wrenching motions. Once. Their bodies smashed into the bed. Twice. Lendsy rammed the both of them into the wall, a choked groan escaping him.

The snap came with the third. The paragon's body fell limp, a heap of muscle and bone and loosening bowels and drooling blood from lips rapidly turning blue. Arn stared at it for a moment, ensuring the death was no act while he recovered from the struggle. Once he regained his breath, he packed his belongings and exited the room. If only he were clever enough to engineer a way to wedge the door shut from the outside. He shifted his chest of personal belongings underneath his armpit, then hurried to the deck. Half the caravel's passengers had already debarked, the rest forming lines in front of the gangplanks. A quick glance around confirmed the ten Seeds missing, likely among the first allowed into the city.

"Damn it," he muttered, even though he doubted any gods of Thanet remained to damn anything or anyone. "Damn it all to darkness."

He retucked the chest under his arm so it was more comfortable and then strolled down the gangplank as if nothing were amiss. The various passengers lined up for inspection at the head of the docks. There were two lines, and after giving a glance at the men at their heads, he chose the left. Arn shuffled his weight from foot to foot, all the while dreading the cries of surprise from within the boat. During the hubbub of docking and disembarking, everyone's attention would be on the outside, or on the cargo holds deep below. Still, a bit of bad luck, and a single crew member checking all cabins to ensure they were empty . . .

"Next," said the pale man with an eyepatch.

"Meffrit Mason," Arn said as he stepped up.

"Purpose for visit?"

"Brought in as a builder for a new temple."

The man with the eyepatch peered up at him from his docket.

"The church brought a builder all the way from the mainland? Surely there were locals who could be more convenient."

Arn gave an exaggerated shrug.

"Don't know who gave the order. Might be your Anointed here, might be some magistrate. My guild master says I go, and so I go. Is it really so strange? I wouldn't trust these islanders with building something like a church. Not if I wanted the walls to remain standing longer than a few winters."

It sickened Arn's stomach how easy it was to bring the man onto his side, but he had participated in many invasions. He knew the attitude of an imperialist toward native populations. A knowing smile crossed the inspector's face, and he chuckled as he marked something down on his ledger.

"Indeed, indeed. I suppose if you have the coin, you might as well spend it on the best instead of relying on the inferior. Almost done, then." He pointed his pencil at the chest tucked underneath Arn's arm. "What have you there?"

"Just some clothes and personal effects," Arn said. Thorda's instructions had made it clear to use this specific inspector's line, and for a very particular reason. He pulled out a finely minted gold coin from the capital in Eldrid. "Nothing worth the hassle to look over, am I right?"

"I'll mark it down," the inspector said as he pocketed the coin. He didn't even try to hide taking it, which impressed Arn in a way, knowing the corruption was so widely accepted. That, or the inspector thought it better to take the bribe than risk landing on the church's bad side. "Try to enjoy your stay, Meffrit, but avoid any dark alleys once night falls. The population has proven...stubborn, in its conversion."

"Don't worry about me," Arn said, and he struggled to hold back a darkly amused grin. "My knuckles are used to having a bit of blood on them."

Once free of the docks, Arn slipped his word-lace over his neck and began checking names on roads. He had memorized his instructions before climbing aboard his caravel, for keeping the scrap of paper from Thorda on his person was much too risky. On it were a series of street names, informing him where to turn and ending with a single number. Arn followed them, hands shoved into his pockets and his head down to avoid catching any stranger's eye. In less than ten minutes, he arrived.

Such an unassuming two-story house hardly seemed the proper headquarters for a mastermind of a half-dozen insurgences, but Arn hardly looked like the average resistance fighter, either. He knocked on the door hard enough to make the hinges rattle. Not good. Using such excess strength showed he was nervous. He took in a long deep breath and counted backward from ten. On four, the door opened, and an elderly Miquoan stepped out to greet him. His arms folded over his chest, and his scowl could churn butter.

"What is it?" he asked.

"Arn Bastell, heretical paragon of the Everlorn Empire," Arn proudly declared. "I believe you requested my presence in this far-flung corner of the Crystal Sea?"

The hint of a smile cracked the older man's leathery features.

"That I did. Come in, Arn. I've been most eager to meet with you since the first letter from Onleda reached my domicile."

The home may not have seemed special from the outside, but inside was finely furnished and belied Thorda's obscene wealth. Arn passed through the entryway to a den with a roaring fireplace. Couches and chairs were spaced about a small table in the center. Arn plopped into a chair that groaned in its struggle to handle his weight. A frown crossed his lips.

"Is something amiss?" Thorda asked.

"Amiss? Nah. Missing? Yeah. Whatever your strongest drink is, I want it, and then I want your second strongest to wash it down with."

"I will see what I have."

Thorda exited to the next room. Arn used the absence to close his eyes and steady his breathing. The ground quivered beneath him, and his stomach, normally solid as iron, fluttered like a frightened animal.

It was only three months, he told himself. *Real sailors spend almost a year at sea. You can handle this.*

Three others silently joined him in the den, a young man and two women, and they said nothing as they took their seats. They were concerned about his presence, not that he blamed them. He probably stank like a pigsty, and there was little hiding his paragon background. In return, he eyed the three, judging their abilities. The taller of the two women seemed promising, her body well honed with muscle. The shorter and stockier woman struck Arn as someone belonging more in a kitchen than on a battlefield. Their dark brown hair matched Thorda's, and he held little doubt they were sisters. As for the boy, if he was out of his teens, it was only barely. At least he had some muscle on him. He could perhaps be useful if he knew how to swing a sword.

Thorda returned carrying two bottles. He set both on the table before Arn and then turned to address the others.

"Everyone, meet Arn Bastell, a former paragon turned traitor, and the last key member of our band. Arn, this is Prince Cyrus, my older daughter Stasia, and my younger daughter Mari."

Arn did a poor job of hiding his disappointment.

"So is this the elite gang of rebels I heard so much about?" Arn asked. "Two girls and a young brat? Consider me unimpressed. Hells, that one looks like she couldn't run a mile, let alone fight an empire."

"Watch your tongue," Thorda snapped. "You speak ill of my daughters. Each can count paragons among their victims."

"Fine, fine, forgive me. Can I speak ill of the brat, at least? When your allies sent me packing on a boat, I was told Thanet would have a legendary killer uniting the populace. That whelp over there barely finished learning how to wipe his own ass."

Cyrus glanced at his master. His eyebrow arched.

"Are you sure we need him?"

"Quite sure," Thorda said. "Though my confidence falters with each passing moment."

Arn twisted the cork off the bottle and then tossed it over his shoulder. When he lifted the bottle to his nose, he smelled honey and lavender. Interesting. Had Thorda brought it with him from the mainland?

"Sorry, it's been a long few months, and my arrival here wasn't much fun." It was the best apology he'd give the group. "Let me make it up to you with a bit of news. I had some interesting passengers with me on my trip. Ten Seeds, all eager and ready to give their lives in service of the Everlorn Empire. I'm shocked the weight of their faith didn't sink our boat beneath the waves."

The local boy showed only confusion, but the three members of the Ahlai family reacted much more appropriately: with worry and confusion.

"You believe they're here for a ritual?" Thorda asked.

"That I do."

"What ritual?" asked the young prince. "Could someone catch me up, please?"

"There is power in faith and belief," Thorda explained. "That power gives glow to the blades of Lycaena's paladins, it creates the divine swords of the empire's priests, and gives rise to the gods themselves. Of all the rituals, prayers, and rites, none are greater than blood sacrifice. The Seeds will offer their lives to their intended recipient, transforming that person's body into that of a paragon. I must say, to have one performed here on Thanet is highly irregular."

"Not irregular, damn well unheard of." Arn drained half the bottle, thoroughly enjoying the burn as it traveled down his throat. Liquor had been painfully lacking on the journey to the island, and he was pleased to see the locals capable of some heady, strong vintage. "All new paragons are birthed at the Bloodstone back in the capital of Eldrid. There's an approval process, a training regiment, all sorts of shit you have to endure. If there are Seeds here, then someone with a whole lot of weight is pulling strings to do something they shouldn't be doing."

"Sinshei," Stasia said. Her hands white-knuckled the hilts of her twin axes. "It must be. Who else has that level of authority?"

"Sinshei vin Lucavi?" Arn asked, lifting an eyebrow the muscular woman's way. "As in one of the God-Incarnate's daughters? Yeah. That'd do it. I take it she's the Anointed One here on Thanet?"

"That she is," answered Thorda.

Arn downed the rest of the bottle, tossed it to the floor, and then ignored the glares as he popped the cork of the second bottle with an easy flick of his thumb.

"Then she's your likely culprit." This bottle was sweeter, its taste reminding him of cherries and perhaps a faint scent of roses. Normally he'd dismiss such a combination, but the kick it gave him on the way to his stomach was most impressive. "I'd say she lied about the real reason she's bringing them over. Based on the prayers and songs I had to endure, they probably think they are here to proselytize to a stubborn populace refusing to convert their faith to the God-Incarnate."

"There's more to this that worries me," Cyrus said. "Let's say you're right, that Sinshei plans to do whatever ritual Arn's describing to turn someone, illegally, into a paragon. First question, who? Second question, why? What does she have to gain from this? It can't be in response to my assassination attempt, or our resistance. Travel here takes months. This was planned before we started."

Nothing but shrugs and confused looks around the room. This only confirmed Arn's belief that the paragon ritual had been organized in secret. Back at the Bloodstone, the creation of a new class of paragons was celebrated widely. What was happening here, he had a feeling word was not meant to reach the mainland.

"Something strange is afoot," Thorda said. "And I loathe being uninformed. We need to find these Seeds and, if possible, disrupt the ritual. Mari, I trust you can handle the former?"

"Of course I can." The chubby woman hopped down from her chair and crossed the room to Arn. She seemed almost giddy with excitement. "Do you have anything belonging to these people, the Seeds? Anything of theirs that might carry a scent?"

Arn tilted his head to one side. A bit of wine dribbled down his cheek.

"Not on me, no, but the boat they came on should be docked for a week or two before the crew's up for a return trip to Garlea. You got yourself some tracking hounds?"

Mari smiled sweetly at him. Something about that smile unnerved him far more than any speech by Lendsy.

"Hounds? No, Arn. Not hounds. *Me.*"

CHAPTER 28

MARI

The stars were not yet out when Mari bounded across the rooftops in the form of the Lioness. Her path led her silently to the boat docks. Finding the right caravel was easy enough. From her perch atop a wharf guild she scanned the area for imperial soldiers. With night approaching and the harbor blockaded against smugglers by five distant warships, there wasn't much reason for military patrols. Of the few ships docked, their crews were expected to use their own men to safeguard their possessions.

Mari hopped to the street and raced toward her destination. The wooden planks rattled beneath her paws. Two sailors sat at a small table atop the deck, playing cards and laughing away the evening. They would be no threat to her. Since they weren't imperial soldiers, they might even be of use...

She landed atop the table in a clatter of cards and chits. The man and woman cursed and fell from their chairs, one reaching for a knife clipped to his belt while the other scrambled in a panic for the gangplank.

"Halt," Mari snarled. The word-lace around her throat shimmered blue, translating the meaning of her words so the two would understand. "Or else I chase."

The woman by the plank halted and slowly turned about. Both were young, and the reek of alcohol on their breath was nauseating to Mari's enhanced sense of smell. No doubt they'd been celebrating their arrival to Vallessau nonstop since that morning.

"Wh-wh-what do you want?" the man with the knife asked.

"I seek the acolytes you brought as passengers," Mari said, glaring at that knife. The man followed her gaze, saw her bone wings twitching eagerly, and immediately dropped it to the deck with a weak thud.

"You mean the crazy fanatics?" he said. "Oh shit. Oh shit. We don't know. I swear, we don't know, do we, Slin?"

"It's true," Slin said behind him. "We docked, they got off. That's it. That's all me and Kirt know."

Mari sighed. Of course it wouldn't be that easy. Both sailors retreated back a step, and it took all her control not to laugh. In her Lioness form, her sigh had come across as a faint snarl.

"Which bunks belonged to the fanatics?" she asked them.

Slin pointed to the door leading to the lower cabins.

"The doors are numbered," she said. "Four, five, and six all belonged to them. You, uh, you can read numbers, right?"

Mari smiled sweetly at her, showing off her sparkling white fangs.

"I can read. Now run to the nearest tavern, drink yourself into a stupor, and tell no one of my arrival. Because if I hear rumors of the Lioness visiting the docks, well…" She flicked her tail. "I'll know who to blame."

The two sailors were all too eager to follow those commands. They fled down the plank, leaving Mari with free rein over the boat. She trotted through the lower doorway, her wings folded in tightly across her back to fit in the ensuing narrow hallway. The doors had numbers carved across their fronts, and at door 4, she nudged it open with her forehead and entered. There wasn't much to it, two tiny bunks on the floor, two hammocks hanging above them, and a tiny glass window so dirty and fogged, she doubt it served much purpose beyond letting in a sliver of light during the day.

"They haven't cleaned it yet," she said. "Thank the gods."

Thanks in particular to Endarius, who gifted her with her enhanced smell. It seemed by focusing upon it with her mind, it enhanced the power. Her world suddenly grew awash with color. A dozen scents struck her, and instinctively she knew that the colors and the smells were linked. She put her face to the nearest bunk and slowly inhaled. The colors shifted. For a brief moment she fought off a wave of disorientation. Her mind was not used to perceiving the world in such a way.

The dizziness cleared, and with it came understanding. The scent of the woman who had claimed that bed, it was a specific yellowish color, weaving together through the air like a thread. Finding the thread was like seeking a particular stripe in a rainbow, not particularly hard once she knew what she was looking for. When she focused upon it, it seemed the other colors of the world faded, and the yellowish thread shimmered that much brighter before her eyes.

"Where did you go, little Seed?" she muttered.

Mari returned to the empty deck. Now in the open air, it was wrong to call it a thread, but more of little scattered flecks of paint marking pieces of the boat. Places the woman had touched the wood, or spit, or had a single drop of sweat fall from her forehead to the ground. Mari followed them, her attention split between them and signs of a patrol. Even after all these years, Vallessau was still under a nightfall curfew. If she was fast, and kept her sharp ears up and listening, she trusted her ability to track the Seeds without being noticed by imperials. If Thanese natives saw her, well...

The people of Vallessau had learned over the past three years whom the Lioness protected, and whom she hunted. No one would seek out guards to mention her passing. Truthfully, she could walk down an open road at high noon and likely get only whispered thanks and comforting embraces, at least until imperial soldiers noticed.

The scent path led her from street to street while skirting along the island edge, the gentle call of the ocean all the clearer to her sharp ears. The yellow thread grew stronger, and she noted familiar scents intermixed with it, of others who had called the caravel home for their three-month journey across the Crystal Sea. They bundled together into a twisted rope of color that she found easier and easier to follow. That rope led directly to a large lodging house that offered rooms to Thanese travelers come to Vallessau for trade or leisure. The building was practically awash in color from the Seeds, but more immediately concerning to Mari was the guard stationed along the front.

A few quick leaps carried her to the nearby rooftops, and she hopped unseen to the lodge's roof so she might peer down at the guard. Bored and tired, he leaned on his spear as if it were an exceptionally deadly walking stick. A cursory circle following the rooftop's edge showed multiple entrances she could use, albeit at a bit of a squeeze. She checked on the soldier one last time, then moved for the opposite end to sneak unnoticed through a window. At least, she tried to move. Instead her entire body locked in place.

You would take my form yet deny me the tearing of flesh? rumbled Endarius's voice like a thunderstorm inside her skull. *I want blood upon my tongue, god-whisperer, not skulking cowardice.*

Mari shivered in place as if suddenly lost in a snowstorm. Saliva dripped from the sides of her mouth. Her wings shuddered, and her limbs tightened so her claws fully extended, their impossibly sharp tips raking the stone.

"We track the Seeds," she whispered, the words coming out as a soft growl. "It is their blood I would give you, not that of a lone soldier who means nothing to Thanet."

I would hunt, girl. My rage cares not for whom. You promised blood. If you would have my gifts, then I would have your offerings.

A sharp hunger stirred in Mari's belly as if she had not eaten in weeks. The drool dripping from her teeth thickened. She could smell the sweat sticking to the soldier's skin. She could hear the steady beating of his heart.

"A pitiful offering," she argued meekly to Endarius.

But one I demand nonetheless.

Mari leaped from the rooftop. Her full weight hit the soldier's back, and he had not a chance to remain upright. A frightened yelp was his only sound before she closed her teeth around his neck. He hit the ground face-first, and when his nose broke on the street, the smell of blood arced through Mari's body like electricity. The jagged tips of her wings pierced each of his shoulders to pin him. Her teeth tightened. A shake, a tear, and his spine cracked. Blood washed across Mari's tongue, and it filled her with elation so strong, it bordered on sexual.

"Happy?" she asked.

Are you not?

Mari dared not answer him. Instead she licked a bit of blood off her front paws and then bounded through the door.

The interior hall of the lodging was wide open, with four tables stacked with benches for daily meals. A cast-iron pot hung over a fireplace. A busty woman with her hair wrapped in a bun emerged from the adjacent kitchen upon hearing the door open, and her tired smile immediately vanished into shock. Her mouth opened and closed, words unable to form as her eyes bulged.

"Flee," Mari ordered, and the woman was only too happy to obey.

It seemed the rooms were upstairs, and so she bounded up the steps three by three to enter a narrow hallway. Mari put her nose to the ground and immediately regretted it. A thousand and one smells assaulted her, tracked in by countless muddy feet. Still, there was no doubt that floating among them were the Seeds. They had lodged here, yet the first two rooms had doors unlocked and interiors empty.

Am I too late? she wondered.

The next door was closed and locked. A soft snarl rumbled out from the throat. Should she break it down? The lodge owner likely had no choice on whether or not to provide rooms to the Seeds. The other doors were still open, and she smelled only the lingering odor of their presence.

Her decision was made for her when that locked door burst open. An armed man flung himself recklessly toward her, his sword gripped in both hands and plunging downward. Mari's initial instinct was not to flee, but to pitch sideways into the attack, meeting him body to body. The sword's sharp edge struck the bone plate of her shoulder, scraped off with a horrid vibration she felt in her teeth, and then nicked her leg. Mari snarled, the pain flooding her with rage she happily embraced. The two collided, and when he staggered back a step, her jagged left wing snapped like a scorpion's stinger. Its spiked end curled as it struck, puncturing the underneath side of his throat, skewering his tongue before embedding into the roof of his mouth. He gargled blood as she lifted him, her paws twisting beneath her for a pounce.

The wing pulled free, he dropped, and she descended upon him with claws raking and teeth bared.

When she was done, and his body a mess of innards and broken bones on the lodge floor, Mari checked her wound. Her rough tongue licked her bleeding foreleg beneath the bone shoulder plate. Nothing deep, and when she reverted back to her mortal body, it would resemble only a deep bruise. Still, she had to be more careful. There'd been so many people crammed into the building, resulting in a chaotic mess of scents, she'd failed to notice the heavy concentration behind the door. A true lioness would have known the difference, but even after years of inhabiting the power of Endarius, she was still akin to a babe when it came to her heightened senses.

I hope you're happy, she thought as she padded past the corpse and into the main hallway.

Never happy, the voice of Endarius grumbled in the back of her mind. *Never enough blood.*

Now convinced of the Seeds' departures, Mari returned to the outside. She tilted her head back and inhaled the night air, drawing in deep lungfuls of it as the world around her steadily blossomed with color. Two paths led from the building, one faint, one strong. The faint she had followed here, and so the more recent collection guided her. To her surprise, it did not go to the castle as she had anticipated. Instead her hunt took her south, a straight path beyond the homes and the steadily rising heights of the city carved into the surrounding mountainside. The jumbled scent trails led out of the city and to the beach, she realized. But why?

She needed no supernatural senses to know she tracked them correctly. Imperial soldiers stood in groups of three along the worn dirt path trodden into existence by thousands of feet. The soldiers chatted with one another, strangely excited and distracted. Mari skirted the outside of the path, trusting the tall pale grass and the harsh light of the setting sun to keep her dark fur hidden. Her destination was the broken stump of what had once been a bronze statue marking the edge of the cliff. The wind blew harder across the grass, warm from the ocean. The waves crashed a pleasant rhythm below.

Mari prowled to the cliff's edge, careful to avoid catching the attention of the patrols. The cliff was sheer, and so to allow access, rope ladders were spiked to the ground beside the bronze pedestal. Mari wondered what it had once portrayed. The Lion, perhaps? She thought a little piece at the bottom might resemble the lower portion of a butterfly wing. No doubt the Uplifted Church smashed it during their purges that filled the first few months of their invasion.

A butterfly emerging from cocoon, Endarius answered within her mind. *The promise of Lycaena. Of course the magistrates destroyed it.*

A wave of anger rippled through her, and once it had passed, she brought her attention to those below. A massive collection gathered on the white sands. Soldiers milled about, as did men and women in red magistrate robes. Mari spotted several paragons also in attendance, but most concerning to her were the collection of ten Seeds sitting in a perfect circle on the beach. They spoke softly with one another, faces beaming with pride. Near them, wearing a plain white robe and locked in conversation with the Anointed One, was Gordian Goldleaf, the island's regent. Blood covered his hands and face, though he acted as if all were normal.

The ritual, she thought. *It happens tonight.*

Then we stop it, Endarius rumbled. *Bring our hunt to the beach. Let us spill blood upon the sand.*

"Yes, but not alone," she whispered, turning her back to the beach and weaving through the grass. Haste was all that mattered now if Thorda's group was to react prior to the ritual's commencement. Once far enough so no soldier might see her, she broke out in a sprint, her long legs carrying her through the night back to her father's abode.

Everyone had gathered in the main den by the time Mari returned downstairs. She'd donned a loose robe, having reverted to her human form. Wearing more seemed foolish, given the certainty she would retake Endarius's form before the night was over. Rayan and Thorda stood together by the fireplace, their quiet conversation halting at her return. Cyrus lurked in the corner, observing but keeping to himself. Stasia and Arn, meanwhile, were taking turns sharing shots from a bottle, and by their grins, each was far more excited about that night's prospects than Mari.

"The Lioness returns!" Arn hollered when he noticed her exit the stairs. "Been through a dozen nations in my time and never seen a trick like that. Tell me, girl, did you find our prey?"

The amusement at her powers as a god-whisperer unnerved her, though she could not voice why. Something about it cheapened her gifts, as if communing with slain deities was a carnival trick instead of a sacred duty.

"I found the Seeds gathering on the beach south of the city," she said. "I know not its name, but there was once a bronze butterfly marking its cliffs."

"The Solemn Sands," Rayan clarified. He looked ready to vomit with disgust. "It is a site most holy, where Lycaena blesses those who are twice-born into their new life."

"Of course they would perform the ritual where it'd be most blasphemous," Stasia practically snarled.

"What were the Seeds doing there?" Arn asked. "Were they scouting the area, or were they singing?"

"Singing," Mari said, and she shuddered at the memory. "Regent Goldleaf was among them, and his face and hands were...bloody."

"Then the regent is the one meant to receive the power," Arn said. "Hardly proper, but it seems the rules are bent out here in Thanet. The Seeds will bring out their knives come midnight, and spill their own blood in worship. Their faith will empower whoever stands within the circle, granting them the might of a paragon."

"So it seems the empire offers the Usurper King power to defend himself in response to my attempt on his life," Cyrus said from his corner. "The question is, do we allow it?"

"I have been to those cliffs many times before," Rayan said, directing his attention to Thorda. "The only way to reach the sands is to swim from afar or descend the rope ladders. Those down upon the shore will have no direct contact with anyone higher up on the cliffs. If we hit hard, and fast, we might interrupt the ritual without anyone the wiser."

"You will be vulnerable during the descent," Mari argued. The distance from cliff to beach was significant, but Mari trusted her Lioness form to endure the fall. The same could hardly be said for Rayan in his heavy plate, nor the other three in their lighter gear. "Even if we can reach the cliffs unnoticed, I don't see how we ambush them without plenty of warning during the climb down. The moon is bright, and they have many torches burning all about the sands."

Rayan flashed a brilliant smile.

"There's more to the rope ladders than you first surmised, I assure you. It will be a bit of a rush, but we can drop in a hurry. Assuming, of course, that our leader approves of the attack."

All eyes turned to her father. So far he had not said a word since Mari's return. Those unfamiliar with his ways might assume he was deep in thought, but she knew from experience that was not the case here. He was observing those around him. He was watching the way Cyrus stood in his corner, the way his fingers patted his sword hilts. Stasia and Arn, putting aside the bottle, eager grins on both their faces. Mari had a feeling her father already knew what he wanted to do. All that mattered to him was whether or not he believed them capable of succeeding. By their behaviors, their ticks and mutterings, he would judge their resolve.

"With Arn here, my desired team is finally assembled," her father said, his decision made. "You are my elite, each individually capable of incredible feats. Together, I hold faith you are unstoppable. We will not allow the people of Thanet to see the empire as a source of anything other than pain. The Uplifted Church offers a gift, and so we deny it with blood and steel. Tonight, the Usurper King dies."

The excitement building throughout the room exploded into smiles and preparation. Mari put a hand to her breast and closed her eyes as those around her gathered their weapons and armor for the last-minute attack. She breathed in slowly, attempting in vain to slow the thunderous beating of her heart.

"It seems you get your hunt, Lion god," she whispered.

Deep in her bosom, the lingering presence of Endarius roared with eager approval.

CHAPTER 29

CYRUS

Masks on."

At Rayan's order, Cyrus and the rest pulled out their face coverings. They stood at the edge of the city, the cliffs visible in the far distance. Stasia tied her black cloth over her face, the snarling skull of a panther vibrant in the moonlight. A touch to her neck, and the word-lace shifted the color of her eyes. Of their group, only Thorda remained behind. Cyrus had questioned why his teacher would not join them, especially when he was so skilled with a blade.

"Someone must ensure you have a way home," the older man had offered as explanation, but given no more than that.

Cyrus slid his own crowned skull atop his forehead, then adjusted it slightly. He tried to ignore how his fingers were shaking. When that failed, he told himself they shook from excitement, and not from fear. When that also failed, he told himself he was about to ambush a secret sacrificial ritual attended by paragons and magistrates. A little fear was rational.

"Have you a covering of some sort?" Stasia asked Arn, who was tugging his weighty gauntlets into a tighter fit. "I didn't think to check before we left."

In response, the former paragon withdrew what appeared to be the upper half of a skull from some sort of canine. A thin layer of leather was attached to the underside, along with several cords to tie it in place. He pulled the skull over his face so that it covered his nose, forehead, and much of his cheeks. The teeth dropped down to hover over his mouth, like a morbid version of a soldier's nose guard.

"You forget I had been helping the rebellion in Onleda before I ever sailed here," Arn said.

"And what of a secret name?" Cyrus asked. "Thorda has us all use secret names to hide our identities."

"Not much point in hiding mine," Arn said. "But I'll use one if it will shut you up. Back in Onleda, they called me Fox, after my mask."

"You're much too big to be a fox," Stasia said. "And that's not nearly intimidating enough. Have you another?"

Arn rolled his eyes.

"Fine then, woman. No reason not to go on the nose with it. Call me Heretic."

That seemed good enough with everyone. Cyrus drew his swords and took in a long breath. No more stalling, no more delays. Ahead of them, Mari crouched before the tall grass, once more transformed into her Lioness form.

"All right then, *Heretic*," she said, her growls translated by her word-lace. "Try to keep up."

The four followed Mari into the high grass. Stasia and Cyrus found it easy enough to keep low and hidden, though Arn had to practically crawl to keep his tall, bulky body out of sight. Mari led the way, the distance between them steadily growing. After several minutes, she suddenly reappeared from the dark grass, ordering them to halt.

"Soldiers," she growled. "Three of them."

"Wait here," Stasia whispered to the others. "We'll handle this."

Together Stasia and Mari prowled ahead. Cyrus waited behind, biting his lip to fight his nerves. He hated letting them go alone, even if it made the most sense. Deciding it a weak compromise, he crawled a bit closer so he could at least observe the ambush. Rayan and Arn lurked farther behind, awaiting their signal to approach.

The trio of soldiers patrolling the path hadn't a chance. The two sisters struck with uncanny cooperation born of a shared childhood growing up amid war and insurrection. Mari leaped into the air, a soft swish of grass the only warning of her attack. She struck the lead soldier directly in the chest with her front paws, her jagged wings knifing downward to tear out his throat before he could let out a single cry. Stasia followed in her wake, twin axes flashing silver in the moonlight. With his weapon still sheathed, her foe had no defense against the double chop that cleaved his face in half, a far less subtle but still effective kill that denied a warning call for the other patrols.

"Ambush!" the final soldier screamed, or at least tried to scream. Only the first half of the word came out before Stasia's heel buried into his gut, robbing him of breath. Mari fell upon him an instant later, teeth in his throat so that second half of the word would never be spoken.

So far so good, Cyrus told himself, but he knew there would be far more resistance at the sacrifice. Mari returned to the lead, while Stasia beckoned the others to follow.

They could hear the chants long before Cyrus looked over the cliff. The sight of it awakened feelings of something deeply wrong inside his stomach. Ten men and women dressed in white acolyte robes, presumably the Seeds that Arn had spoken of, stood in a circle around a naked Gordian Goldleaf. The regent knelt in the center of their circle, his head bowed and his hands raised above him. Golden light sparkled around his body, swirling like a gilded fog. There was no denying the aura's resemblance to the ethereal weapons the magistrates could summon with their faith.

Separate from the circle, leading the chants of the Seeds, was Thanet's Anointed, Sinshei vin Lucavi. Cyrus would recognize her ankle-length hair anywhere. Paragons accompanied her, including Imperator Magus and the blue-armored spear wielder whom Cyrus remembered slaying Endarius during the initial invasion. Keeping much farther away to form protective rings were armored soldiers, pointedly looking anywhere but the sacrificial ritual. Cyrus had never been to the Solemn Sands before, but from what he could tell, both the northern and the southern sides were blocked off by the sheer white cliffs stretching into the ocean much farther than the shore. Arrival meant either swimming, or descending down from above.

Once he'd seen enough, Arn backed away from the cliff's edge and gestured for the others to gather around.

"We cannot let them complete the ritual," he whispered once sufficiently far away. "The gifted strength is always greatest at the moment of sacrifice. If they succeed, Gordian will be close to untouchable."

Cyrus thought of the rope ladders lining the edges, and of trying to descend unnoticed.

"How do we crash their party without raising alarm?" he asked.

Rayan grinned at them, the years falling off his face until he looked like a mischievous kid.

"Didn't I tell you I had a plan?"

While most visitors to the Solemn Sands descended to the holy site via the multiple rope ladders, the Church of Lycaena had constructed a wide platform connected to pulleys to be used by the elderly and the infirm for whom ladders were not feasible. It hung suspended over the edge overlooking the beach, and at Rayan's insistence, four of them climbed atop. Down below, the chanting continued, steadily rising in volume.

"You are certain you can manage?" Rayan asked Mari, the only one to remain on the cliff. She closed her jaws about one of the ropes. The word-lace flared blue as she let out a soft growl.

"Have faith, Paladin."

The platform was meant to descend by the steady, gentle turning of a wooden crank. Mari, however, bashed it with her front paw, her inhuman strength twirling it wildly so that it rocked side to side. The platform immediately dropped. Wind whipped through their hair. The wood groaned beneath their feet.

Might as well have leaped off, Cyrus had the briefest moment to think before the platform hit the sand. His knees buckled, and the rattle of their gear and the rope-bound wood was more than enough to announce their presence to the imperials. Cyrus vaulted off the platform, swords out, cloak trailing in the air behind him. Soldiers formed a ring around the sacrifice, and they shouted out confused orders and reached for weapons in response. Cyrus's grin matched that of his mask, far too wide and amused. They weren't ready. By the time they were, they'd be dead.

Together, the four were an overwhelming ambush of steel. Cyrus easily countered a panicked thrust, the curled end of his sword smashing aside the man's shield that he'd kept back, thinking it would protect his other half. A shift of Cyrus's hips, a turn of his shoulders, and the sword came slicing around with such strength, it decapitated the man. A woman next to him shouted something frightened and mindless as she chopped at him with her sword. He ended that cry with a spin. His sword cut across her face, meant to open up her throat but instead slicing off her jaw. She staggered, clutching her face and howling as her tongue hung limp in an image that would haunt him for days.

Cyrus's first glimpse of the Heretic in battle was most impressive. He charged the lone defending paragon, a man in golden platemail and a massive ax strapped to his back. Arn's gauntlets were a flash in the night, faster than daggers despite their weight and size. Two soldiers tried to block his path. One collapsed with a giant cavity punched into his chest. The other died with a twisted, broken neck from a single blow to his face. Arn's paragon foe proved a much more dangerous opponent. They danced, feet shifting, two masters of battle testing the other, watching their movements, until one made a mistake.

That mistake was for the ax-wielder to remain so patient. Rayan joined Arn, his shield up and blocking a defensive swing of the ax. Rainbow light flared across the shield upon impact, and with its blessing, the paladin held strong. Arn closed the distance in an instant, gauntlets pounding huge indents into the paragon's armor. The metal shrieked as it broke, and beneath it broke bones and flesh as well. As if that weren't enough, Mari descended from her diving leap from high atop the cliff. Her long feline body slammed down upon the paragon's shoulders, collapsing his body to the sand and skidding it several feet. The dangerous foe dead, the three split, each assaulting soldiers still scrambling to ready their weapons and set up position.

Cyrus forced his attention back to his own foe, a soldier armed with a spear. The man thrust it the moment Cyrus was in range, an obvious center-of-weight attack that would do fine if in formation with hundreds of others. Here on the sands, one on one? Too easy. Cyrus swept his left arm sideways, blade and spear shaft connecting. His shove moved both out of the way, easily exposing his foe. Cyrus chopped, the curved hook of his other sword easily sliding into the man's neck, breaking his collarbone, and cutting open the vital arteries within. He collapsed, and in his absence, Cyrus had a clear path to the ring of chanting Seeds.

Sinshei stood on the opposite end of that ring, and her voice cried out to the heavens, perceivable even above the din.

"The time is nigh!" she screamed. "Give of your faith, children of the incarnate!"

All ten acted as one, their movements, their voices, their lives given in perfect reflections of their fellows. Their knives sliced across their throats. Their blood pooled at their feet, sinking into the sand, to form a circle about the regent. They should have recoiled at the pain, but the Seeds only dropped their knives and lifted their arms in worship. They smiled up at the stars as their lifeblood poured from their self-inflicted wounds. They closed their eyes and wept tears of joy as their knees gave out. In return for their collapse, Gordian was uplifted.

For one brief moment, the regent shone gold. The light arced across his body, flowing from the blood and sacrifices like a backward rain. The color seeped into his skin, sparkling across his veins. Gordian screamed, the pain in his cry unimaginable. His muscles bulged. The bones of his body elongated to grant him height and reach, and what could not fit his new form broke and reshaped so it did. Wrinkles smoothed away. Old scars became unblemished skin. The sand shimmered beneath him, grains of it lifting heavenward as if the world itself were in awe of his transformation.

Cyrus dashed toward the circle of corpses and magic. The ritual was complete, but Gordian still endured the change. If he could strike now, cut the man's throat before he recovered...

A flash of color above him, a blue much brighter than the night sky, was his only warning. Instinct took over, and he dug his heels into the sand and then lurched backward. A blue-armored paragon landed mere feet before him, his spear embedding halfway up to the hilt. Cyrus had met him a few times while Gordian's prisoner, the paragon always accompanying Thanet's Anointed One during her occasional trips to the castle. Every visit had given him shivers.

"You weren't invited," Soma said as he ripped his spear free with a flourish of sand.

"I thought it more fun to arrive unannounced."

His foe laughed as if they were casual friends and then attacked with his spear. No shift in his weight, nor turn of his feet, gave away his intentions. Cyrus barely parried it aside, and then only due to the significant distance between him and his foe. Another thrust followed, and Cyrus immediately went defensive, his off-hand weaving back and forth in a constant series of parries for that jabbing, seeking spearpoint. It was like keeping a viper at bay. On the fifth attempt, he saw an opening and lunged with his right hand. The sharp edge bounced upward, the paragon's spear twirling like the sails of a windmill in his deft hands. That rotation ended with the butt of the spear cracking him in the shin, and only pure adrenaline kept him from crumpling. Cyrus pulled back while retreating yet again, expecting the paragon to claim the offensive, but a woman's shout prevented him.

"Soma!" was all the Anointed One cried. His paragon foe reacted instantly. His spear pulled back, and he twirled it once before leaping a dozen feet into the air, making a pure mockery of the earth's downward pull. Cyrus followed his leap and saw Mari ripping apart two soldiers standing protectively before Sinshei. Light shimmered about the Anointed One's hands, the specter of divine weapons ready to lash out, but the Lioness was so fast, so brutal, she must have doubted her own magic.

She need not doubt Soma's spear. The paragon landed between Mari and Sinshei, and his spear twirled in his hands so quickly, it was but a blur. Mari retreated, her bone wings thrusting wildly to provide cover. Cyrus wished he could watch their battle longer, but with Soma gone, the way to Gordian Goldleaf was clear. The regent no longer lay helpless on his hands and knees. He had retrieved one of the sacrificial daggers used by the Seeds, and he held it before him like a fencer. His hair waved wildly in an unfelt wind. His smile reached his ears.

"Stay back!" Gordian shouted to the other soldiers who moved to protect him. He pointed his free hand toward Cyrus. "I need not fear this coward's wrath. Come, Vagrant. Come die to your better."

Such a challenge could not be refused. The regent was their target for the night. His death would be a crippling blow to the imperial government, not just in Vallessau but throughout all Thanet. Still, Cyrus found himself hesitating for the briefest heartbeat. It had nothing to do with the electric power crackling around him. This was the man who had lorded over Cyrus for two horrid years of his life. This was the bearer of the handsome smile that promised him death should he misbehave. That he was here, challenging him, felt more unreal than even the divine glow that radiated from the regent's pale skin.

The rest of Thorda's elite were holding strong, pushing back what was becoming a battle line. The way to Gordian was clear. Cyrus must take it. Bury the child that he was, and rush forward as the Vagrant he had become. Sand kicked in sprays as he sprinted. He flipped his off-hand out of its reverse grip, bent his knees, and lunged with both hands arcing downward with all his strength. Gordian's dagger flashed upward, intercepting both. Though Cyrus pressed with all his might, it was his own swords that trembled. The smile on Gordian's face grew, and he flashed perfectly flawless teeth, so white they glowed like moonlight.

"I am the incarnation of unshakable faith," he said. "You are only mortal."

Cyrus fell back a single step, shifted his weight sideways, and then used his off-hand to block a retaliatory stab from Gordian. Right hand free, he shoved it straight into Gordian's gut in what should have been a killing blow. Instead the weapon skidded off as if he'd attempted to stab a stone pillar. What thin scratch he made was a white line amid the golden hue, and it did not bleed.

Gordian glanced down at the wound, and its insignificance. His reaction was pure, monstrous pleasure.

"You're nothing to me now, Vagrant. Just a dead man."

"I've always been a dead man," Cyrus said. "But tonight you join me."

Cyrus flipped the grip of his off-hand blade again, then shoved it sideways to parry a downward thrust aimed at his collarbone...only to discover he could barely adjust Gordian's aim. The man's strength was incredible. He'd have a better chance pushing aside the path of a carriage. Cyrus buckled his left knee, dropping low and awkwardly curling so that his lower back ached in protest. The stab cut a thin hole across his shirt but failed to draw blood. Spinning on his knees, Cyrus cut twice along his foe's naked thigh and leg. Yet again, the cuts made a sound like metal on stone, and if they did any damage to the newly birthed paragon, it did not show on his bemused face.

Refusing to be deterred, Cyrus danced about his foe, cutting flesh and dodging stabs with the dagger. No more parrying. Instead he read the naked man's movements, watching the shift of muscles and change in footing to predict the next attack. Despite their pitiful impact, he cut and stabbed whenever able. Paragons could heal quickly, but they were still mortal. They could bleed, and they could die. Cyrus knew, for he had killed one himself. He need only convince both Gordian and uncaring reality of that fact.

"Wall off the ropes!" Magus shouted to the soldiers. "Leave them no escape but to drown!"

The rest of his friends battled the soldiers, but their foe's numbers were thankfully split. Half formed a line of battle against Thorda's elite, steadily pressing them toward the beach, while the other half guarded Sinshei and the remaining priests and magistrates at the cliff wall. True to Magus's orders, they blocked the rope ladders leading back up the cliff. There was no way out but the sea.

Only training kept Cyrus's panic in check. His skills outmatched Gordian's. Let his faith reside in that. He scored blow after blow, and though it felt like hacking away at a pillar of marble, he could tell by the flinch on his foe's face and the sweat collecting across his naked body that the onslaught was starting to break through. Gordian's faith in his own invulnerability was wavering. The cuts had begun to bleed. The golden aura about his bare skin had faded like a summer tan into winter. As his strength faltered, so, too, did his confidence tumble into doubt. Again swords crossed against dagger, but this time it was the dagger that trembled.

"Magus!" the regent shouted, his attention breaking for the briefest glance toward the giant Imperator. That doubt, that cry for help, was all Cyrus needed. He dropped low and swept his leg, kicking Gordian's feet out from under him. Cyrus assaulted him immediately, his knees driving down into the regent's shoulders. His swords simultaneously chopped, and were halted mere inches above Gordian's throat by the long sacrificial dagger. Metal rattled against metal. Cyrus pressed his knees harder, pinning the other man to the sand despite his newly granted paragon strength. The two were close, so close. Cyrus's skull mask was mere inches away from Gordian's sweat-coated forehead.

Their eyes met, and time slowed to a crawl around them. Even amid the chaos, bathed in torchlight, awash in screams of the dying and the manic cries of battle, it felt like the two were alone somewhere quiet. Somewhere private, and close, in a forgotten memory of Cyrus's past. Back when he walked the halls of the castle, keenly aware his parents were gone and the building would never be his.

Harder and harder, the edge of Gordian's dagger cracking, the metal groaning, whereas Cyrus's held strong. They gazed into each other's eyes, Cyrus seeing the darkest years of his life, Gordian seeing nothing but hatred he didn't understand.

Until he did.

"Cyrus?"

At last, Cyrus had everything he wanted. He pulled his swords back, spun them around, and stabbed straight down. The ends of both easily bypassed Gordian's stunned defense, ripping twin gashes into his neck. From like another world, a panicked woman screamed in protest. Gordian convulsed, his mouth unable to form words. He died, still with that look of confusion on his face. Cyrus stood, cloak falling across his body, hood fluttering low over his face. He lifted it so it would not block his crown, for he wanted the moonlight to reflect off it as he stood upon the Solemn Sands. Just one more cut to finish the deed, a crown of blood carved across the Usurper King's forehead. It was the only crown he deserved.

A lull had fallen over the battle as the rest of Thorda's elite retreated toward the beach and the remaining imperial soldiers stood aghast. Cyrus relished every second. Their fear, their doubt, it fueled him like fresh coals upon a fire.

"The Usurper King is dead!" he shouted. "What good are your

sacrifices? What purpose is your slaughter, when death still comes for you?"

Still silence. They recognized the Vagrant, he realized. The weeks spent spreading rumors, his nightly excursions, the marks he cut across his victims' foreheads... they knew him now. It wasn't solely Thanet's faithful that believed. His enemies did, too, and it was everything he could have imagined and more.

"Thanet will never belong to you," he bellowed to them. "Not her heart, not her soul."

A long, shrill whistle stole Cyrus's attention to the ocean. Two boats, short and flat like the fishermen used, curved around the eastern edge of the cliffs that formed the outer perimeter of the Solemn Sands. Two to a boat, one on the oars, the other holding aloft lanterns burning hot. Each held a single object in front of their lanterns so they cast long shadows across the shore. One was a long feather, the other, a small piece of wood carved into the shape of butterfly wings.

"There's our way out!" Rayan shouted.

No soldier or magistrate stood between them and the Crystal Sea, for they had thought to trap them against its waters and guard the rope ladders instead. Only Cyrus's path was blocked by the furious Imperator storming over with sword and shield drawn. The other members of the five raced for the boats, Stasia in the lead. She waved her arms to gain the attention of the nearest boat, then pointed to where Rayan fought against the waves.

"Get closer to shore," she shouted. "Paladin cannot swim in such armor!"

"No," raged Magus as he slowly repositioned himself to match any shift Cyrus attempted to slip past to escape. "Stay and fight, you coward. You say Thanet is yours, not ours? Come and prove it."

Surprise was no longer on their side, and time had never been, but Cyrus lifted his swords and crouched his legs low for a sudden dash. He had encountered the paragon's enormous shield once before, but that was in the crowded hallway of the castle. In open air atop the blood-soaked sands, he at least stood a chance. Here, right here, he could end the life of the man who cut down his parents. It was foolish, and reckless, and they were still badly outnumbered...

He glanced past Magus, to where Rayan was frantically pushing against the waves while wading toward their escape boats.

"One dance," Cyrus said. Behind his mask, he felt confidence he could only dream of when but a young man frightfully wandering the castle halls of his captors. "I have time for only one dance."

Magus lifted his enormous sword and shield, each hand holding a single weapon that mere humans would struggle to hold in two. Waves pushed against Cyrus's ankles, and they crashed into a salt spray around the gargantuan Imperator's legs as if he were the prow of a warship.

Cyrus chose that moment to lunge out of his crouch. As with all his other battles against paragons, he relied on speed over strength. He had to be faster than his lumbering foe...yet when the first of his thrusts was parried aside by Magus's deftly shifting blade, he realized that this paragon was not like the others. His movements were quicker, his decisions made faster. Cyrus baited out another parry, then curled around while slashing with his left hand. The blade should have sliced across Magus's eyes, but instead it bounced off the upper half of the shield, leaving not a dent.

Another clash, Cyrus's swords never able to find purchase. Magus kept defensive, for he also knew time was on his side. When Cyrus thrust, it scraped off the shield. When he chopped an exposed leg or jabbed his short sword for the eyes, the Imperator's own sword was there to parry the attack. Desperation growing, Cyrus attempted what he'd done against Rayan, a sudden and overwhelming barrage of strength and speed. His swords struck the shield as if he were beating a drum, then a sidestep, one thrust, two thrusts, another sidestep. Never an opening. Never a maneuver the paragon had not seen coming.

Soldiers rushed closer, increasing Cyrus's growing worry, but it seemed he need not fear their intervention.

"Let them fight," Sinshei ordered from her protected circle of soldiers and magistrates. The soldiers hesitated, torn between helping their Imperator and obeying the Anointed One.

Confused by it as he was, Cyrus appreciated the delay. The Imperator could not be moved. He could not be beaten. He was as indomitable as the cliffs that surrounded them. What did speed matter if his foe were as unbreakable as the tide? Panic replaced his previous confidence. No, he had to push himself even harder. He had to move even faster. This monster, this murderer, would suffer for his sins. Gordian was not enough. Let the true architect of Thanet's invasion die in the sands.

Cyrus closed the space between them, attempting to position his body so his longer sword could thrust past Magus's shield, but the move had been anticipated. Magus's sword came crashing down, eager to perfectly split Cyrus down the middle from head to toe. Despite every lesson from Thorda screaming otherwise, Cyrus pulled both his swords together and attempted to block it. Their weapons connected, and the hit was like being run over by a horse. Cyrus screamed as his weapons rattled and his arms ached from the jolting impact. His knees gave out next, his body collapsing like a broken toy.

The block held, but it didn't matter. The Imperator pulled the weapon back and raised his shield, its edge dripping water, its massive weight ready to pound Cyrus into the sand. He thought to flee, but his breath had been robbed, and his legs felt like mud. Too slow. Too foolish.

"What a pitiful dance," Magus said.

The Lioness collided with Magus's shield, her weight rocking him backward on the unsteady footing of the sands. Her claws dug into the slab of steel, then her paws pushed off, somersaulting her to a landing beside Cyrus. In what must surely have been on purpose, the angle of her paws upon hitting the sea splashed a sharp jet of saltwater straight into Magus's face, blinding and burning his eyes.

"Run, Vagrant," Mari roared. "Or gods help me, I'm dragging you home by your neck."

The spell over him broke. Ignoring Magus's furious challenge, Cyrus turned and sprinted awkwardly against the water until it was up to his waist. Up ahead, two soldiers had rushed past his duel with Magus, foolishly thinking they could chase down Rayan. Mari tore apart one of them before Cyrus even neared the duo, for she glided through the water like an otter. The other, seeing the raging Lioness blocking his way and snarling her blood-soaked fangs, turned to flee. Cyrus greeted him with a skull grin and a thrust to the gut.

"I was afraid you'd be stupid and keep on fighting," Stasia shouted from the farther boat.

"I'm smart occasionally, Ax, give me some credit."

Only when Rayan was safely aboard did Cyrus sheath his swords and dive headfirst into the water to swim. He fought against the waves, moving sluggishly given his cloaks and weaponry, but the imperial soldiers were outfitted far worse than he. As for Magus, he could only walk along the seabed with his heavy plate and enormous shield. Cyrus ignored the closer boat, thinking it already pushing its luck weighed down with both Arn and Rayan, and swam farther out to Stasia's.

"Welcome aboard," the lantern holder said as he pulled Cyrus up by the arm. "The Coin said you might need a trip home."

"The Coin was right," Cyrus said. He collapsed onto his back, sopping wet and not caring in the slightest. His cloak bunched beneath him, and his hood lay heavy on his face. He shook his wet hair and pulled strands of it away from his mask. The man with the paddles immediately set to rowing, and he shifted in his seat so the lantern holder could take one and join him. Stasia sat before the bow, and she leaned back with her palms pressed against the boat's frame. The moon shone behind her, but he swore he saw a smile on her face amid the dark night.

"The Usurper King is dead," she said. "Long live the Vagrant Prince."

Perhaps Thorda would prefer that Cyrus relish his pleasure in silence, a brooding image of assassination and death for the fishermen to describe to their friends and family when they returned home. Instead he laughed, and laughed, until tears were pouring down his face. He couldn't help it. Despite all his training, all his effort, he had never truly believed they could accomplish such a victory against the empire. It had been a hope in the distance, a dream surely meant to be sought but never achieved.

Gordian's blood on his swords said otherwise.

CHAPTER 30

SINSHEI

Sinshei vin Lucavi stood on the white beach of the Solemn Sands, arms crossed over her chest and mind distant. A pyre burned before her. Regent Gordian Goldleaf, meant to be her paragon champion and loyal ally, charred to ash within it.

"In the thousands of years spanning the great history of the Everlorn Empire, I daresay your failure tonight may rank among the most humiliating," Imperator Magus shouted from the other side of the pyre. "Ten Seeds bled out to bless an unworthy man, who died mere moments after receiving it. Has such a gift ever gone to waste so quickly? This is *why* we have rules as to whom we bless and where we bless them."

The two were alone upon the beach, with Soma and the rest of the imperial soldiers gathered up top to give them their privacy. Magus had seethed from the moment the battle ended all the way to the lighting of the pyre, but he had said nothing beyond grunts and one-word commands. It seemed he had been saving all his ire for when he could unleash it without eavesdroppers.

"Given the extreme distance from Gadir, and the dangers posed by assassins of the insurgence, I thought it best if Gordian were able to defend himself," she said. It was a flimsy lie, and they both knew it.

"The regent need not defend himself if he is beloved by the populace,"

Magus argued. "As for his defense, that responsibility falls to the Legion, not your priests and magistrates."

"Yet he lies dead. Why, then, do you send me your ire? Was it not your responsibility to defend the ritual?"

The light of the pyre reflecting off Magus's silver eyes was a paltry blaze compared to his growing rage.

"You would lay this at my feet?" he asked. "You purposefully sprang this upon me with less than a day's notice, in a place and time not of my choosing. You *wanted* me unprepared, Anointed One. Do not dare admonish me for what you yourself caused."

Sinshei looked away. He wasn't wrong. Magus had initially refused, but then she informed him Gordian was already at the beach with the Seeds, the first of many rounds of prayers having begun. Dozens of priests, and every single magistrate, were also there to bear witness. If Magus halted proceedings, it would be abundantly clear he was going against the church's Anointed One, a tricky proposition even for a respected paragon and Imperator like Magus. Even if they disagreed behind closed doors, they were meant to present a unified front to the public.

"Complaining and bickering will not alter the past, so instead let us plan for the future." She gestured toward the pyre. "How might we deal with this? Can we lie about the nature of his death? Or perhaps pretend he returned to Gadir and appoint someone new to take his place?"

"Naïve fantasies," Magus said. "Before the dawn rises every man, woman, and child of Vallessau will hear stories of the Vagrant claiming the life of Thanet's regent. Already we deal with a sudden resurgence. This victory will only strengthen them. Damn it, how in Lucavi's name did they know the ritual was taking place? Have you spies among your ranks?"

"I hand-picked every magistrate and priest who accompanied this invasion," she said with a shake of her head. "Their faith is without flaw. No, I suspect Paragon Lendsy's death is related, a fact that becomes clear only in hindsight."

"Another slain paragon?" he asked. "I heard nothing of this."

"Because it happened only earlier today. Lendsy Moralae, Paragon of Blades. He was found dead in his cabin on the caravel shortly after docking. My priests have been questioning the crew, and we have a primary suspect. A giant man named Meffrit Mason, though likely that is an alias. He vanished shortly after disembarking, no family, no appearance at any of the inns. We'll have posters up for him shortly, but even with a handsome reward I do not expect the populace to aid us much."

"So this Meffrit learned of the Seeds on the months sailing here?" Magus said. "It is a possibility, but how would a civilian know the difference between an acolyte and Seed, or of the ritual?"

"Because he wasn't a civilian. Based on his description, I believe we have already met him. The man with the gauntlets. You saw how he fought, and the strength he wielded. He was once a paragon, now turned traitor. It explains how he would know of the ritual, and the purpose of the Seeds."

She hadn't believed it possible that Magus's mood could worsen, but somehow it did. He stepped around the fire, the shadows it cast upon his face adding a sinister edge to his glare.

"A traitorous paragon, here, in Thanet? Brought on the very boat carrying the Seeds you demanded for your ritual?"

Sinshei stood to her full height and uncrossed her arms. She would not be bullied, not even by an Imperator. A prayer to her God-Incarnate father whispered through her mind, and little sparks of light glimmered along her fingertips.

"This matter must be swiftly addressed," she said. "We'll need an oathtaking ceremony for Katrin's guardianship, and an official proclamation for Uriah establishing him as regent-in-waiting."

"We will do no such thing."

Sinshei tilted her head ever so slightly. She and Soma had discussed fallback scenarios should Gordian die, but those hypotheticals always assumed Gordian died in battle after acquiring his paragon blessing. The idea that the ritual would be interrupted, and the regent murdered, was so outlandish it had never occurred to them. That Magus would deny Uriah his lawful ascension, and his mother her guardianship, never did, either. It seemed she would suffer for her lack of imagination.

"You would not have Katrin fill the role of guardianship?" she asked, hoping she misunderstood his refusal.

"Katrin and her boy are taking a caravel back to Gadir," he said. "*I will be Thanet's new regent.*"

Even her lifetime of plots and lies did not enable her to keep the shock from her voice.

"Imperator *and* regent? It is not done."

"Neither is granting the paragon blessing on a regent. It seems Thanet is a place for setting new precedents, isn't it, Anointed? I do what I must. Harsh, desperate measures are necessary to clean up this mess you created."

Heat flushed to Sinshei's face. This was a nightmare scenario. Gordian's ascension to paragon was meant to be the first in a series of events that would result in him challenging Magus's rule over Thanet. The bothersome Imperator needed to be out of the way if Sinshei was to properly plan for the grand ceremony marking the six hundredth year of her father's reign. Instead, Magus would both command the military and directly control the political court built to replace Thanet's original royal family. His rule would be absolute, with no counter-balances, and nothing to hold back his worst impulses. The stubborn, rebellious people of Thanet would quickly yearn for the relatively peaceful days of the Usurper King.

"My mess?" she asked, blustering as a way to regather herself. "You declare this my mess, despite you ignoring my advice at every turn? Of course the people now riot. You implemented portions of the Joining Laws years too soon. Their hearts were not ready, their heathen traditions still fresh in mind. Ruthlessness and patience, together in equal measure, is how you change a nation. Yet you would instead blame me for your impatience?"

She had known full well what Magus's answer would be. What she did not know was how savagely he would react. His hand was around her throat before she registered the movement. Fingers tightened about her larynx, choking out the needed words to complete her prayer. Deadly light faded from her fingertips. He lifted her up by the throat as if she weighed but a feather.

"Do I blame you?" he asked. She dug her nails into his skin and pulled at his hand, but her meager strength paled in comparison to the divine power flowing through his veins. It felt like trying to carve stone with her fingertips. "Yes, Sinshei, I blame you. The botched ritual, Gordian's death, Vagrant's rise...it all stems from your failure to convert the hearts of the ignorant wretches that fill this damnable island."

Her vision was a blurry blotch of orange fire and a circular shadow that was Magus. Her lungs burned for air, but she couldn't breathe, couldn't break free. Her legs kicked, weak little hits that meant nothing to the Imperator's armor. If only she could speak. If only she could tear apart his body with blades of light. If only the Vagrant had killed Magus during their duel instead of fleeing to the boats...

"We are the Three Pillars of Thanet's Conversion," he said, his words thick and distorted as if her ears were clogging with blood. "Yet two of those pillars are crumbling and weak. One has collapsed. The other is rotten to its core. You may have those in the church fooled, but we of the God-Incarnate's Legion can see the truth. You have risen far above your deserved station, *vin Lucavi*. The others of your family have great deeds and conquests to their names, but they are not thin-blooded and born of a concubine. What deeds can you boast of from your miserable life? Only Thanet, a poorly handled failure. Unfaithful, disloyal, a viper's nest growing unchecked while you play at games that led to a regent's death."

His fingers tightened. Her vision blacked out, and her light-headedness threatened to sweep her away completely. This was it, she realized. This was how she would die. All her plans and preparations for the God-Incarnate's arrival, come to naught. He brought her closer, his voice dropping to a whisper.

"You ordered my men to stay back. You hoped the Vagrant would kill me, didn't you? But I lived, and whatever plans you had for Gordian, they are now dead. Open your eyes to your proper place, woman, or I will open them for you."

Magus dropped her to his feet. She hit the ground and fell to one side, her weight braced on her elbows as she gasped in gulps of air. The Imperator lorded above her, scowling with naked displeasure.

"If not for your father, I would have you join Gordian upon the pyre," he said. "I tell you this so you understand the extent of the mercy I show you this night."

Mercy, she thought as she spat blood upon the sand. At some point she'd bitten her tongue, yet she remembered not when. *I will teach you mercy one day, paragon.*

"I pray you feel better now you have released your frustrations upon me," Sinshei said instead as she rose unsteadily back to her feet, wiped at her dress, and swallowed down her shame. She had to pretend nothing were amiss. The last minute was an aberration none would speak of. That was the key to enduring these insults, these humiliations. Push them into the past, stand up tall, and act like everything was proper and fine. A little death, but she had sacrificed worse in service to the church. "So what now is your plan, Imperator-Regent?"

"We have no more time," Magus said, and for the first time that night, a hint of panic crept into his voice. "The six hundredth year of your father's reign approaches. Thanet must be made ready. Now you may help me, Sinshei vin Lucavi, or you may board that boat with Katrin so I can elevate a magistrate into an Anointed who will. Those are your only two choices. All other paths, well…" He glared at the pyre. "You see where they lead you."

A fire burned hotter than lava in her belly but she dared not let that rage show. The Imperator would view it as a challenge, and his pride would never let him back down from a perceived threat. Only the God-Incarnate himself could condemn Magus for his crime against her. But she knew her father. He would not condemn. He would only approve. So it was either summon her holy blades and spill his blood upon the sands, or feign obedience, and right now she was in no shape for a duel.

"I am not leaving this island," she said. "Nor shall I abandon my honored post."

"Then it seems we have an agreement." He turned for the rope ladders, pausing only to spit upon the dwindling pyre. "Tomorrow, we rebuild the Dead Flags, and we enforce the Joining Laws in their entirety. Make the announcement, as well as news of my appointment as regent. We have coddled the people of Thanet long enough. These spoiled children shall faithfully kneel in servitude, one way or another. If they reject our loving embrace, then we shall give them the clenched fist instead."

CHAPTER 31

RAYAN

Rayan walked the Midtown market as soldiers tore apart the nearby stall.

"You were warned," one of the soldiers shouted. It seemed it was the only phrase he knew in Thanese, and he gave it repeatedly.

Rayan's hand itched for the sword strapped to his thigh. Come Magus's appointment as regent after Gordian's death, he had announced new additions to what were now being openly referred to as the Joining Laws. The presence of soldiers on the streets had increased tenfold. Marriages were being annulled for the flimsiest of reasons, the crossed and twice-born were forced into hiding, and as for the shopkeeper and her stall? Women weren't allowed to own a business, and it seemed she mistakenly thought stubbornness might prevail over hate-filled law.

"Stay strong," Rayan whispered to her when he offered her his hand. She looked at up him, face bruised and dirt on her clothing.

"Don't need 'strong,'" she said. "Need a damn army."

Bootheels smashed the last of the stall and its seashell jewelry. Rayan glanced at the soldiers, then back to her.

"Soon," he promised. "Hope springs anew."

He led the woman safely away, her arm tucked into his as if they were partners for a dance. Whatever fight she'd raised when the soldiers first came for her withered as they walked.

"Let not your hearts cling to the heathen old ways," a priest on the street corner bellowed to a crowd mostly ignoring him. "The dead will not answer your prayers. The slain will give no blessings. You were fooled into worshiping faulty beings from the moment of your birth, but an awakening has arrived upon Thanet! Lift your voices to the God-Incarnate. Confess your sins, and be reborn in both heart and flesh! There is joy in the worship, and freedom in the obedience."

Priests lecturing in public were commonplace ever since the Everlorn Empire arrived, but they were particularly fervent with the arrival of the Joining Laws. No doubt the Anointed One was pressuring them immensely to make better progress, given the rising insurgence. Rayan refused to look at him, and with his free hand he touched the ten winter jasmines in his pocket. Today was a special day. No matter the horrors the empire inflicted, he was determined to find solace in its celebration.

"They never shut up, do they?" the woman said. Despite the bite in her words, she clutched his arm tighter.

"We will silence them," Rayan said. "Every day, we work to free our shores of their poison."

"It seems you need to work faster." She released his arm. A panicked man was running toward her, the relief on his face clear as daylight. The two embraced, and the woman who had been iron when facing the soldiers wilted now with family. Rayan left her, and he tried to soothe his guilty heart with reminders of their deeds.

Thorda's elite band of fighters had not relented in their attacks since Gordian's death. Rayan had participated in most missions large and small, attacking soldiers on patrol, ransacking language schools teaching the populace the imperial tongue, and setting fire to the homes of priests and magistrates. If it represented the Everlorn Empire, it was a target. After two years of relative inaction, he relished donning his armor, readying his shield, and bringing his sword to bear against his oppressors.

Yet their every strike was retaliated tenfold by Magus's soldiers. War loomed on the horizon, and everyone in Vallessau felt it.

"Blessed Midwinter to you, paladin," a shopkeeper said as he walked past his stall. Years prior, the man would have belted out the phrase at the top of his lungs, but now he whispered the words. A faint red

mark of paint had been brushed underneath his left eye. A shadow of
the painted faces men and women once wore to mark the Midwinter
holiday, but like all things involving Endarius and Lycaena, faith had
to be hinted at instead of proudly proclaimed. Everywhere he looked,
Rayan saw the stubborn signs. Shapes cut into the world that resembled
butterfly wings. Swabs of color on wrists, cheeks, and foreheads. A lone
feather tucked into a belt. A lion's paw drawn in chalk.

"Blessed Midwinter to you, too," Rayan said, and he beamed a hollow smile. Again Rayan fingered the jasmines. That was the theme of
today's lesson to the children. Thanet was smothered and buried, no different than the flowers and grass beneath fallen snow. And like the flowers, so, too, would Thanet's people emerge come the spring, brighter
and stronger than ever.

Rayan knew something was amiss as he neared his teaching spot.
Normally parents would be lingering about with their children waiting
for him to come tell his stories. Instead the dead-end stretch of road was
remarkably empty, with not a child in sight. Of the regulars, only the
bearded and big-bellied merchant Jesper waited nearby with a scowl on
his face, a scowl that deepened upon seeing the paladin.

"What happened?" Rayan asked. "Where are my students?"

"I thought it best that I be the one to tell you," his friend said.
"They've all gone home."

"But why? I wasn't late. Was the church prowling about?"

Jesper stared at him a moment. Rayan's unease grew.

"You don't know, do you?" the merchant asked at last. He sighed.
"Fine. Follow me, paladin. And steel your stomach."

The boy, Luke had been his name, hung from a lamppost beside the
road. The rope dug deep into his soft neck. Purple splotches traveled
from it to his lips and down below his throat. His shirt had been cut
apart to reveal his bare chest. A pair of butterfly wings were carved into
his flesh, the cuts deep enough to expose his ribs. His gaze remained
open in death, once beautiful emerald-colored eyes that now bulged in

their sockets. His hands were bound before him, and forced into his grip was a single winter jasmine.

"What was his crime?" Rayan asked. His throat was so dry, his voice rasped as if he were ill.

"A soldier saw him give away one of those flowers while wishing a Blessed Midwinter."

"That is it? But we've celebrated Midwinter every year, even after they invaded our island. Even after they..."

After they slew our gods. He didn't say it aloud, though. He couldn't give voice to that dark past, not even in the face of the swinging corpse.

"Aye, they did let us, if we were quiet about it," Jesper said. "Looks like they're done with that. I don't suspect you'll have much of a crowd at your lessons anymore, paladin. If you plan on keeping them, best you look into somewhere hidden and indoors."

"There has always been a danger to our keeping the faith," Rayan said. "It never stopped us before."

"Yeah, but they never hung kids at the Dead Flags before, let alone at a gods–damned street corner. It's different, and we all can tell."

Rayan drew his sword. He would not leave Luke hanging like this. He pulled back to swing, only for Jesper's hand to close about his wrist.

"Don't. His parents already tried. They're in a prison cell now. Leave it be."

The sword shook in his hand. Rayan glared at the merchant, but he didn't see his bearded face. He saw a swinging body. He saw knives tearing into black skin. Wordlessly, he returned his sword to its sheath. Jesper started to say something, then changed his mind. Instead he sighed, long and deep, and then squeezed Rayan's shoulder with his meaty hand.

"Good luck to you, paladin."

The merchant left Rayan to stand alone before the swinging corpse. The groan of the rope swaying at the top of the pole was a grotesque tick of an unwanted clock. Luke was dead, and his parents possibly condemned. He stared to the ground, not wanting to see those swollen lips or bulging eyes. A prayer, he realized, he should say a mourning prayer.

The words would not come to him. Only bitterness and despair. *Blessed Midwinter, indeed*, he thought.

There was a time when Endarius himself would have flown over the city to mark the start of their annual fast with his mighty roar. Despite the fading winter light, his feathered mane would sparkle with a rainbow of color. Come nightfall, it would be Lycaena's turn to take flight, soaring higher and higher into the sky so the moon would highlight her multicolored wings, which fluttered like an impossibly long dress. His goddess would raise her arms to the heavens and clap thrice. On the third clap, fire would descend over the city, sparkling every color and transforming into a thousand different shapes. The fire would fall like leaves and cats, dancing children and singing birds. Upon landing, the fire would not burn but instead sparkle, loud but harmless.

That fire ended the fast and began the Midwinter Feast. The year was over, and the world reborn. Rayan was too exhausted and drained for tears, but his chest ached remembering those laughter-filled feasts. Songs would fill dining halls. Endarius would prowl the streets, and if a house seemed especially boisterous and cheerful, he would mark its door with a scratch of his claws, marks that any homeowner would bear proudly for years to come. When Lycaena's decorative fire was fully spent, the goddess sang instead, and she traversed all of Thanet so everyone might hear a whisper of her lovely, wordless chant.

The emerald-eyed boy's body swung in the cold breeze. He would hear no songs. He would dance amid no heatless flame.

"I murdered you," Rayan whispered. He pulled out the ten winter jasmines from his pocket. "Forgive me, child. Forgive me."

He scattered the bright yellow flowers at the foot of the corpse and then fled for the solitude of home.

Keles sat on his doorstep when he returned, and she dashed to her feet to embrace him the moment she saw him.

"You're safe!" she said as her arms closed about his chest. Rayan pulled her close and accepted the warm hug.

"Should I not be?" he asked.

"They've rebuilt the Dead Flags," his niece explained. "The Imperator has been leading raids all day, coming down hard on any Midwinter festivals or gatherings. I even heard of Lycaena followers being executed on the street, and I feared... well, it's obvious what I feared."

"Come now, as if I would ever be captured by the empire," Rayan said, and he forced a smile. Keles pulled away, and she seemed far from convinced by his poor joke.

"You've been crying," she said. Rayan cursed the redness of his eyes. He thought he'd wiped them dry on his walk home.

"I might have been."

"Come inside. I'll boil us some tea."

Rayan's pantry was poorly stocked for most trivialities, which meant Keles had little to sweeten the green tea once the iron kettle over his hearth reached a boil. The teacups and plates, however, were exquisite. They were a pale white with intricate carvings painted blue along the sides depicting both Lycaena and Endarius. Queen Holly Lythan had presented them as a gift to one of his ancestors for their loyal service, and the set had been cherished ever since. Possessing them put Rayan's life at risk should they be discovered, but given his lectures and his missions with Thorda, keeping a little tea set paled in comparison.

Rayan let Keles do all the preparations, for she seemed filled with a nervous energy, and the focus of a small, insignificant task did her well. They chatted while she worked, little inconsequential things about her own daily life as a messenger scribe, the position afforded to her given her paladin training in letters and numbers. It seemed absurd, to discuss trade minutiae and the status of the island's roads mere moments after standing before a swaying corpse, yet somehow it made the horror bearable. He immersed himself in Keles's life so he might endure the loss of Luke's and the sorrow of his own.

"This really is quite nice," he said once he had a chance to sip the tea she presented to him. "Though still not better than what I myself am capable of."

"So unbecoming for a paladin to brag," Keles said, but her laughter was light and precious. She sat on the floor opposite him at their little table. "I don't remember the priests teaching us anything beyond swordplay and prayers. My mother taught me how to make tea. When did you learn?"

Rayan smiled at a warm memory of Yvonne, his cousin and Keles's mother. They had played often when children, for both their parents lived in the castle as part of their familial duty to safeguard the throne. He kept the memory to himself. The young rarely wanted to listen to such stories, especially when the telling tended to have little point beyond the teller indulging themselves with fond memories.

"I forced myself to learn over the years," he said. "Our duties as paladins may require the sword to protect Thanet, but they more often mean telling stories around dinner tables or praying over the unwell. A good cup of tea can open up hearts that a thousand sermons may leave closed."

Keles sipped her tea, and he noted a sudden shift in her mood.

"I suppose it's a good thing I forsook my duties. If I can't make tea, I guess I'm not much of a paladin."

That explained her sudden shift in attitude. Leave it to him to botch things. "Our duties as paladins," he had said, despite Keles publicly shedding her title at the forsaking ceremony. He pretended not to notice, and instead tried to inject a bit of cheer back into the conversation.

"You'd have learned," he said. "Like all my talents, you would surpass them with time and training. I remember your schooling. You were a true natural with the blade."

"Only because you thrust a sword into my hand before I was even walking."

Rayan laughed. She was only partially exaggerating. By the time she was three, he'd begun sparring with her using wooden sticks, though if it had been his idea or hers, he could not truthfully remember. He held the tea closer to his mouth, not to drink, only to soak in the oceanic smell.

"Our family has faithfully served and protected the throne of Vallessau for four hundred years. Forgive an old man for being excited to have his niece follow in those footsteps."

"Magus of Eldrid now sits on said throne. Shall I march to the castle and offer up my sword? I'd hate to betray tradition, after all."

The bitterness in her words far exceeded the bitterness of his tea. Rayan had to pause a moment to prevent himself from responding in anger. He didn't want to spoil the mood with a fight, but neither would he allow such an insult to go unchallenged.

"Prince Cyrus carries royal blood in his veins, and holds within him the promise of his parents' legacy. Do not belittle his responsibilities, nor our family's history. The vows we swore, we have honored for hundreds of years since the end of the War of Tides. Nothing, not even the Everlorn Empire, can take away that honor."

"Honor. Vows. A lot of heavy, meaningful words, but what good do they do us now? Words won't cast out the empire's boats from our harbor. They won't put the Lythan family back on the throne."

"The tides have changed," Rayan said, determined to banish the despair his niece so often exhibited. "Regent Goldleaf now resides in the Heldeep, and may Dagon crunch on his bones each and every morning. We've slain priests and paragons. After years of darkness, daylight rises, and that is why they strike harder at us. They're afraid. We must bleed a little bit more, but peace shall come."

"Peace," Keles said. "Would that I could believe you, Uncle. I fail to see its promise."

"With Lycaena's aid, all things are possible."

"And Lycaena is dead!" The plate rattled as she slammed her cup, splitting a thin crack along one of its sides. "I was there, Rayan, same as you. I watched the blood spill as the knives tore apart her flesh. I heard her final scream. I gave Thanet's resistance everything I had, but our goddess is gone. It doesn't matter who sits on Vallessau's throne, be it Cyrus or Magus or some appointed regent. Our gods are dead, and our past with them."

Rayan slowly stood. He wished he knew better words than his own. He wished Keles had been with him in Alliya's house, and witnessed the flurry of moths.

"She is not dead," he said. "She is not gone. Our prayers are heard. She mourns our burdens. She weeps over our tribulations. Hold faith, my dear Keles, even in this darkest hour. Lycaena will return to us from the shadows she currently resides. Her wings shall fly over our city once more."

"Perhaps you're right," his niece said. "Though I doubt it. I wish all of you fighting Thorda's war the best of luck, but I'd rather not hang from the Dead Flags because I won't relinquish a dead goddess's memory."

Tea leaked from the crack in her cup, and she sighed and pushed both cup and plate away.

"I came to ensure your safety, but I regretfully have work to do. Thank you for the drink and the conversation. Stay safe, Uncle."

She left. The door shut behind her, and in the ensuing silence, Rayan's heart plummeted. There was a time when he had considered Keles's faith the strongest of any student he had ever known. A curse in disguise, for it meant the breaking of that faith had resulted in untold damage far beyond his capabilities to heal. If it ever healed.

"Would that I had better words," he said as a moth fluttered in through the open window. He offered it his hand, but it circled twice in the air before retreating outside. Rayan smiled, taking no offense. He prayed that it might fly far to the north, to land on the slowly swaying body of a nine-year-old boy with emerald-colored eyes, to guide the soul within to the flower-strewn fields of the eternal lands beyond.

CHAPTER 32

CYRUS

It had been three days since Thorda last sent Cyrus on a mission, and the delay was enough to ruin his already fitful sleep and send him pacing the halls of their mansion. And so when night fell, and all others slept, the Vagrant donned his mask and cloak, buckled his swords, and slipped out into the night.

Just a quick kill, he thought as he stalked the rooftops. *A reminder to the city I'm here, and watching.*

Magus's rule as Imperator-Regent was one of bloodshed and misery. The number of Dead Flags rivaled those of the earliest purges at the start of Thanet's invasion. By the end of his first week, he ended the unwritten rule that no children would be hung from them. Businesses were being confiscated left and right. Soldiers searched homes at random. No reasons needed, nor given. It was as if the fear and chaos were justification enough. Whenever the bells sounded for mandatory service, the streets emptied, not a soul daring to show their face lest they be confronted by soldiers as to the reason for their absence.

Thorda insisted he had a plan, a raid on a church to kill a magistrate. Three days wasn't that long. The calls for patience might be wise, but they burned in Cyrus's gut nonetheless.

"Is this what you hoped for?" Cyrus whispered unheard to the soldier he stalked along the rooftops. The man marched down the midnight street, clueless to how close death followed. "Was this everything you wanted when you boarded a boat for our island?"

Was it the pay? The bloodshed? Or was it merely a job to him, and the people of Thanet meant absolutely nothing? Cyrus didn't know, nor did he particularly care. The soldier was foolishly alone, and in the poorest parts of Vallessau, having sneaked out for a visit to the brothel at the end of the lane. Cyrus drew his swords and grinned behind his mask. It would be the last fun the man had. The noise of his footsteps upon the rooftops was the man's only warning, and his reaction was far too slow to defend himself as Cyrus descended with swords ready.

The downward curved blade of his longer weapon sank into the soldier's chest. He screamed, but the cry was weak, with one of his lungs already torn. Cyrus easily shoved him toward the nearby alley. No reason to risk remaining in plain sight. The soldier rolled across the ground, leaving a bloody trail to shine slick black in the moonlight. He tried to rise to his feet, his sword gripped in one hand. Cyrus trapped him in that little alley, and he closed in on his foe without hesitation. It was so much easier now, killing these soldiers. But wouldn't it be, given his experience? After battling against the divine strength of paragons, what threat did a mere soldier present?

An upward slash, a kick, and the soldier dropped to his back. Cyrus's off-hand plunged into the man's throat, ending him. He ripped it free, wiped it clean on the soldier's gray tunic, and then sheathed it. He wasn't done with the other blade, though. Slowly, carefully, he cut a crown across the soldier's forehead. There was no denying Cyrus's satisfaction in carving this singular message, repeated upon every kill, to both the empire and the people of Thanet.

The Vagrant was here, and while he lived, the imperials would die.

"It's...it's you. Isn't it?"

Cyrus spun, sword up and at the ready. A young man hardly older than Cyrus stood at the entrance to the alley. His mouth was open, and his eyes wide. Had he also come from the brothel?

"I am," Cyrus said. "Who else would I be?"

"We all know of you," the man said. He walked with a slight limp, made worse by how much of a hurry he moved. "That skull. That crown. You're the Vagrant."

Cyrus grinned behind an already grinning skull despite knowing it would go unseen.

"Guilty."

The man slowed as he neared. He stammered for a moment, struggling for the right words.

"Could you...could you bless me, with your sword?"

Cyrus froze in place. Bless him? How? What did he even mean? The young man took his confusion for rejection, and he dropped to his knees.

"Please," he said. "They hung my brother from the flags. I'm not asking much."

He reached out for the bloody blade. Cyrus allowed him to curl his fingers about the edges, careful not to cut himself on the sharp bottom. Gently, calmly, and with great honor, this stranger pressed the flat side of the sword across his forehead. The blood of the soldier smeared upon his skin, granting him a familiar and yet wholly different crown. The man released the sword, and he leaned back onto his heels. His voice broke when he spoke as the first tears came.

"Make them pay," he said. "Make them all pay."

Cyrus saw the faith in the man's eyes, so fragile and yet so strong. He needed to believe in this. It was the solid ground upon which he stood as everything else around him quaked and fell. Thorda spoke often of Cyrus's need to build a legend for himself, to establish the mystery and power of the Vagrant persona. He understood it now. Those eyes of faith, that crown of blood, revealed it in a way no speech or lesson ever could.

"I will," the Vagrant promised. "They will all pay for the blood they have shed upon my island."

It was exactly what the man wanted to hear, yet to speak such a pronouncement made Cyrus feel strange. *"My island"?* When he'd first returned to Vallessau, he had felt no attachment to the city, nor did he feel that Thanet was truly his to rule. All he wanted was revenge. This change in him...was this a change he even wanted?

The young man dropped his head, and the worship, the whispered words that sounded so akin to prayer, made Cyrus's skin crawl. He sheathed his sword, and he offered no further words. Into the street he ran, then to the rooftops, until he could flee home.

It seemed his midnight excursion would not go unnoticed. Cyrus halted in the hallway when he heard his name called, and he reluctantly stepped into the living room to find Thorda sitting before the fire, carefully manipulating its coals with the iron poker.

"Do you grow impatient with my planning?" his master asked. Cyrus removed his mask and ran a hand through his sweaty face and hair.

"Do you mean, do I feel an urge to 'do something'?" he asked, and grinned in spite of his unease. "No, Thorda, I do not question you. I was careful, and it was a single soldier. Consider it keeping my skills sharp while I await your next orders."

"That is good to hear." The older man glanced over his shoulder. "Get some rest. I've confirmed the movements of the magistrate at the church. You will execute him tomorrow evening, and I would prefer it be done with you on a full night's rest."

"A full night's rest," Cyrus said, and he chuckled as if such a thing were as mythical and rare as any of Thanet's slain gods. He started for his bedroom but then paused. He could not shake the image of the young man bowing before him, nor the worship in his eyes as he pressed the bloody blade across his forehead. Mind changed, he instead joined Thorda in the living room, and he took a seat by the newly warmed fire.

For a long moment he sat in silence, slowly rotating the skull mask in his hands. He thought of the legacy he was building, and the stories he first heard when Thorda began training him years ago. Thorda, meanwhile, stayed on the carpet, legs crossed underneath him, as he soaked in the warmth of the fire.

"Who was he?" Cyrus asked. "The Skull-Amid-the-Trees. What was he like?"

Thorda shifted in his seat so he might directly face Cyrus. Years seemed to have been added onto a face already sporting its fair share of wrinkles.

"My husband was a proud man, confident and deadly. There was no advantage he would not take for his own, no trick he would not employ to even the unbalanced scales."

Thorda reached out his hand, and Cyrus gave him the skull. His master held it tenderly, his fingers brushing the carved and painted wood.

"You would have liked Rhodes, if you met him. Though skillful in murder, he was kind at heart. His dedication was matched only by his compassion. I did not deserve him, even if he never believed that himself."

Cyrus shifted uncomfortably. This was such a tender subject, but for his own sanity, he had to know.

"Where did he err?" he asked quietly. "How...how did he die?"

Thorda looked down to the mask. His shoulders slouched, and his eyes glazed over as the weight of history overcame him.

"It is a difficult tale," he said. "Are you certain you wish to hear it?"

Cyrus thought of the worship on the stranger's face, of the way he had smeared the blood across his forehead into a crown he bore with pride.

"Yes," Cyrus said. "I must know the story of the man whose mask I wear, and whose footsteps I follow."

Thorda breathed in deep and then slowly let it out.

"Though the Everlorn Empire surrounded my homeland of Miquo on all sides, they could not cross the Vermell Mountains into our divine forests without catastrophic death. They tried once. We collapsed walkways and buried thousands beneath avalanches. So we were left alone, a little thorn in the empire's side, but even the most optimistic among us feared it was only a matter of time until we fell. I believed we should act while the advantage remained ours. That is what I told myself, to justify my plans.

"For hundreds of years, we Miquoans squabbled with our neighboring country of Antiev. Their gods were not our gods, their traditions not our traditions, their homes earthbound instead of high up amid the branches. With that in mind, I visited the God-Incarnate in Eldrid and offered him a deal. Promise our little nation of Miquo independence, and I would aid in his invasion of Antiev. He agreed, and so I whispered secrets our people had learned over centuries of conflict, where Antiev's mighty warriors laid out their ambushes, where they smuggled supplies, and where they hid among their tunnels and caves. A campaign that might take years ended in mere weeks. Antiev fell, our longtime enemy conquered, and her gods slain. And I *celebrated*."

Thorda's hands shook as he clutched the skull hard enough, it seemed he tried, and failed, to crush it within his grasp.

"You can guess what happened next. Every promise, every agreement, every treaty…they were all lies. No piece of paper will hold back the divine, for what court may rule against a god? Once Antiev fell, Lucavi turned his greedy eyes to the people of Miquo. He would have our faith. He would murder our gods. His armies gathered, tens of thousands of soldiers and a whole host of paragons, and this time they need not cross the Vermell. They launched their campaign from Antiev, our fallen neighbor, and marched straight into our forests. So began the invasion, and this time, we could not stop it. I'm sure you can imagine what that was like."

A memory of burning fleets and smoke encompassing the entire harbor came unwelcome to Cyrus. Yes, he very much did.

"It took them years," Thorda continued, "but they steadily advanced, their resources limitless compared to ours. When they tired of our ambushes, they burned the forests. I think, by the end, they thought it easier to replace our people entirely with their own citizens than convert our own. It was in that final year, when the people's hope was dwindling, that my husband built his legacy. He used every advantage he could conceive. He fought alone, and hunted leaders instead of grunts. He ambushed from the trees. He poisoned food. With his face unknown, he could still walk among their camps, and walk among them he did…with me, as I argued for peace."

Thorda could not hide his disgust at his past self.

"I begged him to not risk his own life. Trust in diplomacy, I told him. I still had my agreements, and the excuses the God-Incarnate used to justify our invasion were wearing thin. A new peace treaty would be finalized, and all my efforts rewarded. Miquo would become part of the Everlorn Empire, but we would maintain special privileges, and select gods were allowed to survive. And then, on the day the new peace treaty was to be signed, Rhodes promised to set aside his mask. It... it was a lie. As we met at the diplomatic table, he attempted to kill the God-Incarnate. Attempted, and failed."

The older man shook his head.

"They captured him alive. I bribed a guard so I might speak with him one last time before his execution. 'Train them,' Rhodes begged me. 'Train Mari, train Stasia, train them both like I trained you. Teach them to kill. Let the blood of my blood slay a thousandfold more than I did in my time.' And I promised him I would. How could I refuse, given what I must do the following day at the city gates?"

Thorda trembled, sorrow and fury intermixing into a dangerous glare that frightened Cyrus.

"You must understand, I had no choice, not if I wished to protect the lives of my daughters. In full view of my city, my husband, and my children, I rebuked Rhodes for his war upon the empire. I condemned the blood on his hands, and I vowed absolute obedience to the Everlorn Empire. In the quiet prison, I told him one final time that I loved him, for my last words to him below those gates were savage lies."

Cyrus knew but a shadow of that pain. He had been forced to condemn the resistance fighters while under the Usurper King's watch, and he had been forbidden from saying a kind word about his slain parents. But to speak such horrible things to their faces? He tried to imagine cursing his parents just before the sword fell upon them. He couldn't. It was too awful, too cruel, and yet Thorda had endured. His respect for his master increased tenfold.

"It haunts me," Thorda said, after a moment to gather himself. "Those words. Those lies. When my hope falters, or the task of building yet another rebellion threatens to exhaust my will and crush my spirit, I remember my rage in that one moment. I doubted the empire's hunger. I believed peace a viable path. For those great failures, I lost the man I loved most. I have dedicated the rest of my life to retribution. I want to make the God-Incarnate hurt, Cyrus. I want him to feel exactly what I felt as my nation crumbled around me and everything I loved and held dear was brought to the sword."

It was a rare moment of vulnerability, and for once, Thorda did not try to hide it. A twin pair of tears trickled down his leathery face. His hands shook as they clenched into fists.

"Perhaps such desires are the mark of a terrible heart. If so, I am most terrible indeed, and those damn horrid words I spoke to my dying husband only prove it true."

Cyrus didn't know what to do or say. He remembered his own sick anger, especially in his earliest days at Thorda's mansion. He remembered the stuttering speeches he gave at Regent Goldleaf's behest during those awful parties, condemning belief in Lycaena and Endarius and diminishing his own parents' death as a necessary part of Thanet's salvation. Cyrus looked to his master, and he wondered how similar they truly were. All his talk of tales and heroes and inspiring the populace... how much of it was true? Or did he see something else in Cyrus, something so much simpler and easier to understand?

"Do Mari and Stasia know?" he asked after a time. "Who Rhodes was, or why you had to condemn him as you did?"

Thorda hesitated a moment, then slowly shook his head.

"Mari was too young to remember it now, nor understand what was happening. Stasia did, for a time. It drove her during those early years, put a fire into her that allowed her to endure trials that would fell most mortal men. Does she still remember the face of her other father? I do not believe so. Too many lost years. Too many campaigns and war-torn nations."

Thorda offered Cyrus the skull mask.

"I pried that off my husband's swollen, bloodied face and smuggled it out of the prison. Twice before, I have attempted to build a legacy worthy of him. Twice, I have witnessed my chosen warrior die at the hands of paragons. You are my third, Cyrus, and already you have accomplished more than Rhodes did in his time. You give me hope. You make me believe that there is still a chance we can send the empire crumbling into the ashes of history."

Cyrus accepted the mask, and he held it with newfound respect.

"You ask so much of me," he said.

"Only because our need is so great." The older man pushed up from his seat before the fire. His hand rested upon Cyrus's shoulder. That single touch was more affection than he had shown all those years they had trained together. Cyrus had no idea how badly he needed it, craved it, until those hard, callused hands squeezed his shoulder to offer him comfort.

"However great our need, I believe you capable of surpassing it, my young Vagrant. My daughters are my all, but my heart still holds room for a son. Thank you. For everything. And in return, I will ensure you perform miracles. It is in that, and in you, I place my faith."

Cyrus could barely find words to speak. The word echoed in his mind, again and again.

Son.

"I don't deserve it," he whispered.

The hand left his shoulder.

"None of us do."

CHAPTER 33

CYRUS

Cyrus paused at the door to Thorda's home after another successful midnight mission and watched Arn panic in the middle of the empty street.

"Where is it?" the giant man asked, patting his pants pockets. "Damn it. All gods, damn it."

"Something the matter?" Cyrus asked. He pulled off his mask and wiped a bit of sweat from his brow. It was risky to expose his face as such, but the hour was late and Thorda had worked with Clarissa to purchase all the nearby homes and fill them with Thanet loyalists. The two Ahlai sisters had gone inside, leaving only the pair out in the cold.

"None of your business," Arn said. "Maybe I left it back here..."

He burst through the front door like an angered bear. Cyrus tilted his head to the side, eyebrow arcing.

"Huh."

Stasia and Mari shot him a confused look from the couch, the two unwinding together with steaming cups of tea in hand. Cyrus shrugged, having nothing to offer. He followed Arn upstairs to his room, where the door was open and Arn was busy ransacking his dresser. He still hadn't removed his fox mask.

"Not here," he mumbled. "Not here, not here. SHIT."

"There something wrong?" Cyrus asked. He'd not been working

with Arn long, and was still feeling out the man's temperament. He was, paradoxically, both the most laid back and relaxed on missions, while also the crankiest and most stubborn about people following plans and orders. Cyrus assumed much of this was due to his paragon training, holding no fear for his own life while demanding perfection from others. He also put some of this on Arn just naturally being an asshole.

"None of your business, Vagrant."

That he used their secret name in the house did not go unnoticed by Cyrus.

"Something is clearly bothering you, and I'd like to help if I can."

Arn stopped his searching to put his hands on his hips and glare.

"I lost something, that's all," he said. "Now out of my way."

He blasted past Cyrus, connecting shoulder to shoulder for good measure. Cyrus flung his hands in the air, cast his eyes to the heavens in a plea for patience, and then hurried after. He meant to ask another question, but Mari and Stasia were both staring by the time they'd reached the bottom of the stairs. Cyrus had a feeling the paragon wouldn't share while in their presence, so he kept his mouth shut and followed Arn outside.

"Where in blazes are you going?" he asked as Arn pulled his metal gauntlets off the clips to his belt and jammed his hands back into them.

"To the church. I must have dropped it there."

Cyrus momentarily froze from the sheer audacity of the plan.

"You want to go *back*?"

His face may have been covered, but Arn's eyes were visible through the holes in the fox skull, and there was no hiding his absolute impatience with this conversation.

"Yeah? Got a problem with that? Then go inside, make yourself some tea, and stay out of my affairs."

Cyrus's brain hiccupped multiple times as he tried to put his thoughts in order.

"Heretic, we just *left* the church. We killed a magistrate and a half-dozen priests. That whole building is going to be crawling with soldiers, paragons, maybe even the Imperator himself. We can't just...go back."

"Who ever said 'we,' Vagrant?" Arn called over his shoulder.

Cyrus dashed after the burly man while putting on his skull mask.

"I did, because I'm not letting you go alone."

The "church" was known as the Twin Sanctuary, or at least it had been before the Uplifted Church claimed it as their own. Now it was the God-Incarnate's Haven, a name no one on the island used unless forced. From the beginning, the Twin Sanctuary had been built with unity between the gods Endarius and Lycaena in mind. The feathered Lion and floating Butterfly had chased and flown about each other in the original dozen painted windows. Those windows had been smashed out and replaced with transparent glass that didn't seem to ever fit quite right. Statues of the gods had once loomed above the grand double doors at the top of the steps. Now broken, jagged stone was all that remained, looking like a gaping wound.

Cyrus and Arn lurked at the far end of the street leading to the church, observing the lingering group of soldiers standing at the front steps. No doubt those soldiers were there because of the *last* attack Thorda's group had succeeded in earlier tonight, during which they had slain the church's presiding magistrate.

"If you're coming with me, you're going to fight how I like to fight," Arn said with a forced whisper. "That means we won't be doing any of this sneaking around shit Thorda's daughters are so good at. I'm going through the front door, and I'm going over the bodies of my enemies. If you have a problem with that—"

"I can go running back home, tail between my legs, my belly yellow, so on and so forth," Cyrus interrupted. He lowered his hands to the hilts of his swords. "You're part of the team now, Heretic, which means I'm sticking with you through thick and thin. I pray this is worth it."

Arn punched his knuckles together. The metal gauntlets rang once, and the big man grinned behind his fox mask.

"We're killing imperials," he said. "When is that *not* worth it?"

Cyrus returned the grin in kind.

"You have me there. Lead on, crazy bastard."

Arn had not been exaggerating when he declared there would be no stealth or subterfuge. Despite the considerable distance between them and the steps of the church, he cut to the center of the street and then dashed straight ahead. It took about a full second before the soldiers noticed the mad approach of a gargantuan man clad in dark leather, and the cloaked Vagrant chasing after him with the moonlight glowing off his silver crown. Cyrus could see the soldiers' shock by their body movements. They stiffened, jaws dropping, hands fumbling for undrawn weapons. One looked around, whether for help or anticipating additional members of an ambush, Cyrus could only guess.

Despite Arn's significantly greater weight and size, he easily kept pace ahead of Cyrus. His long coat, custom made by Thorda upon his arrival to Thanet, billowed behind him despite its tremendous weight. The soldiers managed to ready their weapons as they approached, but it didn't matter.

Arn leaped at the last possible moment, body rotating to add strength to his long, winding punch. The center soldier lifted his shield while pulling back his sword, as if he might counter once the attack was blocked. Instead Arn's punch caved the shield in at the middle. Metal shrieked, as did the soldier as his arm snapped at the most awful of angles. They collided, Arn's body perfectly positioned to take advantage of his momentum. His shoulder hit the soldier's chest, his legs pumped to keep himself moving, and he carried the screaming man several feet past his fellows. A twist, and Arn lifted the man up high off his shoulder and into his hands. A drop of his muscular arms, and he smashed the soldier upon the steps as if cracking open a melon.

Cyrus debated if he should feel insulted at how completely ignored he was following in Arn's shadow. He slid between the two soldiers, his swords flashing in the light of torches burning atop pillars on either side of the steps. His off-hand blade only nicked his target's face, but the other found much better purchase. The curved end sank into the soldier's throat, at first shallow until Cyrus pivoted all his weight on his left heel and then forced the tip deeper. Blood splashed, warm and sticky upon his hands. He ripped it free, spun, and faced the final soldier.

The panicked man shook in his boots, torn between holding his ground or fleeing for his life. Easy prey for Cyrus, but he didn't have a chance to attack to finish him. A projectile sailed through the air to slam directly into the soldier's chest, blasting him to the ground. Cyrus's eyes widened in surprise. The projectile...it was the gory mess that was the first soldier's body. Cyrus was torn between horror and hysterical laughter. He took two quick steps, flipped his swords, and put a quick end to the final soldier's life. Afterward he carved a line across both their foreheads, for the Vagrant must have his due.

Once finished, he stepped back and flicked blood and gore off the slick edges of his swords. His gaze turned to the impromptu projectile, and then the man who threw it.

"Is this how you fight normally?" Cyrus asked incredulously. He knew the former paragon could pound a hole in a brick wall with his punches, but on their few missions together, that's mostly all he'd done, batter his foes with his fists and elbows. Arn shrugged as if tossing men like rag dolls was no strange thing.

"Paragons are meant to inspire, to stand out in battle, not hide at the edges of a war."

Shouts echoed from above, warning cries of people in the church no doubt hearing the commotion of their attack.

"We're definitely not hiding," Cyrus muttered as he turned his attention higher up the steps.

The sanctuary doors burst open, and four soldiers came rushing to the top steps. A red-robed priest trailed behind them, golden light shining about his fingers as he chanted a prayer.

"The soldiers are mine," Arn said. "Take the priest."

Cyrus wasn't exactly sure how Arn expected him to do that with four soldiers standing between him and said priest, but the question was answered when the former paragon charged straight at them, bounding the stairs with the grace of a deer. It was almost amusing seeing such acrobatics upon the enormous mountain of muscle, but for his foes, it was most certainly terrifying instead.

"Stand firm, and receive strength from the righteousness of our cause!" the priest bellowed. He was a mousy-looking fellow, much of his head balding along the top. The light about his hands rolled forward in a wave that swirled around the soldiers defending him. Strengthening them, if the rumors Cyrus had heard were true, but could it be enough to handle the raging Heretic?

The soldier's body flying down the steps to smash headfirst onto the hard cobblestones suggested no.

Cyrus dashed along the far side of the steps, just shy of the ornate railing. One of the soldiers moved to intercept, only for Arn to grab him by the wrist. A single clench of those gauntlets and the frail bones within broke.

"Get back here," Arn shouted, and he tugged the soldier close, opening the way for Cyrus. He burst onto the flat stretch of stone before the church doors at the top of the steps. The priest lifted his arms, and though his face was beaded with sweat, and panic swelled his eyes wide, his voice spoke with surprising calmness.

"God bless and keep me," he chanted as a golden sword materialized in the air before him. Though it shimmered like light, Cyrus knew it could both cut and be blocked like any other blade. Since wielded by the mind, not by bone and muscle, it could weave and move in unnatural manners. This meant Cyrus had to dictate the fight, and overwhelm the priest quickly, if he were to win.

"Your faith?" he asked as he stalked the priest. His every step was measured. The slightest hint of movement from that golden sword and he would react. "Faith in whom, priest?"

"God watch and guide me," the priest continued, ignoring him. Cyrus tilted his head just so. Moonlight fell across his mask. He paused so the priest might see the mocking grin.

"Your god isn't here, priest. I am."

The priest hesitated, fear pulsing through him like venom, and it was in that moment that Cyrus lunged, left hand held close and defensive, right hand extending for a thrust. The priest mentally recovered, fell back a step, and then clapped his hands together. The holy sword split, becoming two blades, each one bathed with power and swinging to cut off Cyrus's charge.

It was a fine trick, but not enough. The priest had no skill in swordplay, and he struck without imagination. Both blades arced straight down, aiming for no specific body part. Cyrus blocked the left with ease, his arm rising as if he wielded a shield. His right, already pulled for a thrust, shifted so that he instead parried the other chop harmlessly aside. His momentum continued. The space between them closed. Cyrus's butterfly off-hand blade weaved a figure eight before him, crisscrossing an X over the priest's throat. The priest dropped, blood gurgling out his ruined windpipe. The glowing swords faded into nothing.

His appointed foe slain, Cyrus moved to aid Arn, but he should have known Thorda's vaunted Heretic would have no trouble with a mere four soldiers. Three were already dead, and the fourth about to be. The soldier did succeed in punching his spear into Arn's long coat, though Cyrus was not sure if it found purchase. The same could not be said for the double-fisted smash of Arn's gauntlets upon the man's shoulders. Bones snapped, so many it sounded like a bundle of twigs breaking. The soldier howled, his shield and spear falling from his limp hands. Arn caved in the man's chest to end his scream. Lungs suddenly punctured and full of fluid, he dropped, retching pitifully for a few seconds as the light faded from his eyes.

"You all right?" Cyrus asked. There was so much blood and gore everywhere, he couldn't begin to guess what belonged to whom.

Arn lifted his arms and glanced side to side. His coat hung down to his ankles, and though it appeared made of dark leather, that was only the deceitful exterior. Thorda had decided that Arn could not sneak about the city wearing a paragon's platemail. Instead he'd lined the interior of the coat with a single sheet of chainmail. Cyrus had worn it out of curiosity, and though it hung comfortably across his back and shoulders, he couldn't imagine fighting with that additional thirty pounds weighing him down.

"Nothing bleeding," Arn said. "Can't ask for more than that."

Cyrus cut the mark of the Vagrant across the soldiers' foreheads. They weren't his kills, but after so many missions for Thorda, he'd long since learned to ignore his guilt in taking credit for the actions of others. When finished, he hurried to Arn's side. The first time they'd entered the Twin Sanctuary earlier that night, Mari had crept along the roof in Lioness form, dropped in through a high window, and removed the heavy iron latches locking the double doors shut. This time, Arn strode right up and kicked their center with his heel, smashing them inward.

"That's one way to knock," Cyrus said, and he followed Arn inside. Unlike the first visit to the Twin Sanctuary, where he'd been nervous and leading a stealthy assassination attempt on the sleeping magistrate, now Cyrus walked in feeling surprisingly nostalgic. He gazed at the painted windows, basic color patterns that once depicted stories of Lycaena and Endarius. The crimson carpet was soft beneath his feet. He walked between rows of benches with goose feather pillows. Looming over it all was a golden statue of God-Incarnate Lucavi. He seemed less of a man and more an idealized version of one, his chest bare and covered with more muscles than seemed humanly possible. His hair was long, his smile patronizing, his legs so thick, they made his rather normal feet seem comically tiny. Even his groin bulged as if the thin loincloth was overstuffed, an obscene image in a place so holy.

"One day," he whispered, imagining the statue of the God-Incarnate replaced with the proper monument from his childhood, that of Lycaena placing a loving hand upon Endarius's head, the two gods in repose atop a thatched reed raft.

One of his earliest memories was sitting on his grandmother's lap a year before she passed away, attending what would be one of many Calm Tide services in his life. The holiday marked the end of the War of Tides, the appointment of the Lythan family as chosen rulers of Thanet, and the declaration of unity and cooperation between Lycaena and Endarius for the hearts and minds of her people. Given the importance, he attended each one dressed up in his finest, cramped into pews to hear speeches of togetherness and sing the same songs that had been sung for centuries. It took place during what was often the hottest stretch of summer, and he remembered impatiently fidgeting on his grandmother's lap, sweating profusely, while she sang hymns at the top of her lungs. He'd mouthed along, too young for the words and promises to mean anything to him. Those songs now made him ache.

Arn walked the aisle, his head rotating left to right as he scanned the dimly lit ground for whatever it was that he'd lost on their original assassination.

"What is it we're looking for?" Cyrus asked, not bothering to whisper as he followed. They'd made enough noise to alert the entire church, assuming anyone else remained to be alerted.

"Vagrant, you ask that one more time, I'm going to give you a fat lip."

"It's personal, I get that, and I assume something dear to you, but you mustn't be rude about it."

"I'm not being rude," Arn said as he lifted a bench to look underneath it, using as much effort as he might to pick up a mouse. "I'm stating a simple fact so you may act accordingly. Also, it's not here. Let's check the magistrate's room."

The majority of the building was dedicated to the enormous worship room, full of rows upon rows of pews, stages for choirs, a raised pulpit for priests, and a pipe organ older than Cyrus's grandparents. Hidden to the side were doors leading farther in, some to storage closets, others to bedrooms and changing rooms. Alone, and normally locked for the night, was the ornate door decorated with gold, hopelessly scratched and mutilated to remove Lycaena's symbol across its front.

Arn led the way. Having already broken the lock during their initial attack, he needed only to brush it aside to enter the hallway beyond. The magistrate's private chambers were at the far end, and he crossed the crimson carpet with a maddening lack of urgency. They passed several closed doors, and after the third, Arn paused and tilted his head to one side.

"I hear your breathing," he said, the sentence spurring the hiding attacker into action. An acolyte armed with a club burst from the door, howling something about Lucavi and his soul. Before Cyrus could even turn, Arn caught him by the throat, flung him to the ground, and kicked his head. The young man's neck twisted with an audible pop, and it bulged unnaturally on one side. Cyrus winced at the sight. He still had acne on his cheeks, for Lycaena's sake.

"Just a kid," he said softly.

"A kid trying to murder us," Arn said. "No pity for those who worship and serve the oppressor, Vagrant. That'll make you soft."

Cyrus tried, and failed, not to take offense as he knelt down and cut a line across the acolyte's forehead. The stories of a double attack on the newly renamed God-Incarnate's Haven would certainly get around. The rumored explanations would probably be worth a few laughs, for who would properly guess the reason for their return? He didn't even know why, either, and wouldn't until Arn stopped being stubborn and explained himself.

A deep brass ringing of a bell pulled him from his thoughts.

"That's the alarm for the nearby watch tower," Cyrus said. "Which means we're out of time."

Arn kicked the door to the dead magistrate's room open and strode inside.

"Let reinforcements come. It'll give us some entertainment when we make our way home."

Cyrus had thought Arn joined Thorda's resistance out of a sense of morality, or disgust at the crimes of the Everlorn Empire. Now he was beginning to think the former paragon merely had a death wish.

"I'm not trying to recapture my throne for *entertainment*," he hissed as he followed Arn into the room. The paragon lifted the dresser, found nothing, then set it down so he might tear open a few drawers to be sure. Next he tossed the bloodstained mattress aside. The magistrate had died in his bed during their earlier attack on the Sanctuary, but there was no sign of the body.

"Then why do you want your throne back?" Arn asked. "Surely you know that even if we succeed, God-Incarnate Lucavi will send fleet after fleet across the Crystal Sea until he buries this island in soldiers and paragons. I assumed you were motivated by hate and spite. Never took you for one of Thorda's idealistic dreamers."

These issues were problems lurking in the distance, ones on which Cyrus had refused to spare even a moment's thought. What point was there focusing on the difficulties he might face as king when the sheer act of reclaiming his throne was already so daunting?

"If it's so hopeless, then why are *you* here?" he asked.

Arn dropped to one knee and checked underneath the bed.

"There you are," he said, ignoring Cyrus's question. "It must have fallen out of my pocket while I was handling the magistrate."

By *handling* him, Arn meant squeezing the magistrate's head between his gauntlets until it popped like a grape. There hadn't been enough left for Cyrus to carve the Vagrant's crown across the forehead, an issue that, when presented to Arn, had only made the paragon laugh. It was during this head-squashing that Arn must have lost his most precious... whatever the object of his fanatical search was. He shoved the bed frame up with his shoulder and then grabbed it, surprisingly quick for a man so giant. Cyrus caught only a glimpse of something orange and white before it vanished into Arn's pocket.

"Is that it?" Cyrus asked. He felt like he was the butt of some strange joke. "We risked our lives for whatever that little thing was?"

"I don't remember asking you to come along."

Alarm bells were ringing nonstop. No time to argue the matter, not here, as much as Cyrus wished for an explanation.

"Later then," he said. "It's time to get out of here before the entire imperial occupation comes down on our heads."

CHAPTER 34

ARN

I appreciate you coming with me," Arn said as they approached their home, and he did mean it. Their sprint had slowed to a walk as they reached the neighboring housing district and left the ringing of alarm bells far behind. They'd encountered only a single soldier during their way out, outmatched and easily dispatched. "Even if you did so uninvited."

"Oh, we're not finished yet," Cyrus said. He dashed a few steps ahead and attempted to halt Arn's path. "You're not entering our safe house until you give me an explanation, and one I deem sufficient."

Of course, Arn's attempt at kindness was rebuked immediately. He needed to stop being surprised by that.

"Big orders from a tiny man," Arn said, and he blasted right past Cyrus, easily shouldering him out of the way. But while he didn't mind bossing around the princeling, the younger Ahlai sister blocking the doorway was another matter.

"And where have you two charming fellows been off to?" Mari asked. Her arms were crossed over her chest, her pleasant voice not matching the cold, calm look on her face.

"Nothing important," Arn said, trying to brush aside this thoroughly unwelcome prying into his past life.

"Nothing important?" She lifted an eyebrow. "Warning bells have been ringing across half the city, most certainly of your own doing, and you left without even a word of explanation. I sure hope you didn't risk your lives and make me worry all for 'nothing important.'"

Arn rubbed at the back of his head and glanced aside. All the gods and goddesses help him, he towered over this woman, yet he feared to meet her gaze. Why? Was it because he knew who she truly was, what she could become as the Lioness?

"He forgot something at the Twin Sanctuary," Cyrus oh-so-helpfully explained. "As to what, he refuses to say."

Now with Mari's backing, Vagrant seemed brave enough to block his way once more. Arn noted the way his hands lingered near his swords. Surely he wouldn't draw them . . . would he? It was just a charm, a stupid charm; why were they so insistent on knowing what it was?

"Look, I didn't ask you to come, and you saw how easily we mopped up the guards that remained," Arn argued. "Everything was fine. I dropped something, and that could be incriminating, yeah? So I went and got it. Why are you making such a big thing out of this? And who are you to even block me from entering Thorda's home? I don't remember *you* recruiting me."

Cyrus's hands tightened around the sword hilts.

"Despite your bluster, you put your life at risk to retrieve it. You weren't even planning on telling anyone you were going back for it, either. What if you were captured? What if you were interrogated, putting all our identities and plans at risk?"

If Arn's mood weren't so sour, he might have been impressed. Cyrus had training, but he'd seemed so young and timid when they first met. Now he saw a bit of spine, a good thing under most circumstances. Just not when Arn wanted to grab himself a bottle, slump by a fire, and drink himself to sleep. He leaned closer. Let Cyrus realize their size difference. Let him feel the presence and power of a former paragon.

"That's not an answer, princeling. You're not in charge. Move aside."

Cyrus's eyes widened behind his ridiculous crowned skull mask.

"I may not be in charge, but I care for those inside, and you're putting them in danger. That's my reason. If you want my trust, and my cooperation, you'll tell me what we fought and killed for."

Arn glanced over Cyrus's shoulder, and he saw similar sentiments on Mari's face. He signaled his surrender with an exaggerated sigh.

"Fine," he said. "If you're going to be a nosy little shit about it, I'll show you."

Arn removed his gauntlets and hooked them into his belt by the tiny rings carved into their bases. When done, he retrieved the charm from his pocket. It was the tip of a fox tail, hardly larger than a human thumb, with the cut side capped with a bit of bronze. It was mostly orange but for a long, swirling bit of white on one side. Arn held it before him, letting the prince have a good long look.

"There," he said. "Happy now?"

Arn had to admit, the bafflement on the young prince's face was almost worth the annoyance.

"That's... that's it?" he asked. "A simple little charm?"

Arn twirled the cap between his fingers.

"That's it."

Cyrus flung his hands to the air, his frustration overwhelming his attempt at being the calm, cool defender of his home.

"This is ridiculous. How could such a little thing be worth—"

Mari's voice cracked like a whip.

"Cyrus, go inside." He started to protest, but she gave him no chance. "And change your clothes. There's blood on them."

The two exchanged a look, a conversation happening silently between them. Cyrus pulled his skull mask off and wiped strands of hair from his face.

"If you insist," he said, glanced once more at Arn, and then barged through the front door. Now alone, any resemblance of sweetness left Mari's countenance. Her face hardened. She was stone. She was ice. This, this was the savage Lioness he was convinced lurked underneath the façade. So calmly she pointed to the charm, and it was like being singled out by a witness during a tribunal.

"Cyrus cannot see it, but he's inexperienced with the world, and he does not commune with the divine as I do." Her eyes narrowed. "That tail was cut from a god."

Arn pushed the charm into his pocket. His jaw tightly clenched. She was reading him, judging him. What conclusion would she reach? And then her questions assaulted him, one after the other.

"Was it a gift, or was it taken?"

He gave no answer.

"Does the deity still live?"

He gave no answer.

"Or did you kill them, Arn Bastell?"

A memory flashed before him, unbidden. Of a city under siege, thousands of homes burning, the surrounding muddy fields choked with corpses. He said nothing. Silence stretched between them. Those red eyes, seeing into him in an unnatural way. She was a god-whisperer of Miquo. What powers did they possess he did not know? Could she read his memories? His soul?

"Will you block my entrance?" he asked, surprised by the awkwardness in his own voice. It couldn't...he wasn't actually *afraid* of this woman, was he?

Mari let the question hang in the air. A faint smile tugged at the right corner of her mouth.

"Good night, Arn," she said, turned, and stepped inside. The door shut. He heard the rattle of a lock.

Arn patted the charm in his pocket.

"I probably deserve that," he said.

While paragons were often spoiled beyond measure by the Everlorn Empire, battle did not always afford such luxuries. Arn had long learned to make do with what was available. He curled around the home into a dark alcove for privacy, laid his heavy jacket down, and slept on it as a bed.

Halfway through the night he awoke to find his body covered with a blanket.

"Mari?" he asked, glancing about, but there was no one. He fell back asleep within moments, and come morning, no one said a word of what happened, or asked where he had been.

CHAPTER 35

MAGUS

Magus shifted for the hundredth time in his seat, his discomfort growing by the minute. It wasn't the fault of the auditorium's architects, for when they'd built the rows of wooden chairs and goose feather pillow seats, they had no concept of the size and might of a paragon. Mild discomfort greeted him every time his hips brushed the armrests. Not helping matters was the tediousness of the play, an imperial staple carried overseas and taught to the native actors. Magus had watched *The Handing of the Rose* be performed by the Eldrid Acting Troupe, the finest in all of Gadir. These neophyte islanders were a pale shadow compared to such talent.

The approach of Signifer Weiss down the aisle pulled his attention from the four performers on the stage.

"Forgive me, Imperator," Weiss whispered. His military garb stood out among the fancy dress of the scattered crowd. "Once I finished the translation, I thought it best to deliver this immediately."

"Another message from our mysterious informant?" he asked, trying to hide his excitement.

"It would seem so."

His Signifer handed him a piece of paper of Thanese origin, crafted from their pine pulp and bearing the pale brown hue all their documents possessed. The original message was in the Thanese dialect, and inscribed in weirdly blocky lettering meant to disguise the handwriting.

Magus had become familiar with the language, an expected duty of any Imperator, but spared himself the effort by skipping straight to the tight, looping writing of his Signifer, who had done the translation himself.

I trust my last message proved true. Heed this one well. In twelve days, I will deliver you the heart of the Vagrant. You must only be ready.

Magus read it twice, then folded the paper over itself until he could fit it into his suit pocket.

"What do you think it means?" Weiss asked.

"I think this is not the place to discuss it," he said, and shooed the Signifer away. His attention returned to the actors, who were dressed in ludicrous mimicries of the elegant and flowing fashion of Old Eldrid. None of it looked right, not the ruffles at the ends of the woman's dress, nor the length of the prince's suit, nor the color of their wigs, unable to be dyed the proper white and so they seemed more of a piss yellow. Was that not the way of things? The Empire could bring its class and customs to these far-flung uncivilized worlds, it could gift them education and art, but in the end, they'd be poorly trained fools pantomiming in badly fitting costumes.

In twelve days, I will deliver you the heart of the Vagrant . . .

"Who are you?" Magus whispered into his hand as he held his fist to his mouth. "And can you deliver what you promise?"

Magus hated to admit it, but such information was in dire need. The Vagrant and his group of allies were growing bolder, and their victories more pronounced. Rumors spread like wildfire throughout Vallessau. Wildfire, or a plague.

Your cure is coming, Magus thought. *We'll lance you like the boil you are.*

He settled in to watch the final act of *The Handing of the Rose* for what must have been the hundredth time in his life. At least that might offer him some entertainment while he pondered who might be the secret informant. He did hold out hope for the play's climax. The final act involved a sword duel between competing lovers, and if there was anything these wretched islanders might know how to do right, it was murdering one another.

CHAPTER 36

CYRUS

"More parties," Cyrus said as he obediently stood in a circle of Keles, Thorda, and the Coin. They fussed about his clothes, his mask, the angle of the belts at his hips and the shine of his swords in their sheaths. "It's enough to make one think these clandestine meetings are more important than our attacks."

"It's because they are more important," Thorda said. He crossed his arms and inspected Cyrus. "Satisfactory. Keles, Coin, please wait for Cyrus outside."

The other two exited through the door of the parlor in which they prepared. Though Cyrus's knowledge of the city had expanded greatly since launching their campaign, he only vaguely recognized what felt like one of dozens of mansions built along the upper tier of Vallessau, like a wealthy crown carved into the mountains over the port capital. A faint hint of music from the ballroom echoed through the hall, entertaining dozens of guests come for their glimpse of the mysterious Vagrant.

"You seem obsessed with winning over the wealthy," Cyrus said once the others were gone. "Yet revolutions are won by the masses overthrowing the tyrants."

"I see you read through the historical section of my library," Thorda said. The older man pulled a small wooden box from his pocket. "That groundswell of rage takes time, and often requires decades of abuse and punishment. I would rather not wait for either. Instead, I would fund an army, and such campaigns involve coin I cannot smuggle to Thanet without attracting notice. This means cozying up to the wealthy and telling them how important and precious they are. Swollen egos become fatter, true, but if it leads to blood in the streets, then I consider it a worthwhile investment."

Cyrus appreciated that his mask hid most of his emotions, but he knew it would not hide the eye roll he dearly wanted to make in response, so instead he gestured to the little box Thorda held.

"I get it, even if I don't like it. So what is that? A pin or ribbon for me to wear while I prance about your wealthy friends?"

Thorda's hand grabbed Cyrus's shirt before he saw the man react. A fierce tug, and Cyrus leaned close so that their faces were mere inches away. A calm but intense fire burned in the Miquoan's red eyes.

"Have you forgotten what I said I would make you?" he asked. His gaze held Cyrus prisoner. "You are to be a legend, a god among mortals, yet you whine and prattle like a spoiled princeling. Be better. Am I understood?"

Cyrus's initial reaction was to protest, but he recognized it for the immature thought that it was. Instead he softly bobbed his head up and down to his master and said nothing.

"Very well." Thorda released his shirt. "I come bearing you a tremendous gift, and one close to my heart. Do not insult me or the memories attached."

He opened the box to reveal a silver ring resting upon a small white cloth. Faint runes were carved along the side in a language Cyrus could not read. Set into the ring was an oval gemstone unfamiliar to Cyrus, smooth and round and glittering the darkest shade of black.

"It's beautiful," he said softly.

"The gemstone is known as a black spinel," Thorda explained. "My second campaign after Miquo fell was in a nation called Aethenwald. Their beliefs heavily invoked both day and night, and their goddess of darkness, Anyx, was particularly fond of such stones, as were her priests."

Thorda removed the ring and held it up before him. Despite the hearth and the two lit candles upon the table, not a hint of light shone off the gemstone's polished surface.

"I befriended Anyx and fought alongside her, for a time. When the stars were shining and the moon full, she was a terror the empire could not resist. But then the sun would rise, and she was forced to retreat. The Uplifted Church, they...they found her hidden chambers dug deep into a mountain. Magistrates dragged her out to the sun and chained her to a slab of stone." He closed his eyes and looked away. "I found only what was left. They burned away every piece of her body with torches, and to ensure her death, they smashed her bones to powder."

Cyrus cradled the ring, already feeling ashamed of his earlier snark.

"How many gods has the Everlorn Empire killed?" he asked.

Thorda stared at the ring, and it was a long time before the older man spoke.

"Too many," he said. "Far too many."

Cyrus accepted the ring into his palm. Despite his glove, a spark of energy shot through his body from the silver band. He started to remove the glove, but when Thorda shook his head, Cyrus left it on and slid the ring across the leather, surprised by how well it fit despite the interference. He flexed his fingers, mesmerized by the depth of the black in the spinel.

"I can feel it," he said. It reminded him of the faint heat on his neck when he'd worn a word-lace for required meetings with Gordian during the first year of the Everlorn Empire's conquest over Thanet. If that heat was an indicator, then the fire tingling all the way up to his wrist meant an even more powerful blessing. "There's magic in this ring. What does it do?"

"Priestesses of Anyx blessed this ring with their prayers," Thorda explained. "And though Anyx may be slain, faith in her lingers, however muted, in the hearts of her conquered populace. Tap into that faith, and you will walk through shadows as if they are doors. Focus on where you wish to go, step into the darkness, and trust the ring to do the rest."

Cyrus couldn't deny his excitement. A magic ring, just like a hero's in a story. And to walk from shadow to shadow...

"You want me to appear before tonight's crowd using this," he said, and it wasn't a question.

"I do." Thorda smiled. "Already the people view you as an assassin the empire cannot stop. When they see you call the shadows your home, their belief will only heighten. Know that the ring lacks the power and efficiency it once possessed. It will take several minutes between uses, so while it shall have its potential for battle, do not overly rely upon it. Save it for ambushes and escapes."

"So it's mine now?" he asked, having assumed his master only loaned it to him for their nightly parade among the wealthy.

"It is," Thorda said, and he crossed his arms over his chest. "I pray you are worthy of it."

"Well then," Cyrus said, and he clapped his hands together. "Let's not keep the people waiting."

"Not yet. There is more I would have you do than lurk about. Of Thanet's four lords, Lord Mosau is the only one I have investigated and deemed an ally. Yet one of his vassals, Kaia Makris, is proving... troublesome."

"Define troublesome."

"Her dedication to Thanet is beyond reproach," Thorda clarified. "But it is her trust in myself, and in the Vagrant, that falters. She's begun to whisper those doubts in Lord Mosau's ear. I need her convinced."

Cyrus frowned behind his mask.

"How exactly do I do that?"

"Talk to her. Deduce the source of her doubts, and allay them. We cannot allow any impediment to the progress we make."

"Fine. I'll try. How will I know who she is?"

"Clarissa will be at her side. Find her, you'll find Kaia. Hold faith in yourself, and in my plans. Be brave. The time has come, I promise."

Cyrus sensed those words went beyond a conversation with some random vassal. What would be asked of him now? He sensed another test, akin to his public execution of the imperial officer. His excitement over the ring was quickly replaced with a tightness in his stomach.

"Sure," he said. "Whatever you say."

Only the Coin was waiting for him outside the parlor door.

"Keles is amid the crowd, exaggerating your accomplishments as always," he said. "Shall we join her?"

Cyrus flexed his fist with the ring.

"Yes, let's."

The two crossed the hall in the direction of the violin music steadily growing louder.

"I must know, how did you get roped into all this?" Cyrus asked as they walked. "Becoming the Coin, pretending to be Thorda in disguise, this whole bit?"

"My wife was a faithful priestess of Endarius," the flamboyantly dressed man said. "Her faith was rewarded with a rope about her neck. I wanted to make them pay, yet I was a mere actor. What use could I be? Still, I pledged my services to the rebellion nonetheless. Not a year later, Thorda approached me at my home, alone, and offered me this honored role, one I cherish deeply. If I could do more for Thanet, I would, but this is where my talents lie."

They turned off the main hallway before arriving at the ballroom. Cyrus's curiosity was piqued but he kept silent, trusting the man to have a reason for wherever they went. They hugged the wall adjacent to the ballroom, then stopped at what appeared to be a door of a closet. The Coin opened it, revealing not a closet but a staircase. Cyrus followed the masked man up, and they emerged onto a wide balcony, dark and dusty. A shoulder-high railing separated them from the revelry below.

"Where are we?" he asked.

"I was told to give you a high vantage point of the ballroom to make your entrance. This here is the minstrels' gallery."

"A bit of a fall, isn't it?" Cyrus said, and he glanced over the thin wall.

"Aren't you half cat now? You'd survive it."

The masked man slapped a grumpy Cyrus across the shoulder, and then descended the stairs. The shadows were deep, and the candles set into the wall nearby were unlit. In that darkness, Cyrus did his best to remain calm and survey the scene below.

It was like so many other gatherings Cyrus had attended. Men and women, generally in the latter half of their life, milling together quietly talking. A few danced half-heartedly to the soothing music. There was excitement in the air, distinctly different from the tension prior to a battle when Cyrus and his group gathered for a mission. It had a giddiness to it, perhaps even a childlike excitement. They still did not view this truly as war. Would they ever?

Keles's braided hair and black-and-gold dress were easily discernible amid the crowd, and so she was the first he spotted. Stasia hovered near the far wall, face hidden behind her mask, axes hanging from her belt, and her word-lace strapped about her neck to disguise the color of her eyes. No Rayan for this gathering, it seemed. Usually the paladin accompanied the Coin amid his gossipy treks through the people, but not tonight. Cyrus did see Clarissa, though, the tiny woman full of beaming smiles and wearing a ruby dress with a plunging neckline. Beside her was an older woman in an even older style of dress, her gray hair tied into a long braid with silver ribbons that hung all the way to her waist.

This would be Kaia, Cyrus presumed. Perfect posture, and with a sword at her hip. Did she serve as a soldier at one point? How did she earn her vassalage from Lord Mosau? Cyrus clucked his tongue, feeling the first pangs of frustration. He felt woefully unprepared for this. Thorda had given him no lessons on courtship, politics, or the like. Everything focused on killing and survival. On becoming the legendary Vagrant.

What that meant for Thorda, and for Thanet, Cyrus did not know, and he did not like the uncomfortable way the question squirmed within his belly.

The Coin returned to the party a minute later, and he made his way to whisper something to Stasia. It must have been the signal to start, for she nodded to him and then sprang into action. There was no raised stage to use, but Stasia was always one to improvise. The double windows of the ballroom were enormous, and opened by the turning of little levers. She spun one side, then the other, opening the ten-foot-tall spires of glass to allow in the wintery air. Given the windows' size, she had more than enough space to leap up and stand in their center. The gust of wind was more than enough to gather their attention, but she smashed her axes together for a nice ringing clash of metal anyway.

"Glad as I am to meet you, we all know you're not here for me," she shouted. "Come forth, walker of shadows!"

A now familiar panic spiked in Cyrus's breast. Every visit, every party and gathering, awakened it anew. It had never lessened, but thankfully he had at least learned how to better ignore it and focus on the immediate need. Right now, that meant not leaving Stasia hanging and appearing as was expected.

You will walk through shadows as if they are doors, Thorda had instructed. It seemed Stasia was aware of that gift. She had positioned herself so a giant stretch of darkness was behind her. Cyrus clenched his fist and focused on the open window. High up where he was, there was nothing but darkness, though things were a little trickier in regards to his intended destination. Perhaps this itself was a test. All gods and goddesses knew Thorda loved his tests.

The longer he stared at the stretch of darkness behind Stasia, that unlit night in the open grass beyond the windows of the ballroom, the more something stirred inside his chest. The silver band burned like fire across his finger despite the protection of his glove. The window felt so close, so near, as if the distance between them were the width of a fingernail. He stepped forward, never realizing he meant to. His foot should have touched the rickety wood of the high platform. Instead came a rapid sense of vertigo, followed by an entire shift of his surroundings as he emerged from the shadows to land atop the windowsill amid a flutter of his cloak. He grabbed the sill to steady himself, the instantaneous relocation of his entire body from the high balcony to standing beside Stasia beyond disorientating. Based on the gasps of those inside, he could only imagine what his sudden appearance had looked like.

"I'm here," he said. He had meant it only for Stasia, but he must have spoken it louder than intended. The simple words echoed through the silent crowd. The fifty or so present huddled closer, gathering as if for a speech or proclamation. Cyrus gave them none. He hopped down from the window, bowed low once, and then turned away from them. Let it seem like his arrival meant little to him, and the gathering less. He was meant to be an enigmatic figure, and so he focused his attention on Stasia while the guests slowly resumed their hushed conversations.

"Do you know anything useful about Kaia?" he asked.

"Besides her finding way too many excuses to touch and flirt with Clarissa?" Stasia asked. "No, nothing."

Cyrus leaned closer. His eyes sparkled behind his mask.

"Are you *jealous*, O mighty Ax of Lahareed?"

Stasia dropped a hand to her namesake weapon.

"I will murder you in front of the entire crowd, Vagrant, our years of effort and training be damned."

Cyrus used his amusement as the impetus to set his feet to moving. Over a dozen of these meetings, and still he felt his throat tighten and his chest constrict at the start of them. Once he got to moving, to quietly chatting, the nerves would lessen. Not completely, they never faded completely, but it at least became bearable. Cyrus weaved through the crowd, which parted to allow him access. The men and women nodded or offered vague thanks and gratitude. It was mindless, but Cyrus knew it meant something to them. It made the Vagrant real, in ways even the killing did not.

Only after he'd done a total loop did he approach Clarissa and Kaia. He was scrambling at all of this, but making him seem eager to confront Kaia would be bad, right? And should he acknowledge knowing her name, or make her introduce herself? Gods, what he'd have given for Thorda to have spent a few weeks discussing political intrigue and verbal sparring. He'd sacrifice those tedious hours learning lockpicking in a heartbeat.

"It is good to see you here again, Clarissa," he said, going with the safer greeting. The city clerk attended every meeting, and it would be strange if he did *not* know her.

"And you as well," Clarissa said, all smiles. Cyrus hesitated, and she caught it immediately. "Please, meet my friend, Kaia Makris, one of Lord Mosau's vassals."

All the gods bless you, Clarissa, he thought. Cyrus dipped his head in greeting, his hood fluttering the tiniest bit so it better exposed his crown. The older lady bent at the knees and waist the slightest amount, a relaxed imitation of a more formal bow.

"At last we meet face-to-face," Kaia said. "Presuming you have a face beneath that skull."

"What might I have, if not a face?"

"Rumors say shadow and smoke. Others claim you are air. Who is to say they are wrong? Anything can lurk behind a mask."

She is concerned by my identity, Cyrus decided. But why exactly?

"Stories get larger with every telling," Clarissa said cheerfully. "But there is always some truth among them. If I poke you, will you vanish in a puff of darkness, Vagrant?"

She was pretending to be playful, but Cyrus knew she was responsible for most of the rumors regarding the dead prince's return. It was a subtle reminder to Kaia that even rumors held truth, even if disguised in a joke about Cyrus's, or more accurately the Vagrant's, excessive nature.

"I'll scatter like birds," he said, grinning nervously behind his mask. "Little shadow doves to roost across the rooftops, where I can lurk in waiting for another imperial soldier to kill."

Kaia was far from impressed. She waved over a servant for a drink, something so dark and red it bordered on black, and began to nurse it.

"If only our own troops could scatter and hide as such. My lord has gathered soldiers from across the north, but the larger our forces grow, the harder it becomes to hide them from the prying eyes of the Uplifted Church. I lament a free Thanet requires such secrecy."

Cyrus struggled to interpret the remarks. Did the complaint about secrecy involve him, or did it speak to concerns with moving troops and working with the Coin through clandestine communications? There were messages being signaled here; he was certain of it. Or did she want to remind him that it was the army who would eventually free Thanet, not his own ruthless efforts?

"A time comes when we will throw aside this secrecy, and crush the empire amid flames of war," he said. Surely that was simple and safe enough. Thorda liked it when Cyrus made grand, epic statements about the future.

"The flames of war?" Kaia asked. "Are you a poet or an assassin?"

"Perhaps I am both?"

"I pray you are not. The kingdom suffers enough."

Cyrus blushed, and he doubted even his skull mask would fully hide it. The older woman made him feel so young and clueless. This was not the mysterious killer he was meant to portray. He was quickly learning that keeping his mouth shut aided his efforts more than anything else, but Thorda wanted him to win Kaia over, so he forced himself to continue.

"It is good to hear soldiers still come at Lord Mosau's request," he said. "We are ever in need of allies."

Kaia looped her finger along her glass's edge. Her gray eyes studied him.

"The people of Thanet are forever united," she said. "No amount of bodies hanging from the Dead Flags shall break our allegiances."

More messages. Was he even meant to know them? Or did not knowing them signal to her clues to the Vagrant's identity and purpose? He was starting to think it was a criminal offense to state one's actual opinion. Allies, he had said they needed allies, she implied Thanet's allegiances had never been broken. Which meant what exactly?

That he'd never been part of that initial allegiance.

"I would give much to have fought in those first dark days," Cyrus said truthfully. "I wasn't ready, but I am now. Put the burdens of freedom on my shoulders. I am strong enough to carry them."

"He's shown himself capable," Clarissa chipped in. "He's killed paragons, and the Usurper King!"

"A king died, and another replaced him, one arguably worse," Kaia said.

Damn it, now what did *that* mean? Was this what his parents had to do when they attended their dances and gatherings? Heavens help him, was this the future awaiting him should he retake his throne? Maybe it would be better to let it all burn, or declare someone else king and queen. If only he didn't have to wear this mask. The alcohol Kaia drank was starting to look awfully appealing.

"Is that what you think I want?" he asked. "To become a king?"

"Do you not wear a crown?"

There was no right answer; he was learning that now. With every twist of the tongue, she forced him to either confess more and more truth, or flee the conversation completely.

"I struggle to understand this animosity," he said, desperately hoping honesty might get him somewhere, anywhere, that his attempts at subtlety had failed.

"Because I struggle to understand you, Vagrant," she said. "I would see my island regain its independence, but you? Something drives you. A want, a need of some sort, for only the sick and deranged kill for the pleasure of killing. What is it?"

He'd stumbled once; he couldn't do so again. To admit what he wanted, to claim the throne, would either give away his identity or mark him as an opportunist seeking advantage over the chaos. What was left?

"I would ask for trust," he said, echoing Thorda's request in winning Kaia over. "Trust in my blades, and trust in my resolve. Give me that trust, and I will repay it a thousandfold."

"Forgive me, Vagrant, but I have no patience for games of masks and mirrors. Trust, you ask of me. Trust, in a man whose name I do not know, and whose face I cannot see. My loyalty is to Thanet, and her people. It is not to a slippery name, and a mask brought here by boat."

That was it. Kaia knew his entire persona was a creation of Thorda Ahlai, a foreigner come to Thanet in the aftermath of the Everlorn invasion. Anyone could be behind the mask, and the man behind the mask could be replaced with another.

"Your lord trusts me," he said.

"He does," Kaia said coolly, and sipped her drink.

The irony was killing Cyrus. He was the heir to Thanet's throne, yet suffering an accusation of being a foreign pawn come from Gadir. There was a solution to the problem, though, one simple and direct enough Cyrus trusted even his lacking skills to pull it off. He just had to be crazy enough to do it.

"If you will excuse me a moment," he said. Clarissa shot him a worried look, and he winked at her in return. Even if his own nerves were alight, he could pretend at confidence before others. That's all he did, it seemed, pretend at things he was not. Perhaps it was finally time to stop pretending.

Cyrus marched to the enormous window he'd first arrived at. He made no ceremony, and shouted no speeches. All eyes would be on him either way. Standing above them, wrapped in the shadow of the outer night, he turned to face the crowd.

Could he do it? Had Thorda anticipated this course of action? His cryptic words, and their double meanings. *Hold faith*, Thorda had said. *The time has come.* Cyrus's hands trembled. His master absolutely knew this was a possibility, and had given Cyrus his blessing. Months of rumors and stories, come at last to their culmination. Bind one name to another. Prove to Kaia, and the crowd, that Thanet's salvation would come at the hands of her own children.

Cyrus removed his mask. He stood tall and proud, shoulders back, and let the crowd look upon his true face. The bravado was all false. His innards squirmed, the hairs on his neck and arms stood on end, and he wanted nothing more than to replace the mask and flee. Yet the Vagrant was a cold-blooded murderer, righteous in his fury, steadfast in his determination. Cyrus tilted his chin and held his head high.

It had been years since his last public appearance at Lycaena's execution, but many of these wealthy elite had been regulars to the castle. They had watched him grow from a young boy. They had heard his name resurfaced, fed by rumors Clarissa and Rayan carefully spread. Cyrus focused his attention on Kaia Makris. He let her see his face, his true face, of a boy believed dead now returned. Recognition swept over her, her spine straightening, her eyes widening. She opened her mouth to speak. Cyrus waited for his name to grace their lips. It never did. He had a new name.

"The Vagrant Prince," Kaia whispered. "It cannot be."

That name blew across the ballroom like the cold wind from the window. Their silence grew thicker, deeper. Something like fire burned in Cyrus's chest, and he could not place why it bothered him so. It felt like devotion. It felt like worship.

As for Kaia, she stepped back, and he saw the faintest hint of a smile. It was then he knew. Kaia had played her part to perfection. There had never been any doubt. There were no whispers in Lord Mosau's ear.

Do you not wear a crown? she'd asked, and in response, Cyrus had done exactly as she desired. No, as Thorda had desired. The time had come, indeed.

"I have returned to you," he said, acknowledging the whispers and trying not to dwell on such matters. He fought for the words Thorda would have him speak. The path was set, and there was no changing it now. "Know that I will never leave you until the bloody quest is finished."

Mouths dropped. More whispers. Men and women crowded closer, pinning him. The only way out was the window. Tingles crawled up and down his spine. Their eyes looked to his crown, and they understood it now, its true significance. It was no mockery or decoration, but his birthright. Again the name, the latter half emphasized ever harder.

The Vagrant Prince...the Vagrant Prince...

Must they look at him so? Must they keep murmuring, and speak his name as if it were sacred? Standing even taller, he decided to the Heldeep with all of it. He wasn't just the Vagrant Prince. He was Cyrus Lythan, son of Berniss and Cleon Lythan. Let that name grace their lips. Let that truth intermix with the legends and tales and lies.

"You see right, and recognize me well," he said. "For I am...I am the Vagrant Prince."

He couldn't say his name. The words would not come out. His tongue disobeyed. He tried again, but his jaw locked tight. To have his body refuse reignited his panic. He could abide those stares no longer. He pulled the mask back over his face. It helped, but only a little.

Cyrus turned and leaped out the window to the grass below. His relief in escaping the crowded room was indescribable. He walked the garden, following no set path but for the gravel beneath his feet. At last he found a bench beneath a dogwood tree, and he collapsed onto it. The frost of his breath floated out from the teeth of his mask. His wide, grinning teeth, promising grim pleasure at the pain he inflicted and the chaos he sowed.

A lie. A lie. A lie.

Cyrus ripped the mask off and gasped as if he'd been suffocating. The cool air was divine on his sweat-soaked face and neck. If only Thorda didn't insist these meetings were so vital to building the resistance. The thought of doing this again, of standing fully revealed before a crowd of onlookers, set his heart to racing and seared his mind with anxiety. He weathered it, trusting the panic to pass. It always did, so long as he closed his eyes and focused on nothing but his breathing.

Minutes later, footsteps pulled him from his inner silence. Cyrus panicked, and he was halfway to pulling the mask back over his face when he realized it was Keles. Given the night's chill, she'd donned a heavy bearskin cloak over her dress.

"If you would tell me when you wish to leave these parties, I could escort you out," she said. "It would prove much more convenient than hunting you down afterward once something upsets you."

Cyrus laughed weakly.

"Sorry. I've no excuse. This is, what, the twelfth such meeting like this? Thirteenth?"

"But the first you revealed your face."

"Yeah." He bit at the interior of his cheek, trying to fight off a wave of panic. "It was the first doing that."

Keles wrapped the cloak more tightly about her body and joined him upon the iron bench. The garden was much plainer than the one they'd congregated within prior to Cyrus's first dalliance with the wealthy elite. The ground beneath them was a swathe of pebbles smoothed by the tide, and they crunched underneath her dark leather boots. It amused Cyrus, knowing that despite the elegance of her dress, she still wore practical footwear compared to the high-heeled and tightly bound shoes currently in fashion. He had to admit, the sword strapped to her thigh was also a far more impressive accessory than any purse or corsage.

"Why does it bother you so?" she asked. "Is it because you fear having your identity known?"

Cyrus had thought that would be the case. After years of being presumed dead, he certainly felt a vague sense of dread at the empire discovering he had survived Lycaena's execution.

"It seems like that should be it, but it's not," he said. "Standing before that crowd, my face naked...when I removed the mask, it should have made people realize the Vagrant Prince was truly Cyrus Lythan. But the opposite happened. Cyrus Lythan became the Vagrant Prince. Instead of revealing myself, of who I truly am, the reverse happened. Who I am now is inseparable from the Vagrant. I've become him. Or maybe he's replaced me."

"You speak as if the Vagrant and you are two different people."

"Aren't we, though?" Cyrus crumpled deeper into the iron bench. "The Vagrant is an unstoppable killer that will make the empire pay for its crimes. The Vagrant is ruthless, and savage, and feels no remorse for the blood he spills. But me? The one sitting here now?"

He looked to the stars. His lip trembled, and he swore at himself not to cry.

"I'm an exhausted nineteen-year-old with no family, no throne, and the pressure of an entire nation placed upon his shoulders. I barely sleep, and when I do . . ." His fist struck his thigh. Why was he admitting these things? Why open himself up to her? Keles didn't ask for this, any of this, but he couldn't keep the words in. "Fuck. When I do, I see the boats burning. I see the sword falling. I hear my mother's scream. This is who I am. The Vagrant is who I must be. Will they ever be the same?"

He fell silent. That was enough, no reason to embarrass himself further. Cyrus bit his lip and stared at the pebbles, pale and pink despite the cool glow of the moonlight. He waited for Keles to say something, anything, and was surprised by how desperately he craved the sound of her voice.

"From the moment of my birth, I was meant to follow in my father's footsteps," she said. "They sang me hymns to Lycaena while I yet remained in the womb. Before I was nine, I had memorized the Holy Poetics. I trained in both sword and shield, all so I might protect Thanet's throne, and your family's claim to it. And then came those boats. Then fell the sword."

It was her turn to look to the stars.

"I told myself these were the troubled times that our priests and priestesses feared. The ending of days, during which the most faithful of Lycaena and Endarius would rise up to destroy the evil that had come to our shores. I believed it, Cyrus, believed it so fiercely, I tore through imperial patrols with a blade gleaming with light and power. I was two years younger than you are now, but the remnants of Thanet's military viewed me as their finest warrior. I was the hero of their stories, the daughter of murdered parents and a captured goddess who would avenge terrible wrongs. I was their hope then, the same as you are their hope now."

Cyrus wished he could have seen Keles in such glory. His duels against Rayan had taught him the potential power of a paladin, and if she were his finest pupil, she must be equally dangerous.

"And then came the execution," she continued. "Sinshei's dagger tore open Lycaena's breast. I watched our goddess die. That was when I knew. *I knew.* This wasn't the fabled times. This wasn't a story where I would be the hero to save Thanet. The Everlorn Empire had its own stories, its own prophecies, and its own gods. We would be a footnote in them. A small island in the middle of nowhere, finally brought to heel."

Keles wiped at her eyes, banishing traitorous tears.

"The Vagrant is no different than the paladin I once was, Cyrus. I shed my heroic mantle, for I believed you dead, and the bloodline I was sworn to protect forever lost. The thought of believing in something other than my goddess terrified me. I grew up fearful of admitting doubt for even a moment. Lycaena was my heart, my desire, my comfort. Now she's dead, and I am no longer a paladin. My greatest doubt came true, yet I did not crumble, nor cease to be. Only we decide who we are. No one else. The Vagrant is just a mask. It is an identity you slide over yourself like a cloak. It can be removed. It can be rejected. You are not slave to it, no matter the pressures you face or the guilt that weighs upon you. Clinging to it may grant survival, but it may also drag you under. Always know the difference. Always make it your choice."

Cyrus stared at the skull in his hands, at the too-wide teeth grinning back up at him, and was haunted by his inability to speak his true name to the crowd.

"Sometimes it doesn't feel like I have a choice."

She settled her hand upon his and, in doing so, covered the mask with her slender fingers and painted nails. A new kind of panic overtook Cyrus, nothing at all like when he was to reveal his face to the crowd.

"You would choose the right path, but if you let others decide what is right, and what is wrong, you will never make a choice at all."

They sat in silence. He wished he could wrap his arm about her and hold her close. He wished she would place her head upon his chest, and he could take comfort in her warmth. She was beautiful, so beautiful, but it went beyond that. Her faith was lost, yet she seemed so much more secure in herself and her decisions. He had always held little faith, and now he knew nothing but doubt. Thorda would have him counter it with rage. How would Keles?

"So it sounds like you're pretty good with a sword and shield," he said, wanting to banish the last remnants of tension. If he didn't start talking, he might do something stupid like lean closer toward her, or wrap his fingers into hers. "Are you better than Rayan?"

"Sometimes. I struggle with consistency, but on my good days, I can give him quite a challenge."

"Then we must spar! I'd love to see a glimpse of this fierce, imperial-slaying woman that was fighting wars while I was still an untrained princeling brat being held hostage."

"I don't know, Vagrant, that could be dangerous. How might you react if I win?"

"I'd demand a rematch," he said, and he beamed her a grin. "And if you win that one, I would demand another, and another."

Keles laughed.

"That sounds miserable."

"Does it?" he asked. "It sounds instead like I'd have found myself a perfect training partner."

She leaned in close, and his entire body stiffened. His heart leaped high up into his throat. Her lips were close, so close, and it seemed they would brush his cheek, but they veered away at the last second so she might whisper warmth into his ear.

"As I said...it sounds miserable."

Keles flashed him a smile before she left, so playful, so mischievous, that when he slept that night, he dreamed of it instead of burning ships.

CHAPTER 37

MARI

Please, God, please, stop!" Mari's claws sank deeper into the priest's chest. His arm was locked in her jaws. Bones crunched between her teeth. "Please, it hurts, it hurts, it—"

The rest of his sentence ended in a scream of pain as she savagely twisted her head. The arm dislocated in its socket, then tore completely. His cry pitched in scale as new pain hit him.

"Mari?" She turned, arm still in her mouth. Stasia stood in the doorway of the priest's home, her face hidden behind her cloth mask. Fresh gore dripped from her twin axes. There was no reading the expression in her eyes. "Everything good?"

Mari looked back to the sobbing priest. Her jaw relaxed, and the arm plopped to the wood floor and rolled twice before coming to a halt. The man reached for it. She couldn't guess why. Was in he shock? Did he think he could reattach it? As if she would let him live. As if her prey would ever survive a hunt.

Her prey...

With a thought, her wings simultaneously stabbed the man's throat and then pulled, tearing it open. His pained screams became a gargle that quickly ended in death. Mari padded toward the door, her paws leaving bloody prints in her wake. The word-lace about her throat shimmered a soft blue, translating her tired growl.

"I'm fine."

"If you insist," Stasia said. She tilted her head toward the room she'd come from. "The priest is dead. Time to go."

It was just the two sisters inside the priest's home. Their father had plotted a triple kill for the night, Arn and Rayan taking out a different priest while Cyrus would assassinate the most public of the targets, a magistrate who spent far too much time traveling to nearby brothels to remain safe from the Vagrant's blades. Mari followed Stasia to the door, on their way passing overturned furniture and claw marks on the walls. With the strength of her Lioness form, she had easily broken in the front door, purposefully attacking when the priest was believed to be sitting down for his evening supper. His guards had been few, and easily killed. None put up any sort of real fight.

"We did good," she said, and led the way out the mansion entrance with long, feline strides.

Sometimes Stasia carried spare clothes with her in a pack; other times they hid an outfit nearby so Mari might change and walk home incognito. Mari dashed rooftop to rooftop before dropping into the tiny indent between two wealthy mansions. Her bone plates receded, her fur fading away as soft, chubby flesh took its place. Naked as her birth, she took the plain green dress out of the stashed rucksack and pulled it over her head. She had one arm out the sleeve, and was working the other arm through, when her sister caught up with her. Stasia pulled the mask down from her face as she talked.

"I don't think anyone heard us, but it won't be long before someone notices the mess you made of the front door."

"Then we should hurry before that happens."

Stasia nodded in agreement, then slipped past Mari to where they had hidden a long brown coat beside Mari's dress. She pulled it on, the thick leather easily hiding the twin axes belted to her hip.

"I'll meet you at home," Mari said. Wind blew across her skirt, and she fought back a chill. Though the wind was cold, that wasn't why she shivered. It felt like her blood were aflame.

"Are you sure?"

Mari didn't look back when she answered.

"I'm sure."

Vallessau was known as the City on the Cliffs most everywhere else on Thanet, and for good reason. While time and human persistence had steadily flattened out huge swathes of land near the beach where the docks were built, the outer ring of the city steadily rose higher, culminating in a U-shaped ring of cliffs and mountains surrounding the majority of the populace. The ritual sacrifice they had interrupted weeks ago had been along the southern end of this ring, off one such white cliff. Mari traveled toward that end, which sported dozens of roads carved into the cliffside. Homes teetered off wooden platforms. Huge towers rose high above them, ringed with windows and lanterns to form shining beacons to travelers along the main road coming from the southern portion of the island.

Mari had discovered this particular spot during her first year on Thanet. One of the cliffside roads ended abruptly at what had once been a guard tower. Fire had gutted much of the interior. The door was gone, the stone doorway marked with deep cuts that hinted at a forgotten battle. It was hollowed-out rubble now, sometimes occupied by squatters, but it wasn't the tower that interested Mari, but beyond it. The tower's base was built several feet from the cliffside, and with it at her back, she could sit with her feet dangling off the edge and overlook both city and ocean with relative privacy. To get to that private rectangle of land meant climbing out the second-story window of that dilapidated tower, but such obstacles meant little when she was the Lioness.

When not in her lioness form, it meant clinging to the window ledge for dear life and then dropping to a landing most painful to her knees. Mari endured the sting, brushed dirt from her legs, and then sat with her back resting against the cold white stone. Returning to her lioness form was distinctly unappealing right now, after the battle. She craved solitude, not a barrage of senses and a hunger for blood. Mari drank in the precious silence as time marched along and the sun lowered beneath the water's edge.

Only one other person knew of her private hideaway, and she dropped from the window with a far more elegant landing than Mari's.

"Sorry for interrupting," said Stasia, "but anytime you wander off from a mission like that, it makes me nervous."

"You shouldn't worry about me," Mari said as Stasia sat beside her, her longer legs easily dangling over the cliff's edge.

"But it's my job to worry. Inherited position, no resignations. Comes with being a big sister."

"A responsibility you rarely fulfill, I might add."

"I never said I was good at it." Stasia's hair, freed of its ponytail now their battle had ended, blew wildly from the wind, and she tucked strands of it behind her ears in a vain attempt to keep it from her face. "Something bothers you, and I'd rather you let it out before it eats a hole in your stomach. So what's on Mari's mind?"

Mari focused on the ripples in the ocean, highlighted orange with the setting of the sun.

"Remember Noth-Wall?" she asked. "How it felt, right before the enclave was raided?"

Noth-Wall was the last war they had participated in prior to Thanet. Its resistance had been one of the best funded and best equipped Mari had ever seen. Next to Noth-Wall was Arim, and its government had smuggled in soldiers and supplies to help slow the inevitable march of imperial conquest. The "enclave" was what they had called their head-quarters hidden in a deep cave complex throughout the nearby moun-tains casting a shadow over the nation's capital. Noth-Wall had made great strides toward independence, but then the full might of the Ever-lorn Empire had come crashing down. Thousands of soldiers flooded into the caves, and what tunnels they couldn't explore, they collapsed.

"You're scared to feel hope," Stasia said. "Is that it?"

"Of course I am!" Mari gestured to the beautiful city before her. "Who's to say that Thanet isn't the next Noth-Wall? The victories we've had, and the rebellion growing in people's hearts... is it even real? Will the story end any differently than all the others before? Or is it a passing dream that the empire will soon crush?"

Stasia pulled her knees to her chest and leaned her head and arms upon them.

"I hope it's real," she said. "What I have with Clarissa, it certainly feels real. You should know, I've made up my mind. Whatever happens in Thanet, whether we succeed or fail miserably, I'm staying here. I'm going to make this my home. With her. I hope you understand."

But of course Mari understood. Stasia and Clarissa had been together for four years. Mari would have been more surprised if Stasia moved on to whatever new battleground their father chose should Thanet crumble like all the others.

"So will you keep fighting, even if we lose?"

"For my new home? I don't suppose I'll have a choice. I might try hanging up my axes, for Clarissa's sake. Wouldn't that be something?"

Her older sister giving up a warrior's life was too far-fetched for Mari's imagination, so much so that she chuckled at the thought. Yet when she turned the idea on herself, her blood ran cool. The first few wars she fought in, she had spent her quiet nights praying for peace. Even as she descended upon battlefields as Kasthan the Falcon Reaper, or stalked the Ibarah Jungles as the panther god Como-rah, she had never wanted a life of war. So many nights she'd sobbed away the images scarring her psyche. But lately?

Please, God, please, stop.

"The fights, the killing, all the bloodshed..." She slowly breathed in deep to gather the necessary resolve for her confession. "I'm afraid I'm starting to enjoy it."

Stasia cocked an eyebrow in her direction.

"I've always enjoyed it. Are you sure you aren't scared of becoming your big sister?"

Just like that, her deep-seated fears seemed so silly, so easily conquerable. Mari wished she knew how Stasia did it. The talent bordered on magical.

"I'm trying to be serious!" she insisted. "It was never easy for me, you know that. Yet here on Thanet, with Endarius's help, it's become...I was going to say tolerable, but that'd be a lie. I'm looking forward to it now, Stasia. I'm no longer seeing the soldiers as people. Only prey."

"Given the life we lead, is that really so bad?"

"But what happens when the killing stops? What happens when the war is over? Do we shed our violence like old garments? Can we find ourselves a life to live when all this bloodshed and horror turns to peace?"

So many questions with difficult answers, but she was never one to prefer ignorance. Those answers, they mattered. If the future they created was bleak or hopeless, then the path they walked must be changed. She believed that firmly, deeply. Mari protected people. She fought for those who could not fight for themselves. Her form may be monstrous, but she was no monster. She was a god made mortal flesh.

"Do you want the truth?" Stasia asked. "I've never believed in peace, not in my lifetime. How could I? The idea that people could go about their lives free—truly free—to be themselves? That calm is as foreign to me as the towers of Eldrid. It's so much easier to believe in war. The strong enforce their will upon the weak. The one with a sword decides the life of the one on their knees. And so I strive to be strong. I strive to never find myself on my knees before an empire that would see me erased."

The ring of a clock tower interrupted any further thoughts. The two fell silent as the tolls washed over them. A thousand memories rose and fell in Mari's mind. Given the nature of their role as builders of insurgents, they often arrived in lands with the Joining Laws recently enacted. The hurt from it, the bloodshed, was always fresh. Thanet was one of the rare places they had come so recently after conquering, and before the laws had been put in place. Mari doubted it a coincidence that it was here in Vallessau her sister, whose usual whirlwind romances lasted a few weeks to months at best, had found someone she deeply cared about and could remain with.

"If you're staying here in Thanet, I'm staying, too," she said, struggling to find the right words. "We'll make this our home. The best home we can possibly build."

Stasia pulled Mari close for an embrace. Her cheek rested on Mari's forehead. Strong arms held her tight, hard muscle to support her own softness. It was everything she needed, and she wished it could last forever.

"Tell me of Miquo," she whispered.

Stasia thought a moment before answering. Mari had been too young to remember much of anything when the empire invaded. To know of her homeland, she had to rely on stories from her family, or the rare book containing drawings of the godwoods.

"Our blood-mother once took me to the Pantheon Tree in the heart of Azema City," Stasia began, referring to the Miquoan capital. "She woke me up early, a good two hours before the dawn. Just climbing all the ladders and riding the four pulleys to reach the top had taken an hour, and that doesn't count the other hour we stood waiting in line. The Pantheon Tree supported only five or six viewing platforms built above the tree line, and she wanted to make sure we were early enough to secure a spot. The autumn sunrise was worth it, she insisted. And she was right."

Stasia leaned her weight on her other hand as she stared, not at the ocean, but memories far more distant.

"The sun crested the Vermell Mountains, and it washed over the forest like fire. A red-and-orange sea of leaves, as far as the eye could see, shimmering in the dawn light. It was so beautiful. There were dozens of us crammed into those little platforms, and none of us could speak. Not a word. When we climbed down and walked home, I craned my neck looking at the branches and leaves above us. It wasn't until then that I understood, truly understood, the wonder of our city. The gods and goddesses had blessed us to live beneath a burning sky."

The way she spoke those words, "a burning sky," was filled with such longing, it made Mari's heart ache. What she would give to have been there with her sister, holding hands in anticipation of the rising sun.

"I vanished into our mansion library for three days after," Stasia said. "Me, if you can believe it. I wanted to learn everything about our trees. I read about the rarity of the seeds, and how we cultivated the soil around newly planted godwoods. They were the tallest and oldest in the world, and even the other nations agreed there was no comparison! I'd grown up surrounded by trunks and leaf rooftops, so it'd always been normal to me, but for the first time I was old enough to understand how unique it was, how special."

Her jaw hardened. She shook her head.

"Less than a year later, those trees burned for real. The empire realized it was easier to torch everything instead of enduring the ambushes of our rebels. Our family left not long after."

Mari had no recollection of their departure. Her earliest memory was some months later, staying in a shabby inn in the nearby country of Antiev. Stasia and Mari had played fetch with a stray canine missing an eye. She'd bawled hysterically when they left that lodging a week later, and she'd not been able to say goodbye to the pup. The one thing she knew for certain was that it'd been only the three of them, Stasia, Mari, and Thorda. No one else. Whatever family she might have had remained behind in Miquo, or perished.

"Do you miss it?" she asked. "Miquo, I mean?"

"Of course I miss it. How could I not?"

Mari hesitated. This was a thought she'd long feared to share, for how could it not be a betrayal to everything her sister and father had worked for?

"Do you...do you wish we had stayed behind? That we never left Miquo?"

"You've seen what becomes of a conquered populace," Stasia said. "The reeducation centers. The forceful conversions and mandated prayers. The harder a nation fights back, the crueler the Uplifted Church becomes, and none fought back harder than Miquo. Life was rough as a Miquoan refugee, but we had money, and Father's reputation. It was worse at home, I'm certain of it. Better we fought. Better we gave aid to places in need."

"Places that fell nonetheless," she said, surprised by the bitterness in her own voice. She thought Stasia might snap at her, or berate her, but her sister instead surprised her with a moment of thoughtfulness.

"I've held those same fears," Stasia admitted. "It's hard to believe we're helping, when every rebellion we raise up dies beneath an imperial heel. But we only need to succeed once. The empire is too big, too unwieldy. The moment its foundation cracks, the rebellions we seeded will sprout again. The Uplifted Church sows hatred to unite people behind a faith few truly believe in, and that needed hatred will be their undoing. Peace may not come in my lifetime, but I believe victory one day will. The God-Incarnate is no god. He's a man. A wretched man with too long a life."

The final few boats pulled into the dock, last-minute fishermen and merchants from elsewhere on Thanet bringing goods from their villages to trade in the expansive city on the cliffs. The five imperial galleons settled into position, reestablishing the nightly blockade. That a blockade was still in place years after the initial invasion was unusual, but then again, so many things were, on their distant island. Small things, but the more Mari thought about them, the more they struck her. The talk of what had been done to Miquo upon its conquering only made the oddities that much clearer, and she finally broke the comfortable silence to voice these thoughts to her sister.

"Something is strange about Thanet," she said. "I didn't notice it at first, but the longer we stay here, the less normal things seem. The empire's built only a handful of language centers, all here in Vallessau. They haven't recruited any locals into the ranks of their soldiers to help keep order. They've repurposed the churches to Lycaena and Endarius instead of burning them, and built none of their own. Foreign trade is slow to come, if at all, yet at the same time, they've hurried through other rules and changes, such as the Joining Laws and mandatory services."

"Maybe it's because of how far away we are from Gadir?" Stasia offered. Mari shook her head, unsatisfied with that explanation.

"It's a lengthy travel by boat, but there are places on Gadir that take six months of travel to arrive from Eldrid. What of the mountain paths into Miquo, or the desert sands leading into Lahareed? Something is wrong here. Maybe Magus is to blame, or Anointed Sinshei. But it's different than anywhere else we've been, and that worries me."

She clenched her hands and struggled to find the right words.

"It feels like they're not setting roots down, for they are too hurried and impatient. They're creating a shallow, temporary faith, and I don't understand why."

Instead of answering, Stasia gave her a playful smile.

"You keep asking me questions with answers I cannot know. Ask someone wiser. Tell me, what does Endarius think?"

Mari closed her eyes and fell into herself. It was a comfortable act, akin to prayer but even more personal. Dwelling within her was the essence of a god. The presence, the power, was a cherished gift, a part of her to be called upon as she so desired. The nature of a god-whisperer was to seek answers from the divine, and so she offered to Endarius all her hopes and fears. It wasn't a specific question, for she sought no specific answer. She wanted reassurance to her uncertainties. She wanted her faith in victory reaffirmed. He answered not with words, but with a single, rumbling snarl. Mari opened her eyes, and she smiled at the setting sun.

"I think the Lion is like you, Stasia. I think he merely wants to hunt."

"Then let us hunt," her sister said. She offered the horizon a raised fist. "The wise can rebuild a better world from the ashes, but for there to be ashes, we must first burn down the old and the rotten. I say we get to burning."

"I suppose I should have expected as much from you, shouldn't I?"

They shared a laugh, their embrace ending as Stasia hopped to her feet. The life in her, the joyful chaos, could part any cloud that darkened Mari's mood.

"What can I say? I'm an arsonist at heart."

CHAPTER 38

MAGUS

Magus sat at his desk reading a copy of the *Pames Memoirs* by candle-light. Religious study had never been his strong suit, but he found himself reaching for the memoirs of Anointed Catala Enfar more and more as of late. Catala had been responsible for bringing the light of truth to the secluded valley of Pames in the far northwest corner of Gadir over a thousand years ago. The soil of the land was rocky and poor, and the people nomads of no real importance, which meant Catala had been given few resources to work with during his efforts. Given Thanet's distance from Gadir, and her people's incredible stubbornness in adopting faith in the God-Incarnate, the experience grew increasingly relevant to Magus.

To abandon a god is to abandon an identity, wrote Pames's Anointed One. *These simple people meet in caves, they pray to the stars, and they think their rituals, which are shrouded in mystery, make them wise. They refuse to believe their gods are dead. The mystery and ignorance of their practice grants them a veil no logic may pierce. For this reason, I suspect our measures go not far enough. Until they see themselves as imperials, they will never worship an imperial god. We must break the identity. I propose we hasten the replacement of their native tongue. All new homes must be built using wood brought by our traders, and styled like our abodes*

in Everlorn. Any ritual, be it innocent or tied to dead gods, must be
outlawed. I have also ordered an influx of new clothes, and ordered
burned their meager city's lone textile.

These early thoughts were the first inklings of what Catala would codify into the Joining Laws upon his return to the capital of Eldrid. His success in Pames had led God-Incarnate Aristava to adopt them throughout the empire, creating a unified identity for each and every citizen to hold in their hearts.

Magus sighed. The lengthy journey across the Crystal Sea, coupled with their narrow time frame leading up to the six-hundredth-year ceremony, prevented the Three Pillars from implementing many of Catala's perfected methods in Thanet. Sinshei had done her best, as much as her limited skills allowed. She had focused on the language, mandating that the imperial tongue be the only writ accepted for any legal documents and, after two years, requiring that Thanese be removed from all signposts and storefronts. Paid bards sang songs from the mainland. No teachers had been supplied for the language centers, so Sinshei had chosen clever priests among her ranks to spend several days each week amid the city's schools teaching their young the imperial tongue.

Yet Catala was right. These people viewed themselves as part of Thanet, not part of the Everlorn Empire, and so they clung to their lion feathers and butterfly wings despite the ever-present reminders flying from the Dead Flags. Perhaps it was time for even more drastic measures...

A knock on the door pulled him up from his book, and he glanced over his shoulder.

"Enter."

One of Magus's most trustworthy men, Signifer Weiss, walked into the center of the room and then saluted. His face was heavily scarred from a citywide fire started during their campaign subjugating the people of Noth-Wall. It was that campaign that had earned Magus his position as Imperator, and he had made damn sure that Weiss came with him after his promotion.

"Pray, forgive me for coming at such a late hour," the Signifer said.

"But the nature of this communiqué does not allow me to wait until morning."

That got Magus's interest. *Something new from our mysterious turncoat?* He swiveled his chair around and held out his hand for the rolled piece of paper the Signifer carried.

"Let's have it, then."

The scroll was smaller than his hand, and it bore no seal or signature. Magus unrolled it and read the three short sentences. What they promised set his blood to racing.

"You're sure this is from our informant?" he asked.

"It was delivered in secret, in the same manner as all the other messages."

Magus read it a second time. As before, the lettering was in Thanese, with clumsy, ragged lines meant to disguise the writer's actual writing style.

The Villasa mansion. Exactly one hour prior to midnight, no sooner, no later. Come, and capture the Vagrant and his believers.

"Have you located this mansion?" he asked.

"It's in the outer ring," Weiss explained. "According to our records, the Villasa family have fallen under suspicion before, and were punished with a heavy fine for allowing their servants to abdicate their daily duties to celebrate last year's Midwinter."

"Small heresies hide larger ones," Magus said as he stood. "A lesson we learn in Thanet time and time again. We have an hour, so tell everyone to make haste. I'll be leading the mission to grab that bastard myself."

Magus ensured they held exactly to the time his informant demanded. The moment the bells of the city chimed the eleventh hour, he gave his order. Four hundred men accompanied him, each broken into a squad of one hundred positioned on different sides of the mansion so that all four cardinal directions were covered. The Signifer with him raised a horn to his lips and blew a single, long note.

"And so the hounds give chase," Magus said as his soldiers rushed the mansion. "I pray the fox finds the strength to fight instead of flee."

If there was any fighting, though, it was short and pathetic. Magus strode through the front door of the extravagant mansion minutes later, satisfied the location was secure. He moved with a purpose amid the chaos. Men and women were scattered and crying. Tables were over-turned. Soldiers ripped aside curtains and kicked open doors. The Imperator recognized the marks of wealth upon them and, more trou-blesome, relics of the slain gods. Here a small feather, there a butterfly ring. What he did not find, however, was the man he sought.

"Where are you, Vagrant?" he muttered.

No sign of the man in the skull mask. No dark hoods, no finely crafted swords, and no silver crown. It was entirely possible one of the unmasked people was him currently not wearing his disguise, but Magus found that doubtful. His informant had made it clear the Vagrant was meant to make an appearance, and at this exact hour. Hard for him to do that while wearing the foppish clothing adorning the wealthy men his soldiers currently slapped in irons.

"We're sweeping the upper floor, but so far found only servants," his Signifer said, finding him in one of the large dens. Magus ignored him, and instead crouched before a woman sobbing on her knees. Her hands were bound behind her back with rope instead of manacles. Paint ran down her face from her crying.

"You there," he said. "Did the Vagrant make his appearance?"

The woman stared at him dumbly.

"The Vagrant!" he shouted. "Was he here?"

"N-no, of course not," she said. "He's not here, I swear, we never saw him."

Damn it all. She could be telling the truth, or she could be lying to protect Vallessau's newfound savior. Had his informant botched the time? It burned, knowing he was so close to capturing the Vagrant, and yet had failed. A familiar laugh only further soured his mood.

"Such a fine night, Imperator, yet you scowl like a bird shat on your dinner plate."

Magus turned to glare. Soma was one of the few paragons remaining after the island's gods were successfully slain, for paragons rarely stuck around any one place for long. There were always other nations to conquer, gods to kill, and rebellions to put down. Thanet was supposed to have been pacified, her people ready to open their hearts to the Uplifted Church. Of those chosen to stay, Soma was the worst of the lot, no doubt due to being tightly wrapped around Sinshei's finger.

"There is always room for improvement," he said lamely, having no real desire to argue with the blue-armored Paragon of Spears.

"Give it time." Soma's face was fully hidden behind his helmet, but Magus was absolutely certain he grinned from ear to ear. "You'll succeed eventually in capturing the Vagrant. Surely it is worth celebrating what minor victory you achieved tonight?"

"I shall celebrate when all of Thanet kneels in servitude to our glorious God-Incarnate, and not a moment before."

He strode for the mansion exit, preferring no other soldiers see his disappointment. Soma wasn't wrong, after all. To capture so many wealthy and connected members of the resistance was a tremendous victory... it just wasn't the victory he wanted. Once outside, he stomped his feet to work a bit of warmth back into his limbs. The chaos of the raid now dimmed, he scanned the outer grounds, wondering if somehow, despite their hundreds of soldiers forming an impenetrable net, they had missed something.

And then he saw him.

"Running late, aren't you?" Magus shouted.

The Vagrant knelt on the highest point of the nearby rooftop, his body crouched low and hulking like some ancient carved statue. Moonlight shone off the silver crown wrapped about his skull mask. A faint wind teased the edges of his hood. His hands were on the hilts of his swords, but he had not drawn them, not yet.

"You missed your party!" Magus gestured toward the mansion's front door. "Come down and join them. It's not right that they have all the fun without you."

Even with his face hidden, Magus could sense the raw hatred pouring from the Vagrant. The enigmatic killer slowly stood, his head lowered. The hood covered the upper half of his mask. The swords slowly slid free of their sheaths as his arms shifted into a battle stance. Magus's grin grew.

"That's right," Magus said. He hefted his shield, trusting its massive weight to keep him safe. Twice now the Vagrant had matched blades with him and then fled. He feared no third. "We fight alone, I promise. You and me, right here in the cold street. An honorable duel for the fate of Vallessau. The moonlight can witness your execution. Is that not a fair offer?"

The Vagrant's stare lingered. Was this it? Would the maddening wraith finally settle matters one-on-one?

A woman joined the Vagrant's side, her face masked with a black cloth bearing the skull of a roaring panther. Magus recognized her from Gordian's death, the Ax of Lahareed, as she was known. She put a hand on the Vagrant's shoulder and said something Magus could not hear. The Vagrant looked away from her and nodded. Without another word, the two retreated, leaping from rooftop to rooftop as if it were another street accessible only to them. Magus did not give chase, nor order any of his men to do so, either. He let his words do the chasing.

"Thrice now you run from me! The people think you a god, yet I see nothing but a coward!"

He replaced his shield and turned. Weiss waited patiently beyond the doorway, a twitch of his lips and tremble of his shoulders revealing his nervousness at interrupting.

"We've rounded up the last of the guests," the Signifer said. "Not counting servant staff, that puts the total number of traitors at forty."

"Take them to the castle dungeon," Magus said. "Drag them down the thoroughfare, and do it slowly. I want the whole city to know who we've captured."

No, Magus did not need to chase the Vagrant. Forty members of his insurgence were now in his custody. The Imperator cracked his knuckles. One of them would know the Vagrant's true identity.

And if the God-Incarnate smiled upon him, that one person would talk.

CHAPTER 39

CYRUS

Thorda's home was wrapped in a fog of curses and barely contained anger when Cyrus arrived, Stasia at his side. Rayan was the calmest of the lot, and both he and Arn were busy explaining to Thorda what had happened. As for the younger Ahlai sister, she had beaten them home with her long, feline strides and, after reverting form, had come downstairs in a simple green dress.

"Are you all right?" she asked, rushing to embrace them both upon their return. "I worried when you fell behind."

"As well as can be," Cyrus answered softly.

Stasia didn't answer. She pushed past Mari, wandering deeper into the home. Her entire body trembled like a volcano about to erupt. She looked left, then right, as if lost. Cyrus had not spoken with her since fleeing the mansion. She'd seemed trapped in her own mind, but he hadn't understood the reason. Her panic and anger had grown with every step, and now it demanded release.

"*Fuck!*" she shouted. She slammed her fists atop a table, rattling the decorative vase atop it. Cyrus reached for her, then let his hand fall. What might he say to her? What hope could he give that would not be a lie he himself did not believe? The others stared silently. It seemed no one else had any comfort to offer, either. Stasia fumed at the table, her arms and fists trembling, before she suddenly spun.

"I'm going," she announced to no one. She did not get far. Her father blocked the doorway, his arms crossed over his chest.

"And where is it you go?" he asked.

"Clarissa's," she answered. Her hands dropped to the axes buckled to her waist. "I have to know, if she was—if she's caught, if she was there like she was supposed to be..."

Cyrus's stomach dropped. Of course. Clarissa, she was at every meeting, one of Thorda's several go-betweens to keep himself hidden from the public. The idea of her chained in a prison cell sickened him, and no doubt Stasia felt a thousand times worse.

"Calm yourself," Thorda interrupted, and he showed no sign of budging. "Clarissa wasn't there, for I sent her on an errand. Twenty men arrived earlier tonight to join our resistance, come by boat pretending to be fishers. I had Clarissa finding them homes."

The woman's entire body loosened, and her shoulders dropped.

"She's all right?" Stasia asked, as if unable to believe it.

"She is. Put her out of mind, my daughter. We have greater concerns."

Stasia at last released her grip upon her axes. Cyrus breathed a sigh of relief. He feared the woman would storm out into the night, never to be seen again. Worse, he knew he would have gone with her, even if it had been a suicide mission.

"Clarissa may be safe, but there're still the others," Cyrus said, forcing the guilt deep down. He could not dwell on it now. "Such a brutal stroke against us cannot go unanswered. What do we do?"

"We must be patient," Thorda said. "This is not the first time the empire has raided a gathering of our supporters, one of whom likely leaked word of our meeting in the first place. Now is a most precarious time for our resistance. The Imperator is hoping to anger us, to make us panic, and in that panicked anger, commit a mistake. Deny his desire. We listen, we plan, and only when we are fully ready, do we act. Is that clear?"

Magus hovered in Cyrus's vision, haunting him with his smug, insufferable grin.

"Perfectly clear," Cyrus said, each word a bitter drop upon his tongue. "So what, then, is our plan in the interim?"

"For now?" Thorda gestured to his surroundings. "We move to my fallback manse. I hold faith in the resolve of our fellow conspirators, but in case one talks, we must be long gone."

CHAPTER 40

MAGUS

Magus had spent the past several hours going from cell to cell of the castle prison, inflicting misery and punishment with his fists on those he questioned. There were better instruments, for sure, but none were as satisfying as the feel of flesh crumpling beneath his bare hands. The only problem was, the information given was worth less than the blood he beat out of them. A stubborn lot, the whole bunch, including the old man currently before him. His clothes were a garish mixture of blues and yellows, and when they'd taken him in, he'd worn a red-and-green cloth mask, the two colors sewn into a checkerboard pattern.

"The others tell me you are known as the Coin," Magus said. The man's hands were shackled behind him to the stone wall, and he had to lean and arch his back awkwardly to meet the Imperator's gaze. He appeared in his late fifties, his face handsome, and no doubt he'd won many a people over with his smile. Magus had bloodied that smile until teeth were missing from it.

"Aye, that's me," the man said. "The infamous Coin funding the rebellion."

Magus dropped to one knee so they might be closer. He pressed his finger against the man's temple and pushed until his head thudded against the stone.

"It wasn't hard to decipher your identity, nor find others who recognized you, *Coin*. You're not a businessman. You're not a noble or a merchant. Your real name is Hozier Frommeson, some out-of-work actor. Do not try to convince me you are somehow the secret wealthy backer funding the insurgence."

"Then I won't tell you that," Hozier said. "I'll let the others tell you instead."

Magus smacked his knuckles across the man's mouth. Blood splattered across the front of his armor. His temper flaring, the Imperator grabbed Hozier by the front of his shirt and pulled him as close as the wall manacles allowed.

"Do you think this some sort of game?" he asked. "I can bind you here for a thousand days, chained perfectly still as your muscles atrophy and sores eat away at your skin. Your hair will wither, and your teeth will rot and fall from your mouth. You'll suffer, and cry, and beg for death as the pain grows so great, you'll *fantasize* about being able to stand up and stretch your poor, bent back. But you won't have that. You'll shit yourself, and you'll piss in a puddle directly in front of you so often, its smell will be all you know. That is the power I have over you. Think on that before you deign to mock my questions."

Instead of retreating, the older man leaned closer. A smile tugged at the edges of his lips, as if he were direly amused by his predicament.

"A thousand days of suffering, you threaten me with. But it has been a thousand three hundred and twenty since one of your soldiers shoved a sword into my wife's stomach for the terrible crime of publicly praying to Endarius. Your threats mean nothing. They never will. They are the pale curses of a man doomed to spend eternity in the Heldeep."

"Shall I show you how cruel those curses might be?" Magus said. He smashed the man's head against the wall with a satisfying crack, but he waged a losing battle. Hozier may not be the true Coin, but Magus could tell why others believed him. His devotion was unshakable. The way he conveyed his rage was masterful, even as his head rocked side to side from the pain.

"A thousand, thousand years may pass, and they will be but the blink of an eye in the lands beyond. I will not forsake the future awaiting me, nor will I tremble in fear of pain that cannot surpass the hurt you have already given me. My wife awaits. So does my death. Who are you, Imperator, in the face of either?"

Magus almost killed him. Almost.

"Your suffering is not yet done," he said, and shoved the man against the wall. "All of Vallessau will witness your execution, wretch. No noble sacrifice awaits you. No goddess will embrace your soul in comfort. The heavens belong to the God-Incarnate. Hell awaits the disloyal who refuse his grace. If you will not worship here in life, you will kneel and serve in death."

Hozier leaned against the wall, a dazed look in his eye. Blood trickled down his neck from where his head had collided with the stone.

"I shall walk among green fields, blooming flowers, and an eternal song," he said. "No priest of your hateful church awaits me there, only my beloved wife. But you? The Vagrant comes for you. His blades lurk in the shadows, and I hold faith they will spill your blood before the spring's thaw. Your soul will drown in the Heldeep, and lost in its darkness, you will wail and thrash as wretched Dagon consumes all that remains of your vile being. When I am in the eternal lands, I will pray for you . . . if I even remember your name."

Magus shut the prison cell door and stormed down the corridor. Dozens of men and women were crammed into the cells on either side of him, some weeping, some sulking, and a rare few conversing quietly with one another. Magus had worked over many, his results always identical. It was uncanny. In none of his previous campaigns had he encountered such devotion in the defeated populace, especially years after the initial invasion and the public execution of their deities. Whatever made up these Thanese people, it was of a most stubborn, maddening sort.

The frustration could not last in the face of his overall mood. The raid on the mansion was the most significant blow to Thanet's insurgency since it had begun in earnest months ago. And according to the most recent letter of his informant, another great victory hovered in the distance, waiting for him to reach out and take it. The excitement put a bounce in his step he'd not had since Soma ran the god Endarius through with his spear.

What actually could threaten his mood was Sinshei vin Lucavi waiting at the far end of the prison, a blazing torch above her casting gloomy shadows. Her face was perfectly calm, her voice passive, but disgust and contempt radiated off her like unseen heat from a bonfire.

"Unable to make them talk?" she asked.

"How could you tell?" he muttered sarcastically.

"I could try with my magic. The sting of a heavenly sword is most unique."

He shook his head. His shield waited for him beside the stairway, and he lifted its comforting weight onto his arm.

"Do not bother, Anointed One. Their devotion to this Vagrant...it goes beyond the pale. They're fanatics, every last one of them. Even calling them 'fanatic' might be too kind. It feels like they've been branded into a death cult."

"Even fanatics can be broken," Sinshei said. A little shiver ran up his spine. So often he viewed the God-Incarnate's daughter as a spineless kitten, but every now and then he glimpsed a hint of fangs. The idea of torturing these people, of breaking their faith in the Vagrant, excited her.

"They don't need to be broken," he said, putting the thought aside. "Not to serve their purpose."

"So I heard." Sinshei stepped to her left so she put herself directly between Magus and the stairs leading out of the prison. "Word has spread throughout the city like wildfire. You're planning a mass hanging. My priests tell me the gallows is already under construction."

"What of it?"

"You'll hang forty of Vallessau's wealthiest and prominent members solely for being together at a party? We have no evidence against any of them that they conspired against the empire, nor that they provided aid to the Vagrant and his insurgence."

"I don't need evidence," Magus said. "Not when I have an informant feeding me information from the rebellion's highest tiers of leadership."

Sinshei's eyes narrowed, and he caught her digging her fingernails into the bunched fabric of her dress.

"You possess such a valuable traitor? Why was I not told?"

He smirked at her.

"I trust no one in your church, Sinshei, not after the disgrace that was the paragon ritual. Of course I kept this information to myself, lest the men and women at that party flee prior to our arrival."

The Anointed's painted cheeks flushed red.

"Even if you have secret knowledge of their guilt, you already admit it is not knowledge you can share with the populace. Execute them here, quietly and in secret. Let rumors spread throughout the city of their guilt. To hang them before a crowd is too great a risk."

"I am no fool, Sinshei. I know the risk, but with that risk comes the potential rewards. A mass execution of the Vagrant's faithful? The meddlesome bastard won't let that happen unchallenged. He'll inter- fere. He must. And when he does..." Magus grinned. "Then we show the wretches of this city they have put their faith in the wrong man."

"This is a mistake," Sinshei insisted. "You move too quickly, and like with the Joining Laws, you underestimate the resolve of a people—"

Magus slammed his shield to the stone, cracking it with the sharp- ened edge. The noise blessedly interrupted her rambling. He crossed his arms over his chest, directly challenging Sinshei to show him, truly show him, how sharp her kitten's fangs could be.

"The hangings commence tomorrow," he said. "Unless Thanet's Anointed One objects?"

He thought, even hoped, she would strike at him with her magic. Holding her by the throat on the beach after the paragon ritual, show- ing the woman her blood and station meant nothing compared to his strength, had been immensely satisfying. If she lashed out now, no one, not even her father, would blame him for putting her down like a poorly trained dog. If leaving a few bruises on her throat had given him such pleasure, how great would it be to hear her beg for her life? How deep the thrill to listen to the breath leave her lungs as her skinny body broke beneath the fury of his fists?

The Three Pillars had become two. Perhaps the conversion of an island would go even swifter with one.

"My priests and priestesses shall not partake in this endeavor," Sinshei said. Fire burned in her violet eyes. "You laid the failure of the paragon ritual at my feet despite your own ineptitude. I shall suffer no blame unfairly cast my way again. I wish you well, Imperator. This public farce is all yours."

She turned to leave. Her extreme confidence unnerved him so. The public execution, and the planned ambush, was perfect. It was under his control. How could it possibly go wrong?

"Your father shall hear of your refusal," he said, his words freezing her in place. She glanced over her shoulder, her long dark hair rippling like a waterfall. Her smile was a serpent's welcome.

"Indeed he shall," she said. "And to you, I freely give it all, Magus. All the glory...and all the shame."

CHAPTER 41

THE NIGHT BEFORE

Thorda placed a dagger on the table to represent the execution plat-form the imperial soldiers had spent the last day building. Books were stacked side by side to show the positions of homes. An upside-down cup was the nearby bell tower.

"Rayan and Arn will reinforce what soldiers Commander Pilus can afford," he said, and he pointed to an empty circle around the dagger where the crowd would be. He tapped a faded copy of poems behind the platform. "Mari, you'll wait with Stasia in this building here along with a smattering of archers. Your main goal is to secure a vantage point for those archers, but when the fighting starts, do not hesitate to join the fray. We need the two of you spilling blood. As for you, Cyrus"—he pointed to the bell tower—"you'll be at the very top, looking down on the execution platform. No matter how prepared the soldiers are, they cannot prepare for the magic of your Anyx ring."

The members of his elite were gathered around the table, and they all nodded to show their understanding. None questioned him, nor remarked on the difficulty of their ambush. They were resolute. Confident. It made Thorda's heart swell with pride.

"I've already contacted Clarissa's band. They shall be setting fires to distract any potential reinforcements. As for myself, I will be at the far end of the crowd, and leave the moment the fighting begins." He crossed his arms and stared at the dagger. "This is my resistance, and the lives of those forty are in my hands. On my whistle, we unleash fire and blood. I may not be able to do more, but at least this one responsibility will fall upon the shoulders of he who deserves it most."

He glanced at the five, giving each a chance to interrupt. All stayed silent.

"Very well," he said. "We'll move out early tomorrow morning, and be set up long before the hangings begin. All else pales in comparison to the importance of this mission. If Thanet is to believe we can stand up to the empire's might, we must show them we protect our own. I will not lie to you. We have never attempted something so dangerous. My friends, my family, spend this night as you see fit. Tomorrow may well be your last."

Stasia and Clarissa walked along the moonlit beach, afforded a rare privacy in the city. With the docks heavily patrolled by the five distant warships, the beaches themselves were left alone. Here in the late dark, they could be together and talk openly amid the waves.

Hold hands, without fear of the eyes of a priest.

"I swear your mother almost locked the door on me to keep me there," Stasia said. She paused to kick a shell with her toe, enjoying the way it flipped along the wet sand toward the waves. Stasia had joined Clarissa and her mother at her tiny cliffside home for a rare meal of seasoned bluefin tuna and freshly caught oysters as they laughed and talked as if tomorrow meant nothing at all.

"It's just her way," Clarissa said. "If you're with her, she can keep you safe. She always thought the same for me, too. That I don't move in with her, or with my grandfather in North Cape, drives her up the wall."

The city was a fading collection of torches and shadows behind them. A particularly strong wave washed along Stasia's ankles, and she paused momentarily to recapture her balance. Clarissa's hand slipped out of hers. The wave receded, and amid the ensuing silence, her lover suddenly confessed beneath the stars.

"They'll be ready for you."

Stasia shrugged as if unconcerned.

"I know."

"It's a trap. It has to be a trap. There will be soldiers, patrols... what if something happens to you?"

"That's never stopped me before."

"I've never asked you to stop before."

They turned, faced each other. Clarissa looked hesitant, frightened.

"Will you ask me?" Stasia carefully asked, revealing nothing.

Her lover cast her gaze to the sea.

"I want to. I'm scared, Stasia. I'm so tired of being scared. Is it wrong of me to want that to end? And even if you win tomorrow, there will be another fight, and another, battles unending..."

Stasia turned and knelt in the sand before her cherished, her beloved, her everything. There would be no secrets between them, no unspoken fears. She'd put so much thought into her future, and what she wanted it to be. Come whatever may be, it would be done in naked, painful truth.

"I've made up my mind," she said. "And I think I have known for a long while now. I'm fighting for you, Clarissa. Not Cyrus, not my father, not those men and women doomed to hang. Just you. It means nothing if you aren't waiting for me when I return. If you want me to stay, then I'll stay. Whatever life follows, it will be enough, because you'll be with me."

Clarissa leaned closer, her messy red hair covering her face in waves.

"Do you promise?"

Stasia thought herself a killer, cold and brutal, yet she realized tears were falling from her eyes. Was it relief she felt, or guilt? She didn't know.

"Yes," she swore. "I do."

Clarissa wrapped her arms around Stasia and pulled her close. Trembling fingers slipped through Stasia's hair. The softness of her body enveloped her. The embrace renewed her.

"Then I want you to fight," Clarissa said. "Because if you're not fighting, then you're not the Stasia I love."

More tears, wetting her lover's shirt.

"Thank you," she whispered.

Arn slumped at the table in the dining hall. A tall glass sat unused before him as he drank straight from the bottle. He'd opened it fresh, and had made decent progress on the final third of it by the time Cyrus descended the stairs, silent as a mouse. The young man looked to the front door, then paused upon realizing Arn was watching him from the dining hall in the opposite direction.

"Heading out?" Arn asked, amused by the young man's conflicted mood. "Seems like everyone's got an itch to go somewhere."

"Maybe it's this house," Cyrus said. "It's unfamiliar to me. I would rather sit among the stars."

"Sit and what? Think? Piss on that." Arn lifted the bottle. "I'd rather be drunk."

Cyrus joined him in the hall. Whatever plans he had, it seemed he could put them on hold for a moment.

"I must confess I am not the wisest when it comes to paragons," he said with a smile. "But I remember reading once that your divine bodies cannot be intoxicated."

"Yeah, we tell people that," Arn said. He took another chug. "It's mostly true. Our stomachs are little miracle workers. We can eat rotten food and feel fine. It's damn hard to poison us, and even snake venom does little more than make our skin swell up like a mosquito bite."

"So why drink the wine? Do you enjoy the taste?"

"The taste? Hah!" He gestured to the two other bottles he'd set out before him. "With perseverance and dedication, we may all reach our desired goals. I'm a stubborn man, Cyrus, and by the time I'm done with these bottles, I'll be a drunk man, too."

Cyrus reluctantly settled into the chair opposite him.

"Don't take it too far," he said. "We need you in top form for tomorrow. I'd rather not fight alongside a traitorous paragon discovering for the first time what a hangover is."

"You barely look like you could grow facial hair, and you want to lecture me on hangovers?" Arn's boisterous grin didn't last. "Besides, you don't need me. You got a good head on your shoulders. A lot better than, say, that Stasia woman. She's death in a fiery body. Someone's gonna get burned when it comes to her. I pray it's not you."

Cyrus crossed his arms and leaned back in his chair. Arn had to admit that, for a young brat, he managed an impressive scowl.

"You are one of the finest fighters on this island, and a fine ally. Former paragon or not, you're risking your life for our sakes. I am glad to have you with us. We all are."

"You show me too much kindness, young prince." Perhaps the first bottle was finally starting to hit him, because he felt uncharacteristically honest. "What help I've given you is nothing when compared to my past. The weight of my sins is massive. Fighting with you? Killing some soldiers in Thanet's name? It's me removing a few measly feathers resting atop a pile of stone. It won't equal out the scales. It won't even make them twitch."

"Let's say you're right, and it is but a few feathers," Cyrus said. "At least you're removing feathers and not adding more stones. That still has to mean something, doesn't it? Better that you struggle one inch higher up the mountain you're climbing than fall another dozen feet."

"I see the young prince is now a philosopher," Arn said with a chuckle.

"I'd rather hit things with swords like Stasia taught me, but you looked so sad drinking in the dark, I had to try my best."

"Sad?" He thudded the table with the empty bottle. "I'm drinking to celebrate another victory tomorrow. Get out of here with that 'sad' nonsense. Go sit under your stars, boy. Leave this tired adult to his wine."

Cyrus smacked him playfully on the shoulder.

"If you insist," he said, and departed for the front door. Arn watched him go, and it wasn't until he was certain the young man was gone that he reached into his pocket and pulled out his charm. He twirled it in his fingers, feeling the fur against his fingertips as the red and orange he'd long ago memorized turned in kind.

"Feathers," he whispered, put the foxtail away, and reached for another bottle.

To possess any religious symbol of Lycaena and Endarius risked public floggings, imprisonment, or worst of all, hanging from the end of a rope at the Dead Flags. Rayan's small stone altar of rising butterfly wings would certainly earn him the worst of the three punishments. He kept it hidden in the closet of his home, behind a false board. In preparation for tomorrow's mission, he retrieved it and set it in the center of his modest living room, along with a bag of incense. He put his back to the hearth so its warmth would wash over him while he prayed. When he loosened the bag's tie string, his nose was greeted with a welcome burst of rose and sandalwood.

"Your kindness and mercy be upon me," he whispered as he prepared for his meditation.

Rayan sat with his sword drawn, its naked blade resting atop his legs. The incense burned in the little bowl at the base of the butterfly wings. The bright smoke filled his house with the welcome aroma. Eyes closed, he lifted his hands heavenward, and he pretended he wasn't hiding in a closet. Instead he imagined himself in the great fields west of Vallessau. He imagined tall grass swaying against his legs when the breeze blew. He imagined shining stars above, and a choir of the Twin Sanctuary singing hymns to Lycaena to hasten the arrival of the coming spring.

A knock came from his door, interrupting the meditation.

"Uncle?" Keles asked from outside. "May I come in?"

He'd not locked it, foolish in hindsight.

"Enter," he said.

His niece stepped inside and, upon seeing the altar, quickly shut and locked the door.

"I was with Pilus when we were told our part in Thorda's plan," she said. She'd wrapped an orange scarf around her hair to protect it from the nighttime chill, but Rayan's home was always warm (too warm, his wife used to complain). She removed the scarf, stuffed it into her pocket, and crossed the room to join him at the tiny altar.

"Our part?" he asked.

"I would like to fight alongside your group instead of Pilus's . . . if you'll have me."

"Of course I'd have you," Rayan said. "Why wouldn't I?"

In answer, his niece reached for the sword that lay across his lap. She lifted it by the hilt and held it before her face. The finely polished steel shone in the lamplight, but it didn't glow with faithful energy the way a paladin's should.

"I will be a soldier, like any other," she said. "Not a paladin of Lycaena. I'm sorry, Uncle. I'm not doing this for her, or for Endarius. I'm doing this for you. I'm doing this for my family, and my friends, and everyone else the Everlorn Empire has trampled. I hope...I hope that will be enough."

"Though your skills may be rusty, I would still put your swordplay above many an imperial soldier. You are offering yourself, Keles. It is enough. It will always be enough." He gestured to the little altar to Lycaena he had removed from his closet. "I know the path you walk is no longer my own, but would you join me in prayer nonetheless? Even if only for tonight, as a way to humor an old man?"

"This may sound terribly rude, but I do not understand the point."

"Do you speak to your parents sometimes, when you're alone, your heart is hurting, and the memories won't let you sleep?"

"I do," Keles said. "But I don't expect my parents to speak back. You would have me pray to a slain goddess. Why should I expect an answer to those prayers?"

"What does death even mean to a god?" Rayan asked. "I do not know that answer, Keles. I do not pretend to have that wisdom. But I believe in her, and I hold faith that she remains, perhaps no longer here on this world, but in the evergreen fields beyond. I believe your parents are with her, as is my wife. And though our goddess has fallen, she yet lives on in our hearts, and in our memories. It is through both she empowers us."

He reached out and took his sword from her grasp. Faint light shimmered across the steel.

"I do not know if she listens," he said. "But I hold faith that she does. The Butterfly may be dead, but the moth remains."

Keles's eyes watered from the light of the sword. She stepped back and retrieved the scarf from her pocket so she might wrap it about her head.

"I cannot do it again," she whispered. "Do not ask me to do it again. I prayed, and prayed, and *prayed*, and for it, I watched my parents swing from the Dead Flags. I watched the Anointed One's dagger pierce our goddess's breast. I will not pray again, not until I see Lycaena spread her wings before me. With all of Thanet as my witness, I forsook my faith, and as much as it pains me to admit it, I spoke no lie."

His niece turned for the door. Rayan wished to stop her, but a life-time of wisdom told him it would only make things worse. He let her final words hang in the air, far heavier than any incense.

"For once, the goddess must earn *my* faith."

"You're gloomier than usual," Mari said as she joined Thorda on the couch facing their new home's hearth. "And that is truly saying something."

"Is it so obvious?"

Mari's father had stared into the fire for several minutes without him noticing she had entered the room. Normally he'd be aware of her every movement, with senses she swore bordered on the divine. To be so completely lost in his thoughts meant something troubled his soul.

"Yes," she said, declining to elaborate further. "So what bothers you?"

Her father shifted against the arm of the couch, away from her. Phys-ical connection had always been complicated with him. He loved her and Stasia, she knew that in her heart, but he did not show it with a kind embrace or a playful touch of their hair while they were children. His fight for a free Miquo, and a free Gadir, was for his two daughters more than it was for himself. At least, that's what she told herself as they rode a carriage to yet another nation, to fight yet another war.

"I find my sins weighing heavily upon me this evening," he said, eyes locked to the hearth. "Especially the lives of the forty who will hang on the morrow. They trusted me. I offered them promises of a free Thanet, and now they rot in a prison, their only future a knotted rope."

"Imperials love to blame punishments on those who resist," she said. "No different than a drunken abuser blaming his wife for her bruises. The empire is responsible for its actions, not those who rise up to point out its crimes. Those forty, they chose to fight back. They *wanted* to fight back. We both know this. You've given the same speech a hundred times before, to men far less intelligent than yourself."

"Yet it does not absolve my involvement," her father said. "These men and women, they die because of me. They die because of my choices. They die because I sailed across the Crystal Sea, scattered gold and silver coins across Thanet's sands, and bade them to rise up and believe. Forty men and women, set to hang from a rope. I will not pretend their blood belongs on anyone else's hands but my own. I must put that guilt upon my shoulders and bear it, for who else will?"

"We will," Mari said. "Stasia and I, we'll keep going, for as long as we must. Everywhere we go, there are people willing to help. You don't need to carry the burden alone."

"I would if it means sparing you two, my precious daughters," he said. "These choices I make, they are mine, and mine alone. I do not fear them. I have long since moved beyond guilt and doubt. If I am to be judged, let it be by gods wiser than I."

Mari took his hand into both of hers and squeezed his bony fingers.

"There will be nothing to judge," she said. "Tomorrow morning, we're going to free those people from their hangings. We'll save them, every last one, and if we're lucky, we might even put the Imperator and the Anointed One into early graves. Wouldn't that be a day? A good day, great day even, so don't worry tonight. Smile instead. At least, smile for me, all right? I know a frown fits you better, but if you don't, those lines around your mouth will become deep as canyons."

Thorda laughed, and it warmed her heart to finally see her words pierce through his veil of gloom.

"Thank you, Mari," he said. "I know you doubt yourself, and that you think yourself a poor comparison to your sister. She's a cold killer, true, more brutal, more eager to act, but you're the stronger one. You've kept your kindness despite this world's hate. You've kept your vulnerability despite this world's cruelty. Holding on to your humanity amid death and war...that is so much harder than rage. In Stasia, I see what Miquo once was. In you, I see the future I would give our people, if I were but clever enough to grasp it."

Mari bit her lip. A thousand times she'd wished to say this. Perhaps due to her father's own encouragement, she finally possessed the necessary courage.

"Please don't compare us," she said. "No matter how you do it, it always feels like one of us falls short of the other. Can't we both be enough?"

Thorda did not speak for a long moment, though his jaw shifted and his mouth chewed as if he were eating his own tongue.

"You two have ever been the world to me," he said. "And I could never have asked for better daughters. You are beyond what I deserve. I may show it poorly, but I thank the heavens for you two. You give me the strength to walk the lonely, jagged path that must be walked. If Miquo is to be free of the God-Incarnate, it will not be by my hands, but yours and Stasia's. I believe that, I truly do."

Mari slid across the empty cushion so that her weight pressed against him. She settled her head on his shoulder. He tensed at first, then slowly relaxed. It reminded her of befriending a stray cat, and the thought made her smile.

"It's been hard," she said. "But you've done your best. I know that. Stasia does, too."

Her father gently leaned his head upon hers. Together they watched the three logs within the hearth char and fade to gray.

"Do not hate me, Mari," he whispered.

"Why would I ever hate you?"

He did not answer. The fire crackled, silence followed, and she lay there until the fire faded and sleep came.

Cyrus was glad to be outside, for his feet craved a walking path. Hood pulled high up over his head, he traversed the dark streets, his gaze locked mere steps before him. His mind, however, was a thousand miles away.

Forty men and women, prominent members of Vallessau's high society, set to hang. And why? Because they sought to meet him again. They wished to be in his presence, to watch him move, to fight, perhaps even execute another member of the imperial army. They desired the hope he offered, and in return, the Imperator stormed the mansion and dragged them into prison cells.

"Everywhere I go, people are dying for me," he whispered. He dared not voice the thought that followed: *Am I worth it?*

His path led him southwest, to the outer wall where the city could grow no farther due to the rising Emberfall Mountains. The particularly clever or desperate citizens had carved their homes into the rock, with both wood and rope ladders granting access. Cyrus focused on a distant section worn into the cliff by wind, rain, and time. There. That would suffice.

Cyrus clutched his hand into a fist, and he enacted the magic of the Anyx ring so that when he stepped forward, his entire body transported to the deep shadows atop that cliffside. He calmly crossed the tiny space to the edge, and from high up he gazed upon the sleeping city. He soaked in the faint streetlamps, the torches surrounding the castle, and the five blockading ships lurking on distant starlit waters.

"Does it end?" he whispered to the night. "Does it ever end?"

People had fought and died for him from the first moment the army of the Everlorn Empire invaded Thanet's shores. Those better than him had sacrificed their focus and time to train him. Years of others' lives, spent and gone, to make him useful. Thorda whispered stories, and his daughters sowed chaos so he might claim the credit. Mari had insisted he didn't need to own the city to wish the best for its people, and Cyrus believed that, he did, but he also understood the unspoken promise connected to that belief.

The people believed in him, in the Vagrant. They believed, and with that hope came bloodshed. His hope. His bloodshed. There would be no washing his hands of that.

"I won't let you win," Cyrus told the phantom image of the Imperator who had murdered his mother and father. "I'm tired of people fighting for me. I'm tired of people *dying* for me. Others carry the burdens meant for my shoulders. No longer."

Will you be stronger, Cyrus Lythan? had asked the island's Lion god. *Will you carry their legacy?*

He would. For Thanet. For her people. For her gods. His swords were not with him, but he imagined drawing them anyway. He lifted his arms, wrists crossed, and gave his vow to the city his family had ruled for generations. He offered it to the forty people imprisoned, who had refused to name the Vagrant, and were willing to die to protect his secret.

"Tomorrow, I prove myself worthy of your hope," he whispered. "Tomorrow, I prove your faith in me is not a death sentence."

CHAPTER 42

CYRUS

The entire square was heavily patrolled, but those patrols meant nothing to Cyrus when the bell tower had few windows and lots of shadows. A flicker of the spinel in his ring, a step into an unlit corner, and he emerged on a familiar set of stairs. Cyrus climbed to the belfry, remembering the first time he had come to this tower. It was on the night of his return to Vallessau, when he had feared his need for vengeance would make him a poor hero for the city. Mari had come to him and, with her kindness and her dedication, given him the hope he needed.

Looking down on the hanging platform, he prayed he would be the hope *they* needed, if they were to survive.

"The church and the Imperator will both want to revel in the murderous excess," Thorda had reminded Cyrus prior to donning his mask and leaving for the tower. "They'll want speeches and posturing, and we will deny them all of it. Before the pomp and circumstance, but after the prisoners arrive, I shall sound my whistle. So begins the battle. So begins your final step in becoming Thanet's hero."

Cyrus clung to his teacher's confidence as the first of the prisoners arrived, escorted by soldiers toward the hanging platform. Skilled woodworkers had built it over the past two days, and if its purpose wasn't so ghastly, it might have been impressive. Multiple beams were nailed overhead, crisscrossed so that they formed four rows deep and ten across. Forty ropes hung from the beams, awaiting their victims to climb the five steps to their doom.

The base was made up of six wide, flat pieces of wood, each held up by dozens of unseen gears and braces underneath the hollow platform. With a single pull of a lever, the bottom would drop out, and all forty would simultaneously plummet to their deaths.

If only such engineering could be used for a better purpose, Cyrus thought dryly.

The announcement leaflets distributed throughout Vallessau indicated to Cyrus it was a good half hour before the entire macabre ceremony began, but the soldiers brought the prisoners early, as expected. A small crowd had gathered around the platform, just a few dozen men and women come to ensure themselves a good view of the spectacle. Many were plants from Thorda's resistance, armed with daggers and knives hidden in trouser legs and coat sleeves. They wouldn't fight once the assault began in earnest, but instead ambush the soldiers scattered throughout, killing them the second Thorda's signal sounded.

The crowd parted for the soldiers, which numbered at least a hundred. Cyrus crouched low along the edge of the belfry as the soldiers adjusted the nooses so they were nice and secure about the necks of their victims. Forty men and women of all ages, remarkably calm as they marched with their hands bound behind their backs up the steps and to their spots. Did they somehow know of Thorda's plan? Or did they merely hold faith in the Vagrant to rescue them from execution?

Time ticked along, painfully slow. Cyrus studied the area in preparation for the ambush. The platform was built at a T intersection of streets, and soldiers formed lines checking arrivals at all three sides. Beyond the platform were several multistory homes, all currently empty as soldiers swept through them. Lioness and Ax would arrive mere moments after Thorda's whistle, along with a group of archers, to kill the few stationed on the opposite side of the buildings. Once done, they could climb in and attack from the windows with their bows while the battle raged below.

Cyrus turned his attention down the street closest to him. Waiting at the far end would be the rest of Thorda's elite, fully armed and dressed in their armor. They would attack in unison when given the signal, relying on surprise and superior strength to make up for a lack of numbers. If all went well, they would be greeted by chaos caused by Clarissa and Pilus. Clarissa had formed a loose alliance with those most harmed by the Joining Laws, and they were positioned in a half-dozen places in the surrounding neighborhood. When Thorda gave his signal, they would start fire after fire to delay and confuse reinforcements.

Back on the platform, all forty were now securely prepared for the sudden drop that would snap their necks and crush their windpipes. Their confidence was starting to waiver as the crowd swelled with new arrivals. One woman near the front began to weep, and when a nearby soldier yelled at her, she cried only louder.

"Soon," Cyrus whispered, pretending the woman could hear him. "I'll be there for you soon, I promise."

The crowd had begun to amass in earnest. Imperial soldiers formed a thin line to scan arrivals, and they had anticipated people coming equally from all three directions. Thorda had worked with Commander Pilus to intermix his own fighters with large groups of civilian volunteers meant not to fight but to interfere with the imperial soldiers' ability to do their jobs. These volunteers loudly grumbled and pushed back against any and all attempts by the soldiers to pat down arrivals for weapons. Pilus's armed soldiers held back, waiting, as the exaggerated impatience before them grew. Once soldiers were sufficiently distracted, they pushed inward, slipping past the line unchecked.

Cyrus smiled at the efficiency. They would have dozens of armed men and women in the crowd, their swords hidden beneath their cloaks and coats. Once Cyrus arrived, they would draw their weapons and form a battle line along the west. Rayan, Arn, and Keles would charge from the south, while Stasia and Mari joined the archers along the north. The eastern road they would leave open for civilians to escape.

Starting it all would be Thorda's whistle, but that would not be what most remembered. The real start, the one that would mark the tales, would be when the Vagrant appeared upon the stage with the power of his Anyx ring, his swords cutting the ropes and saving those who had put their faith in him.

Cyrus clenched his hands together, feeling the magic of his ring grow warm. It was ready. The shadows underneath the execution platform were more than deep enough, and they'd already confirmed the platform's back was open, meaning he could immediately dash out and then up. He bit his lip. His thumb slowly curled the silver band back and forth. So close now. The prisoners were ready, but still no sign of Magus or Sinshei. Any moment. He only waited for...

A single, shrill whistle pierced the dull hum of conversation.

Cyrus lurched to a stand. This was it. Runners would be sprinting to Clarissa's friends, crying out to start the fires. The initial assassins crept their way to the guards within the crowd. Cyrus stared at the platform, envisioning the darkness beneath. One step into shadows, one step out, and his arrival would begin the assault.

Except something went very deeply wrong.

He never had a chance to leap down from the tower. He never enacted his magic. There were no speeches. No priest or priestess of the Uplifted Church denounced the prisoners for their heresies. No official stood with scroll in hand to declare the multitude of crimes to the crowd. Upon hearing the whistle, the lone soldier stationed near the execution platform's lever calmly turned, grabbed the lever, and pulled.

Up in the belfry, Cyrus did not move. He did not save anyone. He only watched.

The platform opened, and the forty prisoners dropped until the ropes snapped taut. Necks snapped with them. He heard screams, not from the executed, but the shocked crowd. Cyrus couldn't look away. The image burned into him with the same savage fire as when he'd witnessed his parents' murder. The way their legs kicked. The bulging of their eyes, for none of the forty were hooded. The growing redness of faces of those not instantly killed as the air was choked from their ruined throats.

The signal to start the attack had been the signal to execute the prisoners. No pomp and circumstance. No expected traditions. Just sudden, unheralded death. A maelstrom grew in Cyrus's breast, twisting with emotions he could not fathom. Betrayal. Confusion. Guilt. It struck his body like a physical force. Energy vibrated throughout his muscles. Time itself slowed. His anger boiled in his blood, hot enough to burn down a city. Too late. Yet again, he was too late.

Footsteps thudded upon the wooden stairs behind him. The trap door creaked open. Cyrus turned to be greeted by laughter, and a grin so wide, it matched his mask's own.

"There you are, Vagrant," Imperator Magus of Eldrid said. "Did you enjoy my surprise?"

Cyrus pulled his swords from their sheaths and crouched at the edge of the belfry. Magus came dressed in his full platemail, and he carried his enormous sword and shield. The trap door that allowed access to the top of the tower could not fit his girth, so he casually smashed aside a board with his shoulder as he climbed the last step.

"You monster," Cyrus seethed in the imperial tongue. If only he had learned more curses and insults during his days in Thorda's mansion. His knowledge of the imperial language was woefully incapable of conveying his rage.

"Now, now, there is no need for insults. Save your anger for the traitor in your midst, for this glorious day would not be possible without them."

The sounds of battle erupted behind him, but he dared not take his eyes off his foe. What glimpses he saw from the corners of his eyes were dire. Soldiers approached from all three directions to seal off the crowd. A trap for a trap.

"Those people deserved better," Cyrus said. "All of Thanet will hear of this cowardice."

Magus shrugged. It seemed nothing could diminish his grin.

"I do not care if those prisoners died without appropriate grandeur. You're the island's real hope, Vagrant, not those wealthy fools pretending at rebellion. Is there no better stage for a duel?" He spread his arms wide. "Let us fight, here and now, while all the city watches."

Cyrus glanced at the giant bronze bell positioned between them.

"A bit cramped, wouldn't you agree?"

"Too true. One moment, please."

Magus smashed the bell with his shield. It rang out, sounding weirdly dull and cut off, as the supports along the top cracked. The bell broke free of its crossbeam, flew out from the tower, and fell to the crowd, smashing both imperial soldiers and civilians alike as it rolled.

"There now, we have our space," the Imperator said. "Not the best footing, perhaps, but sacrifices must be made for spectacle."

Sacrifices, like the lives of forty men and women who had trusted Cyrus to save them. Those forty had refused to name him despite their imprisonment and torture. They had held faith in him. And oh, how he had failed.

Cyrus crouched for a lunge, his swords feeling electric in his hands. To engage a paragon one-on-one in cramped spaces, let alone an Imperator, was suicide. He knew he wasn't as strong as the stories claimed. He knew he couldn't defeat Magus without the help of Stasia or Thorda or Arn. He knew that. But he no longer cared.

"Spectacle," he said. "Yes, Magus, I shall give the city a spectacle. They will watch as I throw your severed head from the tower. A pittance compared to the lives you have taken, but not all debts may be paid at once."

Cyrus exploded into motion, determined to take the offensive. The belfry was small, and would limit his mobility, but so, too, did it limit Magus in his bulky plate and oversized weaponry. If he could overwhelm the Imperator with his rage, bury him in a barrage of attacks...

His blades rattled off Magus's sword. Back and forth the Imperator weaved it, quick, sharp movements that seemed to understand Cyrus's patterns. Cyrus scraped his off-hand blade against the golden bull emblazoned across the shield, then pressed against it to avoid an overhead chop. He rolled, head ducking underneath Magus's arm, and came out swinging. The shield followed him, but while his off-hand carved a new groove into its surface, the other crossed above it. Magus tilted his head so his helmet took the brunt of the hit. A faint gash opened across his lower jaw.

"Think the city saw that part?" Cyrus asked.

Magus brushed blood from the wound across his gauntlet and sneered at it.

"First hits don't matter, only the last."

The Imperator hopped forward, his shield leading. In such close quarters, Cyrus could only retreat. He fell back again and again, tracing a circle around where the bell had once hung. Magus's sword cut and weaved, always a shadow's width behind. Cyrus dared not try to block it. Twice he countered, his superior agility allowing him to sidestep or duck underneath a swing. The first time, he tried using the curved end of his sword to beat the Imperator's shield aside. Instead his sword

scraped off, lacking the strength to make it budge. The second time, he
flipped his off-hand and extended his entire body into a thrust for the
gap in armor at his armpit.

Magus's shield smashed into his chest before he could make contact.
He fell back and tried to gather his footing, only for the shield to bash
him a second time. It was so huge, so heavy, he doubted an angered bull
matching the one on the Imperator's shield could crash into him any
harder. He swiped low, a hit meant to open up a gash along the shin,
but yet again came the shield, only lower. His sword screeched metal
on metal, and he only barely withdrew it in time to keep it from being
pinned to the floorboards.

Not enough room! he thought as that shield bashed again. He felt
mocked. He felt belittled. The Imperator was toying with him, amusement in his eyes and teeth exposed in a grin. Cyrus flipped his off-
hand to a regular grip (there'd be little parrying and blocking with
it anyway, given the paragon's enormous size) and attempted to bury
his sword right between those grinning teeth. Magus batted it aside
with an upward swipe of his sword, then brought it right back down to
block Cyrus's attempted follow-up. His speed was incredible, his honed
reflexes surpassing even Stasia's. And always, always that damn shield!
Cyrus pushed his shoulder against it and then rolled, hoping to come
out of it with an open angle of attack.

Instead the paragon shifted with him, his footing careful and deliberate,
given their tight conditions. Cyrus's next few hits bounced off the shield.
Magus shuffled forward, inch by inch, his sword darting left to right so
Cyrus could not dance away. His goal was obvious. Trapped against the
edge of the belfry, Cyrus had nowhere to go when the shield came, all of
the paragon's weight flung into the charge. Nowhere but out, and so he did.

Cyrus leaped through one of the belfry openings, grabbed the edge
of the corner pillar, and swung round it to slide right back through the
adjacent window with his heels leading. They slammed into Magus's
upraised shield, yet despite all his momentum and weight, the Imperator moved not an inch. Cyrus somersaulted, back arching to curl over
a quick slash meant to cut him open at the waist. He landed lightly,
springing once more off the belfry floorboards. Magus had pulled aside

his shield to swing, and Cyrus thrust both his swords for that slender opening. His left hand jammed against the shield's side, delaying its retreat for a fraction of a second as his longer blade sought the thin exposure between armor at the waist.

Magus moved with speed belying his bulky, muscular body. The thrust missed by a hair. The Imperator then clutched his elbow to his side, catching Cyrus's sword and pinning it harmlessly against his chestplate.

"Damn fool," he said.

Cyrus yanked with all his strength, pulling the sword free, but the delay was all Magus needed. Instead of swinging his sword, he opted for a faster hit with his elbow. Its hard gold plate smashed into Cyrus's mask.

He screamed through gritted teeth as he pivoted in a desperate attempt to soften the blow. Blood splattered from his nose across his lips and teeth. His hood fluttered off, and the mask cracked, then broke. A diagonal portion running from his ear, underneath his left eye, and to his chin fell to the belfry floorboards. Cyrus staggered down to one knee, separating from the Imperator.

A follow-through attack could have killed him, but the paragon chose to refrain. Instead he calmly watched as Cyrus grabbed the broken piece of his mask and jammed it into his pocket.

"It's only a matter of time until you die," Magus said. "I confess, I expected better."

Cyrus stood tall. His eyes shone with rage. He said nothing, for what else was there to say? This brute had murdered his parents and conquered his nation. He'd hanged dozens, just to lay a trap for him. Few alive deserved death more than the Imperator. If only Cyrus's swords could be faster. If only his need for revenge could burn hot enough.

Magus shook his head, as if disappointed, then suddenly froze in place. He focused on the exposed portion of Cyrus's face. On his eyes. His jaw. His brown hair.

"No," Magus said, his smile stretching ear to ear. "It can't be. He lives. The boy prince lives."

Smoke billowed from the intersection below, accompanied by the screams of the injured and dying, yet high atop the bell tower, Imperator Magus of Eldrid laughed.

CHAPTER 43

STASIA

Stasia took her sister's hand in the dark alley.

"You ready?" she asked, her mouth crooking into a lopsided grin. Nervousness and excitement formed a heady cocktail flowing through her blood. Soldiers gathered around them, bows strung across their backs.

"More than ready," Mari said. "The Lion is eager for blood, and so am I."

Stasia took a step back to give her room. She had witnessed her sister's transformation countless times, and in multiple forms in nations outside Thanet, but the Lioness was the most frightening. There was a wildness to it the others lacked, a savagery previous gods and goddesses had not imparted. Mari's spine snapped rigid, and she screamed a cry of pain as her body changed. Her clothes, a simple ruddy dress bought for the occasion, ripped and tore to make room for muscle and claw. Pale gray fur sprouted across her skin. Her jaw unhinged, teeth growing, sharpening, while her knees broke backward. Wings sprouted from her back as she dropped to all fours. Bones pierced through her flesh to form armor akin to plate.

The word-lace about her neck shimmered blue.

"The Lioness shall lead this hunt."

The archers with them muttered prayers, for while they knew the

Lioness battled on their side with Endarius's blessing, they had never seen such a sight, nor known Mari was her true identity. Some cursed in shock. Others wept. Stasia clanged her axes together to draw their attention.

"Move out," she told them, then lifted her mask over her face. "Save your awe for later."

They had already placed ladders in preparation, and the collected twenty men and women climbed them to the rooftops. Ahead were the homes that lined the northern border of the chosen clearing for the hangings. Those homes had been swept repeatedly, hence why Stasia and Mari's group would reclaim them only moments before Thorda's whistle. The Lioness led the way, dashing across rooftops as the group stealthily approached their destination. They slowed only when reaching the gap of the road splitting their current cluster of homes and their destination. While the archers remained crouched low atop the shingles, Stasia and Mari crawled on their bellies to the edge so they might observe.

"Just three," Stasia said, and pointed. The soldiers stood watch, but their eyes were on the roads to either direction, not above. A fatal mistake.

"The nearest are mine," Mari growled. The shingles rattled beneath her as she leaped. Stasia kicked to her feet and then dove after her, axes above her like the wings of a hawk. She rolled shoulder-first to absorb the landing blow, then burst out of it with speed challenged only by her sister. Frightened cries greeted them. Her back was to Mari, but she heard the tearing of metal, heard the gargling screams. Her own foe lifted her spear and thrust it wildly. Stasia knocked it aside with both her axes, snapping the shaft in half. She kicked her heel into the woman's stomach to kill her momentum, then swiped the axes back the other direction. One hit chopped off her shoulder, the other buried deep to the spine.

Stasia pulled the weapons free of the corpse in a spray of blood, then turned back toward their archers in hiding. She beckoned to them, for the way was clear, but before they could move, a sharp whistle pierced the relative quiet. Their father's whistle. They were behind schedule.

The archers dropped and climbed down from the rooftops, hurrying after the two Ahlai sisters. Stasia kicked open the first door, axes ready for the guards she anticipated. Instead a finely furnished and empty home greeted her.

"To the windows," she hissed to the archers. "Half here, half the top floor."

Mari bounded up the stairs, Stasia at her heels. Again, no soldiers in wait. The discovery left her uneasy. Such an obvious vantage point over the execution should have been guarded more thoroughly. Did the Imperator believe the resistance so easily broken by capturing a few wealthy backers? Stasia spun about, checking the bedrooms, but still nothing. When she returned to the stairs, Mari faced the window, whiskers twitching. A whimper escaped her throat, dutifully translated by the glowing word-lace.

"No...no, it can't be."

Stasia joined her side, and her unease twisted into full-blown dread.

The shrill whistle should have signaled the start of their rescue. Hidden members throughout the crowd would execute the watchful guards. The armed men and women near the back would draw steel and charge the stage to form a true battle line against any reinforcements. The archers hurrying to the windows on either side of her would take full advantage of the chaos to pick off scattered targets. Amid it all, the Vagrant Prince would descend upon the stage to cut free his faithful while the crowd cheered. That was the plan, a good one, as far as Stasia was concerned.

Instead the bodies hung from the ropes, each and every one of them dead. The Imperator was nowhere in sight, nor any magistrates. The Vagrant had not arrived. Battle raged, but it was wild and uneven, with hundreds of innocent men and women caught in the middle.

"They suspected an attack," Stasia said.

"No," Mari growled. "They knew how. They knew when. We were betrayed."

The wall collapsed inward to their right, confirming their every fear. Wood and plaster clattered from a pair of soldiers wielding enormous mauls, bashing a way open for the other four soldiers armed with swords and spears. They rushed the nearest archers setting up at the windows, and they faced little resistance. Blood quickly stained the floorboards.

"You bastards," Stasia shouted, and she flung herself into them. Rage replaced her dread. Her axes decapitated the closest soldier, for his attention was not on her but instead the archer he was busy impaling. Two more rushed her, one with a maul, the other a long blade he held in both hands. Stasia trusted her speed to dodge the bulky maul, and instead focused on the longsword. Given their cramped conditions, the soldier thrust it forward, aiming to disembowel Stasia during her charge. Anticipating the attempt, she hooked the underside of her right ax down and out, catching the thrust and locking it aside. Steel scraped against steel as she closed the gap. The maul swung, she ducked underneath, and then she was between the two men.

Their weapons were in awkward positions. Hers were not.

The Lioness dashed overhead as Stasia hacked down her foes. The remaining three gathered, attempting to fall back into the neighboring home they'd burst in from. Instead they discovered the jagged bones of Mari's wings cared not for the defensive swipes of their swords. She pierced one woman through the chest, lifted her up, and ripped her in half. A frantic thrust reflected off the bone guard of her shoulder. Mari's teeth closed about the wielder's wrist. Even across the room, Stasia easily heard the crunch of bones.

The last soldier fled the sisters, but his speed was nothing compared to the Lioness. Mari dove upon his back, her claws raking bloody grooves into his flesh. Stasia did not watch. Her eyes were out the window, and on the squads of imperial soldiers sealing the streets from all three directions.

More shouts from downstairs, followed by screams of pain. Stasia spun. The other archers with them had rushed to the bottom floor to help the others. How had they missed a squad of imperials waiting in ambush? Or had they hidden in a nearby home? There was no way to know, nor time to ponder their growing list of mistakes.

"What do we do?" Mari asked as she padded over. The red blood across her mouth and face was a stark contrast to the gray of her fur and white of her bone armor.

"You join the war out there," Stasia said. "I'll help downstairs."

Her sister nodded in agreement, then dashed out the window. Her roar was in Stasia's ears as she sprinted down the steps. She expected to find an ambush. What she did not anticipate was to find a red-cloaked paragon with coppery-red hair towering over the bodies of the slain archers. He turned her way, and he beamed with excitement upon seeing her.

"Ax, isn't it?" he asked. "You've been quite a thorn in our side."

There was zero chance Stasia could defeat a paragon alone in such cramped conditions. She lifted her ax, acting as if she would fight anyway, then grabbed a flower vase from the shelf next to her and flung it for his head. He shifted his weapon to block it, but the clay shattered upon hitting the steel, covering his face in soil. The paragon swore up a storm as it stung his eyes and covered his tongue.

Stasia dove out the window to join the chaos beyond. Perhaps out there she could link up with the others, or at least get Mari to help her. Frightened people shouted as she landed amid the crowd. With battles erupting in all directions, it seemed the people were of two minds. Half pushed near the stage, seeking to avoid the bloodshed. The other half rushed the exits despite the fighting, hoping to either be let through by the soldiers or sneak past during the confusion.

Stasia maneuvered quickly through their numbers, fearful that the paragon already gave chase. She let the sound of battle guide her, especially the roars of her sister. It seemed the soldiers positioned by Pilus had formed a line to the west, and so to them she ran. Mari dashed among them, a predator most vicious, to form the backbone of the entire force. Soldiers fell to her bone wings and razor-sharp claws. Stasia could only catch the occasional glimpse, given the people between them, but the screams and sprays of blood marked her location well. She spared a glance behind her, but so far it seemed the ax-wielding paragon did not yet chase.

Before she could reach the line, an enormous brass bell came crashing down through the center of the crowd. Stasia leaped aside, narrowly avoiding being crushed as it rolled to a stop. Baffled, she looked to the bell tower from whence it came. For a moment she thought her eyes deceived her, but there was no mistaking either combatant. High up where all could witness, Cyrus fought against Imperator Magus. An impossible fight, even for someone who had shown such promise as Cyrus had over the past months. And should he somehow win, there was the matter of soldiers filling the intersection. If everyone in the resistance fled, Cyrus would find himself surrounded and alone. They had to ensure no one remained.

The answer came in the smoke that billowed to the air from Clarissa's groups scattered throughout the city.

"Lioness!" Stasia shouted, calling her secret name again and again as she closed the distance between her and the battle. Mari's ears perked up, and she bounded over the line of Thanet rebels to land before Stasia. Her head tilted sideways.

"What?" she asked, her impatient snarl translated by the word-lace.

"Set the houses aflame!" Stasia demanded.

"Which ones?"

"All of them."

Mari turned her attention to the houses, thinking for a moment, and then nodded. Stasia had thought her sister might take a torch in her mouth. Using her feline speed, she could easily leap from home to home, spreading fires so that the entire square was ablaze and Cyrus might have a chance to escape amid all the smoke and ash.

Stasia clearly did not have her sister's imagination, nor her understanding of the power of gods. Mari threw back her head and roared to the heavens. The word-lace offered no translation, for it bore only pure emotions. Pain. Rage. A desire for chaos. A need to hunt. The air rippled, and within it, Stasia felt the power of the divine.

In life, Endarius's wings had borne long white feathers tipped in red, at least according to the paintings of the god Stasia had seen. In death, he granted no feathers, just jagged bones. In death, Mari demanded something more. The roar deepened. The air shimmered. Fire burst from the long bone wings, rolling across Mari's body into the perfect shape of folded feathers. They unfurled to her sides, and the sight was so beautiful, so terrifying, Stasia gaped in awe of her sister.

Mari turned to face her, and at last the word-lace had speech to translate, echoing a sentiment Stasia had offered in a much more serene setting.

"I say we get to burning."

Stasia whooped as her sister leaped to the rooftops of the homes over-looking the gallows. Her wings fluttered, casting fire upon the shingles. Within moments black smoke billowed overhead, the dozen buildings quickly becoming an inferno. Stasia slammed her two axes together, their parts interlocking with expertise that was incredible even for her gifted father's handiwork. The haft she kept clipped to her side like any other weapon, and she slid it free of her belt so she might lock and twist it into the base of the axes. No more dual-wielding. She needed the reach and power of using it two-handed.

Weapon ready, she sprinted straight into the thick of the chaos. She never slowed. She never hesitated. Stasia announced the Ax of Laha-reed's arrival with a massive downward chop that cleaved a soldier in half from shoulder to hip. The screech of metal and snapping of bone turned nearby eyes her way, and she relished the attention. Gore coated her weapon, and she would paint a thousand new layers atop it.

"With me!" she screamed to Pilus's soldiers. "Let the empire break against my ax!"

Soldiers rushed her. Fools. Dead men. The Lioness landed amid their number before Stasia lowered her ax. The fire had faded from her bone wings, but her teeth and claws were more than enough to tear through their ranks. Once Stasia joined her, and the sisters linked up side by side, none could withstand them. Her great-ax weaved back and forth, a lumberjack cutting down tree after tree in a drunken stupor. Blood spilled across the streets, and Pilus's soldiers surged in the wake of every assault made by the Ahlai sisters. Stasia's ax broke shields. Mari's claws shredded open plate without a care to their attempted blocks and par-ries. Forward, always forward, pushing the imperials back until they had no choice but to break lines and collapse before superior might and a growing numbers advantage.

Through it all, Stasia whooped and hollered like a child on her naming-day. Her pulse pounded in her ears. Her lungs burned, and her heart pounded in her chest, but never did she feel so alive, and so at peace with herself, than in such a carnage-filled frenzy.

It might have been minutes, it might have been hours, but the last of the soldiers broke before Stasia. The way was clear. Smoke billowed across the entire intersection, and what people had not already fled south dashed around and over the corpses. The remnants of Pilus's soldiers sheathed their weapons and sprinted along with them. The battle was over, and there was no objective to fight for beyond survival. The way would be clear for Cyrus, should he survive.

Mari bounded near, and it seemed she had reached the same conclusion.

"It is time we flee," she said.

"And the others?"

"We pray they endured."

Stasia hoisted her ax onto her shoulder, thankful for her mask. It took the bite out from the smoke when she sucked in gulps of air. Mari climbed up to one of the rooftops opposite the rows that were aflame and led the way. Stasia sprinted after her, feeling the first hint of exhaustion starting to weigh down her tired legs.

She should have known her escape would not be so simple. A familiar blue-armored paragon emerged from the smoke directly ahead, his spear thudding upon the dirt as if it were his walking staff. His long blond hair blew wild in the ashen wind. Men and women of the crowd fled past him, and he paid them no attention. His grin was reserved solely for Stasia.

"Oh, hey," she said. "It's that horse's ass."

"I prefer the name Soma."

"Same thing."

Prior experience told her a duel against him was hopeless, but this time she wasn't alone. Mari stalked the rooftops. If Stasia could only distract him long enough, they might catch him by surprise.

She screamed as she charged, trying to will energy back into her tired limbs. He parried aside the initial swing of her ax, so she kept on turning, spinning to maintain the momentum and bring the giant steel edge back in a second time. Soma closed the gap between them, his spear shifting to catch the interior handle with the shaft. The clang of metal on metal filled Stasia's ears. The ax-head was close to the paragon's jaw, so close, but he tilted his neck the slightest amount to spare himself.

"Impressive," he said. "And so very good for a mere mortal. Too good."

He shoved aside her ax, his divine strength more than she could match. Her feet danced, pushing to regain distance between them. His fist struck her side as she retreated, and overwhelming pain flared throughout her chest. Ribs had to be broken with how much it hurt to breathe. Instead of chasing her, he calmly approached.

No roar, no motion, no tell of any kind marked Mari's attack, and yet Soma sensed it nonetheless when she leaped from the rooftops. His spear twirled above his head, the butt jamming into Mari's belly to halt her leap. She whimpered as her paws flailed impotently.

"The soldiers here think you a monster," Soma said. "The locals believe you the reincarnation of their god."

He flung Mari like discarded trash. She landed on her side and rolled back to all four feet. A little bit of blood dribbled down her lips as she bared her teeth at Soma.

"They're all wrong. I know what you are, god-whisperer."

Stasia exploded into motion. Her ax swung high overhead. Up came the metal shaft of the spear, and it held strong as it blocked her attack. Dimly she wondered if that spear were of her father's make, for how else might it endure such a blow?

"You talk too much," Stasia said through clenched teeth. Try as she might, she couldn't force her ax closer. The strain reignited the pain in her side. The rush of battle was helping her ignore it, but by all the gods and goddesses, it was going to hurt tomorrow.

"I am told that sometimes."

He shoved the ax high, rotated his spear, and swung it for her side. She blocked it with her own weapon's handle, kicked him in the stomach, and then brought the weapon back down. She struck dirt. The paragon twirled twice as he retreated, then uncoiled into a savage lunge that would have impaled her if not for Mari arriving in time to slap the weapon aside with her bone wings.

"A god-whisperer and a demigod." Soma laughed. "What an intriguing pair. Are you both Miquoan? Or did shared treason lead to strange bedfellows?"

Stasia glared to hide her worry. So far as she knew, god-whisperers were unique to the nation of Miquo. If he pieced that connection together, the trail to them and their father should be immediately apparent. It seemed he understood her worry, for he held a finger to his lips and shushed as if addressing children.

"Don't worry, I won't tell. I would be so disappointed if someone stole my fun."

Mari thrust with the jagged ends of her bone wings, forcing the paragon's spear into motion. Undeterred by his blocks, she dove, teeth successfully closing around his leg. The platemail held, and the butt of his spear hit her ribs in payment. Her grip lessened, and she rolled across the dirt. The weapon looped up and around, eager for a killing thrust with the bladed end. Stasia swung her ax for the paragon's neck, forcing him to turn and block instead.

"Fun?" she asked as steel hit steel. "You're a madman, and I am no demigod, just a very, very pissed-off woman."

"You don't know?" Soma asked. "How precious. How quaint. A distant spawn, perhaps? But the blood of gods flows through you, Ax of Lahareed. It is unmistakable."

Their weapons separated. She struck his stomach with the lower half. He backhanded her across the face. By all accounts, hers should have hurt him worse, yet he remained upright, hardly noticing the hit that would have taken the breath away from any normal foe. Stasia, meanwhile, saw bright lights swim across her vision as blood poured down her face from her nose and split lip.

"I have slain many gods," he said. "I know how they fight. I know how they bleed."

It made no sense. What insanity possessed the paragon to call her the daughter of a god? Yet he seemed so confident, so sure of his guess. That he so quickly identified Mari as a Miquoan god-whisperer unnerved her. Who was this blue-armored paragon?

Such thoughts had to wait. If the sisters were to survive, no part of her could be distracted. Whatever game Soma played, let it die with him.

"If you're right, then you're dead," she said. "Even paragons can't slay a god in a fair fight."

His grin grew. Disdain and mischief sparkled in his blue eyes.

"A small god, with diluted blood. And you, Lioness, you walk in the skin of a god I have already slain. I fear neither of you, but please, come try. Give me the challenge Thanet has failed to offer since our boats stormed these shores."

Stasia and Mari assaulted the paragon simultaneously, in coordination few alive could match. They were sisters, born and raised amid rebellion after rebellion. There was no one else Stasia trusted to keep her safe when the paragon's spear thrust for her side at an angle she could not block. No one else could read her movements, accompanying them with a slash of her claws or bite of her teeth so the paragon could not retake the offensive. They circled around him, giving no quarter, Stasia's entire world becoming one of snarls, whirling axes, and the striking of steel.

It wasn't enough. Stasia couldn't overwhelm his strength like she could most foes. His speed was faster. His spear moved with mastery that baffled her. There was no positioning it wrong. No feint proved successful. Stasia had fought paragons before, even killed a few prior to arriving in Thanet. She had never fought anyone like Soma. If anyone was a god, it was him, not her.

"Is this it?" he asked as they battled. "Is this the best a broken Thanet may offer? Your priests, your paladins, your champions...I have found them all wanting. What a pitiful fate. Endarius and Lycaena made you weak. The land is far better with their deaths."

And then, as if to prove it, he retook the offensive. No more parrying. No more dodging. His spear hit Stasia's hip, and a scream tore from her lungs as she collapsed. His elbow bashed Mari across the nose. Blood splashed across his armor. Another elbow, then a thrust with his spear. It hit one of her bone plates, breaking the plate in half. Mari roared in pain, and yet when her wings thrust in retaliation, he twirled his spear to bat them aside with ease.

Stasia staggered forward, determined to help her sister even to the death. She swung her ax in an upward arc, hoping to cut him in half from the crotch up. The paragon sidestepped it. A flick of his wrist, and the butt of his spear clacked the underside of her chin. Her head whipped backward, and her stomach heaved as the awkward motion reignited brand-new waves of pain from her already injured ribs. Mari attempted to protect her, and in reward, Soma barreled into her with his shoulder. His fist pumped twice, blasting the wind out from her lungs. She staggered, and amid her weakness, he bashed the bone plate armor upon her forehead, cracking it down the middle.

Mari collapsed before him. Soma towered over her, his spear twirling with such speed, it was but a blur.

"Nothing can describe my pleasure in killing Endarius," he told her. "Thank you, god-whisperer, for the gift of experiencing it twice."

Mari's wings sliced inward the moment the spear dropped. Her exhaustion was exaggerated, her weakness the one trap the paragon fell for. The jagged edges closed onto either side of the spear's steel tip, locking it in place. The rest of her body twisted, paws pounding the dirt. Again Mari closed her teeth around his leg, and this time she crunched the platemail with a savage bite. She rotated as her momentum carried her, twisting the shin plate sideways and scraping teeth along the skin beneath. Soma held strong despite the obvious pain it caused. His other leg slammed into Mari's underbelly, lifting her several feet into the air. Stasia feared the bruises her sister would sport should they escape this. Still, the bastard's attention was stolen. Up came her ax, tired muscles forced into movement, and then she sent the weapon screaming back down again.

He pulled back his head and twisted his face aside, the rapid movement sparing his life. Her ax should have bashed right through his skull, but its sharp edge only caught his cheek. It ripped a gash into his flesh, not once slowing. Stasia twisted her arms so instead of burying the weapon into the dirt, it shifted sideways, pulling her into a spin that she continued into a dance that retreated her several steps away from the paragon. Only once separated did she return her attention his way.

Soma clutched the wound with his free hand, and he muttered something she could not hear. He withdrew it just as quickly and stood to his full height. Blood should have been pouring down his face from a gash so deep. Instead, the wound was clean and already sealing. Stasia saw a hint, not of bone, but the blue glint of what looked like sapphire.

Her ax lowered. Her mouth dropped.

"What *are* you?"

There would be no answer, not that day. Mari collided into Stasia, and she grabbed ahold on instinct. Her legs wrapped about the Lioness's sides, and her hands clasped a circle around her throat. A single leap of Mari's tightly wound feline muscles and they bounded off into the smoke. Even if he chased, and Soma's leg were uninjured, there would be no catching them. Her speed was unmatched. Yet even if he could chase, she doubted the man would.

Stasia glanced over her shoulder to see the paragon watching their departure. Twice now, they had fled from him. Twice now, she had been defeated.

"One day, you bastard," she muttered, then turned away. Her rage bled dry, and her thoughts turned to the others. Had anyone else escaped the ambush? What of Clarissa? Was her band safe, or had their interventions been predicted, too?

They fled, the street a blur, yet high above, Stasia could still see the distant bell tower. The Vagrant and the Imperator faced off, dueling shadows, and she prayed at least one victory might be had amid this horrid, awful nightmare of a day.

CHAPTER 44

RAYAN

Rayan knelt in prayer, his head bowed and his eyes closed, as he listened for the signal to start the attack. That sharp whistle opened his eyes. Three of them were hiding in a small home, Keles watching from the window, Arn leaning beside the door while steadily clacking his gauntlets together. Rebel soldiers and archers would sow chaos, and then when the Vagrant made his entrance, the three of them would come crashing in from the south to overwhelm the distracted soldiers. This was it, the time come at last. Rayan stood, taking strange pleasure in the groan of his joints and slight pain in his back. He was far from a young man, but with his goddess's blessing, he would still be a terror upon the battlefield.

"Guide us now and forever," he whispered. "Be it moth or butterfly, may your wings fly watchful above."

"Ready to lead?" Keles asked. Her face was covered below the eyes with a long black cloth sewn by Mari in preparation. It resembled Stasia's, only instead of a panther skull, its front bore the white outline of a butterfly. She wore her shining plate for the first time since the forsaking ceremony, and the sight lifted Rayan's heart. Her sword bore a similar winged hilt as Rayan's, though her shield was smaller than his, and perfectly circular. It once bore a rainbow of color, but was now painted a pure sheet of black.

"Almost," he said. "You still haven't told me your secret name."

She may have worn a mask, but the curl about her eyes gave away her mischievous grin.

"Who else would battle alongside a Paladin and a Heretic but a woman named Doubt?"

"Then may we prove your name untrue this day," he said, and stepped out to the street.

Screams of the crowd greeted him. The platform was distant, but he could see it above the panicked mass. Cyrus should have been standing upon it, his swords slicing free the ropes. Archers should be firing from the homes overlooking the stage. Assassins amid the crowd should have been burying knives into the scattered soldiers. Instead, the bodies hung, the platform beneath them opened up to drop them to their deaths. The rescue. It was over before it had begun.

"We've been betrayed," Rayan said. "Lycaena have mercy."

"There's no mercy here, from gods or otherwise," Arn said. "Run, old man! We are needed!"

Rayan drew his sword. Faint light swirled across the naked steel, the blessing of his faith as a paladin. The sight of it gave him meager comfort, and it spurred him into a sprint. His shield led the way. Keles and Arn accompanied either side of him, a deadly trio.

A thin line of six soldiers formed along the southern edge of the clearing. Their weapons were drawn, but their backs were to Rayan as they focused on the increasingly panicked crowd. The first died with Rayan's sword in his back. Not the most honorable kill, but nothing about this bloody day was honorable. Arn caved in the second soldier's head. Only Keles's target even offered a defense, but Rayan saw not how it went from the corner of his eye, only heard the man scream in sudden, horrid pain. The closest imperial spun, saw Rayan, and swung wild with her sword in both hands. Rayan blocked it high with his shield, stepped close, and punched with his shield arm. The sharp edge of it broke in her teeth. The pain doubled her over on reflex, and that brief span of vulnerability was all it took for Rayan to jam his sword into her neck.

With the nearby soldiers dead, the three took in their surroundings. Fires spread across the homes overlooking the gallows, forming a backdrop of smoke and flame to outline the macabre sight of so many hanging bodies. Soldiers positioned by Pilus had rushed to the west, where they fought against a large contingent of imperial soldiers. A glance to his right, and he saw a smaller group of soldiers coming in from the east. It couldn't be coincidence. This was an ambush, set by someone who knew every single detail of their planned rescue.

Cyrus? Where was Cyrus? Seeing him nowhere on the ground, Rayan looked to the bell tower from which he was meant to observe the battle. His discovery only confirmed his suspicions that the ambush was planned with the aid of a traitor. Up in the belfry, as many in the trapped crowd watched, Magus of Eldrid battled the Vagrant Prince.

A sound of horns. Rayan turned, and behind them marched over fifty imperial soldiers, approaching in tight lines to seal off the southern road. How far back had they waited? They must have been prepared to come in such numbers and at such speed while ignoring the distant fires set by Clarissa's gang. The only blessing was that they held back, content to seal off anyone's escape. And why wouldn't they? Time was on their side. More soldiers would come, an entire army to bury the resistance if it must. The crowd currently surging their direction slowed considerably upon seeing their approach. With their tightly packed lines, and the scowls on their faces, the soldiers showed no intention of letting the innocent pass.

"Can't think about it now," Arn said, interrupting his thoughts. His bloody gauntlet settled atop Rayan's shoulder. "Keep your mind on the fight at hand."

Rayan prayed the young prince could withstand such a foe alone, for Arn was right, he had to focus on what he could directly influence. With Stasia and Mari tearing through the western part of the battle, Rayan faced the soldiers coming in from the east. Unlike those to the south, they did not linger back but instead went on the offensive. There were none to counter them, and so they swept through the crowd. It was chaos, absolute chaos. Men and women fell to their swords, some rebels with hidden weaponry, but most not. They had come to distract at Pilus's request, or wished to witness the execution of so many of Vallessau's wealthy and elite. Their reward was butchery.

They were only three, but Rayan trusted the skill of Thorda's hand-picked elite. He pushed through what few people did not part for his passing. His aim was for the nearest soldier, always the nearest, and never beyond that. One kill at a time, he would fell this army. One by one, he would slay an empire. The first few never even saw him coming. His shield knocked them off balance. His sword ended them before they knew a fight had begun. As he cut through, more soldiers shifted toward him in an attempt to surround and subdue him.

"I thank you!" he shouted. "You spare an old man a tiresome chase."

His confidence unnerved them. The glow of light upon his blade frightened them. Their attacks were frantic, clumsy, and he defended against them with ease. Another kill, his sword tearing through a soldier's belly. He ripped the weapon out through the man's waist, a shower of blood accompanying the following block. Sword crossed sword, and when strength met strength, it was the imperial who retreated a step, groaning in protest. Rayan surprised him by suddenly pulling back, and when his foe attempted to counter, he was met with the paladin's butterfly shield to the face. His nose broke. His blood splattered across the gray surface. Dazed and blinded, it was easy to cut him down.

The panicked screams of the trapped crowd faded into the background. Another foe, a woman wielding a spear and shield that seemed more together than most. Rayan positioned his shield directly between them, and he approached with quick shuffles of his feet. He never left himself vulnerable. He never dared attempt a swing, not until he knew it was safe. The woman tested his defenses, her spear thudding into his shield each and every time. On the fourth strike, he lunged instead of blocking it. The spear struck the side of Rayan's breastplate at a poor angle and deflected off. Rayan's sword passed right over the defending shield and into the soldier's face, ending her.

The paladin kicked her body aside. To the next soldier. The next foe. Two men rushed simultaneously, but a body thrown by the wild and savage Arn blasted one of them off his feet. Rayan made easy work of the other, suddenly alone and confused, opponent. He killed the first for good measure, though the man lay on his back with his eyes glazed and his thoughts clearly jumbled.

Next soldier, next foe, until his surroundings cleared and Rayan stepped out from the crowd. Ahead of him gathered the remaining soldiers sealing off that part of the intersection. Smoke billowed overhead as fires started in the homes behind the hanging platform spread eastward. More blazed farther behind them, at such speed he suspected some of Clarissa's friends were responsible. Seemingly every building surrounding the execution grounds was aflame. A good plan, given how dire matters were. The greater the chaos, the more likely any of them made it out alive. Chaos and fury were the greatest counters to such an expertly laid trap.

"Fire behind you, death before you," Rayan shouted to the nervous soldiers. "Make your choice!"

The ambush, the slaughter, the fires; it was all beyond anything they had trained for. Some fled east into the fire. Others held their ground. The majority, though, tried to charge Rayan and overwhelm him. He screamed back in protest to get his blood to pounding. If they thought him alone and easy prey, the arrival of Arn and Keles disabused them of such a notion. Together the three formed the bulwark against the onslaught, a thin line of soldiers planted into the crowd forming up on either side of them. They were poorly armed with knives and swords, but they needed only lurk and strike amid the fury of Thorda's elite.

The battle here paled compared to that raging to the west, but that did not diminish the bloodshed. Rayan fought along the northern edge of it, steadily retreating as he cut down soldier after soldier. He would not allow them to overwhelm him, not when numbers were his foe's only advantage. Arn didn't even bother to retreat. He punched through their ranks, coating his gauntlets with blood and gore. Keles followed in his wake, cutting down any who still attempted to fight. They were a terrifying pair, and despite the mask covering her face, he could tell his niece was laughing.

Fight on, he thought, seeing the absolute carnage the pair unleashed. *Let poets sing of this day, and of this betrayal turned into victory.*

An explosion of wood and smoke stole his attention. An enormous man leaped out from one of the burning buildings overlooking the hanging corpses, soaring overhead in mockery of gravity. He landed with a rattle of armor and flourish of his red cloak. Rayan stood proud before his newly come foe. It was one of the few remaining paragons on Thanet, a pale-skinned man with coppery red hair and a long scar sealing his left eye shut. A scorpion marked the front of his gold plate, and so, too, did a yellow one flutter from the center of his cloak. He wielded an enormous ax, the wood haft of it carved along the bottom to resemble a stinger.

"I thought we butchered every last paladin of the Butterfly bitch," the paragon rumbled. His hoisted his ax up and onto his shoulder. "Did you not hear? Your goddess is dead. Our priests carved her up like a pig."

"My goddess yet lives," Rayan said. "And she is greater than any god you serve, imperial."

The paragon took the ax into both hands and smashed it to the ground.

"Let us see, paladin. I haven't fought one of your kind since we first slaughtered Endarius. Try not to die immediately. I've been lacking entertainment."

What few rebels scattered through the crowd could never hope to harm a paragon. It was only Rayan, and so he held his blade before him. The power of his faith made manifest across the steel, a faint white glow that left a trail of red-and-orange light when he swung it through the air. He took strength in its glow. His goddess watched. Even in death, she bestowed her blessing, and with every attack they had launched against the empire over the past months, it had grown stronger.

The paragon charged, his ax dragging along the ground to carve a groove. He belted out a mindless cry, and it reached a crescendo upon ripping his weapon free to strike. Dirt and stone pelted Rayan's armor. Up came the ax, and so he met it with his shield. A prayer whispered through his mind.

By your strength, not mine.

The shock wave rolled through Rayan's body. His armor should have crumpled. His bones should have shattered. Buildings would quiver from such a blow. Rayan screamed, but though the pain was intense, he held firm. The ax-head grinded against his shield, denting the gray surface inward an inch. His arm quivered, and his legs shook. Yet he held. By the goddess, he held.

"Stubborn as ever," the paragon muttered. His words belied the hint of doubt Rayan saw growing in his eyes.

"You have no idea."

Rayan shoved the ax aside and swiped sideways along the paragon's chest. His foe pulled the long handle of his ax to block. The moment wood and steel made contact, he twirled the ax, attempting to throw Rayan's positioning off. The sword went up wide, but Rayan fell back a step, using his shield to protect him from the sudden shoulder slam. It hurt, but nothing like the direct blow of the ax.

His training dictated decisive, firm movements, but the paragon denied Rayan the chance to settle into a rhythm. There was no forcing a block from a man with such massive armor. At the same time, he could not rely on his shield to hold, or his sword to parry, when he defended. The paragon may have decorated himself with a scorpion, but his strength matched that of a bull. Rayan moved quicker, his lungs aflame, as a lifetime of training and battle took over. His shield arm was almost completely numb, yet still he heaved it up and about to defend against the ax. Blood dripped from a split lip, an errant hit by the paragon's fist, yet he ignored the pain. Stab in, retreat with shield up. Slash twice in a V-shape, then pull back to parry. At last he scored a significant hit, the tip of his sword cutting a thin line along the paragon's waist, his shining steel easily parting the padded leather to draw blood.

"Enough," the paragon snarled. "This insolence ends."

He gave no pretense to defending himself. Their dance became decidedly one-sided, and all Rayan could do was attempt to survive it. Again and again, the head of the ax battered the direct center of the shield. Rayan retreated with each hit, allowing the momentum to transfer into him lest he break completely. Still, he could not suffer this long. Twice he attempted to counter, but the paragon was too swift.

"You are alone, paladin," the paragon said as he rammed the scorpion stinger of his ax directly into the shield, wielding it as he would a spear. Rayan skidded backward but held strong. "All alone. Your goddess bled out while we watched. Weren't you there? Didn't you hear her screams?"

Heard them? They had haunted his nightmares for months. Despite all his efforts, and the combined soldiers and paladins of the two gods, they could not break the line of paragons protecting Sinshei and the now-deceased regent. But despite that failure, there had been hope. The boy prince had lived. Cyrus had practically rolled to a stop at Rayan's feet after being flung through the air by an explosion of energy marking the death of the goddess's physical body.

Rayan had never told the boy what his arrival interrupted. He'd never admitted the truth after he disguised the prince with mud and cloak.

When Cyrus came rolling to his feet, Rayan's sword had been pressed to his own throat. He had been ready to give his life, for the goddess he loved was dead, and the royal family he'd sworn to protect had come to a bloody end. For Cyrus to survive? To escape the clutches of the empire, and through Rayan's aid? It had to have meant something. He had clung to that fact to keep fighting, even as the last of his order dwindled, the few survivors casting aside their armor or dying in the ensuing purges across Thanet.

"Your words cannot bring me despair," Rayan said as he braced his legs and readied his shield. "I have known the lowest of depths, and I have emerged stronger. You are a blight upon our island, paragon. It is only a matter of time before we burn you away."

"Stronger?" asked the paragon. "Show me."

He swung his ax directly into the shield. The impact tore a scream from Rayan's lips. He staggered backward, pain flashing up and down his arm in waves. His balance faltered. He tripped, not realizing over what, until he collapsed down to one knee.

The body of a man lay before him, mouth open in a frozen scream. Blood pooled beneath him from a vicious wound across his abdomen. In Rayan's peripheral vision, he saw the approach of the paragon's enormous boots. Each step echoed in his mind, as if the weight of the paragon's armor shook the world with a quake only he might hear. The ax whistled through the air as he twirled it overhead. His eager laugh stung like vipers.

Alone, the paragon had mocked. *All alone.*

Rayan used his shield hand to close the dead man's eyes, then pushed back to a stand. The paragon clutched the shaft of his ax and raised it high. A smile blossomed upon his lips. He knew Rayan would not flee. He knew the fight had reached its end.

"Not alone," Rayan whispered as he braced his shield for a blow that would surely break him. "Are you with me, Lycaena? Do you watch, even in death?"

One last step to close the distance. The paragon's boot crunched down upon the rib cage of the slain man.

"Are we still loved?"

The boot should have broken bones. It should have spilled gore across the street and left a stain upon the plate. Instead the body dissolved, every drop of blood and water, every bone, every sinew. A thousand moths erupted into flight, a swirling gray whirlwind that encased the stunned paragon. They slammed their powdery bodies into his eyes. They flowed into his mouth by the dozens, choking his throat as he gagged. Amid the flutter, Rayan heard his name whispered, sung in a song that reached only his ears.

Rayan lifted his sword. Light blazed across the steel, as hot and blinding as the sun. He thrust the divine blade forward. The moths broke to either direction, opening the way. The sword sank straight into the paragon's chest, the steel of his armor not even slowing its push. The pale-skinned man gasped, blood gargling out his lips.

He lifted his ax, determined to attack even in death, but Rayan gave him no chance. His legs planted, and before the ax could fall, he ripped the blade upward at an angle. Armor melted. Bones parted. He cut the paragon's shoulder off from his body, dropping the ax harmlessly to the ground, the shaft still clutched tightly in the ghost grip of his fingers.

The moths burned away like embers released from a fire, leaving nothing behind but a faint whiff of smoke. Rayan stood over the body, eyes cast to the heavens, as he whispered a prayer of thanks.

Slowly the song faded, and the sounds of battle returned to him. The fires had spread quickly during his duel, and their smoke flooded the entire intersection. Thanese soldiers fought to the west, and while Rayan's initial instinct was to aid them, he realized the bulk of the crowd that had come to witness the execution remained trapped in the clearing. Why had they not fled?

"Heretic!" he screamed, grabbing the attention of the former paragon. Arn punched a soldier thrice in the chest, bending his armor inward to ruin his own innards, then turned to aid Keles beside him. She was parrying a series of sword strokes, and when she finally stepped forward to counter, Arn flung the body of his recent foe into a direct collision.

"What is it, Paladin?" Arn asked, sounding annoyed by the interruption.

"We need to get these people out of here!"

"Then offer up a path!"

An inferno sealed off the east, and soldiers battled to the west.

"What of the south?"

"Blocked off, from what I can tell," Keles said, rushing to his side.

"Then we unblock it."

Rayan lifted his sword high above his head. His spirit soared, and he refused the temptation to doubt. Light blazed across his steel, a beacon of white that pierced the haze of smoke and fire. Though his heart cried the name of his goddess, his own lips shouted a different message.

"To me, people of Thanet! Follow the goddess's light!"

Rayan waited a few more seconds for all to see his lifted sword, then sprinted south with the blade held high like a torch. As he neared, he better understood the situation. The imperial soldiers had formed a two-man deep barricade, and were determined to keep everyone locked into the intersection. Once things were calmed, they'd imprison everyone within, then beat confessions out of the innocent under the guise of locating the rebels among them. Though fires raged wild, and smoke choked their lungs, the soldiers refused to relent. A scattered dozen citizens pleaded and cried to be let through, to no avail. Bodies of those who pressed too hard lay bleeding at the soldiers' feet. Their decision was clear. Better these people of Thanet be dead and ash than escape. That knowledge filled Rayan with fury that knew no limit.

The paladin dashed toward the line of soldiers, sword blazing with white fire. It shone with every ounce of his faith. Frantic soldiers readied their shields as the civilians moved aside. Doubt and Heretic followed a few paces behind, and though they were three against many, it was the soldiers who were afraid.

As they should be.

Rayan batted aside a spear thrust with his shield and then brought his sword crashing down. It pierced armor like butter, cleaving his foe in half from shoulder to hip. He curled the blade up and around, catching an attempt to impale him. The imperial's sword shattered in half. Rayan kicked him aside, smacked the nearest soldier in the face as he attempted to seal the gap left by his butchered ally, and then slashed at a third. The blade sliced off his jaw and opened his throat. Blood soaked the ground, smearing in circles beneath his feet as he fought. Block a hit, counter with his holy blade. Step by step, one after another, he worked to tear down those who would see the innocent die.

Arn blasted into the line, his paragon strength breaking their defenses. With each punch, another body went flying. Panicked screams marked the line's imminent collapse. On the opposite side, Keles was the only one to struggle. She lacked the gleaming holy blade, and so, too, did she lack the paragon's gifted strength. Rayan rushed toward her, sweeping across the line. He trusted his shield and plate to protect him from their errant blows. He swept spear thrusts aside, and jammed his sword into their mouths and chests. No armor could withstand that edge. Upon reaching Keles, he put his shoulder to hers, shield up alongside shield, and dared any to attack.

"I have no need of a nanny," she said, even as she gasped for breath, the exhaustion of battle taking its toll.

"I offer you a sword and a shield, not a blanket."

The soldiers closed around them, trying to form a front against their chaos, but then came the crowd. They crashed into the soldiers, some fueled by panic, others by rage. No imperial could focus anymore, for their foes were everywhere, and even if unarmed, the people thrust fingers into their eyes and pulled at their arms in desperate struggles for their weapons. Rayan separated from the defensive formation beside Keles. Unlike the crowd, he sought not to escape, only to fight. He waged war against a backdrop of smoke and bleary sky. He fought amid a gray world, and within it, he was a light.

"Damn it, Paladin!" Arn shouted as he smashed two soldiers' heads together. They cracked like eggs within their helmets. "Leave some for me!"

But the line had already broken. The crowd fled, men and women sprinting past the fires and then scattering. Rayan lowered his sword, and the entire world dimmed. The light upon the steel faded. It was done. The people were safe.

He looked back to the gallows, and to the bodies that littered the street.

No, not all of them. But those he could help, he had helped. Nothing less, yet sadly, nothing more.

"Time to go," Arn said, patting Rayan across the shoulder. He jogged off into the smoke without waiting for an answer. Keles lingered, and he followed her gaze to the bell tower overlooking the intersection. High above, Cyrus and Magus faced each other, their duel seemingly halted so they might speak.

"If we hurry, we can reach the tower before more soldiers arrive," he said.

"No," Keles said. "We've done our part."

Rayan shook his head. Cyrus was the last living member of the Lythan bloodline. The one man his family had sworn their honor and reputation to protect.

"We can't leave him," he protested.

Keles sheathed her bloody sword. Hand now free, she touched his face with the fingertips of her gauntlet, and she peered up at him with her dark eyes.

"Hold faith in him. He has earned that much from us."

Rayan stared at the tower, wishing he could be up there with the young prince, wishing he could hear the words spoken between the two most important and powerful people on all of Thanet.

"'Hold faith,' says the woman calling herself Doubt." He smiled. "What fool shall listen?"

But he followed her nonetheless, joining the surge of the crowd to flee into Vallessau, to vanish amid the smoke and the fires to where the soldiers of the empire could not find them.

CHAPTER 45

VAGRANT

I cannot decide if I am amused or disappointed," Magus said as he overcame his laughter. Smoke billowed across the belfry, thinned by the wind. The sounds of battle rang constant. "This entire rebellion, the masks, the cutting of bloody crowns, the outlandish stories of the Vagrant...it was all to put you back on your throne. Cheap theatrics for a deposed little boy angry about his parents. I hoped for something special from you, *Vagrant*, yet all I find is petty revenge and a desire for power."

Cyrus fixed his hood and then pointed a blade Magus's way.

"I fight for more than revenge," he said. "I fight to overthrow your tyranny, and save Thanet from your evils."

"Evils?" he asked. "What evils have we to our name that your own family has not committed?"

Cyrus tensed for another lunge. Whatever nonsense the Imperator was spouting, it had to be a trick to throw off his guard. Yet Magus showed no interest in attacking. His eyes widened, as did his smile.

"You don't know? I thought royalty still whispered the stories, but alas, I must be the truth bearer. The history of this island is but a blink of the God-Incarnate's eye, the centuries of your existence a mere nothing to an empire spanning thousands of years. Our spies have always lived here, and we have recorded the history your people sought to bury. Tell me, boy, have you ever wondered why your island was embargoed hundreds of years ago?"

"We accepted refugees fleeing the empire's grasp," Cyrus said. That history was well-known, for the economic hardships that followed were the reason for the ensuing War of Tides that established the Lythan family rule.

"They were no refugees," Magus said. His disgust dripped off every word. "They were the wealthy and powerful upper strata from the nation of Mirli. They saw our march across Gadir and demanded the lower strata offer sword and coin in defense. Once collected, they fled, abandoning the people they swore to protect. They sailed the Crystal Sea, to a distant, unimportant island they thought far enough to escape our reach. They did not come to Thanet as refugees. They came as conquerors."

Cyrus took a step toward one of the belfry windows. It couldn't be true. Thanet was an island of unity and peace, and had been ever since the War of Tides.

"You lie," he said, a childish defense against the Imperator's words.

"I have no need of lies when the truth suffices. Your family sailed to Thanet with swords and spears, overthrew the crown, and declared themselves kings and queens. Who are you, son of conquerors, to wag your finger at the Everlorn Empire and call them evil?"

Cyrus's hands shook as he clutched his swords. No, it couldn't be this simple. There was more hidden from him, something in the past to blunt such a condemnation of his family. They were good rulers, fair rulers, beloved by Thanet. They were nothing like the empire.

"You slew Thanet's gods!" he shouted. At least in this, he knew they were blameless.

Magus met his eye. No laughter this time, only cold finality.

"As did you."

"No," he said. He shook his head with each word. "No. We would never. My family, we would *never*."

Magus sheathed his sword and jammed his shield into the floorboards. He spoke not with laughter, but disgust. It made it so much worse.

"Lycaena was birthed upon Thanet, but not Endarius. The feathered

Lion sailed with his faithful Mirli across the sea. He was a proud god, and would not bend his knee to anyone, not even other deities. Nor would he have his favored people be servants in another kingdom. The War of Tides that set your family upon its throne? Another god of Thanet, the deity Dagon, sought to protect the rule of his own chosen family, the Orani, from the Mirli royalty's takeover."

Magus pointed an accusing finger.

"That war ended with Dagon slain, his corpse dumped to the ocean to float among the countless dead of his priests. Endarius declared the Lythan family eternal kings and queens of Thanet. Dagon's followers were ostracized, if not executed. His religious symbols were banned. Whatever books your family could not lock away in the royal archives were instead burned. But your purging fires could not reach our own imperial libraries safely tucked away on Gadir. Dagon became a villain in your stories, his true history forgotten as the centuries passed and the memories of the war faded. As for the Orani? Your family, ever so wicked, ever so cruel, forced them into servitude. Let all of Thanet see them humbled and broken, they loudly decreed, forced to feed and clothe the conquerors that stole their throne. So, too, would their children serve, and their children's children, until the end of days."

Each word was an arrow to his heart. He wanted to scream. He wanted to silence the doubt that grew like wildfire in his breast. Yet the Imperator was so certain, so convincing...

"You seek only to break my will," Cyrus said. "Such crimes would stain us forever. We could never bury them so deeply that the island would forget."

"Oh, I'm sure there are those who remember," Magus said. "But they live far from Vallessau, where their trinkets and prayers might go unnoticed by the Lion and the Butterfly. They tell their stories to their children over midnight campfires, these wicked worshipers of the even more wicked Dagon. None would dare whisper them to a spoiled little princeling. Yet you call me a liar? The proof is self-evident, Cyrus, if you were to but open your eyes."

Magus took a step closer. He loomed over Cyrus, seeming so tall, so mighty.

"The heathen gods worshiped outside the empire are manifestations of people's faiths. They adopt incarnations the populace understands, most often as variations of animals. If I walk the verdant fields beyond Vallessau, the butterflies soar like clouds, wondrous and beautiful. Lycaena is equally beautiful and wondrous, and she bears their wings, their skin. But Endarius? Did you never wonder? Did you not once see the obvious truth before you, little prince?"

Another step. His voice shook with rage.

"There are no lions on Thanet."

The strength in Cyrus's legs faded. His stomach churned, vomit eager to travel up his throat. He met Magus's silver eyes and wished he could fade away into nothing. What might he say in response? What worth did his stories and family traditions carry against such obvious truth?

"All we have done, your family did the same," Magus said. His tone softened. "But there is wisdom in the past, if you seek it. Lycaena remained neutral in your War of Tides, and so she bonded with Endarius, and ruled alongside his chosen family. While Dagon was forgotten, the Butterfly goddess blossomed. The same can be said for you. The Lythan family, it was not evil, any more than the Everlorn Empire is evil. What purpose does a god serve if they lack the strength to protect their people? But just as Thanet knew peace after war through unity, so, too, do we offer that unity, not to a mere island, but the entire world."

He offered Cyrus his hand.

"You have grown strong, little prince, and Thanet lacks a true regent since Gordian's death. I can relinquish that title to you. I can forgive your many crimes in the name of a greater good. Reveal your identity to the populace. Tell them you have seen the mercy of the God-Incarnate. The Vagrant shall bend the knee and serve. Beg your subjects to do the same. Turn their hearts from their dead gods. What greater purpose could you serve for your people? End this rebellion. Bring them peace. Bring them safety."

Cyrus stared at the paragon's offered hand. In his mind, it clutched a sword still wet with the blood of his parents. He saw bodies hanging from the Dead Flags, their hands bolted together. He saw forty bodies dropping with nooses around their necks. He watched boats burn, heard Lycaena's keening death cry.

There was no argument Cyrus could make that the Imperator could not refute, but it did not matter. In his heart, he clung to a simple belief, and he spoke it amid the growing cloud of smoke.

"Whatever we are now, it is better than what you would have us become. I deny you to my final breath, Imperator."

Magus pulled back his hand. He unsheathed his sword.

"Then draw that final breath, prince. One way or another, your people will confess their faith to the God-Incarnate."

The time for discussion was at its end. Cyrus knew the tight confines of the belfry were too favorable for the well-armored paragon. He needed open spaces to dodge and weave, which meant changing the arena. He tucked his arms to his chest and dropped into the small square opening in the center of the belfry meant for the ropes that had once been tied to the support beam above the broken bell. Down into its shadows he fell. He needed somewhere dark and hidden to reappear, and despite its morbidity, Cyrus could think of only one.

The ring on his finger burned. Again he felt a deep vertigo and a sensation of movement. His feet struck dirt instantly. The smell of smoke was overpowering, and the air burned hot. He crouched in the hollow space beneath the gallows. With the lever pulled, the bodies dangled around him. Men and women, necks snapped and throats crushed, for daring to hold faith in a free Thanet. For their faith in him.

Did it matter if what Magus said was true? He spoke of crimes in the past. He laid guilt upon Cyrus's shoulders for deeds committed long before his grandparents walked the island. Amid these sacrifices, Cyrus breathed in the choking smoke. People were dying, perhaps hundreds, and they had trusted him to deliver victory. How did he weigh one atrocity against another? If these sins were passed down from generation to generation, how did one make amends? Or was the sin in the denial and refusal to let the truth be known?

"Vagrant!" Magus screamed. Through cracks in the gallows side boards, Cyrus watched him land from a direct leap atop the belfry to the square. He prowled about the intersection, a frustrated hunter unable to track his prey amid the chaos of smoke, fire, and corpses. "Come out, Vagrant, you coward! Will you flee me yet again?"

The Everlorn Empire murdered innocents. It executed priests and priestesses. It sacrificed gods in a jealous need for faith. No matter their justification, it was wrong. Cyrus had to believe that. There was no evil in the Thanese tongue that must be replaced by their imperial language. There was no blasphemy in the gods they worshiped instead of bending the knee to the God-Incarnate in distant Eldrid. There was no sin in the marriages and lives that the Joining Laws would eradicate. This forced melding, this erasure, was worse.

Cyrus closed his eyes and lifted his blades to the corpses above him. They seared his mind with light. They banished his doubt, replacing it with rage, determination, and something akin to fire. He didn't need to fight for a throne and its tainted legacy. He could fight for the dead and dying. He could fight so it never happened again.

"Thank you," he whispered to the hanged. "For your sacrifice. For your faith. I swear to honor it in blood."

A leap, and he soared up and onto the thin front of the stage. Homes about him burned. Bodies of soldiers, rebels, and innocent bystanders littered the gore-slick streets. No sign of his friends. He prayed they'd safely escaped. Most everyone of both sides had fled, but some survivors cowered in front of doorways and crouched in alleyways, while others remained with injured or slain loved ones regardless of the flame. Amid this smoke and ruin, Cyrus lifted a sword and pointed.

"Imperator!" he screamed.

Magus spun to face him. The amusement that lit his eyes lasted but a moment. Even he could see something had changed. Standing before the rows of the sacrificed, purpose flowed through Cyrus, indescribable in the strength it lent.

"Perhaps you're not a coward after all," Magus shouted back. He batted his sword against the front of his shield. "Come, boy, and meet your fate."

From the moment he climbed those bell tower steps, Magus had kept Cyrus reeling on his back foot. He'd been on the defensive, in heart, mind, and body. No longer. He vaulted off the platform, the great distance between them seemingly nothing. Magus lifted his shield, and once more blocked the kick. Cyrus crouched atop the steel, legs coiling, and then somersaulted high into the air, for now there was no tower to constrain him.

Magus kept his shield angled to cover much of his body, while his sword readied to skewer Cyrus upon landing. Cyrus read those movements while upside down, anticipated the trajectory of his fall, and twisted his arms and legs to reposition. The upward thrust passed between the crook of his arm, and though his swords could find no purchase, his heel collided with Magus's head. The impact traveled up his leg, the hurt nothing compared to his ensuing amusement. He landed on his back and rolled, avoiding a furious stomp that would have crushed his bones.

"There," Cyrus said as he came up bouncing to his feet. "Now both our noses are bleeding."

Magus grabbed his bull helmet, which had been twisted askew from the kick, and ripped it off. It clattered to the dirt as he snarled and spat blood.

"I should never have spared you," he said. "I should have cut off your head and tossed it atop the corpses of your parents."

It was meant to hurt him, to distract him. Instead it only tightened Cyrus's focus. Every single agonizing second of training had brought him here. Every mission. Every kill.

"Yeah," he said, and he grinned. Gods help him, he felt intoxicated by his own strength. "You probably should have."

Cyrus zipped left to right, relishing the open field of battle compared to the cramped belfry. He need not limit his dodges, nor worry for his footing. His speed was greater than the paragon's, he realized that now. Whatever weight had lain upon his limbs, it had vanished amid the hanging corpses. He pirouetted on his heels, carving hit after hit over the painted bull of the Imperator's shield. He would scrape it raw to wear the paragon down. He parried when needed, and dodged when Magus overextended, causing the weapon to carve grooves in the dirt.

When at last he found his speed lacking, Cyrus tightened his grip and demanded the Anyx ring to obey. It had been but moments since its last use, yet perhaps Thorda misunderstood its true power. This reaction was instinctive, an understanding he could not explain if asked, but the shadows were his. They pooled beneath his feet, and he fell through them to deny the paragon his kill. After a wave of vertigo, Cyrus reemerged once more below the gallows. He laughed at the paragon's bewildered fury, and he leaped from the stage with a flurry of swords.

With each passing second, and each hit across the paragon's armor, Cyrus's confidence grew. He had broken down the impenetrable wall that was Rayan and his shield. He had weathered the fury of Stasia's ax. His mind was honed to every proper action and reaction due to Thorda's instruction.

Magus was greater than them all, and yet still lesser. He lacked their heart. Arrogance stood in place of their desperation and righteousness. The Imperator fought with the certainty he would win. With every cut, every parry, Cyrus robbed him of that certainty. He revealed the hollowness beneath it. His blades promised a new fate, one the Imperator had never before believed possible.

"Enough, damn you!" Magus hollered. Anger was his only counter. Though he was a Paragon of Shields, he tossed the bulky slab of metal aside and clutched his sword in both hands. "You may buzz about like a bee, but your stings are equally meaningless."

He thrust for Cyrus's abdomen. Cyrus risked parrying it, and though the paragon's grip was strong, it still shifted aside when pressed with both blades. The excitement of battle rushed through Cyrus. The energy he'd felt since leaving the tower refused to abate. Cyrus slashed with his off-hand, but Magus was faster than his size should allow. He lifted a shoulder, deflecting the hit off his platemail pauldron.

They danced, Cyrus trying to close the gap while Magus sought a medium distance that favored the longer reach of his sword. Another thrust, another parry, yet it was the Imperator on the retreat. The pace of the duel was in Cyrus's hands, and he did not relent.

Without the shield, Magus relied solely on his armor, and truthfully it was magnificent. There was no hope of penetrating its thick steel, but there were gaps along the joints, little spaces to afford the giant paragon movement. Cyrus cut across them, seeking blood in every which way he might find it. His swords raked over wrist and knee. He whirled about Magus, the sharp edge of his curved sword slashing along the waist. Nothing deep, just enough to cut through the underpadding and carve a line across vulnerable flesh. A bee, Magus had called him, and so he buzzed about, swifter, angrier. A thousand stings it might take, but he would bring this bull low.

Sweat caked Magus's neck and pasted his hair to his face. His skin flushed red. He swung his sword with wilder and wilder abandonment, as if pure desperation would be enough to overcome his foe. Cyrus's every movement became instinct. He ducked underneath a slash, danced left while parrying the looping counter, and smacked Magus's chest plate twice with his sword. Mocking him. Enraging him. Magus swung wide and horizontal, and when Cyrus curled underneath it, the Imperator hopped closer, hip-checking Cyrus's side. He rolled with it, came back up to his feet to find Magus barreling down upon him, his sword raised high above his head for a powerful double-handed chop.

Every shred of wisdom within his skull said to dodge, but Cyrus was done fearing the might of paragons. He crossed his swords before him and held his ground. His legs and arms braced. Steel hit steel like a thunderclap. Dust billowed outward. The strain pulsed through his every muscle, but his strength held.

"How?" Magus asked. "It's not possible."

Cyrus slid to his left. His short sword remained pinned underneath Magus's sword, keeping it harmlessly at bay, while his free hand pulled back for a thrust. Its razor-sharp edge tore through the leather padding underneath Magus's armpit, then sank halfway up to the hilt. A pained cry marked his efforts.

"This is for my mother," Cyrus hissed into Magus's ear. He slammed the sword deeper into his armpit, then twisted the steel. "This is for my father."

Another twist, making a mess of innards and puncturing lungs. Magus's breathing turned wet. Cyrus shifted his hips so he could jam his shorter blade into the small of the Imperator's back. The giant man's entire body locked, and he gasped out an unintelligible protest. His legs buckled, and he collapsed to his knees. Cyrus knelt so he might whisper his final words to the dying paragon.

"I am the Vagrant Prince, and I will have my crown."

He ripped both weapons free in a glorious spray of blood, then curled around, facing the dying Imperator. The Endarius blade cut him temple to temple, for the Vagrant must have his due. Magus crumpled to a heap of clattering armor. Cyrus stared at the body, his pulse pounding in his ears, and waited for the relief he thought would come. He remembered the screams of his mother, the rage and horror of watching this bastard paragon cut them down, and waited for this vengeful murder to soothe his hurt. He waited for the world to change, now this monster was dead.

But the world did not change. The homes still burned. The bodies remained hanging from their nooses, legs swaying in the smoke-filled wind. Magus was dead, but the words he spoke lived on. The fate of the Orani. The legacy of his family. Thanet was an island of dead gods, and there were so very many to share the blame.

"Damn you for all you've done," Cyrus said. He clenched his fist, felt heat on his finger from the ring. The whole world was dark with smoke. He fell into that darkness, now a doorway, and fled for home.

CHAPTER 46

MAGUS

Fingers to the dirt tightened, pulled, dragged Magus's body along the ground, leaving a crimson smear to mark his agonizingly slow progress. Fire and smoke filled what vision was not blocked by the blood from the Vagrant's "crown" stinging his eyes, but he swore to survive it. The foolish prince had not finished him off. Like many throughout the history of the Everlorn Empire, Cyrus had underestimated the strength and willpower of an imperial paragon.

"Almost..." he groaned as his healthy arm outstretched. Fingers flexed, the tips clawing the beaten road. The other arm dragged behind him, limp and bleeding. "Almost there."

Citizens, soldiers, and rebels alike had all fled the burning intersection. From what shouts he could hear, bucket brigades were setting up along the outer ring of the flames, preparing to halt the fire's spread from claiming the rest of the city. If he could only reach them. They would summon the surgeons. The divine nature of his body would allow it to heal, should he be given proper care. That meant not dying amid the smoke, his battered flesh burning away in unchecked fires.

The metal of his armor scraped along the ground. More blood leaked despite keeping his injured arm clutched tightly to his body to seal the wound. A mortal would have fallen. Blood would have pooled within their pierced lung, and they'd have choked to death on dry land. Magus would die in no such manner. He forced air into both his lungs despite the dreadful pain. He demanded his body move despite the dizziness in his head and the weakness that kept his legs limp.

Hatred gave him the willpower to move. To endure the way his skin along his face and forehead flapped loose, like a mask not properly tied.

"Cyrus," he whispered. The name alone set a fire to his bleeding insides. "Find you. Kill you."

He was out of the street. Buildings burned to either side of him, but the heat was a pleasant sensation to his strangely cool body. Arm out. Hand down. Drag. Move. Into the alley, continuing toward the sounds of people and buckets and salvation.

Regrets savaged his discordant thoughts. He never should have let the boy prince live. A quick sweep of his sword, and the brat would have died next to his parents. A hostage would make the transition easier, he'd thought. Foolish. Naïve. Better to excise former royalty immediately. Better to lance it all like a boil.

"I'll kill you, Cyrus. I'll kill you."

Not quickly, either. Slowly. Publicly. Strip him naked and hang him from the Dead Flags by his wrists. Magus would flay the skin from his body while all of Vallessau watched, peel it back to show the ignorant believers the guts and bones and veins of their supposed savior. A mere man, dying in agony. The fate the prince deserved. A tired grin came to Magus. No, not just the prince. The fate *all* of Thanet deserved, and they'd get it soon enough. When the appointed hour came at last. When the God-Incarnate set foot upon the island, and looked upon a faithless, ungrateful people.

Fingers curled, hand down, flex, then drag. To the end of the alley now. The fire was brighter, the sky blotted out with smoke. The shouts of what he presumed to be the bucket brigade were close, so close. Magus craned his neck to stare at the exit, doing his best to ignore the horrible way it made the skin on his forehead slump to one side. There, in the smoke, he saw the dark shape of a man.

"Here," he called out, and he lifted the one arm that had brought him all this way. "I'm here!"

The shape stepped from the smoke. The red and orange of the flames reflected off his armor, blending its hue, casting it to purple. Magus lowered his hand.

No, not a man. A paragon.

"You always were a stubborn one, weren't you?" Soma said. He pulled his spear from his back and twirled it like a dancer. "In a way, I am grateful. When Sinshei ordered me to kill you amid the chaos, I thought for sure the Vagrant would do you in first. How lucky I am, for the pleasure to be mine."

A faster twirl, the spear *whooshing* through the air.

"So you're just...Sinshei's dog after all," Magus coughed out. "Pathetic."

Down flew the spear. The jagged point pierced Magus's back and ripped through his chest, easily tearing aside his plate armor in the process. Magus gasped. His entire body convulsed. Blood pooled beneath him, and his lungs hitched, and hitched, but could draw in no air.

Soma knelt beside him, bending low so he might whisper cheek to cheek as if they were confidants.

"Sinshei is but a useful fool, Imperator. She'll share your fate one day, I assure you." His pale blond hair fell across Magus's sweat-and-bloodstained face. His lips brushed Magus's ear. "I have but one regret, and that is you will not live to see the collapse of your beloved empire. As you die, try to imagine it instead. That alone must suffice."

Soma ripped the spear free in a shower of gore, then turned his back and departed into the flames. He would not even grant Magus the dignity of observing his death. Magus's head collapsed to the dirt, and his only movements were involuntary convulsions. Blood pooled in his mouth. Even while dying, he defied his murderer. Instead, he imagined a young Cyrus, fourteen years old, sobbing before the bodies of his parents. Imagined cutting the boy down like he always should have, before the dark took him, and his heart beat its last.

CHAPTER 47

VAGRANT

Smoke filled the air behind him as Cyrus walked the final stretch to Thorda's new hideout. His nose hurt like mad, and he had no strength left to run, even if that was smarter than walking. He had left everything in the battle against Magus. Perhaps people would see his arrival at the small house, and they'd need to move in case a neighbor wagged a loose tongue to the wrong person. At that moment, Cyrus was too tired and too drained to care.

The door to their newest home was unlocked. He took it in hand and then hesitated. His fight atop the bell tower had occupied his entire attention. He knew nothing of the others, nor their fates. Had they died in the ambush? Did they burn even now in the fires? Stepping inside meant finding out. It meant removing the doubt and confirming the truth, however joyful or terrible. Cowardice held him in place, but only for a single heartbeat. He pushed open the door.

"Cyrus!" Mari cried. She crossed the space between them in a flash to bury him in a hug, and things, while not quite perfect, were now so much better. The shorter woman pressed her forehead to his chest, and her words were muffled through his shirt. "We were so worried."

Cyrus's tension eased away. There they were, his friends and allies in this war. Arn and Thorda sat at the table, their quiet conversation interrupted by Cyrus's arrival. Stasia lay on the long couch, cuddling with Clarissa with their arms and legs entangled, and she barely moved to greet him other than to laugh and toss him a thumbs-up. His heart skipped a beat at seeing Keles with her uncle beside the fire, and it skipped again when she flashed him a warm smile. All here, all safe. His relief shocked him with its strength. He returned Mari's embrace, arms wrapped around her waist, and allowed a few stubborn tears to vanish amid her hair.

"Never worry," he whispered. "I'll always come back."

To his surprise, it was Arn whose excitement almost mirrored Mari's.

"Bloody good show, Vagrant," he said, smacking Cyrus across the back once Mari had pulled away. "Did you give that Magus bastard everything he deserved?"

"That I did," Cyrus said, and he couldn't help but smile. "The Imperator is dead. I daresay my parents would be proud."

That earned him a round of cheers and applause.

"We fought as best we could before fleeing," Rayan said as he rose from the table. "I hope to Lycaena that the chaos helped you escape."

"That it did," Cyrus said. "Nothing like a good citywide fire to distract to empire's soldiers."

He accepted Rayan's embrace next. When separated, he removed his skull mask and then pulled from his pocket the other broken half of it. Cyrus quietly offered both pieces to Thorda, who had not risen from his seat.

"We didn't save them," Cyrus said softly. "All those people who trusted us are gone."

"It is a rare victory in war that comes without a cost," his master said, accepting the pieces. "I know it hurts, Cyrus, but believe me when I say this was a victory. You faced the greatest paragon of Thanet while all her people watched, and you brought him low. The island will believe now. In rebellion. In a future free of the empire. You gave them that." He turned his attention to the others. "You *all* gave them that. Thank you, my friends. You are far better than I have ever deserved."

Thorda pushed the chair back and stood. He clutched the two halves of the mask to his chest, cherishing them as he would a child.

"The damage is fixable," he said. "I shall be in my study."

Cyrus's master retreated from the crowded living room and kitchen, leaving the rest of them in an awkward silence. Cyrus removed his hood and ran a hand through his hair.

"You know what?" he said. "I feel confident saying I deserve a damn drink."

"I can handle that," Arn said. He gestured to one of the chairs at the table he and Thorda had occupied. "Sit your ass down. For at least today, you're the man of the hour."

Cyrus did as he was told. The former paragon vanished momentarily into a pantry, a comical sight in and of itself, given how he had to turn sideways to fit, and then he returned holding three bottles in a single meaty fist. He popped the cork off one and set it in the middle of the table.

"I know it was still a bit of a mess, but this is a huge deal," Arn explained as he poured the wine into one of the glasses Rayan had brought from the kitchen and set between them. "An Imperator has *never* died during either invasion or occupation. The forty people who died today, they died as martyrs. Their loss will infuriate Thanet, and Magus's death with simultaneously give them hope. All things considered, I'd say there's plenty to celebrate."

"Tell that to the martyrs," Cyrus muttered.

Arn bit back his next retort, and his cheeks flushed red.

"You're right," he said. "Sorry. You spend so much time as a paragon, with every man and woman you know kissing your ass as if you're half god, and you lose sight of some things."

"It's fine," Cyrus said as he sipped the glass's contents. "You're only trying to cheer me up."

Despite his friend's attempts, Cyrus could not shake his dour mood. Magus's taunts echoed in his mind, again and again questioning his understanding of the world.

"Lycaena teaches us that our descendants do not fade away immediately," Rayan said, having quietly listened to the exchange. "In time, yes, the allures of the beyond will occupy our attention, and we will revel in the paradise fields and crystal streams, but not at first. The dead may still look into the shallow pools and see the world before, and gaze upon their loved ones." The paladin reached out to pat Cyrus's hand.

"Your parents see you now, young Cyrus. They see you, and they are proud. I know that with all my heart. Do not despair at what you could not accomplish. What you've done for your home, and for your people, will be enough. I doubted you once, and spoke those doubts to Thorda. I regret each and every one."

Cyrus grinned even as he wiped at his face.

"You're going to make me cry, Rayan. Cut that out." They shared a laugh. A bit of the horror faded from Cyrus's mind. Not much, but some. "Did you...did you know my parents well?"

"Of course I did," Rayan said. He leaned back into his chair and resumed nursing his drink. "My family has served the Lythan line for four hundred years. It is a vow our family made, one we inherit with pride as children and honor as adults. My great-uncle was Queen Jessica's bodyguard, and my grandfather Martin was shield hand for King Tolbert, ever at his side during the bandit skirmishes. A favorite story for family gatherings is of my great-grandmother Lelia, who foiled not one but three different assassination attempts made against your grandmother."

Cyrus stared at his own drink, refusing to touch it. Four hundred years...

He asked the question he was fearful to ask but knew he must nonetheless.

"Does the name 'Orani' mean anything to you?"

Rayan's eyebrows shot to the top of his head.

"It does, actually. It was my great-grandmother's family name prior to marrying my great-grandfather and taking on the name 'Vayisa.' I suppose you *have* heard a few of my family's stories then?"

Your family, ever so wicked, ever so cruel, forced them into servitude.

"A few stories, here or there." Cyrus pushed back against the table and stood. "Maybe wine was a bad idea," he mumbled as an excuse to leave. He retreated up the stairs, pretending not to see their concerned faces. Once in his room, he collapsed onto his small, lumpy bed. Too much. It was all too much. He couldn't decide how he felt, nor why. Innocent faithful were dead. He had failed. Imperator Magus was dead. He had succeeded. How did they balance on the scales? Could they ever?

A knock on the door pulled him from his moping.

"It's unlocked," he said.

The door creaked open, and Keles stepped inside.

"I thought you might need some company," she said as she joined him on the uncomfortable bed.

"Thanks," he said, for what else was there to say?

Silence fell between them. After a brief hesitation, she reached for his hand. He accepted it, cherishing the touch of her fingers upon his, the shared warmth, but he dared not look at her. His gaze bored into the floor, mind awash in memories of the previous hour. The hanging bodies. The fire. Magus's amused grin as he tore down Cyrus's every understanding of Thanet, her people, and her gods.

"You keep seeing them, don't you?" Keles asked softly.

Cyrus took in a long, deep breath, and then let it out.

"The moment the platform dropped," he said. "The moment they all fell, and I realized I wouldn't be able to save them."

Even now, Magus's laughter echoed in his ears, and the way Keles responded, it was almost as if she could hear him, too.

"The Imperator is dead," she said. "Thorda and my uncle both consider this a great victory."

"Heavens save us from another such victory. We'll have no one left on our island but corpses."

Keles squeezed his hand. His mind grew ever more aware of her presence. He heard her every breath. He felt every twitch of her arm and fingers. She was far better than he could ever deserve, he knew that, but that didn't change that she was there, with him, choosing to be in this moment. He was afraid to look in her direction. His emotions were high, and he wasn't thinking straight. Part of him was convinced he would say or do something very stupid if he saw her beautiful brown eyes, her small button nose, and the soft curve of her jaw.

"Am I wrong to feel this way?" he asked, then immediately clarified. "About the executed. About my failing to save them."

"You can't save everyone, Cyrus. You know that. It wasn't your fault Magus was more ruthless than any of us predicted."

"But it's...it's not the guilt that eats away at me. I'm *angry* that I feel this guilt. I don't want it. I'm furious at the world for thrusting this burden on me. And then others who have spent far more years fighting the empire, people like Mari, Rayan, and Stasia, congratulate me. It feels like a twisted joke. Forty hanged, dying in my name, and yet I receive adulation. I don't deserve it, Keles. I don't."

"Why are you so harsh on yourself?" she asked softly.

Cyrus leaned back and exhaled long and whistling through his clenched teeth.

"When Thorda first brought me to his countryside mansion, he gave me a choice. I could stay, and become what I am now, or I could run. I could run away from my responsibilities. I could turn my back on everything I had been, adopt a new name, and become a war orphan, merely one among thousands. And do you know what I did? *I ran.* I sprinted out into the rain and fled all the way to the gate of his property, but I couldn't go through it. The guilt would haunt me. I knew the choice I wanted to make, yet I lacked the strength to make it, and so I stayed."

He let out a broken laugh.

"The people who died today considered me a savior, yet all I am is a coward. I am a selfish, angry child wishing nothing more than to have his parents back and his easy life returned. All throughout Thanet, every soul has suffered as much as I have, if not more. Everyone has lost someone. I want to scream at how unfair my life has been, but who else would have been given this chance at revenge I have been given? Would Magus have kept a servant's brat hostage in the castle? Would Thorda have brought the son of a fishmonger to his mansion to train into a hero? Of course not. A blessing and a curse intertwined. I lost much because I had much to lose. But if I wasn't who I was, if I wasn't a prince...then this burden would not be mine. Thanet's fate would belong to someone else. Surely that other person would be stronger than I am, and wiser, too. Anyone but me. Is that so horrible to ask? Is that so wrong to wonder? A life free of this guilt. A life without this godsdamned burden on my shoulders."

He was clutching Keles's hand in a death grip, he realized. Surely hard enough to cause her pain, yet she said nothing. He relaxed his fingers, and he closed his eyes in a futile attempt to gather his thoughts.

What evils have we to our name that your own family has not committed?

"The hanged men and women died believing in me," he whispered. "And yet I do not believe in myself. What greater insult could I possibly offer them than that?"

Silence fell between them as she pondered her answer. It wasn't heavy or awkward, for he could sense her piecing together the words. The hesitation showed only that she cared.

"The life we wish for, and the life we have, will never meet," she said. "If your parents weren't king and queen, they might have survived Thanet's invasion. They also might have been soldiers who died defending against the initial wave of boats. They might have been priests executed in the early days when the Dead Flags filled not a crossroad but whole streets. We cannot judge ourselves by the unreal worlds we spin about ourselves. In this world, the *real* world, your parents were cut down before your eyes. Your sorrow is real, as is your pain. It could have broken you, but it didn't. You lived on. You grew. You are not defined by your doubts, Cyrus, but the path you walked to bring you to where you are now."

She leaned against him, forehead to his cheek, her words vital whispers of life.

"And where you are now is in a small room, burdened with guilt and regret, revealing deep wounds to a friend who would heal them if she could. You're here, struggling to save an island against impossible odds, willing to die so others may feel hope. It's enough, Cyrus, I promise you. You have nothing more to offer, for you have already offered everything."

Cyrus used his free hand to wipe away the stubborn tears that had built up over the past minute.

"Such kind words, and ones I needed to hear. It's almost like you used to be a paladin or something."

"Or perhaps you're not alone in living with 'what if's." She sat up straight, and a phantom of her own pain shimmered across her face. "By all rights, I should have hung with the rest, yet random happenstance spared me. Life is like that, Cyrus. A thousand decisions on top of a thousand more coincidences. There is no going back, only looking forward."

"What do you mean, you almost hung?" he asked. "I don't remember hearing about this."

"Normally I'd have been in the mansion crowd before your arrival, spreading a few choice rumors. Thorda contacted me half an hour prior, asking me to run a message to a resistance cell down near the docks. Such a random little thing, yet without it, I hang from the gallows." She ran her hands over her braided ponytail, tightening the knot at the top with practiced motions he knew meant to hide her unsteady emotions. "It could have been me, but it wasn't. I tell myself... I tell myself there is a reason. Maybe luck. Maybe fate. Maybe a goddess. Regardless the reason, I'm going to make sure I give my everything to justify this life I have."

Luck? Fate? Fire burned in Cyrus's belly. No. None of those, not even a goddess, were to blame for this.

Save your anger for the traitor in your midst...

Cyrus jumped up from the bed. He tried to hide his nervousness, his anger, but there was no disguising the shaking of his hands.

"I need to speak with Thorda," was all he offered in explanation as he strapped his swords about his waist. Keles glanced at his swords, then at him. The question floated unspoken between them in the air, but he did not answer it.

"All right, then," she said instead. "Stay safe, Cyrus, will you?"

There was no pleading in her eyes, but the invitation to remain with her was there. He didn't have to go. He could stay, and talk, and perhaps do even more than talk. The weight of the day was heavy, but she was willing to share it with him.

"Of course," he said, and he smiled as if all were well, and his mind wasn't a wildfire. He left the room, his legs feeling thick and heavy, his every footstep pushing as if walking through wet sand. Down the stairs, and to Thorda's study, with each passing moment a dragged, bloated thing. It couldn't be. It couldn't. Such a truth, such a betrayal, was more than he could bear. He was overreacting, reaching conclusions based only a few convenient coincidences.

Calm yourself. Clarissa wasn't there, for I sent her on an errand.

Two errands. Two lives saved. It couldn't be chance.

Cyrus's hand touched the handle to the door and held still. He didn't have to do this. He could walk away, and turn his back to the nagging questions. Doubts could be ignored. The truth could be buried and forgotten. Hadn't Thanet's past proven that, with the Orani? He could still be the Vagrant Prince. The war they waged didn't have to change because of a few words spoken by a dead Imperator who might have easily lied.

Yet just as with the Orani, the truth lingered, never quite gone. Cyrus would cower before none of it, no matter the guilt or the shame. He had to believe he was strong enough to face it. To be the person he needed to be, the person Keles thought he was, he must stand tall before the truth.

No matter how much it hurt.

CHAPTER 48

VAGRANT

Thorda sat on the floor of his study, facing his beloved fireplace. His back was to the door, but hearing Cyrus enter, he slowly rotated until he faced his pupil. A sword lay across his lap, its hilt a beautiful gold, its shining steel curved downward at the end. Cyrus had never seen the blade before, but he could guess whom it once belonged to. It belonged to the man who wore the broken mask Thorda cradled in his hands.

"Yes, prince?" Thorda asked, and he arced a bushy eyebrow.

Cyrus cleared his throat. It felt like he had swallowed shards of glass. A single word bounced around his skull, scraping him with its edges.

Son.

"The ambush," he said. "It was intentional, wasn't it?"

Thorda stared into Cyrus's eyes, meeting his gaze for a long, interminable stretch of silence. Recognition sparkled in them. He knew. They both knew. The mask lowered in his lap, and his hands instead settled upon his sword, one with palm gently pressed to the flat edge, the other holding its golden hilt.

"What do you mean?" he asked, his question nothing but feigned innocence.

"Before I killed him, Magus said there was a traitor in our organization. Someone who leaked word of the meeting, and gave warning of our rescue attempt."

Cyrus paused to give his master a chance to defend himself. He clutched to some faint hope of an explanation, one that did not leave the man a monster in Cyrus's eyes. Once his master spoke, it was clear none was coming.

"You need not voice the accusation," Thorda said. "I see it plain in your eye, and you have the right of it. I sent the Imperator communiqués under the guise of a resistance traitor. I engineered the obtaining of prisoners. I ensured he knew of the signal, and your prepared ambush from within the bell tower."

"But why?" Cyrus asked. Again and again, he saw the platform bottom out. He saw the bodies drop, the ropes snap tight, necks snapping with them. They weren't even given hoods to cover their faces, so their tongues bulged outside their mouths and their eyes popped loose from their sockets. "Why would you do something so hideous to the people who trusted you?"

"You already know the answer," his master said. "Or you would, if you viewed your battle with Magus with open eyes. There is nothing special about the paragon ritual you interrupted weeks hence. Gods are but manifestations of belief and faith, for there is power in both. Ancient power, older than the world itself. To die for that belief? To sacrifice oneself for another? Nothing compares. They may not have been Seeds, but the men and women who died today, they died believing in you. They knew your face, and your name, but they kept it hidden in their hearts. They gave their lives, convinced it would mean something, that *you* would mean something."

Thorda slowly stood, mask in one hand, sword in the other.

"Did you not feel it?" his mentor asked. "The power flowing into you as the men and women breathed their last? As you moved through shadows? As you matched a paragon's inhuman strength blow for blow?"

The entire house collapsed around Cyrus. He remembered Thorda's insistence that his every action magnify an otherworldly appearance. How he wasn't allowed to ever lose a battle. How his face must be hidden, his bloody crown spread across Vallessau, and his name spoken in whispers. Soft, prayerful whispers.

"This was always your goal," Cyrus said. "You knew Magus would challenge me. You wanted us to battle while the city watched."

"And you *won*. This is a day I never dreamed would arrive, and yet it has. Can you not see? Can you not understand the great lengths I went to for such a victory? Just as the empire utilizes Seeds to bless its paragons, so, too, did I build my garden in Thanet. I arranged the meeting with only the most loyal and faithful members of our resistance. And faith in you grew, as it did with my husband. When the Skull-Amid-the-Trees hung from the city gates, I swore I would not repeat the same mistakes I did with him. I had begged him to cast aside his rising faith, to rebuke his growing powers, for it was not his place as a mortal to ascend to godhood. I put doubt in his mind, and it cost him everything. It robbed him of his power when he attempted to kill the God-Incarnate. But with you, Cyrus?"

His pleasure, his twisted satisfaction, made Cyrus's insides tremble far worse than any battle against a paragon.

"You, my Vagrant Prince? In you, I re-created the demigod that was the Skull-Amid-the-Trees, only this time instead of pleading for you to deny your ascension, I had you embrace it. From the first moment of your training I impressed upon you the need to transcend the limits of the mortal realm. And did I not succeed?"

How could he deny it? Against Magus, he had moved through shadows far sooner than his ring should have allowed. He had blocked direct blows from a paragon, blows that mere weeks ago would have broken the bones in his arms. Exhaustion had never touched him. His speed and skill had defied even the legendary Imperator's understanding. Cyrus had thought it the excitement of battle, the single-minded focus that often filled all hardened fighters...but this was more. Lightning sparked through his veins. The dark corners of rooms called to him, and he viewed them not as shadows, but doorways.

"I never asked for this," Cyrus insisted against the panic rising in his throat. "You forced a change upon me with your lies."

"I never lied," Thorda said. "I made my intentions clear that first night you arrived at my countryside mansion."

I want a weapon. I want a god of death the empire one day fears. Is that you?

"You know I didn't understand," Cyrus insisted.

"I gave you your choice, and an open door to flee through should you lack the strength. You stayed. You knew, deep down, that I would craft you into something greater than human. You knew others would die so you might live, and fight, and free your people. Does it matter if they died in battle, or hanging from a rope, so long as it advances the cause? Close your eyes, Cyrus, and listen to the prayers that flow through Vallessau. They pray to the Vagrant. They pray to *you*. Do not deny them! Do not let their sacrifice be in vain!"

"You would put this on my head?" Cyrus asked. "You would murder innocents, then demand *I* show them honor?"

His movements were of their own. His swords were in his hands, and they attacked. Steel rang against steel as Cyrus slashed and cut, each blow expertly blocked. Thorda, his teacher, his master, would die for his betrayal. It was inevitable as the rising of the sun. The rage within him, it allowed no other possibility.

Son.

So many times they had dueled in the past, and during each clash his master had seemed unbeatable. His understanding of positioning had been second to none, and his sword weaved through the air with a blinding speed. Now Cyrus followed it with ease. He hammered it thrice, always predicting its defenses accurately. It was as if the older man's movements had slowed, but no, that was wrong. Thorda wasn't moving slower. Cyrus was moving faster. His swords weighed air. Their hilts were his own flesh. Thorda blocked a downward strike at the last possible moment, his sword held horizontal above his head. Cyrus pressed down with his own, challenging the older man's strength, defying him, breaking him. Thorda's knees buckled. His breathing turned labored.

"I would be no god!" Cyrus screamed as his legs tensed and the muscles in his arms bulged.

"Yet Thanet's gods are dead!" Thorda thundered back. Even on his knees, he revealed no fear. "Let a new one take their place. The people must believe in something, lest their faith rot. Turn that faith into a weapon, Cyrus. Wield it as a blade to cut the empire's throat."

"I would rather cut your own."

Their swords pressed tighter together, the edge of Cyrus's sliding closer and closer to Thorda's exposed neck. The metal rattled as his master struggled to hold back the killing strike.

"I knew your rage was fire the moment I met you, boy. I am not afraid of being burned."

The door opened behind them. Cyrus spared a glance over his shoulder to see Stasia standing in the doorway. Her hands rested on the handles of her axes, but she had not yet removed them from her belt. Her face was passive, but her glare more intense than a hurricane.

"What nonsense is this?" she asked coldly.

A momentary sliver of calm pierced through Cyrus's angry veil of thought. Stasia would not permit the death of her father. The Lioness would also hunt in vengeance for her family. He could not bring himself to harm either of the sisters, not even in self-defense, which meant Thorda must also live. He reined in his fury. He pulled back his sword and stepped away from his master. No, his *former* master.

"I am done with your rebellion," he seethed at Thorda. "I renounce your Vagrant god. I am not your puppet. It is only for your daughters' sakes that I let you live, for they are each worth a thousand of you."

Thorda lowered his sword to his lap, and he faintly smiled. There was something frightful in his eye when he spoke.

"Godhood cannot be so easily cast aside, Cyrus, as you will soon learn."

Cyrus jammed his weapons into their sheaths and stormed for the exit.

"I would have an explanation," Stasia said, blocking his way. Cyrus pushed past her with a collision of their shoulders.

"Ask your father. He will tell you, if he is not a coward."

The sound of anger and steel had clearly reverberated throughout the house. The others stared at him in silence, but only Mari moved to intercept his path to the front door.

"Cyrus, wait," she asked. "What...what's going on?"

He wished he could explain himself. He wished he could say goodbye properly, but how could he do so when it meant revealing the monstrous and vile nature of her father?

"I'm sorry, Mari," he said. "But you will not see me again."

Cyrus slammed the door shut behind him, pulled his hood high up over his face, and vowed never to return.

CHAPTER 49

SINSHEI

If Sinshei vin Lucavi was certain of anything, it was that the world conspired against her. She sat in a chair before the grand mirror of her bedroom, having recently finished tying the last of her braids. The messenger from the docks had just left. His words echoed in her mind, each syllable mocking her plans and her ambitions. Anger and indecision mixed to lock her in place in that chair. When the door opened, and Soma entered without knocking, she did not turn, only observed him in the mirror. By the smile on his face, things must have gone well for him, and terrible for Magus.

"Did the Vagrant and his allies attack as predicted?" she asked.

"They did," he said, and he gestured wide as if thoroughly pleased with himself. "The square burns, the prisoners are hanged, and Magus himself is dead. The Vagrant, I'm sure, believes himself the one responsible, but the heavens were kind enough to grant me the honor of finishing off the bastard."

The paragon strode to her chair, and he clapped his hands together.

"Everything you wanted, achieved in a single day. I daresay you should even thank the Vagrant for killing Gordian, for now you do not have to keep him under your thumb. You are the lone Pillar upon Thanet, Sinshei vin Lucavi. The island is yours, to prepare and mold as you see fit."

Again the words of the messenger taunted her, turning her heart to ash.

"No," she said. "It is not."

The smile slowly faded from the handsome man's face. She saw a hint of something in his blue eyes, a reaction she could not decipher.

"This is a moment to celebrate, yet you look ready for a dirge. Explain why."

"Word from the docks beat you here. A priest with a spyglass spotted a trio of galleons newly come from Gadir." She inhaled slowly, then exhaled. "The flag of the lead ship bears three red stars above the clasped hands of the God-Incarnate."

Soma crossed his arms, and his only reaction was a mildly annoyed grunt.

"He's early."

Months early, in fact, and for reasons Sinshei wouldn't know until she met with her brother. Even favorable winds did not explain as much. Was he impatient? Or did he not trust her to prepare Thanet for the ceremony?

"There is nothing we can do about that now," she said as she forced herself up from the chair. "Come with me. The Heir-Incarnate must have his greeting."

The fires had grown by the time the pair exited the castle. Smoke from a dozen different locations formed pillars in the air. Sinshei eyed them as they made their way to the main road descending the hill toward the docks. Putting the ceremony entirely on Magus's shoulders had been a gamble. It was never in doubt that the Vagrant would take the bait. If the Imperator had crushed the resistance's hero while simultaneously executing tens of their wealthy backers, Thanet would be unquestionably his, as would credit for its successful conquering.

Instead Magus was dead, the Vagrant alive, and the resistance limping along despite its casualties. Sinshei should have been ecstatic, but instead she walked with her head bowed and shoulders stooped, a perfect picture of contrition and shame to greet her eldest brother.

"How did things go so wrong?" she wondered as the pair descended the slowly sloping road down to the docks.

"We are not owed easy paths to walk," Soma said. "That which was within our grasp, we manipulated to our best circumstances. It was a waste of ten good Seeds, Gordian's death, but I always found him a poor ally regardless. And the Vagrant repaid that annoyance by utterly humiliating Magus and his hanging ceremony."

"If only both had happened much sooner. Thanet should have been cowed and ready for my brother's arrival. Instead he will be greeted by chaos. I shall receive all the blame, and none of the rewards."

Soma smirked at her.

"Is that not the way of things for all daughters of the God-Incarnate?"

The closer the docks, the more troubling her surroundings. What began as a few straggling followers grew in number. At first they said nothing, only glared with arms crossed or hands thrust into pockets. Sinshei pretended not to notice. Of course the people would be emboldened after Magus's death, but to acknowledge it might only increase that confidence.

They turned a corner, to the final slope down to the docks, and found the pathway blocked entirely. Men with knives and clubs. Just a rabble, not an army, but they numbered at least fifty to a mere two.

"It seems the fun doesn't stop today, does it?" Soma said.

The angry crowd closed in, surrounded them, blocking their pathway on all sides. They weren't silent, not anymore. Men called her names. Women insulted her honor. They cast crimes at her feet, some deserved, most not. Despite their anger, they kept out of reach. They weren't ready, she knew, not yet. The violence was coming. It needed to be sparked first, be it by Soma readying his spear or her attempting to flee. If they hoped to frighten her, they failed. If they thought to intimidate her, she proved it false by openly laughing at their attempts.

"Louder," she said. "I cannot hear you."

Sinshei gave no thought to the words they hurled at her. Accusations of murder, of denying trial to the hanged. Blame for the fires. Lingering anger over dead loved ones hung at the Dead Flags, as if she were the one choosing the victims instead of Magus. It meant nothing to her. More troubling were those with dark cloths tied over their faces. Through paint, sewing, or chalk, they all bore a now-familiar skull grin.

It seems you gain disciples, Vagrant, she thought.

Sinshei's clenched-tooth grin spread wider. These people hating her, casting their curses and insults, should be *thanking* her. Magus was a heartless brute, who cared nothing for the suffering of those on Thanet. Yes, they would still die. Come the moment of divine inheritance, they would all die. But at least with her in charge, their deaths might be orderly, and painless.

"Shall I disperse them?" Soma asked, calm as could be. His right hand reached for the spear still clipped to his back. "Won't take long, I promise."

"No," she said. Her hands clenched into fists. "I shall prepare the way."

Sinshei took a single step toward the group. They were working up the nerve for bloodshed, hovering at the edge. Every shout, every curse, was meant to give them courage. They knew many would die, such was the reputation of a paragon and the magic of a magistrate, but their primitive islander minds thought their numbers would be enough. Such ignorance. Such foolishness. Perhaps Magus had been right when he condemned the lack of progress made by the church in converting their hearts. They were not loyal, not faithful, and certainly not afraid.

That would not last long.

"God bless and keep me," she prayed. "God watch and guide me. Thy blade, thy mercy, become one."

Four divine weapons manifested in the air about her, hovering perfectly in place. Two were swords, and two were axes. From handle to blade, they shimmered with golden light. Sinshei commanded each and every one of them like a limb. She needed only to whisper her faith, keep it manifest, and the divine weapons would obey. The weapons lashed through the air, wielded by invisible hands. Each shift, each motion, imagined in her mind and re-created in the real.

And then she turned them upon the crowd.

"Thy blade."

Flesh meant nothing to those perfect edges. Blood sprayed, bones cracked. People screamed as she walked amid them, the four weapons a whirling sphere of death around her.

"Thy mercy."

One man threw a spear, only for it to be chopped in half on its approach. She lopped his head off without a thought. She stabbed each of his neighbors, then had the two swords rip straight out their backs so they might continue their arcs. Always in motion. Always protecting their divine master.

"Become one."

A few meager heartbeats, and the slaughter was done. Her prayer ceased. The weapons faded. Sinshei unclenched her fists, and she rolled her shoulders to loosen a knot growing at the base of her neck. Over a dozen corpses lay about her, and a dozen more injured fled with missing limbs or bleeding wounds. She looked over the mangled bodies twisted in pain. Her eyes narrowed at the sight of those bearing masks, especially the one with a skull sewn into the front.

"The Vagrant may have been useful in defeating Gordian, but his inspiration grows dangerous," she said as she stood among the corpses. "We will need to find and break him soon, lest this spiral out of control."

Soma nudged one of the dead with his boot.

"Hold faith in my spear, Anointed One. Its tip has claimed gods. It will one day claim him, too."

None dared challenge them the rest of the way, not with so many dead and the rest scattering to safety. Sinshei briefly debated calling for guards to clean up the bodies, then decided against it. The whole city was awash in fire and death. Let the mess remain as a reminder, at least until their loved ones came to collect the corpses for a pyre. She and her paragon crossed the remaining road to the docks bustling with activity in preparation for the arrival of the three ships in the distance, the lead galleon bearing the signature three stars on its flag.

"I should have sharpened my spear and cleaned my armor," Soma said, somehow still making light of things despite the horrid turn of events. "There's blood on both. It presents a poor picture."

"We're a poor picture regardless," she said as she waited at the end of the pier. "Clean armor won't change that."

A proper greeting would have placed magistrates on either side of Sinshei, along with rows of priests, imperial soldiers, and a crowd of faithful citizens of Thanet eager to worship, or make a good show of pretending to worship, the Heir-Incarnate. Instead her priests were scattered throughout the city, preaching the need for faithfulness amid this newly arrived turmoil. Soldiers were chasing after dissidents or putting out fires. There would be no faithful crowd. What crowd she could have summoned was at Magus's failed execution.

Just her and Soma. It wouldn't be enough. She knew that. Hands crossed before her, she stood tall and prayed for the strength to maintain her resolve.

The gangplanks shook as the three galleons pulled in amid the cries of sailors, the groan of ropes, and thud of boots. Hundreds of soldiers flowed down the gangplanks of the other two warships. From the third came her brother, escorted by a half-dozen paragons. Despite their armor, and their incredible size, Galvanis towered over them all. He was the chosen vessel, the Heir-Incarnate, and the prayers and worship of the legions of imperial citizens empowered him alongside their father. His armor was sleek yet impossibly heavy, painted golden with its edges silvered. A sword heavier than most men hung from his back, and he carried it with ease.

"My dear sister," he said as he stepped off the gangplanks and atop the docks. "Though it is good to see you, this is a disappointing welcome for the Heir-Incarnate of the Everlorn Empire. And is that smoke I see rising all across your city?"

"The result of a series of missteps and failures by Imperator Magus of Eldrid," Sinshei said. "Culminating in his death at the hands of rebels."

"The Imperator, slain? Do you jest, little sister? What of Regent Goldleaf?"

Sinshei kept her eyes locked on his face, perfectly square and with such hard features, he appeared carved from marble. His hair, looking like spun gold, trailed down to his waist. His irises sparkled like sapphires. His smile belonged on a painting.

"Gordian was killed two weeks ago by members of a newly formed rebellion," she said. "Likely the same group responsible for today's ambush. The remainder of his family was sent back to Gadir by Magus's decree."

Galvanis turned to the paragons at his escort.

"Leave us," he commanded. "All of you."

Soldiers, sailors, and paragons, they all hurried down the dock without any real apparent destination beyond escaping the presence of the two children of the God-Incarnate. From the corner of her eye, Sinshei caught Soma staring, waiting for a signal. Openly refusing an order was too risky, and there wasn't much the blue-armored paragon could accomplish. She nodded at him ever so slightly, and upon seeing it, he casually saluted her with two fingers and marched off with the rest of the paragons.

Moments later, the two stood alone atop the creaking wood. Galvanis stared at her with his arms crossed over his chest. He was judging her, and making no attempts to hide it. Her skin crawled at the feeling. It had always been this way, even as a child. She was not a person to him. She was a set of expectations to be met. Those expectations were ever his to decide, and ever hers to fail.

"Things are not so dire," she said, unable to bear the silence.

"Aren't they?"

Galvanis grabbed her by her long hair. A single, vicious yank tumbled her toward him. He knelt, lowering himself so that when she landed on her hands and knees, he was there, his face against her face, whispering to her. His words, somehow, were spoken calmly, almost lovingly. It made it so much worse.

"Look upon your city," he said. "Look upon this beating heart of the island. Can you see it like I can, little sister? Perhaps you don't. Perhaps the blood of our father is too thin within you, and you do not feel the pulse of the divine. I do. I see the faith wafting off the populace like mist off a lake. I see it crimson against a pale sky. That faith is a pittance compared to the smoke your unchecked foes unleash with their fires. It is an insult. A tragedy. The hearts and minds of these people were meant to be carefully fostered by the Three Pillars, yet what do I witness upon my arrival?"

He tugged harder so that the pain forced her to tilt heavenward.

"Two dead Pillars, and a third making excuses before the burning rubble meant to be her grand accomplishment."

"Magus was a damn fool," she seethed. "He and Gordian showed no patience, and little skill. I have done what I can, but it is in spite of their actions, not in concert with them. There is still time. The gods of Thanet are dead, and only the Vagrant gives them hope."

"And now you blame others. You are *vin Lucavi*, little sister. Cease sniveling. You disgrace your own divinity."

His cheek pressed tighter to hers. Did he mean it lovingly? Did Galvanis even know what it meant to be loved? Growing up in Eldrid, surrounded by faithful servants, and raised in the shadow of Lucavi...no, she doubted that he did. He understood loyalty, obedience, and servitude. Love? Sinshei had experienced no love from the God-Incarnate, and she expected no love from Galvanis. He might think his words love, but they were a pale facsimile, and it would not save her.

"This city was to be prepared for the ascension," Galvanis seethed. "*My* ascension. I will not have my inheritance squandered because these savage hearts cling to their lost independence and their slain gods. I came here to ensure all was ready, and it is clearly not. From this day forth, I am Imperator of Thanet. For our entire empire's sake, I pray I came soon enough to rectify these colossal errors."

His pull tightened, hard enough that tears swelled at the corners of her eyes. She clenched her teeth, not to hold back any cry of pain, but to choke down her rage. If only a storm had delayed her brother. If only she'd had time to solidify herself as regent, and present Vallessau to him as a gift instead of a chaotic mess caused by the dead bastard, Magus. His errors, her blame, the accepted way of all the world.

"Thanet will surely prosper in your hands," she said, knowing it was exactly what he wanted to hear.

"So much as it must, before the sacrifice," he said, and released her hair. "Any other member of the empire, be they soldier, magistrate, or imperator, would suffer death for this magnitude of incompetence. But I will spare you that disgrace, dear Sinshei, for I cherish you still. I will not ascend to godhood while stepping over the corpse of my own sister."

No, he wouldn't, Sinshei knew. He would have her there, to fall to her knees, bow her head, and offer him her prayers. Even her obedience would not be enough. He sought her worship. If the world was cruel, he might even get it.

"Thank you," she said, each syllable a needle stabbed into her tongue. "For your kindness."

"You are most welcome, little sister. I trust my kindness will be rewarded in the coming years. Faithful Anointed Ones are key to reaffirming the faith of the populace at the start of a new age." He stepped away to give her some space, and he spoke so calmly, she doubted his heartbeat had even increased while he held her life in his hands. Her own, meanwhile, thumped a frantic drumbeat in her chest. "Answer me, who is this Vagrant that gives the people of Thanet undeserved hope?"

"I don't know," she said. "A man who appeared only months ago, hooded and bearing a skull mask. I presume him the leader of the resistance, or at least their champion."

Her older brother's reaction surprised her, for instead of seeming frustrated or angered, the description intrigued him. He rubbed his chin as he pondered.

"A man in a skull mask," he said. "And now the people pin their hope to him, do they? Whisper his name, hide his symbols, that sort of thing? I have seen this before. He seeks to be a new god for a broken populace."

Sinshei held back a shudder as she straightened her hair as best she could. The violence of her brother's motion had made a mess of her careful braids, and there was little she could do on her own.

"He is no god," she said.

Galvanis walked past her toward the city. He reached over his shoulder for his sword, holding on to its leather-wrapped hilt as he gazed at the rising smoke.

"Just like Miquo," he said softly. "You were too young then to pay attention to such matters, but I remember. I remember the pain he caused. I remember the faith he built with his every kill. Troublesome, but only in that we have such limited time to deal with his interference."

Her older brother turned to her, and though he wore no mask himself, his face was as white as bone and his smile without joy or kindness. Instinct would have her wither beneath it, but she stood, defying the crawling fear. All her plans, her slow seduction of Gordian, the Seeds, Soma killing Magus; it had all been done so she might prepare Thanet for Galvanis's arrival. Not to greet him. To murder him. Sinshei pulled back her shoulders and swore to remain strong. She had outlasted Magus and Gordian. Here on this wretched island, with Soma at her side, she would outlast even her father's chosen heir.

In the three-thousand-year history of the Everlorn Empire, no woman had ever been named Heir-Incarnate. No matter what lies she must tell, what blood she must shed, or what family must perish, she vowed to be the first.

"Shall we do here as we did in Miquo?" she asked Galvanis.

That cold smile of his grew.

"We have no forests to burn, dear sister, but there are other ways, other methods. The Vagrant will suffer the same fate as his forbearer in Miquo. When his corpse hangs before the gates of Vallessau, the people shall learn once and for all we suffer no gods other than the God-Incarnate of the Empire."

"And how will you catch him?" she asked. "The wraith has proven infuriatingly elusive."

In answer, he gestured behind her, to the galleon Sinshei had presumed empty. There was one last set of passengers, and they descended together down the gangplank. Two were acolytes dressed in white, and they each held an arm of the one between them. Sinshei's insides ran cold. Her mouth opened in shock.

"Rihim shall handle that matter for us," Galvanis said.

Rihim was naked from the waist up, and though his muscled body resembled a man, it was covered with a thin layer of dark blue fur. He towered several feet over his escorts even with the heavy stoop of his spine. His face was that of a panther, with golden eyes glinting in the sunlight. Manacles wrapped about his wrists, each two inches thick of solid steel. Runes were carved across their surface, in an ancient language of Old Eldrid that only chosen priests knew how to read.

Those manacles were used only on captured and imprisoned gods of conquered nations, beings that were taught their proper place in worship of the God-Incarnate. They were the Humbled, and Sinshei knew that Galvanis had been working on one from Antiev for years. Never had she thought he would bring the god with him across the Crystal Sea. Again her lack of imagination might cost her dearly.

The Humbled stopped at the bottom of the gangplank. His ears flattened against his head, and he sniffed the air twice, long, deep draughts to fill his lungs. His deep voice purred as he spoke.

"You name this place Thanet." His golden eyes narrowed. "Yet I smell Miquoan gods here."

Miquoan gods? What did he mean? Sinshei swore to investigate, but for now, she turned to her brother and bowed her head. She must be deferential. She must be obedient. Loyal. Faithful.

Galvanis touched the Humbled's face, and it was with far more care and love than he had ever shown Sinshei.

"Then it is well I brought the perfect hunter for them."

Rihim bared his white teeth with twin broken fangs, and the manacles about his wrists rattled as he growled, eager for the hunt.

EPILOGUE

VAGRANT

Cyrus sat in the farthest, darkest corner he could find in the tavern. He'd never been much of a drinker, not that he'd had the chance to become one over the past years. Tonight, he was going to give it his best go. An enormous tankard sat before him. He'd drained it once already, and was halfway through the second round. Cyrus kept his hood up, his head low, and his eyes on the table. He trusted time, the poor lighting, and his drawn hood to protect his identity. No one would suspect the down-on-his-luck young drunkard in the corner of being a long-dead prince. Cyrus hardly believed it himself. Thorda's words echoed in his mind, mocking him and his plight for solace.

Godhood cannot be so easily cast aside . . .

"You weren't there!" a man shouted from the nearest table.

"I was!" a burly, bearded man hollered back. His left eye was scarred over, but he pointed to his right eye with the hand that wasn't busy holding his drink. "Saw it all with my one good peeper. I was in the crowd when it started, and I couldn't get out even if I tried, what with the fires. Found myself watching the fight, and what a fight! I'm telling you, I'm gods-damned *telling* you, the Vagrant killed Imperator Magus, straight-up gutted him and bled him dry."

Cyrus wished the man would shut his mouth. This was the second tavern he'd visited. He'd left the first after a few minutes. All talk had focused on the execution, and Magus's death. He thought here, on the other side of Vallessau and the farthest he could possibly get from the scene of the battle, he might find some peace. He was wrong.

"You're full of horseshit, Justin," someone shouted from a table positioned before the enormous hearth blazing along the wall. "Endarius died to the empire's paragons, and he was a god. You saying this Vagrant took down their leader, just like that, all by himself?"

"Yeah, I am," the man apparently named Justin said. "His swords, they danced, man, they danced!"

Cyrus put his hands to his ears and bit his tongue. He stayed like that, wondering if there was relief to be found anywhere in the city from the inescapable rumors, until the son of the tavern keeper came over holding a heavy pitcher in both hands.

"A hard day?" he asked.

"The hardest," Cyrus said, surprised by the gravel in his voice.

In response, the young man filled Cyrus's tankard, and he waved away the attempt to pay.

"On us," he said. "It's a day to celebrate. Sorry you're alone. Come on up by the bar if you'd like a friendly ear."

"Thank you," Cyrus said, so softly and insecurely he hardly made any noise at all. The boy, a handsome fellow really, smiled and then hurried away. Cyrus watched him go, but it wasn't long before his attention returned to his tankard. He stared at his rippling reflection in the beer. Distorted. Dark. Not worth believing what he saw. Just his tired, overworked imagination, that's all. That's what he told himself.

"Call me crazy, but he ain't a man!" the boisterous Justin bellowed. "Men don't move like that. They don't go from shadow to shadow, and it ain't no ordinary man that can best a paragon."

"Not living ones anyway," his friend added, and they both shared a laugh.

"So you're saying a dead man killed the Imperator and all his soldiers?" the bucktoothed woman with them asked.

"Dead? Alive? What's it matter? The Vagrant ain't neither." The braggart's tone lowered, and it seemed he realized everyone else in the tavern was listening. The attention made him stand up taller, and he met the eye of any willing man or woman.

"The Vagrant is something else. Something we all need. He is Thanet's own heart and soul. There's a reason he's black as night, and his face is a skull grinning at those damn imperials. He's the killer come to drag their souls to the Heldeep. He's the death they deserve. And to that, all I have to say is, a good and rowdy amen!"

Drinks were lifted throughout the tavern as the crowd cheered. Justin led the cheer.

"To our god and goddess!"

Even now they were fearful to say Lycaena's and Endarius's names aloud, for the damage the church had inflicted ran deep. The rest of the tavern echoed him, eager to celebrate. Every man and woman there but Cyrus, who stared at his reflection.

He wore no mask. The reflection did.

"To the Vagrant!"

The mocking smile stretched all the way to his ears.

"To a free Thanet!"

Cyrus slowly, fearfully pressed his fingertips to his cheek, feeling for soft skin.

Felt hard bone, and grinning teeth.

The story continues in . . .

BOOK TWO OF THE VAGRANT GODS

Coming in 2023!

A NOTE FROM THE AUTHOR

Welcome to my little space at the end of the novel, where Orbit still graciously lets me ramble for a few pages. I've written twenty-nine of these at this point, so you'd expect I would be good at them, or have an idea of what I wanted to accomplish with them. Hah! With some books it is easy. I'll tend to talk about a moment that was particularly important to me, the reasons why events unfolded as they did, or the decisions that led to it (see the end of, say, *Voidbreaker* for an example of that). A lot of it comes down to what the book means to me and what I wish to say about it that I cannot do explicitly within the text itself.

But what *Bladed Faith* means to me is a bit more complicated. My first...nineteen novels, I believe, were all set in the same world of Dezrel. So, despite writing a lot, it was mostly in one setting. The Seraphim trilogy was my first-ever attempt at doing something in a significantly different world, and to stretch my world-building skills beyond the more traditional Dungeons & Dragons–inspired setting. With Seraphim, I wanted to capture a more energetic feeling, with a more modern setting, akin to something you'd find in an anime like *Attack on Titan* or *Fullmetal Alchemist*.

Then came The Keepers. I wanted to return to monsters and magic, but this time all of my own creation. Crawling mountains, onyx faeries, an adorable sentient fire pet named Puffy, who basically became the mascot of the book. The storytelling changed with it, as I tried to let the story build and expand based on the characters' decisions, a seemingly small initial conflict blossoming into world-shattering implications (as I did so long ago with my very first series, The Half-Orcs). I was trying to recapture the past while growing as a world-builder. Success or failure obviously rests on the reader to judge, but I'm pleased with how personal I was able to keep such a project.

The Bladed Faith, however, started out unique among my entire catalog. I did not start with an overarching plot thread that I then filled out with characters (as I did with Seraphim). I did not build up a setting, and then try to figure out which characters would be most interesting to follow (as I did in Keepers). I was actually in the middle of finishing up *Voidbreaker*, the third book in the Keepers trilogy, when I took a two-week break. During those two weeks, I did something I'd never done before. I wrote short stories, one for each character, for the cast I would follow for my next project.

They're all still here, in this book you've just read. Stasia meeting Clarissa after Lycaena's execution. Mari becoming the Lioness. Cyrus choosing not to execute Gordian's son. Rayan praying over Alliya's corpse. Their first fight fully together against a magistrate and his paragon bodyguard. For a blistering two weeks, I wrote these chapters, because I had been developing the cast in my head over the course of months and I just...didn't want to lose them. I go on daily walks, listening to music while imagining scenes and moments from novels already written, or those I will soon write. I felt like I knew the main cast before I ever decided on where they were, who they were fighting, or how they all even knew each other.

All this worked because I left key aspects blank. I didn't know why Stasia was so upset when she met Clarissa, only that something had gone wrong, and that her need for vengeance was conflicting with her desires for a loving, normal life. Rayan's goddess was slain, but when and how were only vague ideas. What mattered was the moment of doubt, and the eruption of moths that followed. I knew Cyrus was a deposed prince, but the enemy at the time wasn't the Everlorn Empire, nor even the Reborn Empire, as I called it for much of the first draft. What mattered was whether or not he could murder a child, a child that was so very much like himself many years ago.

I wrote these chapters and then shelved them. Had to finish *Voidbreaker*, after all! But I had the cast. I had this group I wanted to spend time with, to discover how they interacted, and learn why they were together. And for my first attempt, let's just say I went big. Massive gateways linking thousands of worlds, a timeline taking place over thousands of years, and a main character who was similar to a paragon but with a bone arm that possessed ancient magic. It was weird and unfocused and the plot blended tons of elements of science fiction with ancient facilities performing auto- mated surgery, world-gates, and robots inside bone skeletons.

And Orbit passed on pretty much the whole concept.

There's a reason *Bladed Faith* is dedicated to my wife. Because at this point, it was like…April of 2020, the pandemic lockdowns were in full swing, my grandiose and genre-breaking pitch was not impressing people, and I was ready to sink into full self-pity and declare my writ- ing career dead and buried. Melodramatic, yes, but reading this novel should be proof enough that I can be a melodramatic person. Sam kept me grounded for my day or two of moping. My career was not over. My skills as a writer had not spontaneously combusted. Hell, I'd reworked trilogy pitches before (such as with The Keepers' original outline ver- sus what Orbit eventually accepted). So what was really bothering me? Why did this one inspire such panic?

So, I thought on it, and I knew the reason. I did not want to lose these side characters. Mari, Rayan, Stasia, Cyrus…I was emotionally invested in them. I knew they were good. I knew they were some of the best I'd done in my entire career. And so I stripped my plot back down to those first few chapters and rebuilt the story once more. Gone were the sci-fi elements. Gone were the thousands of worlds and the gate- hopping. Gone was the main character, far too intricately tied to the bone robots and the worlds-spanning religious empire. I started fresh, and I thought on what exactly I wanted to do.

As I mentioned earlier, each series of mine tends to have a goal or idea that I'm trying out for how I want to tell the story. For The Vagrant Gods, I decided it would be less of an experiment and more of a cul- mination. I would take what I loved from my various series and try to create what I would view as my path forward. This would be the series that, if you asked me what a definitive Dalglish novel was, I would no longer point to *A Dance of Cloaks* or *The Broken Pieces*. It would be this book. This trilogy.

A band of powerful friends/family like the Eschaton Mercenaries of The Half-Orcs and Shadowdance. The religious conflict of The Paladins. The anything-goes philosophy of The Keepers. And as always, my over-the-top battles, in a setting that would allow me to stretch my chops, like the aerial battles of The Seraphim. It's a new world with new characters, but for so much of it, it felt like a homecoming.

I wrote up the much more tightly focused pitch, reworked the character intros to fit the revamped setting, made Cyrus the main character instead of a side character, and then sent it to Orbit. Given you're reading this book, their response should not be a surprise. Plenty of worldbuilding followed, and I have lots to say about the newer additions, such as Soma and Keles or how reading Megan E. O'Keefe's *Velocity Weapon* dramatically altered the initial outline, but that's for another note in another book.

Which means it is time to give thanks to those who deserve all of it and more. Thank you, Brit, for still believing I have stories worth reading. Thank you, Angeline, for the much needed second pass. Thank you to Lauren and the entire Orbit Art deptartment for consistently giving me some of the best covers in the business. Thanks to Megan and Essa for being the earliest readers of this book, and for being there when I needed to ramble, question, or rant about writing nonsense (or just wanted to talk *Final Fantasy XIV*). Thank you, Michael, for being the best agent a guy like me could ask for. Thank you again, Sam, for being the perfect person to spend months locked down together with.

Last, and most important, thank you, dear reader, whether this is the first book of mine you've read, or your twenty-ninth. You allow me to live a dream I never imagined could become real. I get to tell stories for a living. Thank you. Truly.

David Dalglish

July 3, 2021

extras

orbit

meet the author

DAVID DALGLISH currently lives in Myrtle Beach with his wife, Samantha, and daughters, Morgan, Katherine, and Alyssa. He graduated from Missouri Southern State University in 2006 with a degree in mathematics and currently spends his free time tanking dungeons for his wife and daughter in *Final Fantasy XIV*.

Find out more about David Dalglish and other Orbit authors by registering for the free monthly newsletter at orbitbooks.net.

if you enjoyed
THE BLADED FAITH

look out for

VAGRANT GODS: BOOK TWO

by

David Dalglish

In the blockbuster second novel in USA Today *bestselling author David Dalglish's new epic fantasy trilogy, a usurped prince must master the magic of shadows in order to reclaim his kingdom, his people.*

Cyrus wants out. Trained to be an assassin in order to oust the invading empire from his kingdom, Cyrus is now worried the price of his vengeance is too high. His old master has been keeping too many secrets to be trusted. And the mask he wears to hide his true identity and to become the legendary "Vagrant" has started whispering to him in the dark. But the fight isn't over, and the empire has sent its full force to bear upon Cyrus's floundering revolution. He'll have to decide once and for all whether to become the thing he fears or lose the country he loves.

PROLOGUE

Keles stood in the center of the empty tent, her arms crossed and her hands bound behind her back. The rope dug into her skin as she slowly twisted her wrists. The rational part of her mind said she should be afraid, but oddly enough, she felt no fear. She had suffered imprisonment at the hands of the Everlorn Empire. What threat did loyal followers of the slain Lycaena present to her?

Of course, they might not be truly loyal to the Butterfly goddess. Based on their claims, they might even be insane...

The tent flaps opened behind her. She tilted her chin and turned, determined to present herself as calm and honorable as possible despite her current predicament.

"I am Keles Lyon, faithful servant of Thanet, and I demand that you remove my bindings," she told the new arrival. Her intended authoritative tone wilted into surprise at seeing the man towering a good foot taller than her.

His head and face were clean-shaven, and twin butterfly wings tattooed in black ink rose from his eyebrows to curl across his bald pate. His face was thin and bony, as if he were a few harsh days shy of starvation, and his nose crooked from being broken and not allowed a proper chance to heal. He wore a red robe tied with a rope sash. A silver dagger was tucked into it. His arms crossed over his chest, and the loose sleeves of the robe fell back to expose his bare arms. Where there weren't tattoos on his pale skin, there were scars, deep and winding ones that seemed more fitting to a man of war than a priest.

"No," he said. His light brown eyes studied her as he paced a circle around her. "I don't think I will."

"Why not?" she asked. "Surely you do not think me a threat?"

He continued circling her, his right hand gently stroking his chin. His voice was deeper than the sea and smoother than any wine.

"There's not much left in you of the little girl that I once saw," he said. "But war tends to strip away the vestiges of childhood. I know your face, and I remember your name, but it was not the one you used when we last met."

Keles's insides twisted. She knew what the man meant, as much as she had tried to bury that past.

"I'm not her anymore," she said.

"What did they call you?" this strange priest said, ignoring her protest. Around and around he walked, and she felt like a lamb being prowled by a wolf. "If I remember right, you were 'the Light of Vallessau,' were you not?"

She flinched at the title. It had been foisted upon her when she was sixteen, the heroine paladin fighting the invading forces of the empire. She had not gone by that title since her imprisonment and Lycaena's public execution.

"I forfeited any such title at the forsaking ceremony," she said.

"And yet now you are here, so very far from Vallessau. Might you explain, Keles? Set my mind at ease?"

Keles met his narrowed gaze with a faint smile.

"I will confess no secrets to a man whose name I do not know. Only a fool would do so under such a disadvantage."

The priest drew his dagger.

"Are you a fool, Keles?" he asked.

"Do you think me a fool, stranger?"

At last, he smiled. It lit up his narrow face.

"I think you are many things, daughter of Vallessau, but a fool is not one of them."

He stepped around her and cut the ropes that bound her wrists. The pieces dropped to the dirt floor of the tent. Keles stretched her shoulders as she rubbed at the raw skin. When he curled back around to face her, he dipped his head in apology.

"My name is Ramund Dymling, faithful servant of our beloved goddess, Lycaena."

Tradition would have her salute with her sword, then lay the blade flat over her left arm, but she was no paladin, and he no true priest, so instead, she slightly dipped her head in greeting.

"Well met, Ramund. I must admit, I expected a better welcome when I came to your little camp at the far end of the forest."

"We must always be watchful for imperial spies. A little silver and an empty belly can loosen the tongues of even the most loyal."

Now that he had ceased his circling, he faced her directly, arms crossed and openly staring. She felt judged, but was she found worthy, or wanting? And why did she suddenly care?

"Your wrists are freed, and our names are shared," he said. "We are as equal as we can be, so I ask you again, Light of Vallessau, why have you come to my village?"

Voicing her reasons filled her with embarrassment. Childish, delusional hopes, yet here she was, two weeks of hard travel into the northern reaches of Thanet, through the Cliffwoods, to an unremarkable little camp lost amid the trees. All for a fool's hope. All for a dream that could not be real. But oh, what a dream it was...

"Certain rumors have reached us in Vallessau," she said. She stared him dead in the eyes and challenged him to lie. "I have to know. Is it true?"

Ramund crossed the wide tent to the entrance, pushed aside the flap, and gestured for her to follow. He still held his dagger.

"Nothing I tell you would ever be enough," he said. "So come see for yourself, if you are willing to endure the blood it costs."

A shiver ran through her. Was it fear, or excitement? This handsome man, he was watching her, studying her. A need to prove herself rose in response to those light brown eyes. She would not cower. As the Light of Vallessau, she had stridden the front lines of the battlefield, her blade gleaming and her shield unbreakable. She held no fear of blood.

Together they stepped out into the center of the bustling camp. Her first impression when she had arrived in the waning evening hours had been of a loose collection of tents and huts built from the surrounding ash trees and covered with linen. It was orderly despite the obvious newness and rush. While bound and marched into Ramund's tent, Keles had estimated maybe thirty or forty people lived there, but that number had been off by a wide margin.

"Stay with me," Ramund said, as the train of followers swelled. Hungry, distrusting eyes watched her, and Keles made sure to keep beside him at all times. They walked a well-worn path through the trees to the white cliffs that gave the forest its name.

The crash of waves greeted the forest edge. Beyond were steep cliffs, rising out in defiance of the Crystal Sea. The path they walked led to the highest of the cliffs, six lit torches already waiting. Ramund led the climb up the slope, where a half circle of stones, six in total, lined the narrow edge. These pillars were wide at the bottom but slender and curling near the top, so they appeared to be fingers of a buried giant reaching out from the ground. Moss grew along their wind-blasted gray surfaces. Walking into their center felt like walking into the presence of history. These stones were *old*. Who had placed them, and how many centuries prior to Keles's existence?

The sacredness of this site was clearly felt by the others. The people accompanying their walk fell silent. No one spoke. The only sound was the muffled shuffling of feet, the rustle of cloth, and the heavier breathing of the elderly. Even the children knew to hold their tongues, which was a miracle in and of itself. The young certainly had never shut their mouths during the lengthy sermons she'd attended at the Twin Sanctuary.

Then again, the Twin Sanctuary did not possess a massive stone slab at its heart. A slab that could be only an altar, and whose deep red stains were most certainly dried blood. A man lay upon it, hands tied behind his back in the same manner the villagers had bound Keles. His mouth was gagged, and his eyes blindfolded. He had been stripped of all clothing but his undergarments. Whether he was unconscious or sleeping, she did not know, but there were at least visible movements of his bruised chest. Two men stood guard over him, clubs in hand.

Keles tried to remain calm when she spoke. To her relief, there wasn't the slightest quiver or hint of worry in her voice.

"Who is that man?"

Ramund halted just shy of the half circle. The accompanying villagers fanned out to either side, and they moved with a purpose. Those carrying torches lifted them high, casting light about the cliff.

"An imperial soldier we captured on patrol to Chora," Ramund said, referring to the nearby village whose elder had guided Keles into the forest. Ramund shed his robe so that he was naked from the waist up. All across his muscular body were winding tattoos, and for every curve or circle there was a matching scar, some a full foot in length. Whatever had been done to this man, it had been brutal. He turned to her, no more smiles on his face or sharp banter on his tongue. His voice lowered, meant only for her. "There is no coming back, Keles. If you stay, you become a part of this, all the way to the necessary end. I will not blame you for leaving... though I would be disappointed."

The movement of the people ceased, for they had taken their places. Completing the ring, Keles realized. What had been a half circle was now full. Stone and flesh, the everlasting and the ephemeral. Torches burned in the human ring, while only moonlight lit the six weathered pillars. In the center, the prisoner and the man with the knife.

"Lycaena has never preached a need for blood sacrifice," Keles said, feeling the first hints of panic nibbling at her mind.

"And what need was there in a time of peace?" Ramund asked, this time louder and for all in attendance. "On calm days, the sword stays sheathed, but let it be drawn when night falls and the burglar comes prowling."

The bound man rolled onto his back, a faint moan escaping his lips. He sounded drugged, which would explain his lack of struggle. Whatever hope had dragged Keles here vanished as she watched Ramund lift the knife. This couldn't be right. This was madness. The people would indulge Ramund's slaughter of imperial soldiers because they were frightened and angry. It was rebellion framed as ritual. It was war disguised as worship. Stars help her, there were *children* in attendance.

"On this night, we give to our beloved goddess," Ramund continued. The deep rumble of his voice was thunder, the moonlight shining off his raised dagger, his lightning. Perhaps it was a trick of the light, but it seemed like the tattoos across his face and arms glowed a faint crimson. He stood at the altar, the bound man before him, the stones behind him, and a field of stars above. There was something primal about his presence, wild and unchecked by the laws of the priesthood and the structure of faith Keles had learned during her paladin training within the Heaven's Wing.

"To Thanet, we give our prayers," Ramund instructed.

"*To Thanet, we give our prayers,*" echoed the crowd.

"To the goddess, we give our all."

"*To the goddess, we give our all.*"

Keles hated herself, but she repeated those words. She would be no innocent bystander, not in this. Whatever blood flowed this night, it would coat her hands equally with all the rest.

"From blood and bone, shadow and fire, from the land and the sea, we scream your rebirth," Ramund shouted.

"*The rebirth comes,*" the people answered.

Down came the knife, opening the man from breastbone to crotch. Whatever drugs keeping him tame were of no match, and the bound imperial shrieked in pain. The chants of the crowd rose in volume to match it. Keles glanced aside. Nothing felt real. A small girl, no older than ten, clutched the hand of her mother, and she belted out those words at the top of her lungs.

"*Blood and bone. Shadow and fire. We scream rebirth.*"

Ramund dove his hands into the open chest. He sank his arms up to his elbows, coating them in blood and gore. His eyes closed as he began his prayer, one echoed by those in attendance. Keles wondered how many times they had performed this atrocity. How many bodies did it take to create a red stain so wide and deep as the one across that stone altar?

"Fly to us, one of wing and flower, of storm and sun," he chanted, once more taking lead. The rest repeated in kind. "Give us light, give us heat, so we may sing."

Her legs felt wooden. Her feet were buried in the earth. To move, to break this spell, was impossible. Ramund had warned her, had he not? If she stayed, she must see this to its end. At least the screaming had stopped.

"Wing and flower, storm and sun," continued his chant, shorter and quicker. "Give us light and heat, we sing."

Fire shimmered along the base of the six stones. It formed in silence, and it spread higher across the surface without consuming the moss. Its color shifted from a natural fire to a more ethereal mixture of blue and crimson. Keles gasped, but the others continued their chant, this revelation a normal part of their ritual.

Light, she thought as the flames burned across the stone pillars. *Heat.*

A shiver collected at the base of her neck and then shot down her spine to her arms and legs. Wind swirled around the crowd, and it smelled not of the sea, but like a blooming field of flowers. Ramund bowed so his forehead rested against the opened rib cage. His arms sank deeper into its core. The corpse shimmered, flesh curling and peeling as if it were within a furnace. The wind howled. The cliff shook beneath them. Ramund cried out, wordless, primal, and then tore his arms free.

The corpse exploded into flame, consumed with such fury not a shred of ash or bone endured to fall upon the witnesses. Ramund stood to his full height, bare chest heaving, tattoos rippling, and they were fire, the tattoos, they were *burning.* He tilted his head back as the communal prayer ceased. Blood trickled down his face, mixing with his tears as a wave of emotion overcame him. His voice, normally deep as the ocean, suddenly trembled as he whispered.

"Lycaena, return to us, even if it must be in blood."

Dark flame burst from the six pillars, flowing in thin streams to the space above the altar. It collected together, shaped, took form. Fire became flesh and cloth. Light and heat became wing and dress. Keles dropped to her knees, and she wept with dozens of others in the crowd. "Return to us," Ramund had demanded, and Lycaena answered. Somehow, despite her death, despite the knives of the church's priests, she answered. She came. She lived.

"My goddess," Keles said, eyes wide, hands reaching, soul offered once more to the wondrous being of compassion and love to whom she had sworn her life since the day she knew how to walk.

A touch upon her fingertips, hot and dripping with blood. In that moment, Keles knew she would never leave. What price Ramund demanded, she would pay. What lives must be offered, let them be offered. The empire had taken their goddess. Let their soldiers be sacrificed for her return.

"It's true," she said, and wept uncontrollably. She closed her fingers and clutched her fists to her breast so she could still feel the residual heat. The years of warfare and despair, of crushing doubt and self-hatred for failing to prevent the death of the one she loved most, bled away.

"You live. Goddess, you live."

if you enjoyed
THE BLADED FAITH

look out for

THE PARIAH

Book One of
The Covenant of Steel

by

Anthony Ryan

The Pariah *begins a new epic fantasy series of action,
intrigue, and magic from Anthony Ryan, a master
storyteller who has taken the fantasy world by storm.*

*Born into the troubled kingdom of Albermaine, Alwyn
Scribe is raised as an outlaw. Quick of wit and deft with a
blade, Alwyn is content with the freedom of the woods and
the comradeship of his fellow thieves. But an act of betrayal
sets him on a new path—one of blood and vengeance, which
eventually leads him to a soldier's life in the king's army.*

*Fighting under the command of Lady Evadine Courlain, a
noblewoman beset by visions of a demonic apocalypse, Alwyn must
survive war and the deadly intrigues of the nobility if he hopes to*

claim his vengeance. But as dark forces, both human and arcane, gather to oppose Evadine's rise, Alwyn faces a choice: Can he be a warrior, or will he always be an outlaw?

CHAPTER ONE

Before killing a man, I always found it calming to regard the trees. Lying on my back in the long grass fringing the King's Road and gazing at the green and brown matrix above, branches creaking and leaves whispering in the late-morning breeze, brought a welcome serenity. I had found this to be true ever since my first faltering steps into this forest as a boy ten years before. When the heart began to thud and sweat beaded my brow, the simple act of looking up at the trees brought a respite, one made sweeter by the knowledge that it would be short lived.

Hearing the clomp of iron-shod hooves upon earth, accompanied by the grinding squeal of a poorly greased axle, I closed my eyes to the trees and rolled onto my belly. Shorn of the soothing distraction, my heart's excited labour increased in pitch, but I was well schooled in not letting it show. Also, the sweat dampening my armpits and trickling down my back would only add to my stench, adding garnish for the particular guise I adopted that day. Lamed outcasts are rarely fragrant.

Raising my head just enough to glimpse the approaching party through the grass, I was obliged to take a deep breath at the sight of the two mounted men-at-arms riding at the head of the caravan. More concerning still were the two soldiers perched on the cart that followed, both armed with crossbows, eyes scanning the forest on either side of the road in a worrying display of hard-learned vigilance. Although not within the chartered bounds of the Shavine Forest, this stretch of the King's Road described a long arc through

486

its northern fringes. Sparse in comparison to the deep forest, it was still a place of bountiful cover and not one to be travelled by the unwary in such troubled times.

As the company drew closer, I saw a tall lance bobbing above the small throng, the pennant affixed beneath its blade fluttering in the breeze with too much energy to make out the crest it bore. However, its gold and red hues told the tale clearly: royal colours. Deckin's intelligence had, as ever, been proven correct: this lot were the escort for a Crown messenger.

I waited until the full party had revealed itself, counting another four mounted men-at-arms in the rearguard. I took some comfort from the earthy brown and green of their livery. These were not kingsmen but ducal levies from Cordwain, taken far from home by the demands of war and not so well trained or steadfast as Crown soldiery. However, their justified caution and overall impression of martial orderliness was less reassuring. I judged them unlikely to run when the time came, which was unfortunate for all concerned.

I rose when the leading horsemen were a dozen paces off, reaching for the gnarled, rag-wrapped tree branch that served as my crutch and levering myself upright. I was careful to blink a good deal and furrow my brow in the manner of a soul just roused from slumber. As I hobbled towards the verge, keeping the blackened bulb of my bandaged foot clear of the ground, my features slipped easily into the gape-mouthed, emptied-eyed visage of a crippled dullard. Reaching the road, I allowed the foot to brush the churned mud at the edge. Letting out an agonised groan of appropriate volume, I stumbled forwards, collapsing onto all fours in the middle of the rutted fairway.

It should not be imagined that I fully expected the soldiers' horses to rear, for many a warhorse is trained to trample a prone man. Fortunately, these beasts had not been bred for knightly service and they both came to a gratifyingly untidy halt, much to the profane annoyance of their riders.

"Get out of the fucking road, churl!" the soldier on the right snarled, dragging on his reins as his mount wheeled in alarm.

Beyond him, the cart and, more importantly, the bobbing lance of the Crown messenger also stopped. The crossbowmen sank lower on the mound of cargo affixed to the cart-bed, both reaching for the bolts in their quivers. Crossbowmen are always wary of leaving their weapons primed for long intervals, for it wears down the stave and the string. However, failing to do so this day would soon prove a fatal miscalculation.

I didn't allow my sight to linger on the cart, however, instead gaping up at the mounted soldier with wide, fearful eyes that betrayed little comprehension. It was an expression I had practised extensively, for it is not easy to mask one's intellect.

"Shift your arse!" his companion instructed, his voice marginally less angry and speaking as if addressing a dull-witted dog. When I continued to stare up at him from the ground he cursed and reached for the whip on his saddle.

"Please!" I whimpered, crutch raised protectively over my head. "Y-your pardon, good sirs!"

I had noticed on many occasions that such cringing will invariably stoke rather than quell the violent urges of the brutishly inclined, and so it proved now. The soldier's face darkened as he unhooked the whip, letting it unfurl so its barbed tip dangled onto the road a few inches from my cowering form. Looking up, I saw his hand tighten on the diamond-etched pattern of the handle. The leather was well worn, marking this as a man who greatly enjoyed opportunities to use this weapon.

However, as he raised the lash he paused, features bunching in disgust. "Martyrs' guts, but you're a stinker!"

"Sorry, sir!" I quailed. "Can't help it. Me foot, see? It's gone all rotten since me master's cart landed on it. I'm on the Trail of Shrines. Going to beseech Martyr Stevanos to put me right. Y'wouldn't hurt a faithful fellow, would you?"

In fact, my foot was a fine and healthy appendage to an equally healthy leg. The stench that so assailed the soldier's nose came from a pungent mix of wild garlic, bird shit and mulched-up leaves. For a guise to be convincing, one must never neglect the power of scent.

extras

It was important that these two see no threat in me. A lamed youth happened upon while traversing a notoriously treacherous road could well be faking. But one with a face lacking all wit and a foot exuding an odour carefully crafted to match the festering wounds this pair had surely encountered before was another matter.

Closer scrutiny would surely have undone me. Had this pair been more scrupulous in their appraisal they would have seen the mostly unmarked skin beneath the grime and the rangy but sturdy frame of a well-fed lad beneath the rags. Keener eyes and a fraction more time would also have discerned the small bulge of the knife beneath my threadbare jerkin. But these unfortunates lacked the required keenness of vision, and they were out of time. It had only been moments since I had stumbled into their path, but the distraction had been enough to bring their entire party to a halt. Over the course of an eventful and perilous life, I have found that it is in these small, confused interludes that death is most likely to arrive.

For the soldier on the right it arrived in the form of a crow-fletched arrow with a barbed steel head. The shaft came streaking from the trees to enter his neck just behind the ear before erupting from his mouth in a cloud of blood and shredded tongue. As he toppled from the saddle, his whip-bearing comrade proved his veteran status by immediately dropping the whip and reaching for his longsword. He was quick, but so was I. Snatching my knife from its sheath I put my bandaged foot beneath me and launched myself up, latching my free hand to his horse's bridle. The animal reared in instinctive alarm, raising me the additional foot I required to sink my knife into the soldier's throat before he could fully draw his sword. I was proud of the thrust, it being something I'd practised as much as my witless expression, the blade opening the required veins at the first slice.

I kept hold of the horse's reins as my feet met the ground, the beast threatening to tip me over with all its wheeling about. Watching the soldier tumble to the road and gurgle out his last few breaths, I felt a pang of regret for the briefness of his end. Surely this fellow with his well-worn whip had earned a more prolonged passing in his time. However, my regret was muted as one of many lessons in outlaw craft drummed into me over the years came to mind: *When the task is a killing, be quick and make sure of it. Torment is an indulgence. Save it for only the most deserving.*

It was mostly over by the time I calmed the horse. The first volley of arrows had felled all but two of the guards. Both crossbowmen lay dead on the cart, as did its drover. One man-at-arms had the good sense to turn his horse about and gallop off, not that it saved him from the thrown axe that came spinning out of the trees to take him in the back. The last was made of more admirable, if foolhardy stuff. The brief arrow storm had impaled his thigh and skewered his mount, but still he contrived to roll clear of the thrashing beast and rise, drawing his sword to face the two dozen outlaws running from the treeline.

I have heard versions of this tale that would have you believe that, when confronted by this brave and resolute soul, Deckin Scarl himself forbade his band from cutting him down. Instead he and the stalwart engaged in solitary combat. Having mortally wounded the soldier, the famed outlaw sat with him until nightfall as they shared tales of battles fought and ruminated on the capricious mysteries that determine the fates of all.

These days, similarly nonsensical songs and stories abound regarding Deckin Scarl, renowned Outlaw King of the Shavine Marches and, as some would have it, protector of churl and beggar alike. *With one hand he stole and the other he gave*, as one particularly execrable ballad would have it. *Brave Deckin of the woods, strong and kind he stood.*

If, dear reader, you find yourself minded to believe a word of this I have a six-legged donkey to sell you. The Deckin Scarl I knew was certainly strong, standing two inches above six feet with plenty of muscle to match his height, although his belly had begun to swell in recent years. And kind he could be, but it was a rare thing for a man does not rise to the summit of outlawry in the Shavine Forest by dint of kindness.

In fact, the only words I heard Deckin say in regard to that stout soldier was a grunted order to, "Kill that silly fucker and let's get on." Neither did Deckin bother to spare a glance for the fellow's end, sent off to the Martyrs' embrace by a dozen arrows. I watched the outlaw king come stomping from the shadowed woods with his axe in hand, an ugly weapon with a blackened and misshapen double blade that was rarely far from his reach. He paused to regard my handiwork, shrewd eyes bright beneath his heavy brows as they tracked from the soldier's corpse to the horse I had managed to capture. Horses were a prize worth claiming for they fetched a good price, especially in times of war. Even if they couldn't be sold, meat was always welcome in camp.

Grunting in apparent satisfaction, Deckin swiftly turned his attention to the sole survivor of the ambush, an outcome that had not been accidental. "One arrow comes within a yard of the messenger," he had growled at us all that morning, "and I'll have the skin off the hand that loosed it, fingers to wrist." It wasn't an idle threat, for we had all seen him make good on the promise before.

The royal messenger was a thin-faced man clad in finely tailored jerkin and trews with a long cloak dyed to mirror the royal livery. Seated upon a grey stallion, he maintained an expression of disdainful affront even as Deckin moved to grasp the bridle of his horse. For all his rigid dignity and evident outrage, he was wise enough not to lower the lance he held, the royal pennant continuing to stand tall and flutter above this scene of recent slaughter.

"Any violence or obstruction caused to a messenger in Crown service is considered treason," the thin-faced fellow stated, his voice betraying a creditably small quaver. He blinked and finally consented to afford Deckin the full force of his imperious gaze. "You should know that, whoever you are."

"Indeed I do, good sir," Deckin replied, inclining his head. "And I believe you know full well who I am, do you not?"

The messenger blinked again and shifted his eyes away once more, not deigning to answer. I had seen Deckin kill for less blatant insults, but now he just laughed. Raising his free hand, he gave a hard, expectant snap of his fingers.

The messenger's face grew yet more rigid, rage and humiliation flushing his skin red. I saw his nostrils flare and lips twitch, no doubt the result of biting down unwise words. The fact that he didn't need to be asked twice before reaching for the leather scroll tube on his belt made it plain that he certainly knew the name of the man before him.

"Lorine!" Deckin barked, taking the scroll from the messenger's reluctant hand and holding it out to the slim, copper-haired woman who strode forwards to take it.

The balladeers would have it that Lorine D'Ambrille was the famously fair daughter of a distant lordling who fled her father's castle rather than suffer an arranged marriage to a noble of ill repute and vile habits. Via many roads and adventures, she made her way to the dark woods of the Shavine Marches where she had the good fortune to be rescued from a pack of ravening wolves by none other than the kindly rogue Deckin Scarl himself. Love soon blossomed betwixt them, a love that, much to my annoyance, has echoed through the years acquiring ever more ridiculous legend in the process.

As far as I have been able to ascertain there was no more noble blood in Lorine's veins than mine, although the origin of her comparatively well-spoken tones and evident education are still something of a mystery. She remained a cypher despite the excessive time I would devote to thinking of her. As with all legends, however, a kernel of truth lingers: she was fair. Her features held a smooth handsomeness that had survived years of forest living and she somehow contrived to keep her lustrous copper hair free of grease and burrs. For one suffering the boundless lust of youth, I couldn't help but stare at her whenever the chance arose.

After removing the cap from the tube to extract the scroll within, Lorine's smooth, lightly freckled brow creased a little as she read its contents. Captured as always by her face, my fascination was dimmed somewhat by the short but obvious spasm of shock that flickered over her features. She hid it well, of course, for she was my tutor in the arts of disguise and even more practised than I in concealing potentially dangerous emotions.

"You have it all?" Deckin asked her.

"Word for word, my love," Lorine assured him, white teeth revealed in a smile as she returned the scroll to the tube and replaced the cap. Although her origins would always remain in shadow, I had gleaned occasional mentions of treading stages and girlhood travels with troupes of players, leading me to conclude that Lorine had once been an actress. Perhaps as a consequence, she possessed the uncanny ability to memorise a large amount of text after only a few moments of reading.

"If I might impose upon your good nature, sir," Deckin told the messenger, taking the tube from Lorine. "I would consider it the greatest favour if you could carry an additional message to King Tomas. As one king to another, please inform him of my deepest and most sincere regrets regarding this unfortunate and unforeseen delay to the journey of his trusted agent, albeit brief."

The messenger stared at the proffered tube as one might a gifted turd, but took it nonetheless. "Such artifice will not save you," he said, the words clipped by his clenched teeth. "And you are not a king, Deckin Scarl."

"Really?" Deckin pursed his lips and raised an eyebrow in apparent surprise. "I am a man who commands armies, guards his borders, punishes transgressions and collects the taxes that are his due. If such a man is not a king, what is he?"

It was clear to me that the messenger had answers aplenty for this question but, being a fellow of wisdom as well as duty, opted to offer no reply.

"And so, I'll bid you good day and safe travels," Deckin said, stepping back to slap a brisk hand to the rump of the messenger's horse. "Keep to the road and don't stop until nightfall. I can't guarantee your safety after sunset."

The messenger's horse spurred into a trot at the slap, one its rider was quick to transform into a gallop. Soon he was a blur of churned mud, his trailing cloak a red and gold flicker among the trees until he rounded a bend and disappeared from view.

"Don't stand gawping!" Deckin barked, casting his glare around the band. "We've got loot to claim and miles to cover before dusk."

They all fell to the task with customary enthusiasm, the archers

493

claiming the soldiers they had felled while the others swarmed the cart. Keen to join them, I looked around for a sapling where I could tether my stolen horse but drew up short as Deckin raised a hand to keep me in place.

"Just one cut," he said, coming closer and nodding his shaggy head at the slain soldier with the whip. "Not bad."

"Like you taught me, Deckin," I said, offering a smile. I felt it falter on my lips as he cast an appraising eye over the horse and gestured for me to pass him the reins.

"Think I'll spare him the stewpot," he said, smoothing a large hand over the animal's grey coat. "Still just a youngster. Plenty of use left in him. Like you, eh, Alwyn?"

He laughed one of his short, grating laughs, a sound I was quick to mimic. I noticed Lorine still stood a short way off, eschewing the frenzied looting to observe our conversation with arms crossed and head cocked. I found her expression strange; the slightly pinched mouth bespoke muted amusement while her narrowed gaze and drawn brows told of restrained concern. Deckin tended to speak to me more than the other youngsters in the band, something that aroused a good deal of envy, but not usually on Lorine's part. Today, however, she apparently saw some additional significance in his favour, making me wonder if it had something to do with the contents of the messenger's scroll.

"Let's play our game, eh?" Deckin said, instantly recapturing my attention. I turned back to see him jerk his chin at the bodies of the two soldiers. "What do you see?"

Stepping closer to the corpses, I spent a short interval surveying them before providing an answer. I tried not to speak too quickly, having learned to my cost how much he disliked it when I gabbled.

"Dried blood on their trews and cuffs," I said. "A day or two old, I'd say. This one—" I pointed at the soldier with the arrowhead jutting from his mouth "—has a fresh-stitched cut on his brow and that one." My finger shifted to the half-bared blade still clutched in the gloved fist of the one I had stabbed. "His sword has nicks and scratches that haven't yet been ground out."

"What's that tell you?" Deckin enquired.

"They've been in a fight, and recently."

"A fight?" He raised a bushy eyebrow, tone placid as he asked, "You sure it was just that?"

My mind immediately began to race. It was always a worrisome thing when Deckin's tone grew mild. "A battle more like," I said, knowing I was speaking too fast but not quite able to slow the words. "Something big enough or important enough for the king to be told of the outcome. Since they were still breathing, until this morn, I'd guess they'd won."

"What else?" Deckin's eyes narrowed further in the manner that told of potential disappointment; apparently, I had missed something obvious.

"They're Cordwainers," I said, managing not to blurt it out. "Riding with a royal messenger, so they were called to the Shavine Marches on Crown business."

"Yes," he said, voice coloured by a small sigh that told of restrained exasperation. "And what is the Crown's principal business in these troubled times?"

"The Pretender's War." I swallowed and smiled again in relieved insight. "The king's host has fought and won a battle with the Pretender's horde."

Deckin lowered his eyebrow and regarded me in silence for a second, keeping his unblinking gaze on me just long enough to make me sweat for the second time that morning. Then he blinked and turned to lead the horse away, muttering to Lorine as she moved to his side. The words were softly spoken but I heard them, as I'm sure he intended I would.

"The message?"

Lorine put a neutral tone to her reply, face carefully void of expression. "You were right, as usual, my love. The daft old bastard turned his coat."

Deckin ordered the bodies cleared from the road and dumped deeper in the forest where the attentions of wolves, bears or foxes would soon ensure all that remained were anonymous bones. The Shavine Forest is a hungry place and fresh meat rarely lasts long when the wind carries its scent through the trees. It had been dispiritingly inevitable that it would be Erchel who found one of them still alive. He was just as hungry as any forest predator, but it was hunger of a different sort.

"Fucker's still breathing!" he exclaimed in surprised delight when the crossbowman we had been dragging through the ferns let out a confused, inquisitive groan. Jarred by the unexpectedness of his survival, I instantly let go of his arm, letting him slump to the ground, where he continued to groan before raising his head. Despite the holes torn into his body by no fewer than five arrows, he resembled a man woken from a strange dream as he gazed up at his captors.

"What's happened, friend?" Erchel enquired, sinking to his haunches, face drawn in an impressive semblance of concern. "Outlaws, was it? My fellows and I found you by the road." His face became grim, voice taking on a hoarse note of despair. "What a terrible thing. They're naught but beasts, Scourge take them. Don't worry—" He set a comforting hand on the crossbowman's lolling head. "—We'll see you right."

"Erchel," I said, voice edged with a forbidding note. His eyes snapped to meet mine, catching a bright, resentful gleam, sharp, pale features scowling. We were much the same age but I was taller than most lads of seventeen, if that was in fact my age. Even today I can only guess my true span of years, for such is the way with bastards shucked from a whorehouse: birthdays are a mystery and names a gift you make to yourself.

"Got no time for your amusements," I told Erchel. The after-taste of murder tended to birth a restless anger in me and the exchange with Deckin had deepened the well, making my patience short. The band had no formal hierarchy as such. Deckin was our unquestioned and unchallenged leader and Lorine his second, but beneath them the pecking order shifted over time. Erchel, by dint of his manners and habits, foul even by the standards of outlaws, currently stood a good few pegs lower than me. Being as much a pragmatic coward as he was a vicious dog, Erchel could usually be counted on to back down when faced with even marginally greater authority. Today, however, the prospect of indulging his inclinations overrode his pragmatism.

"Get fucked, Alwyn," he muttered, turning back to the crossbowman who, incredibly, had summoned the strength to try and rise. "Don't tax yourself, friend," Erchel advised, his hand slipping to the knife on his belt. "Lay down. Rest a while."

I knew how this would go from here. Erchel would whisper some more comforting endearments to this pitiable man, and then, striking swift like a snake, would stab out one of his eyes. Then there would be more cooing assurances before he took the other. After that it became a game of finding out how long it took the benighted wretch to die as Erchel's knife sliced ever deeper. I had no stomach for it most days, and certainly not today. Also, he had failed to heed me which was justification enough for the kick I delivered to his jaw.

Erchel's teeth clacked as his head recoiled from the impact. The kick was placed to cause the most pain without dislocating his jaw, not that he appreciated my consideration. Just a scant second or two spent blinking in shock before his narrow face mottled in rage and he sprang to his feet, bloodied teeth bared, knife drawn back to deliver a reply. My own knife came free of the sheath in a blur and I crouched, ready to receive him.

In all honesty, the matter might have been decided in favour of either of us, for we were about evenly matched when it came to knife work. Although, I like to think my additional bulk would have tipped the scales in my direction. But it all became moot when Raith dropped the body he had been carrying, strode between us and crouched to drive his own knife into the base of the crossbowman's skull.

"To be wasteful of time is to be wasteful of life," he told us in his strange, melodious accent, straightening and directing a steady, unblinking stare at each of us in turn. Raith possessed a gaze I found hard to meet at the best of times, the overly bright blue eyes piercing in a way that put one in mind of a hawk. Also, he was big, taller and broader even than Deckin but without any sign of a belly. More off-putting still were the livid red marks that formed two diagonal stripes across the light brown skin of his face. Before clapping eyes on him during my first faltering steps into Deckin's camp, I hadn't beheld one of Caerith heritage before. The sense of strangeness and threat he imbued in me that day had never faded.

In those days, tales of the Caerith and their mysterious and reputedly arcane practices abounded. Never a common sight in Albermaine, those who lived among us were subject to the fear and derision common to those viewed as alien or outlandish. Experience would eventually teach us the folly of such denigration, but all that was yet to come. I had heard many a lurid yarn about the Caerith, each filled with allusions to witchy strangeness and dire fates suffered by Covenant missionaries who unwisely crossed the mountains to educate these heathen souls in the Martyrs' example. So, I was quick to avert my eyes while Erchel, ever cunning but rarely clever, was a little slower, prompting Raith to afford him the benefit of his full attention.

"Wouldn't you agree, weasel?" he asked in a murmur, leaning closer, the brown skin of his forehead briefly pressing against Erchel's pale brow. As the bigger man stooped, his charm necklace dangled between them. Although just a simple length of cord adorned with bronze trinkets, each a finely wrought miniature sculpture of some kind, the sight of it unnerved me. I never allowed my gaze to linger on it too long, but my snatched glances revealed facsimiles of the moon, trees and various animals. One in particular always caught my eye more than the others: the bronze skull of a bird I took to be a crow. For reasons unknown, the empty eye sockets of this artefact invoked more fear in me than its owner's unnaturally bright gaze.

Raith waited until Erchel gave a nod, eyes still lowered. "Put it over there," the Caerith said, nodding towards a cluster of elm a dozen paces away as he slowly wiped his bloodied blade on Erchel's jerkin. "And you can carry my bundle on the way back. Best if I don't find anything missing."

"Caerith bastard," Erchel muttered as we heaved the crossbow-man's corpse into the midst of the elm. As was often his way, our confrontation now appeared to have been completely forgotten. Reflecting on his eventual fate all these years later I am forced to the conclusion that Erchel, hideous and dreadful soul that he was, possessed a singular skill that has always eluded me: the ability to forgo a grudge.

"They're said to worship trees and rocks," he went on, careful to keep his voice low. "Perform heathen rights in the moonlight and such to bring them to life. My kin would never run with one of his kind. Don't know what Deckin's thinking."

"Mayhap you should ask him," I suggested. "Or I can ask him for you, if you like."

This blandly spoken offer had the intended effect of keeping Erchel's mouth closed for much of the remainder of our journey. However, as we progressed into the closer confines of the deep forest, drawing nearer to camp, his tongue invariably found another reason to wag.

"What did it say?" he asked, once again keeping his voice quiet for Raith and the others weren't far off. "The scroll?"

"How should I know?" I replied, shifting the uncomfortable weight of the loot-filled sack on my shoulder. The bodies had all been stripped clean before I could join in the scavenging, but the cart had yielded half a meal sack, some carrots and, most prized of all, a pair of well-made boots which would fit me near perfectly with a few minor alterations.

"Deckin talks to you. So does Lorine." Erchel's elbow nudged me in demanding insistence. "What could it say that would make him risk so much just to read it?"

I thought of the spasm of shock I had seen on Lorine's face as she read the scroll, as well as her contradictory expression as she stood and watched Deckin coax deductions from me. *The daft old bastard turned his coat*, she had said. My years in this band had given me a keen nose for a shift in the varied winds that guided our path, Deckin always being the principal agent. Never fond of sharing his thoughts, he would issue commands that seemed odd or nonsensical only for their true intent to stand revealed later. So far, his guarded leadership had always led us to profit and clear of the duke's soldiers and sheriffs. *The duke…*

My feet began to slow and my eyes to lose focus as my always-busy mind churned up an insight that should have occurred to me back at the road. The messenger's guards were not ducal levies from the Shavine Marches but Cordwainers fresh from another battle in the Pretender's War. Soldiers in service to the king, which begged the question: if his own soldiers couldn't be trusted with escorting a Crown agent, which side had the Duke of the Shavine Marches been fighting on?

"Alwyn?"

Erchel's voice returned the focus to my gaze, which inevitably slipped towards Deckin's bulky form at the head of the column. We had reached the camp now and I watched him wave away the outlaws who came to greet him, instead stomping off to the shelter he shared with Lorine. Instinct told me neither would join us at the communal feast that night, the customary celebration of a successful enterprise. I knew they had much to discuss. I also knew I needed to hear it.

"There's something I feel you should know, Erchel," I said, walking off towards my own shelter. "You talk too fucking much."

Follow us:

/orbitbooksUS

/orbitbooks

/orbitbooks

Join our mailing list
to receive alerts on our
latest releases and deals.

orbitbooks.net

Enter our monthly
giveaway for the chance
to win some epic prizes.

orbitloot.com